# Dragon's Teeth

An Alex Rogers Adventure

Book 2

By CW Lamb

To my Wife, whose patience and understanding helps make these books happen.

Edited By: Patrick LoBrutto
Cover Design: www.art4artists.com.au

Copyright © 2016 by CW Lamb  WWW.CW-LAMB.COM

All rights reserved. No part of this publication may be reproduced, distributed, or transmitted in any form or by any means, including photocopying, recording, or other electronic or mechanical methods, without the prior written permission of the Author, except in the case of brief quotations embodied in critical reviews and certain other noncommercial uses permitted by copyright law.

First Edition
14 13 12 11 10 9 8 7 6 5 4 3 2

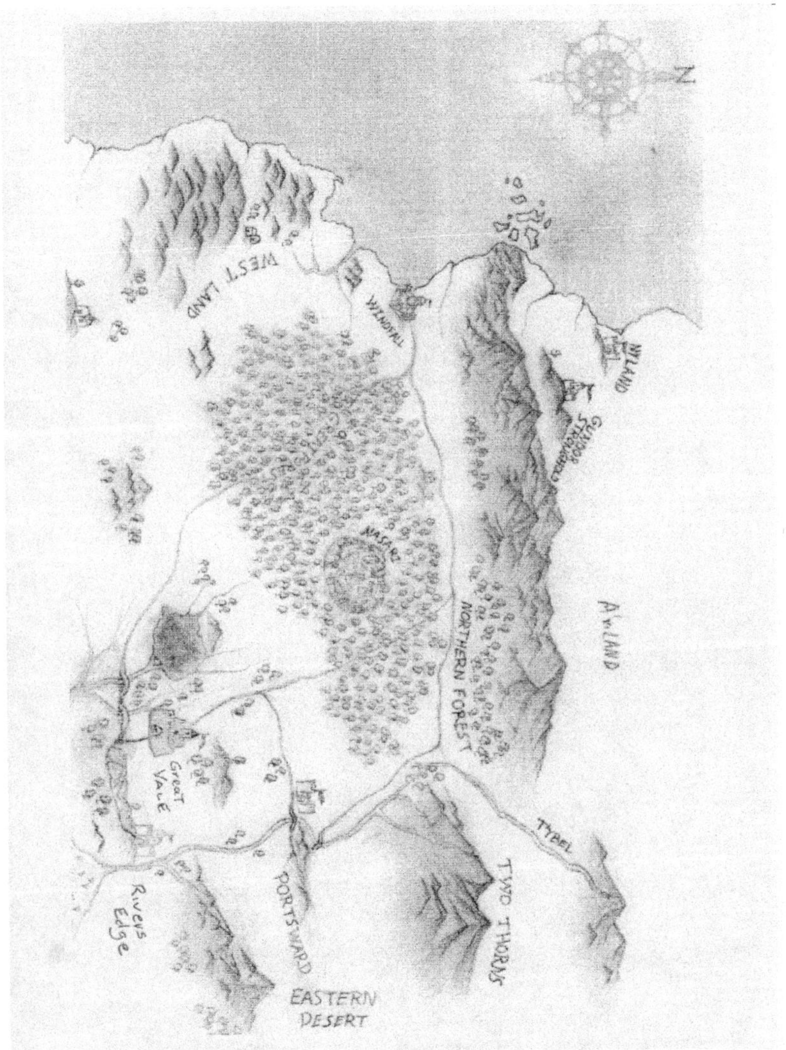
WEST LAND
WINDFALL
NORTHERN FOREST
Great Vale
Rivers Edge
PORTSWARD
EASTERN DESERT
TWO THORNS
TYBEL

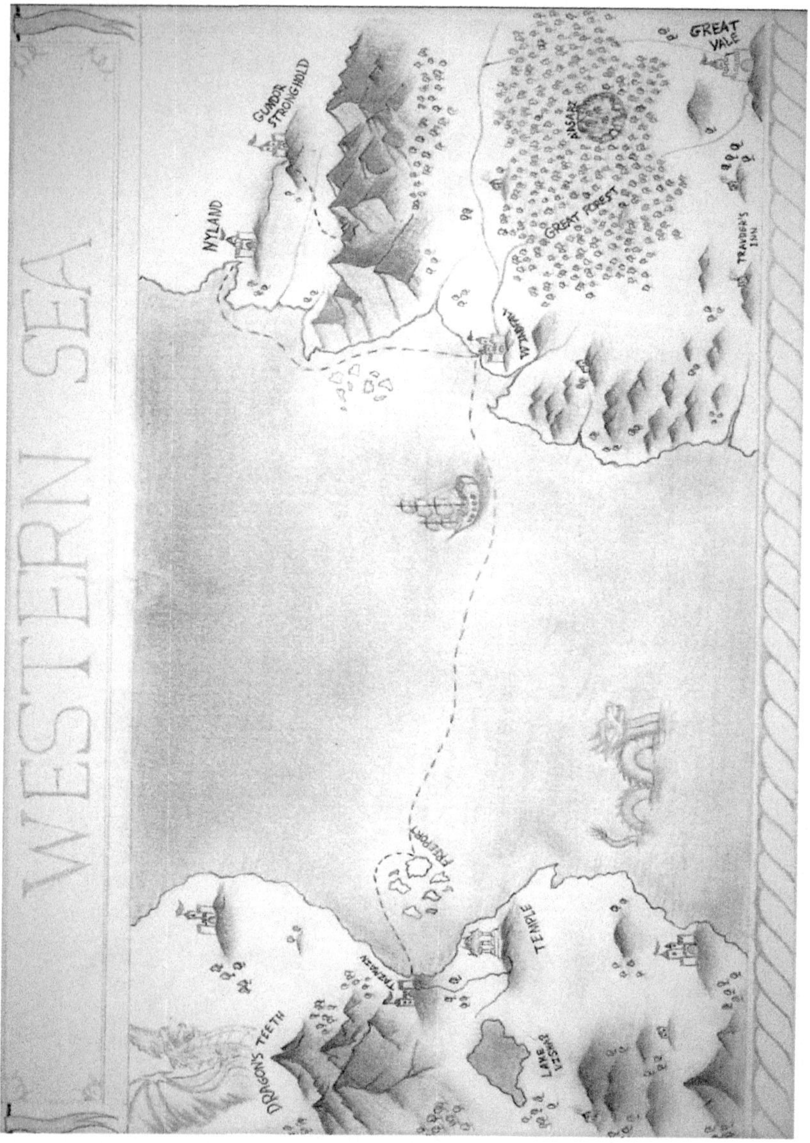
WESTERN SEA
GUNDOR STRONGHOLD
NYLAND
GREAT VALE
NASARI
GREAT FOREST
FREEPORT
TEMPLE
DRAGON'S TEETH

# Prologue

Lady Amelia of House Griffin, sister to the King of Great Vale, stood quietly in the darkened corner of the hallway, dagger in hand. In her free hand she fingered the pendant hanging around her neck, a gift from her brother. The weapon in her hand did little to ease her anxiety as she listened to the two men rummaging through her room.

She was startled as she watched another guest of the inn arrive in the hall at the far end and enter their room without giving her even a passing glance. The setting sun provided little light through the far windows to betray her hiding place. Even so, she tried to press herself deeper into the shadows.

"Where is she? She was supposed to be here!" she heard a man ask his companion in hushed tones.

"I don't know. The boss said her guards went to that mermaid bar, so we were supposed to grab her while the others took care of them," a second voice replied.

Amelia had been fortunate enough to catch the two men as they were entering her room without being seen. She had been in the small private parlor downstairs, reviewing letters of intent she had collected from the trading houses earlier that day. Since arriving in Freeport, she had been meeting with every trade house in hopes of establishing overseas trade with Great Vale.

The haste with which the two men had entered the inn had raised her curiosity as she watched them dart up the stairs. It was the fact that both men drew their weapons as they topped the flight that had caused her to become concerned.

Leaving her things behind, she hurried up the stairs, stopping just before the turn for the hallway at the top. Peering around the corner, she had been in time to see the second man as he presumably followed the first into her room and closed the door.

She had then rushed to the corner of the hallway where she hid in the shadows as she listened at the wall separating her rented lodgings from the hallway itself.

"Her things are still here, so she must still be in the building somewhere," the first man declared.

"Should we go look for her or wait here?" the second asked as they stopped whatever they had been doing that made the rustling noises masking their discussion.

"We can't just snatch her in front of everybody, you idiot. Let's wait here, she has to come back sometime," the first replied.

By now, Amelia had moved to the door so she could better hear the two men talking. With the last comment, she decided it was best for her to retreat until her guards returned from their mission. During their meetings, they had heard rumors that one of the trading houses was aligned with Prince Renfeld of Windfall and that there was a plot to attack Great Vale.

She was about to turn when she suddenly felt a blade at her throat, its cold metal pressing lightly into her skin.

"Lady Amelia, I presume," she heard whispered in her ear.

Driving the dagger in her hand into his leg, she spun away from the blade at the throat and attempted to push past the man as he howled in pain. The noise however, brought the two men in her room into the hall as they threw the door open wide.

"There she is, grab her," she heard from one of the two as she slipped between her attacker and the wall, ducking his grasp as he flailed wildly for her.

Amelia dashed for the stairs, hoping to reach the front door where she could lose herself in the evening crowd on the streets outside. Unfortunately, she had no such luck as two more men appeared at the end of the hallway before her. Turning, the men who had broken into her room blocked her retreat while the third lay on the floor still grasping his leg and whimpering.

"Take me to your master," Amelia announced, sighing in resignation as she drew herself up, projecting an aura of authority.

"That's the idea," replied one of the men.

Amelia let the men lead her down the back stairs of the inn and out into the alleyway between the buildings. Normally traveled by the inn staff and other traders providing food and supplies during the daytime, it was now completely deserted. In the fading sunlight it was also almost completely dark out.

She could hear the man she had wounded complaining as the rest of the group hurried to their destination. Even in the darkness, Amelia could tell they were headed to the warehouse district where she had earlier spent the day talking to traders.

"In here," one of the men ordered as they reached one of the large structures that acted as collection points for the goods traded in Freeport. As she passed through the doorway, she entered a small room, lit by a single candle on a small table. Next to the table was a stark wooden chair, barren of any padding. One of the men placed her next to the chair.

"Sit," he instructed as he pointed at the chair. Doing as instructed, she sat quietly, waiting for their next move.

"Ah, Lady Amelia, so good to see you again," a voice in the darkness finally announced. As she watched, she saw the familiar form of the master of House Drakon appear before her.

"Master Tantalus, have you lost your mind? My men will have your head when they return to find me missing," Amelia declared as she started to rise. The man standing behind her placed a firm hand on her shoulder, stopping her progress and motioning for her to sit once more.

"Ah yes. I am afraid your men ran into a nasty incident at the Siren's Song. Apparently involved in a drunken brawl, I hear. Both quite dead, I am afraid. Put up a considerable fight. They will be missed. It is so hard to find good men these days," he said sarcastically.

The statement drove a bolt of pain right through Amelia's heart as she considered the death of the two. She had become quite fond of them as they traveled, both handpicked from her brother's personal guard to ensure her safety. She expected that Tantalus had lost twice their number in the attack, something that seemed to trouble the man not at all.

"What is this about?" she asked sternly as she recovered her composure.

"Power, wealth...what else would it be?" he replied lightly.

"My brother will ransom me, that is true, but what will be the cost to you in the end?" Amelia replied, insinuating the vengeance the King would inflict on her kidnaper.

"Ransom? Oh no my dear Lady, this is far more audacious than a mere kidnaping. You are a pawn in a power play for the rule of kingdoms. But fear not, you have great value," Tantalus replied with a flourish.

"How?" Amelia asked, not happy where this was going.

"Once your brother is dead, his daughter will be married off to Prince Renfeld of Windfall who will then be master of both lands. Should she resist, or worse yet, succumb to some unfortunate accident, then you could marry the fine Prince, insuring his rule. If all goes well then maybe we shall find happiness together."

"NEVER!" Amelia replied in disgust.

"Ah, I suspected as much, however I hear you have a lovely daughter as well, perhaps she could marry me?"

"Over my dead body!" Amelia spat.

"Let us hope not," Tantalus retorted as he motioned to his men to take her away.

# Chapter 1

Alex Rogers stood at the window of the castle's keep, overlooking the bay. As the newly appointed Lord Protector for the city of Windfall, it was his responsibility to insure the safety of its people and the ships that came to trade here. As he watched the activity on the wharfs below him, he marveled at the changes in his life.

"Sire, do you require anything more?" asked his personal steward as he placed an ornate silver tray on the small table nearby. He noted the teapot and pastries that had become his daily mid-day reward. He sighed. What he wouldn't do for a pot of coffee!

"Not for the moment, thank you," Alex replied as he waved the man out the open doorway.

Hardly more than a few months ago, he had been a successful engineer in a prestigious Seattle engineering firm. He had been responsible for hundreds of millions of dollars' worth of construction projects worldwide. His technical expertise was sought by peers and competitors alike.

Then, he had fallen into a sinkhole while hiking in the forest, and found himself transported into a world straight out of his imagination. Literally dropped into the heat of battle, he had been fighting for his life ever since.

Standing next to him as he looked out the window was a large black wolf, his companion on this adventure. Kinsey had been a mixed breed dog in his previous life, transformed by the same magic that brought them both here. Alex found her current form much closer to her real personality than her former shape. Here, she had protected him from humans and mythical creatures alike, and was always nearby and ready to act in his defense.

Dropped here in the clothes of a Ranger of the Ranger's Guild, an organization created to protect nature's balance, Alex had fought his way across the foreign countryside. It seemed that every time things started to quiet down, another creature from his encyclopedia of mythical critters would appear to threaten his very existence. So far, he had managed to avoid death, at times by the thinnest of margins. The current lull in his life was a welcome break.

Unfortunately, the parchment Alex held in his hand indicated that everything was about to change once more. He had longed for some extended downtime since the battle to take the castle here at Windfall. He hoped the reprieve would give him time to prepare for his wedding. He was betrothed to the niece of the king of the adjoining Kingdom of Great Vale.

Her name was Lady Cassandra, Cassie to those close to her, and she was the redheaded daughter of a woman King Ben had saved when he first arrived here. He had been transported here from the same reality as Alex, many years earlier. Adopted by that family, Ben had risen to the position of Royal Wizard of Great Vale, eventually marrying the King's daughter and becoming King himself. No one but Alex and Cassie's mother knew the King's real origins. His name, Ben, was just assumed exotic for the locale. Only Cassie's mom knew that the House Griffin was really his last name and she was sworn to secrecy, as was Alex.

At the thought of Cassie's mother, Alex looked at his hands again. One contained a parchment, and the other a pendant and chain. The items had been delivered earlier that day, intended for the previous occupants of the keep. Prince Renfeld had perished in the fight for the castle, a passing mourned by only a few.

Scanning the words written on the parchment for the hundredth time, willing that they might turn to something other than what they were, he read them to himself.

*"Have taken King's sister as ordered. Holding her at an agreed location, awaiting further instructions. Included royal pendant as requested for proof."*

Alex examined the pendant, recognizing the insignia. He had seen it all over the Royal Court at Great Vale. Someone had Cassie's mom, and the only person Alex was aware of that knew the referenced location, was now ashes spread across the bay below.

Currently, Cassie was with her uncle, returned to Great Vale after the last of Prince Renfeld's forces had yielded to Ben's authority. Once the declaration of Alex's position as Lord Protector was settled with the community leaders, Ben had decreed a period of mourning for the dead King of Windfall, Prince Renfeld's father. While the Prince was a puke, his father's passing deserved the respect his many years of peaceful rule had earned him.

During this time of mourning, Alex had sent for Kinsey, while he and Ben established themselves with the various factions running the commerce of the city and port. With assurances of support for the new leadership out of Great Vale, Ben took his leave, taking Cassie and a large portion of his army with him.

Alex was left with enough Vale troops to staff the castle walls, and had the additional protection of the newly returned Rangers of Windfall. During his rise to power, Prince Renfeld had implemented a plan to root out any of the Ranger's Guild that might oppose Ranger involvement in his grab for dominance in the region. In so doing he had gutted the local Guild.

The Rangers were an organization dedicated to the preservation of nature and harmony, and had been historically apolitical. Its origins went back for hundreds of years, and was created and sponsored by the Woodland Elves. They had fashioned the Rangers to help instill a sense of ownership in humans with their surroundings. Alex recalled how Cassie had described their charter when she thought him a real Ranger, "You are sworn to protect nature and slay foul creatures."

"Come on Kinsey, time to go back to work," he said absently.

Turning away from the window, Alex went over to a desk against one wall of the study. As Lord Protector, he had taken up residence in the royal bedchamber. It was the very same room where he had discovered the remains of the former King of Windfall, not so long ago. This room had been the king's personal study, conveniently located across the hall from his bedroom and with a commanding view of the bay.

Taking up a quill, Alex dipped the tip and began a message to Ben, King of Great Vale and his new magic instructor. While Alex was actually the more powerful of the two, Ben had decades of education and experience in magical manipulations. It was Ben who had placed Alex in charge of Windfall, proclaiming him Lord Protector, and making Windfall a vassal state to Great Vale.

Alex wrote out a quick explanation of how he had received the message about Cassie's mom and asked for permission to go in search of her as soon as possible. Once he was satisfied with the message's contents, he sealed it, the pendant, and its parchment companion into a leather pouch.

With that completed, Alex got up from the desk, and with Kinsey at his side.

"Please inform the magistrates I will return shortly," Alex passed to one of his ever present guardsmen as he exited the room.

"Yes sire, right away," the man replied before he hurried off. Alex had left a room full of people downstairs when he received the message.

He then headed down to the stables with Kinsey close behind. As they passed through the halls of the keep, Alex recognized a mixture of Vale and Windfall troops going about their duties. It would be quite a while before there was enough confidence in the local military to allow Alex to rely on them for his complete protection. He continued to carry his sword everywhere he went, although it was now at his side, rather than strapped across his back, as he had done in Ranger garb.

He and Ben agreed that the people of Windfall needed time to adjust to their losses on the field of battle, and learn how their fortunes had actually turned for the better. Every day, Alex worked hard to undo the negligence Renfeld's regime had shown to the people here.

Once on the ground level, Alex exited the keep and crossed the open courtyard, heading to the stables near the east gate which opened into the city. With a message this important, Alex knew he needed to expedite its delivery. Unfortunately, the pendant precluded the normal method of magical message birds.

Still a marvel to Alex, the message birds were carried as acorns, but once the sender scribed his message, the two transformed into a small magical bird, with the recipient imprinted in its mind. Once delivered, the bird disappeared in a puff of smoke, leaving the message with its intended recipient. While certainly not the equivalent of texting, it was still a marvel.

Alex entered the stables, searching for his mount, Shadows. He found the black mare in a stall near the entrance, her head and neck over the lower half of the stall door, watching him approach. She looked well cared for, and apparently happy to see him as she buried her head in his chest. He opened the lower stall door and led her out into the open courtyard. A gift of sorts from Elion, the King of the Woodland Elves, Shadows had been Alex's constant companion since the day he arrived here.

The horse was a marvel, tirelessly carrying Alex everywhere he traveled. However, it wasn't until after the battle at Great Vale that he learned she was more than a mere horse. He wasn't sure what the elves called them, but to him, she was a Pegasus, or flying horse. He had flown with her on several occasions and enjoyed the experience greatly. Besides the exhilaration, it cut a lot of time off any trip. As the journey to Great Vale was four to five days on foot, depending on the urgency, he had no choice but to use his prized mare as a messenger.

Attaching the leather pouch around her neck, ensuring it was secure, he led her out into the center of the courtyard.

"Shadows, take this to Ben and Cassie," he declared as he released her from his grasp.

Stepping forward, the mare produced wings, magically hidden under normal circumstances, and spread them wide. Her wingspan was magnificent, first spreading them as if in a stretch, and then she sprang forward in a leap. With the first flap, she was airborne and gaining altitude fast. Alex continued to watch until she was lost in the distance, headed southeast at a good rate.

Looking down at Kinsey by his side, Alex scratched her between the ears in affection, and then turned to head back up the steps and into the keep. While he intended to try and make a dent in the never-ending line of individuals seeking an audience, he doubted his mind would be on his work.

----*----

Cassie was going out of her mind. Her uncle had insisted on her returning with him to Great Vale, leaving Alex to handle the transition of power in Windfall undistracted. Why in the world he thought she was a distraction, she had no idea. Between her and Alex, she had far more experience at court, and would be a great asset to him there.

She had finally conceded when her uncle pointed out she had a wedding to plan, and that required her to come home for a bit. Upon their return, Abrianna had been thrilled at the news of her engagement. Since her return, a day hadn't passed without the two of them busy with preparations. Cassie had never considered the amount of work required in planning a royal wedding and soon found herself overwhelmed.

The only damper on the otherwise joyous situation was that her mother was still away. While not overly concerned, as she knew these things took time, she had expected some word from her by now, if nothing more than a message bird. Cassie had tried to send a few to her, without reply, causing some doubt. She suspected her uncle was worried as well, but kept his thoughts to himself.

One of the more exciting distractions after their return to Great Vale had been the royal visit of King Elion of the Woodland Elves. He had appeared the day following their homecoming and had brought hordes of gifts. She and Abrianna secretly believed that Elion supplied her uncle with his specially made elven goods and weapons. While publicly proclaiming neutrality, Great Vale never seemed short of the things they needed to defend the peace.

Of special note was the wedding gift Elion presented Cassie, a beautiful Chestnut mare named Rose. Her magnificent red coat was spectacular, and Cassie learned she was a sister to Shadows, Alex's horse. The implications of that did not escape anyone, as it was well known that Shadows was one of Elion's prized flying horses. Technically a loan, Cassie was gifted the horse for her lifetime, after which Rose would return to Elion on her own.

With the thought of Rose on her mind, Cassie heard a commotion outside the open window of her room. With Alex gone, she had returned to using her own quarters, if for no other reason, than the familiarity tempered her longing for the man. Sometimes she hated that nymph part of her that drove those raw emotions. Looking out the window and into the castle courtyard below, she could see Shadows, held by one of the stable hands.

Dashing for the door, her heart leapt as she expected Alex had ridden Shadows and was waiting below. Cassie raced down the main staircase and out into the courtyard, her excitement at seeing Alex urging her along. As she passed through the main double doors to the keep, she could see a small crowd surrounding the black mare. But Alex was not to be seen anywhere.

However, her uncle was easily identified, standing in the center of the men encircling the flying horse. Cassie could see he was reading something, a deep frown on his face.

"Uncle, where is Alex?" Cassie asked as she continued to search the small crowd.

"He is not here, Cassie. He sent an urgent message, but he couldn't come himself," her uncle replied while appearing extremely distracted by what he was reading.

Cassie felt herself deflate. After a moment's disappointment, her curiosity got a hold of her.

"What message?" she asked.

Her uncle seemed to consider the question before replying, "Let's go inside."

Motioning for the stable hands to care for Shadows, Ben waved for Cassie to follow.

Cassie trailed him into the keep, passing through the throne room, and into his study beyond. On their way there, Ben had asked someone to find his daughter, Abrianna, and have her sent to him immediately. Ben and Cassie entered the study and both sat quietly as they waited for her to arrive.

Even with her curiosity eating at her, Cassie knew better than to push her uncle when he looked like this. Whatever the message was, it was not good. She doubted it was about Alex, as he had already declared him the sender.

Abrianna entered after a brief knock, and then scanned the room to find only the two occupants seated and waiting.

"Sit," was all the king said, as Cassie watched her cousin take the chair near hers. After a brief silence, her uncle started.

"As Lord Protector of Windfall, Alex was presented a message this morning, from a ship's captain. The vessel had just made port, and the man was delivering the royal pouch from their foreign representatives across the western sea. The message included this," Ben said as he held up the pendant.

"That's my mother's!" Cassie declared as she surged forward to take it from her uncle for closer inspection.

"Yes, apparently Renfeld had your mother kidnapped as part of his grand plan. This message is a confirmation that they were successful and are holding her while awaiting further instructions."

"Then let's go get her!" A worried Cassie blurted.

"Unfortunately, the message doesn't say where she is. It only refers to a previously agreed location that the now extinct Renfeld knew," Ben replied sadly.

"Uncle, we have to go find her!" Cassie cried out, while holding back tears, as Abrianna slid next to her to give her comfort.

"Yes, Alex's separate message says that very thing. He indicated to me that the captain was presented the missive with the pouch at the port of Tazmain. He has requested my permission to lead an expedition to retrieve her," Ben replied.

"I'm going!" Cassie heard herself announce.

"Yes, I expected that," her uncle replied with a sigh. "That is why I asked Abrianna to come in. Abrianna, can you please get in touch with Leander? As Guild Master of the local Rangers Guild, he may be able to reach out to his resources overseas and discreetly start the search before you get there."

"Father, I want to go as well," Abrianna asked as she held her cousin.

"Yes, I expected that as well," he replied with an even bigger sigh. "I would hope a healer would be unnecessary, however, your presence will comfort Cassie."

Cassie felt herself nodding in agreement, her fear over her mother's safety ruling her emotions.

"OK, you two go prepare to travel. Cassie, I expect you will be taking Rose?" her uncle asked.

At the mention of the flying horse, Cassie got a slight surge of fear. While she had ridden the mare, she had yet to take flight.

"Yes, uncle," she replied, knowing it was the fastest way to reach Windfall and Alex.

"Abrianna, you are prepared to ride Shadows?" she heard her uncle ask. Abrianna got the same wide-eyed look that Cassie suspected she had displayed. With the same resolute tone, she replied with a firm yes.

"All right then," was all her uncle could say.

----*----

Leander was still cleaning up the mess Alex had made of the Guild building. Between the blood that had been spilt, and the burnt wood from the fires he had set, they had to rip out entire sections of the main hall for replacement. Leander wanted the Guild to be restored to its former splendor, before receiving the black mark of Renfeld's corruption. As Guild master of the Great Vale Rangers, he knew that Rangers from all over the lands were looking to him to set the example they would all follow.

No more would they be meddling in the politics of the cities, steeped in corruption and greed. He was pushing hard to restore the true nature of the Rangers, as he knew they were meant to be. His feelings for Abrianna did put a bit of a damper on his altruistic attitudes, though. After the great battle, their true emotions for each other were exposed to everyone, themselves included.

Much to Leander's relief, the king seemed to harbor no ill will over their affections. It did, however, create a hurtle for Leander and others in the community. He had to go above and beyond, to prove no royal manipulations were occurring with every one of his decisions.

It was with all this hanging over his head that Abrianna had come to him begging favors. With Cassie by her side, the two explained the dire nature of their circumstance. Leander immediately dispatched several of his message birds to overseas contacts within the Rangers Guild.

His real concern was raised however, when the women explained their intention to accompany Alex overseas. While Leander had nothing but the greatest respect for the man, he had participated in enough of Alex's adventures to know that the women would be in jeopardy. It seemed as if the man attracted conflict while standing idly by.

The final straw was the flying horses. Leander was not going to allow the most important person in his life to fly off, unprotected, while he stayed behind selecting stains for the woodwork. After sending the two back to the castle keep with promises not to leave without him, he set to the task of organizing his assistants to run things in his absence.

----*----

Ben was in his study leafing through everything he had on the overseas ports. While he had some information on Tazmain, he doubted very much that the trail started or ended there. As he was working, both Cassie and Abrianna stopped by on their return from seeing Leander at the Ranger's Guild.

He had suspected that Leander was not about to let Abrianna run off on her own. Ben admired the young man, and felt he was a great match for his daughter. He was patient with her headstrong nature, while a stubborn man himself when necessary. Best of all, she seemed quite taken with him as well. Considering his own roots, Ben had a great admiration for someone who had risen from nothing.

Ben also understood very well the thin line the new Guild Master was walking, considering all that had occurred. He knew that he could not go, himself, to ask for Leander's assistance. The political backlash of Renfeld's war was still being felt throughout the lands.

However, everyone would understand Leander's motivations in protecting his beloved. While they might make jokes, no one would dare challenge the decision as politically motivated. Leander would be a great help to Alex, and Ben felt better knowing Leander was there watching over Abrianna.

Cassie would be Alex's to protect, and he would be a very busy man. She was clearly distraught, worried sick over her mother's safety. Ben was worried as well, although not as much as she, for he understood the nature of things. His sister had been taken as a bargaining chip, so her abductors needed to keep her safe and in good health. The real danger was if they were to discover Renfeld's fate before she could be rescued.

Should that happen, they still might attempt to ransom her. Ben's real fear was that the captors would kill her to remain anonymous, hidden from Ben's wrath. For that reason, Ben had ordered his people to start spreading rumors of Renfeld's survival and that the prince was in hiding. He hoped the deception was enough to forestall any rash action, until Alex could recover his future mother-in-law.

----*----

Elion was in the stables, brushing one of his prized flying horses. While it was not popularly considered a kingly task, he had never been one to stand on ceremony. In addition, he found spending time with the animals to be both soothing and beneficial.

Unbeknownst to most in E'anbel, the horses here were quite intelligent and very old. They were much smarter than their lookalike cousins the humans rode. These stallions and mares were kin to the Greek stallion Pegasus, a winged horse from these very stables.

Before cutting ties to the world Alex and Ben knew as home, the elves had interacted with humans there from all over the realm. Those associations gave rise to many of those stories the humans referred to as myths. In this particular case, Elion recalled, Pegasus had decided to leave the stables and go exploring.

The stallion landed in Athens and accepted the offerings of the Greeks there, staying long enough to leave his mark on the people. Before becoming bored and returning to the elves, he had been paraded around the city, and his legend had taken root.

Elion's current thoughts were around the gift he had personally delivered to Great Vale. All indications were that Alex was preparing to travel across the Western Sea to attempt a rescue of King Ben's sister. As Shadows had proven to be a valuable asset to Alex's adventures so far, he hoped providing Lady Cassandra with Rose would prove just as beneficial. He had little doubt the fiery nymph wouldn't accompany him on the quest.

Elion was aware there were many challenges waiting for the humans should they travel across the sea. There were hidden dangers there that he worried the humans might not be prepared for. Worst of all, a dormant evil lay in wait there.

It was these concerns over the possible escalation with the Dark Elves that motivated the gift of the mare. The failure in rescuing Lady Amelia could escalate things out of control, by prompting Great Vale to take revenge on those involved, wherever they might be.

Finishing his task, Elion dismissed the mare he had been grooming and stowed the brushes before returning to the duties he was avoiding. His last thought before leaving the stables was a hope that the couple survived long enough to see themselves married.

# Chapter 2

The following morning, Ben entered the small dining room, only to find Leander, Abrianna, and Cassie all there ahead of him, and already eating. Ben was not big on formality, and as such had no issues with them starting without him. What happened next, though, did cause him to laugh.

Leander was first to see him enter, and immediately jumped to his feet, causing his chair to topple. Even with as much time as the two had spent in close proximity, Ben noted the boy still got the jitters in his presence.

Both Cassie and Abrianna turned to see the cause of his behavior, and then giggled. What made Ben laugh was that both women were in the Ranger tunic and tights, the outfit Alex had first dressed Cassie in, while the Guild Master himself was in nondescript clothing, attempting to hide his identity.

The irony lay in Leander's attempted discretion while the women broadcast their allegiance to the world. Ben assumed that protective garb, similar to the Ranger attire, was beneath Leander's apparel. However, from his outward appearance no one would see an affiliation to the Rangers. He couldn't help but laugh at the juxtaposition.

"Morning uncle," Cassie bid as he rounded the table and took his traditional place at its head.

By the time Ben had seated himself, Leander had recovered his chair and re-seated himself.

"Sire," the man said as he tipped his head in respect.

"Good morning," Ben replied before adding, "I see the entire female branch of the Ranger's Guild is in attendance."

"I felt it might be best if I didn't appear in Ranger's garb for this mission," Leander suggested in way of an explanation.

"And we wanted to be ready for anything," Abrianna added.

"I understand completely," Ben offered to the obviously relieved Leander.

"I assume you are suitably protected beneath?"

"Oh yes, Sire," Leander replied, while lifting his shirt to show the protective tunic beneath.

"It has been recorded in the Guild records that I am assisting in rectifying a wrong done in the service of Prince Renfeld," Leander explained as a justification for his participation.

"An entry I expect to be unnecessary, but prudent none the less," Ben replied with a smile.

"We are packed and ready to leave," Cassie stated, as Ben accepted the plate provided by his serving staff.

"Traveling light I hope?" Ben asked between bites.

"Only saddlebags for each of us," Abrianna said while indicating herself and Cassie.

"I have a traveler's knapsack," Leander added.

"Well then, let's not keep Alex waiting," Ben replied as he finished the last bite on his plate.

----*----

Alex had received a message from Ben the same day, acknowledging Shadow's arrival, and indicating there would be more to follow. As such, he spent most of that day and the following morning preparing for a message approving his proposal, and releasing him to pursue Cassie's mom.

Besides the preparations for his departure, he needed to get the administrative duties for the city in order, permitting his absence. Thankfully, either by negligence or by design, Renfeld had taken a very hands off approach to governing the city. So long as the taxes were collected and paid to the royal treasury, he left the merchants and the shippers to their own devices.

In fact, one of the immediate benefits of Alex's governing was his redirection of revenues back into the community. The civil engineer in him had initiated public works projects to repair the docks and upgrade the streets damaged by heavy wagons over years of neglect.

Additionally, he had sponsored the construction of shipyards, initially intended to repair trading vessels, but with the possibility of new production in the future. With the knowledge he had of sailing ships from his world, versus what he saw in the bay, he imagined they might be able to introduce some innovative designs.

All these changes had endeared him to most of the population and the local merchants, as it created jobs and improved the facilities supporting their businesses, without cost to them. In addition, the increase in paying jobs allowed the other trades to prosper, as workers spent their hard-earned wages throughout the city. Only a corrupt few felt the sting of the changes.

Although he had only been Lord Protector for less than a month, his efforts had been positively received. Even those in charge of the accounts had reported they still maintained a positive cash flow from the treasury, after the additional outlay.

His initial travels throughout the city were all accompanied with a small contingent of Vale guards. It was a precaution that soon became unnecessary as Alex's reputation as a wizard and a benefactor grew. The positive impact of his changes had been so great that he was now able to wander the city freely, without fear of attack from some disgruntled faction.

And that's how he and Kinsey came to be crossing the inner courtyard alone as they were returning from a meeting. They had traveled to the site that the new shipyard was to spring from. There, Alex was outlining his design to the construction supervisors, explaining his vision before returning to the castle. Half way across the courtyard, he heard one of the tower guards hail him.

"Sire!"

Alex looked up to see one of the guards motioning at him and then to the sky.

Following the direction that the man was pointing, he scanned the sky up and to the southeast of the castle. Alex could see two distant spots in the sky from the direction the guard was indicating. As he stood watching, they grew larger until he could see one was Shadows, with two riders. Accompanying her was a red-coated flying horse he had never seen before, with a rider astride suspiciously similar to Cassie, her red hair flowing loosely behind her.

Moving to one side of the courtyard, he watched as the two flying horses circled once and then landed inside the walls of the castle. By now, Alex confirmed the riders as Cassie, Abrianna, and Leander.

"Alex!" he heard Cassie cry, as she all but leaped off the moving horse. Rushing to meet her, the two embraced, and held a lingering kiss that only a forced separation could inspire.

"I missed you," he declared, after releasing her.

"Uncle told me about mom," she replied.

"Yes, we are here to accompany you on your quest," Leander added as he and Abrianna crossed to where the couple stood.

"Father asked me to give you this," Abrianna said as she handed Alex a leather pouch.

"He said it contains everything he has on Tazmain and the lands across the Western Sea."

"Thank you. So where did the other horse come from?" Alex asked while indicating the beautiful chestnut mare.

"A wedding present from King Elion!" Cassie replied with delight. As he moved closer to the red mare, Alex could see Cassie greeting Kinsey with a rub and a scratch. Motioning for the grooms to come take care of the horses, Alex led the trio into the keep and upstairs to the private study he had assumed possession of.

With everyone seated and provided for, he opened the pouch Abrianna had presented him, and started flipping through its contents.

"Father said he apologizes for the lack of information; however, we don't do much trade overseas yet, so the need has been minimal."

"On a positive note, the Guild has many contacts there, including a House in Tazmain. I have already informed them of our intent and they are discreetly scouring the area for information," Leander added.

"Can we trust them?" Cassie asked, referring to the troubles the Ranger's Guild had encountered.

"Yes, those in the west had not been corrupted as they had in the east. These Rangers are still true to the belief," Leander replied.

Alex was aware that Leander had received assurances from Elion, King of the Woodland Elves, of such but chose not to voice it.

"I have been compiling all I can find here," Alex said, while indicating the stacks of books and papers already cluttering the table.

"Anything usable?" Leander asked, surveying the piles of materials.

"Not much. It should be no surprise that the Royals of Windfall would want maps of the coastal ports. However, they apparently had no interest in the peoples, cultures, or geography inland."

"Once we arrive in Tazmain, the Ranger's Guild there can help with that," Leander provided.

"Yes, but we need to be discreet. If whomever is holding Cassie's mom hears that we are searching for her, it could spook them," Alex said cautiously. He didn't want to feed the fear that he imagined was already flaming inside Cassie.

"How are we to get there?" Cassie asked, apparently avoiding the topic as well.

"Ah, that is all arranged. Good Prince Renfeld had a two-masted schooner at his disposal, though I hear he never used it. She is fast and can carry Shadows and….." Alex stalled, not knowing the name of Cassie's mount.

"Rose," she supplied with a smile.

"And Rose, as well as mounts for you two," he finished indicating Abrianna and Leander.

"Although there was a small issue in the beginning," Alex added. He could see the three looking at him questioningly.

"She was named *Renfeld's Pride*," Alex supplied.

"That will never do!" Abrianna retorted.

"Was?" Leander questioned, catching the reference.

"She was recently rechristened *Cassie's Quest*."

----*----

25

The four stayed in the study for hours, reviewing what little information they had, while Kinsey snoozed happily in a corner. Ben provided an outline of the mission Cassie's mom had been assigned. They also discussed possible locations where she might be held. Alex had food and drink brought up, and other than the occasional break, the group worked well past dark. Kinsey would wander out and back in of her own volition.

"Ok, I guess we have covered just about everything," Alex stated to the weary group.

"I fear it is not enough," Leander replied, concern written across his face.

"For now, it's enough to get us on the right path," Abrianna added, with a quick glance in Cassie's direction. Everyone had been dancing around the subject of Cassie's mom, and the possibility that she may already be dead.

"Let's all get some rest, and tomorrow we will get the ship loaded and ready for departure the following day," Alex said, anxious to prevent any digression in the conversation.

While the four had been occupied, the staff had prepared rooms for the new arrivals. Alex had little doubt Cassie was intending to stay with him, but the arrangements for Leander and Abrianna were far from certain. As the King's daughter, he had a sneaking suspicion that the two would not be sharing a room prior to any official declaration of marriage.

His suspicions proved true as first Leander, and then Abrianna bid them a good night, each taking a room opposite the other and next to the royal bedchamber Alex occupied.

"Alex, I'm worried. What if mom is already dead?" Cassie declared as the door closed to their room.

"I know you're worried. Just remember, the note indicated she was to be held, which includes safekeeping. Hostages are no good to anyone dead. Can you imagine how bad your Uncle's anger would be if his sister was abused in any way?" he finished.

"Not nearly as bad as mine," the redhead replied, her eyes flashing as the thought passed through her mind.

With that, the two undressed and climbed into bed, their exhaustion not nearly enough to prevent them from enjoying a moment of intimacy before drifting off to sleep.

----*----

Captain Yeagars was no stranger to the western sea. He had been sailing the trade routes between Windfall and the ports to the west for nearly forty years. He had gone to sea at an early age, as his parents had been too poor to pay the apprentice fees for any of the local guilds. Thus, growing up on the water, he no more considered Windfall home than any of the other ports he visited in his travels.

So, it was quite a surprise to him when the new Lord Protector had provided him the opportunity to be the master of the newly rechristened *Cassie's Quest*. She had fine lines and was reportedly fast, but her prior owner, the Crown Prince Renfeld, had never used her for more than a daysailer.

That was about to change as the sunrise brought word that he was to prepare to sail on the morrow's tide. They were already tied to the wharf, taking on provisions for a lengthy voyage. As he had yet to receive instructions on their destination, he simply wandered the deck, his experienced eye insuring all was properly stored as it came aboard.

At one hundred and twenty-one feet long and a twenty-four foot beam, she required only five men to sail her, though the current complement counted eighteen plus two cooks. That permitted for three watches, with himself, his first officer, or the second officer overseeing the watches. Yeagars was a bit confused that the Lord Protector had made no provisions for cabin stewards or royal cooks. When asked, the reply had been, "We can eat whatever the crew eats." From the stores he saw arriving, they would all eat well.

About mid-morning, he watched from the deck as the Lord Protector, accompanied by three others he had never seen before, came down the wharf, stopping at the boarding ramp. The large black wolf accompanying them was well-known to all as the Lord Protector's pet and bodyguard.

"Permission to come aboard?" the man asked as he stood waiting for a reply. Those with him appeared slightly confused at the request, but made no comment.

"Permission granted," Yeagars responded. The request was unnecessary as the ship belonged to the requestor; however, the respect it displayed was noted and appreciated.

As he watched the four come across the boarding ramp, he was taken by the beautiful redhead following the Lord Protector. She was followed by another woman, just as attractive, and finally by a man that Yeagars took to be a soldier.

"Captain, may I introduce Lady Cassandra, my fiancée. And this is the Crown Princess Abrianna of Great Vale."

"It is my great pleasure," Yeagars replied, curious as to why the man had been left out of the introductions.

"You may call me Leander," the man suggested, after an exchange of looks passed between the man and the Lord Protector. The Captain suspected there was much more to this man, but accepted that his employer wished it to remain unspoken.

"Your message indicated you wish to sail with the morning tide?" Yeagars asked.

"If at all possible. We also have special cargo to consider; will the ship's hold accommodate four horses?"

"Yes, but no more," Yeagars replied after a moment's consideration.

"But a wolf and horses in such close quarters?" he commented after a moment while indicating Kinsey standing nearby, calmly watching everyone.

"They are all known to each other, well, most anyway," Alex replied with a smile.

"Sire, I presume that you four are the passengers, so I ask again. Are we to add a royal cook and stewards to our complement given the circumstances?" Yeagars asked while indicating the women of royal birth.

"We will be just fine, Captain, but thank you for your concern," Lady Cassandra replied before anyone else. He got the impression that these women of the court had a hardier constitution than those he had met previously. He would not underestimate them, as he noted the dagger in the redhead's belt. It looked far more functional than decorative.

It was then that Captain Yeagars understood for whom the ship had been named.

----*----

Alex had stayed behind with the Captain, while the others went to prepare for the voyage. The two men reviewed the charts they had on hand and Alex supplied what little details he could on the goals of the voyage. He had chosen Captain Yeagars based on the fact that he had no known allegiance to the previous Royal Family and on his reputation as an honest and trustworthy man. Even so, he was only intending to share the destinations, not the intent of the trip. That information was on a need to know basis.

Once the two men were satisfied that everything required for the extended voyage was covered, Alex left the Captain to his duties and returned to the keep. There, he held a final round of meetings, intended for transferring his administrative duties to those he had selected to govern in his absence.

Once he was satisfied all was in order, he went off to find Cassie and Kinsey, as the wolf had not left her side since her arrival. He discovered them waiting in his room, Cassie bathed and ready for an early bedtime, anxious to begin their voyage.

# Chapter 3

A bright, sunny, morning found Alex on the deck of *Cassie's Quest* as they sailed westbound across a calm sea. With the schooner in full billowing sail, the ship sliced through the water at a surprising rate of speed. While it seemed faster to him, the Captain reported them at eight knots. With approximately 1,300 nautical miles to go, the trip would take about a week.

Everyone, including Kinsey, had boarded before sunrise and were shown their cabins. The horses for the four, including Shadows and Rose, had been safely stowed in the hold. Once informed of the special cargo, Captain Yeagars had the hold reconfigured to accommodate the horses safely.

"Isn't it beautiful?" Cassie asked as she joined him at the rail near the bow. She was always in great spirits when in or near the water, and this was no exception. Even with the worries about her mother's safety, it was like a balm to soothe her worried mind.

"The Captain says we can expect to be at sea for five to seven days before our first stop, depending on the wind."

"First stop?" she asked, breaking the trance being on the water had placed on her.

"Captain Yeagars says there are some barrier islands, just off of the mainland. Freeport, the main harbor there, acts as a trade center for the region. I checked your Uncle's instructions, and your mom was to stop there first before pushing on to Tazmain. Leander's contacts at the Ranger's Guild report seeing her arrive in Tazmain from Freeport, but no one recalls ever seeing her leave town."

"So you think someone followed her from the islands?" Cassie asked, her attention completely on Alex now.

He hesitated before answering. "Leander said that both her bodyguards were killed in Freeport, in an apparent bar fight. She was forced to hire locals in Freeport to replace them."

"That doesn't sound right at all. Uncle's men are a very disciplined group; they would never abandon their duties to go drinking," Cassie replied immediately.

"Yes, we thought the same. I am sure it was a setup, to get her unprotected. Anyway, we will stop there first, and then go on to Tazmain to meet with Leander's contacts."

----*----

Ben Griffin had been doing everything he could think of to find his sister once he became aware of her kidnaping. Over the decades he had been in Great Vale, he had acquired a great number of contacts and they were spread throughout the lands. Some he hardly knew, while others he called friends. None, however, seemed to have any knowledge of Renfeld's associates overseas.

What was most disturbing to Ben was the lack of information provided by the Elves. Elion was most apologetic, but was unable or unwilling to provide any information on the subject. When pressed, he confessed that any attempt a scrying the woman had been met with utter darkness, and that was not a good sign.

----*----

It was late in the afternoon when the lookout hailed the officer of the watch. Alex had been on deck, reading a book he had borrowed from the Windfall Harbormaster. The man had been quite resistant to loaning it as it was his only copy and contained the listings of all the ships and cargos delivered to Windfall in the last year.

Though he had no idea of what he was looking for, Alex hoped something in the book would give a clue in finding Cassie's mom. Perhaps preferred trading partners or someone struggling to gain favor with Renfeld had acted as his agent in the abduction.

He did note the House of Drakon, sailing mostly out of Freeport, had a constantly increasing number of visits in the last year. Although the cargos were listed as nonmilitary in nature, the Harbormaster had noted that Prince Renfeld had personally flagged them as "inspection not required." As he was considering this, Alex heard a declaration from the rigging above.

"Sails Ho!" the lookout had bellowed.

Looking up from his reading, Alex first looked at the man shouting from above, and then checked the direction he was indicating. In the distance, he could just make out the shape of square rigged sails of at least two distinct ships. As he watched, the Captain joined the First Officer at the rail near the helm. He could see the two men talking quietly while using binoculars, the image totally ruining his pirate movie replay without a spyglass.

Rising from where he was sitting, he wandered over until he stood next to the Captain.

"Trouble?" Alex asked calmly.

"Maybe," Yeagars replied without looking at him.

"Those are two brigantines, ships favored by the pirates in the region. Normally our schooner could outrun them, but they have the wind for an intercept as long as we hold this course," the First Officer said while the Captain continued to watch the sails on the horizon.

Alex realized he had never even considered there might be pirates sailing the waters off Windfall.

"Why haven't I heard about them before?" Alex asked.

"Until recently, they had been staying to the western side of the sea. They mostly harass smaller vessels heading to and from Freeport carrying trade goods or payments," Yeagars replied.

"And now?" Alex asked.

"You are being tested. It is known that you now rule Windfall, though for how long is uncertain. Rumors persist that the true fate of Prince Renfeld is still in question. Renfeld was ruthless in his persecution of the pirates in the eastern waters; they now challenge you to see if you are weak."

Alex was happy to see the misinformation campaign about Renfeld was working, giving them the time they needed. The unexpected side effect was incidents like this.

As the men had been speaking, the sails had grown close enough to confirm there were two ships on an intercept course. With a nod from the Captain, the First Mate began barking orders to the crew. Scanning the schooners deck, Alex could see the crew readying several stout crossbows, mounted to hardened points along the railing. He suddenly realized he had never seen a cannon nor guns since arriving here. He needed to ask Ben about that.

"You think those are going to matter?" he asked the Captain while indicating the preparations.

"Normally, Royal travelers are accompanied by warships or other armed escort vessels. We appear as either a wealthy traveler or merchant," the Captain explained.

"Pirate ships carry one or two Ballista aboard, allowing them to fire grapples, trapping their prey. Once secured, they swarm the ship, overwhelming the crew and killing any who resist," the First Officer supplied.

Alex was aware a Ballista was an oversized crossbow, capable of firing over hundreds of yards, much farther than the miniature versions being prepared at the rail. According to the First Officer's version, they would be tethered and awash in pirates long before a good fight could be presented.

"You have another option?" the Captain asked, not quite challenging Alex.

Alex had several thoughts, all requiring them to close the distance between the vessels. After a moment's consideration, he asked a question.

"Is fire still a concern to sailors?"

"Dear lord yes!" the man at the helm answered before any of the officers could reply.

Satisfied with the reply, Alex rushed below, returning a short time later with his Elven bow and a strip of parchment with writing on it. Securing the parchment to the shaft, he nocked the arrow and sized up the distance to the pirates. Both the Captain and the First Officer watched him in disbelief.

"Sire, they are far out of bow range, and will be in Ballista range before you can reach them," the First Officer commented.

Smiling, Alex paused a moment checking the wind, and then let the shaft fly. Concentrating on the closer of the two vessels, the three men watched as the arrow carried the distance between the two ships, landing firmly on the deck.

Alex turned to see the look of disbelief in the First Officer's eyes, while the Captain was using the binoculars again.

"A sailor has retrieved your message. It is being passed to someone I suppose is the captain," Yeagars relayed.

"There seems to be a disagreement aboard; what did the note say?" the Captain asked, dropping the binoculars long enough to look at Alex.

Before Alex could reply, they heard the lookout call out from his position up in the rigging.

"They are heaving to!"

Sure enough, Alex could see both ships slowing and starting to change course, heading away from the schooner.

"What did your message say?" the Captain asked again.

"It simply said my next arrow will be aflame," Alex replied with a smile.

"What's going on? Who are those guys?" Cassie asked, suddenly appearing from below decks and joining the three men, while pointing at the two ships now shrinking in the distance.

"Nothing sweetheart, just a case of mistaken identity," Alex replied.

"Mistaken identity?" the First Officer asked, falling for Alex's trap.

"Yes, they mistook a predator for prey," Alex replied with a smile as he led Cassie away.

----*----

After the pirate incident, the remainder of the trip to Freeport was uneventful. The winds had turned even more favorable, delivering them at the earlier end of the Captain's estimate. Rather than tying *Cassie's Quest* up at the wharf, as they had nothing to load or unload, Alex asked the Captain to anchor in the bay. The Captain agreed that would be best if they needed to leave in a hurry.

As the town of Freeport wasn't very large; Alex, Leander, Cassie, and Abrianna had no need to offload the horses for transportation. While an option, Alex didn't want to attract additional attention by flying Shadows and Rose into town.

Therefore, he had the jolly boat dropped in the water to ferry the four to shore. While the Captain remained on board with Kinsey watching through the railing, the First Officer supervised the transfer of the party to shore.

Alex was surprised to see the large number of ships, both in the bay as well as the ones tied up at various docks around the small harbor. Considering the quantity of ships he had seen in Windfall since taking governorship there, he wondered where the rest of these were headed, saying so aloud.

"Many of these ships will never cross the western sea," the First Officer replied.

"They travel up and down the coastline, trading with the many small towns dotting the seashore. Of those that do cross the sea, some are smugglers, anchoring off the coast of Westland, attempting to bypass Windfall tariffs. Others will head north to trade with those beyond the Northern Mountains, like Nyland."

Alex realized there was much he did not know about the world he now lived in. As the First Officer spoke, he watched Leander nod in agreement. At some point, he needed to sit down with the man for some much needed geography lessons.

Reaching an open spot along the dock between two piers, the seamen who had been rowing tied off the boat so that the four passengers could safely climb out and on to the wharf. For the trip, he and Leander had their swords, while Cassie and Abrianna were dressed more formally, although not in dresses. He pretended not to notice the dagger Cassie had hidden under her attire, and suspected Abrianna had the same.

"We will return to the ship, but there will be a man on watch. Just wave from here and we will return to get you," the First Office said to Alex, as he was the last to climb out. He nodded and started to leave.

"Thanks. We should be back before dark," he replied as he climbed up onto the dock.

Alex turned and watched the jolly boat cast off and head back out into the bay, before returning to his three companions. While all three were in nondescript clothing, wearing nothing that tied them to either a Royal House or the Ranger's Guild, he had verified all wore protective garments beneath their clothes. He, himself, wore the same undergarments Cassie had used as leggings, with her Ranger tunic, on previous outings.

"Where to?" he asked.

"Father said that Aunt Amelia was to meet with the Masters of the local Trade Guild Houses, introducing each to our trade proposal," Abrianna answered.

Alex realized that this was the first time he had ever heard the name of Cassie's mom.

"Then we start there. Do we need appointments?" Alex asked, unsure of the protocol.

"No, most Trade Masters are always open to conversation. I am told they hold the belief that the only bad conversation on trade is the one they didn't have," Abrianna said with a laugh.

With that, the four headed away from the wharfs and into the warehouse district, where the Trade Houses were located. Abrianna led the way, with a protective Leander always at hand. As they walked, Abrianna gave a running dialog.

"This area is where we will find the Trade Guilds, as opposed to the Craft Guilds. While the two are tightly aligned, it is the former that controls the movement of goods."

"Wouldn't it be smarter to go straight to the suppliers?" Alex asked. "In my world, that's called cutting out the middle man. You can keep the prices down and shorten the time to market."

From the horrified look on Abrianna's face, he assumed he had spoken heresy.

"That would be disastrous!" She replied, "Any craftsman caught bypassing the Guild regulations on trade would be banned from practice in any Guild city. While small local sales are not regulated, any sizable transfers, such as the type we desire, are strictly controlled by the Guilds. We would soon find that no one would consider doing business with us at all if we bypassed the traders."

Feeling duly chastised on the subject, Alex nodded and dropped the subject. He recognized a protectionist system when he saw one. By now, they were walking down stone streets, wide enough to allow two wagons to pass unhindered.

Looking down the long causeway, he could see building after building on both sides of the street. All were two-story structures, with large wooden loading docks, set at a wagon bed height, for easy transfer of goods.

Above each loading dock, Alex could see large wooden signs, with what he assumed were the names of the owners, rather than the goods they distributed. He was sort of expecting to find dealers of wine, grains, and so forth rather than house names.

"What's with the signs?" Alex asked as they stopped at the first such structure.

Apparently confused for a moment, Abrianna looked at the sign hanging above them before suddenly understanding the question.

"Oh, each denotes the Trading House, not the contents. For example, this is the House of Cybele, and they may belong to the Textile Guild, the Spice Guild, and the Coopers Guild. As such, each house may distribute differing goods. Transport to and from the harbor is by house and ship names."

Alex could see the simplicity of it. You make your pickup at Cybele, and deliver to the vessel *Sally Mae* for shipment at sea. He was sure there was a lot more to it, but for now, he need not concern himself with the subtleties. Climbing the small flight of wooden steps that led them to the loading dock, the four entered the small door next to the large cargo doors.

During the trip across the sea, they had discussed the best way to conduct their search without raising suspicion. All assumed that many of those they encountered would have no idea that Amelia was missing and therefore have no reason to react to a follow up contact from Great Vale.

Entering into a small alcove located at one side of the side of the warehouse, Alex turned to see the expanse beyond the space they occupied. Inside he could see stacks of crates and barrels throughout the warehouse. Looking up, he could see there was a second level, the floor above open straight down the middle to allow items from above to be lowered. Every now and then, there was a bridge-like section connecting one side to the other. He could see men crossing with small carts, moving goods around.

"May we see your Master?" Alex heard Abrianna ask a girl sitting behind a table. There were neatly ordered stacks of sheets, the top containing itemized lists with words he could not make out.

"And your business?" she asked, while appraising the four as one might a potential suitor.

"We follow the emissary from Great Vale. We are here to confirm relations and to place an initial order,"

At the mention of an order, the girl quickly rose from her seat, asking the four to wait. Within seconds, an older woman appeared, with the girl in her wake.

"My name is Cynthia; I am the Master of the House of Cybele. How may I be of service?" she asked.

"Cynthia Cybele, are you kidding me?" Alex mumbled with a laugh to Leander. The comment caught the man off guard and caused him to choke in reply.

"Yes, we are here to follow up with you on Emissary Lady Amelia of Great Vale's last visit," Abrianna replied, doing her best to ignore the sounds behind her.

"That was some time ago, we had assumed things had not fared well with Windfall," she replied while scanning the four before her. Alex got the impression she was holding back something.

"There are rumors?" the woman added without completing the sentence.

"No, the misunderstanding with Windfall has been resolved and Great Vale is prepared to begin trading," Abrianna replied.

"Wonderful!" Cynthia replied, looking relieved, "My assistant will take down the necessary information and we will contact your Trading Houses. What ports are you registered with?"

Before departing on this trip, Alex had identified several of the better Trading Houses in Windfall, at Abrianna's request, should they need reputable references. From the look Cynthia gave them and the gushing responses to their names, he had chosen well.

Once their business was complete, the four retreated to the street.

"Well, that was a bust," Cassie commented in despair.

"Not entirely. She knew your mother and was expecting someone like us sooner. That tells me we are on the right track," Leander replied, causing Cassie to brighten some.

"And the rumor of Renfeld's survival is working. On to the next one," Alex added, ushering the others further down the street.

# Chapter 4

The rest of the day was a repeat of the House of Cybele. Each trader that they contacted remembered Amelia, and was supposedly delighted to begin trading with Great Vale. As the day grew late into the afternoon, they had reached the House of Drakon, a name Alex recognized from the Harbormaster's book.

While outwardly no different from any of the warehouses they had visited earlier, Alex felt a negativity in the atmosphere. It was a feeling that was amplified when the Master appeared to greet them, summoned by his assistant as they approached.

"Hello, you must be the party from Great Vale. I am Tantalus, Master of this house."

"You were expecting us?" Abrianna replied.

"Ah, news travels like the wind on this street. It is quite rare that new trading partners of such importance appear."

Alex took an immediate dislike to the man. He reminded him of the worst kind of salesman, one who profited from the misery of others. As he was scanning the area around them, noting several workmen busy nearby, he caught a comment that snapped his attention back to Tantalus.

"A horrible business that, the death of the Emissary's guards."

"You have knowledge of the incident?" Leander asked, breaking protocol for someone who was supposed to be a guard.

"Only that they abandoned the good Lady to run off to a tavern. I do not know which one, as I do not frequent such places," Tantalus replied curtly at having to talk to one of lesser importance.

"My Lady, it is getting late. Perhaps we can return tomorrow to continue our business here?" Alex said to Abrianna while glancing at Tantalus.

"Of course, he is right. You should not be wandering these streets after dark. My man will see you out. I will look forward to tomorrow, then," Tantalus replied, while indicating one of the nearby workers. With that, he turned and retreated up a flight of stairs with his assistant close behind, leaving the four standing by themselves.

Holding up one hand, Alex indicated the others should wait while he moved over to the closest man, outwardly appearing to stack the same items over and over. Subtly producing a gold from his pouch, he stood next to the man with the coin protruding between two fingers as he set his hand, palm down on the counter.

"You were listening?" Alex asked the man quietly.

"Oh, never, sire," the man replied without looking up from his tasks.

Setting the coin on the table where the man was working, but keeping two fingers on it, he added.

"And you were not listening the day Lady Amelia and her guards arrived?"

The man glanced sideways and then gave the slightest of nods.

Alex slid the coin over and watched the man slip it into a pocket.

"I heard those men talking while the lady went upstairs to speak with Tantalus. They said they were headed to that mermaid bar, out on the point," the man relayed as he continued his work.

"Mermaid bar?" Alex asked, confused by the reference.

"Yes, it's called The Siren's Song. Popular with the fisherman and sailors from the harbor. You know, a pretty face to drown your sorrows type of place. Maybe even get lucky," he finished.

"Do you know why they would be going there?" Alex asked.

"Something about needing information on shipments to Windfall. I think they suspected Tantalus of supplying nasty Prince Renfeld with weapons," the man replied before moving off to the back of the warehouse.

Moving back to the others, he led them out into the street before passing along the information the man provided.

"Aren't mermaids half fish? How can they run a bar?" Alex asked quietly, not wanting to draw attention from the others passing by on the street.

Alex's confusion caused Abrianna to speak up, after the men were out of earshot.

"Mermaids do take that form when submerged, yes. However, when on land, they appear as normal as any human woman might. They are said to all be quite beautiful. I understand they can stay out of the water for days, requiring only an occasional dunking. I'm told even a bath will suffice," She stated, only to be interrupted by a snort from Cassie.

"If you call that normal," she remarked snidely.

Alex was taken aback at the comment, realizing he hadn't seen such a response from his intended since the early days when he first arrived. He realized she was jealous.

"So they have legs?" he asked, trying to ignore the outburst.

"Yes, and I understand they can be as flirty as a nymph!" she added, while looking at Cassie.

"They do nothing as well as a nymph!" she snapped, and then smiled at her cousin, slightly embarrassed by the outburst.

"Sorry," she managed with a blush.

With that, the four left the front of the warehouse and started out for the point on one side of the harbor. As they walked, Alex considered what he thought he knew about mermaids. He was pretty sure a mermaid and a siren was not the same thing, so the name of their destination confused him. Secondly, he was positive that mermaids had a reputation for drowning sailors, so the man's reference to drowning their sorrows was right on.

"So what's the story here? Mermaids running a bar? What about the mermen?" he asked openly.

"First, there are no mermen. Like nymphs, they are all female and mate with human men. Mermaids apparently only bear female children." Abrianna replied while eyeing Cassie. Without the expected outburst, she continued.

"The legend I know says the first mermaid was the beautiful, vain, young wife of a fisherman. Unaccustomed to the long separations from her handsome husband, and longing for his attention, she begged the gods to transform her into something that would allow her to go to sea when she chose, to be with her man. Taking pity on her, the gods granted her wish and made her mermaid, allowing her to swim out to his boat whenever she chose."

Abrianna paused in her tale, waiting to see if Alex had any questions before continuing.

"However, as it always is with the gods, her blessing turned to tragedy. When she appeared at her husband's boat, he was so horrified at what she had become that he rejected her. In her fury, she lured the crew into the sea with her beauty, drowning them, leaving her husband alone and devastated."

"Wow, bummer," Alex replied.

"Ah, yes..." Abrianna replied, looking confused at the comment, "so, from her came the first mermaids, vain and beautiful, like their mother."

"Ok, so why a bar?" Alex asked, still not understanding the connection. This time, it was Cassie that jumped in on the answer.

"Like other creatures of magic, they both need and despise interactions with humans. If they continued to drown sailors, they would become extinct or at a minimum, hunted to nonexistence. The bar gives them a very lucrative revenue stream, a constant supply of willing men, and the chance to take revenge on the very sailors that wronged them so long ago."

"Take revenge?" Alex asked, not liking the implications of the comment.

"Oh, these days they simply relieve them of their purses, while the lucky ones might receive a few moments of pleasure in the process. Every now and then, a sailor disappears, some found later, floating in the sea. There is never any proof that the mermaids drowned him, but there is almost always a tale of misbehavior on his part," Cassie added casually.

"Do we have a mermaid bar in Windfall?" Alex asked, curious as to why he had never heard of it before.

"Most likely, however, you are not permitted in such places!" Cassie replied with emphasis on the last.

Following the path from town, Abrianna led the way as they traveled along the edge of the bay until Alex could see a two-story structure of wood and stone. There was a beautiful, hand-carved wooden sign, depicting a topless woman from the waist up, playing what appeared to be a lyre and singing.

"Sirens are the same as mermaids, aren't they?" Alex asked as they entered the tavern.

"Absolutely not!" someone answered from inside.

As his eyes grew accustom to the darker interior, a stunningly beautiful redhead stood a few steps away, eyeing Alex as if he was a treat to be devoured. Her outfit barely covered her goods.

"Sirens are a winged creature, though they too love the sea. It is the siren's song that draws the sailors to us," the redhead finished with an evil smile.

"May I get you a table?' a blonde asked, just as alluring and immodestly dressed as the redhead eyeing Alex.

"Yes, please," Alex replied, seeing the appeal of this place as he scanned the room. Everywhere he looked, there were scantily clad women wandering among the tables of men, providing drink or sitting and socializing. He was beginning to appreciate the lure of the place, until Cassie's steely gaze that brought him back to earth.

"Um, yeah. Let's take a seat," he added, following the blonde, with Cassie at his side running interference. All four sat, with Cassie sliding her chair to be closer to Alex.

"And what can I get for you?" the redhead asked as she came around Alex's left side and attempted to sit in Alex's lap. It was Cassie's arm she found nudging her away.

"Nymph," the girl responded, as if swearing at Cassie.

"Mermaid," Cassie replied, making the word sound an insult.

"Ladies! May we have a pitcher of ale please?" Abrianna interrupted.

The two redheads glared at one another for a second, and then the mermaid made a show of spinning in place and heading to the bar, almost losing her top in the process.

"Cassie, we need information. Angering the mermaids is not going to help us get what we need. Let her flirt with Alex and see what we can learn," Abrianna whispered.

"Fine!" Cassie replied, her green eyes flashing.

A few moments later the redhead returned, her tray carrying a pitcher and four mugs. This time, she walked to the far side of Alex, on his right, standing between him and Leander. Serving Alex first, she saved Cassie for last, sliding the empty mug across the table so it tumbled into her lap.

"So sorry," she said absently as she poured for the others.

Holding her tongue, Cassie placed the mug on the table, holding on to it to prevent any further accidents. After serving Alex and Leander, the mermaid set the pitcher near the women, letting them fend for themselves.

"Now what else can I do for you?" she asked while sliding up next to Alex and running her arm around his shoulders. Alex could see the fire in Cassie's eyes, but she held her tongue.

"How long have you worked here?" Alex asked as he raised his left hand to touch the mermaids arm affectionately.

"A year," she replied, confused at the question.

"Ah, then you were here when the two men from Great Vale were killed?" Alex asked.

As she started to withdraw her arm, Alex grasped it in a firm grip, while slipping his free arm around her waist. Tugging until she realized she could not get free, she then relaxed.

"Yes, I know the men you speak of," The mermaid replied.

"What can you tell us?" Abrianna asked, while glancing at Cassie, who was staring daggers at the mermaid in Alex's grasp.

"They came in asking a lot of questions, spreading money around."

"What kind of questions?" Leander asked.

The mermaid scanned the room, as if looking for help, before replying.

"They wanted to know what we had heard from sailors on the trader's ships. Everyone knows that the men come here for company, and drunken sailors talk. About everything," she replied.

Before she could say any more, Alex felt the presence of several others behind him and even more around the table.

"Is there a problem here?" a brunette asked, her jet black hair framing a face so stunning as to startle Alex, breaking his concentration. The knife in her hand was being held in an uncomfortably threatening and familiar position. The reaction caused him to go into defensive mode, gathering the free energy around him in preparation of action.

"Apologies white wizard, we did not know," the brunette uttered as she backed away. Alex realized he must be glowing white to the magical mermaids. Although the mermaids around his table knew what had just happened, the men at the surrounding tables took no notice of the exchange.

With that, Alex released the redhead, although she made no effort to retreat from his side.

"It's alright, we were just talking," he replied.

With a signal from the redheaded mermaid at his side, the others went back to their duties while she pulled up a chair from a nearby table and slid in between Alex and Leander.

"What do you want to know?" she asked Alex, all of her previous insolence suddenly evaporated.

"Why the change in attitude?' Alex asked, with the others watching intensely.

"You are powerful?" she asked in return.

"Very!" Cassie replied before Alex could.

"We have need of a wizard such as you. There are problems here, things that we cannot correct ourselves, though many have tried. One such as you could right many wrongs, should you choose to do so," she replied, never removing her eyes from Alex. All the flirtiness was gone now; in its place was an earnest plea for help.

"Perhaps. What can you tell me about the men I spoke of?" he asked, not wanting to commit to anything without understanding exactly what he was being invited into.

"These things are entwined. They wanted to know about which trading houses were honorable and which were aligned with the darker elements of the region. These elements are the same ones I speak of, preying on myself and my sisters."

"In what manner?" Leander asked the mermaid.

"We have been pressed to dispose of certain sailors, and a sea captain or two. We have even been put upon to see that certain vessels never make port again," she answered, this time turning to face Leander as she did so.

"You have abilities. How can they force you?" Cassie asked, showing concern for the first time.

"Yes, we have great influence over human men, but they send other creatures immune to our ways. If we refuse their demands, we lose sisters to the sea, devoured by despicable creatures controlled by dark magic."

"And you know which of these houses are involved?' Abrianna asked.

"Yes, and that is what we told the men. We had learned of the Windfall plan to attack Great Vale and the efforts of Prince Renfeld to rule in the east. He has allies here in the west and we heard rumors of the plot against Lady Amelia as she arrived. We told all this to the two men, and they left straight away, anxious to return and report their findings. I understand they were killed before they ever reached the Inn of Serenity, where she was staying."

"Meaning someone either followed them here or they were betrayed while here?" Alex commented.

"My sisters would never betray us. It had to be someone from the outside, either a patron or a spy."

Alex sat back from the table and scanned the room. There had to be forty or fifty sailors in the tavern, all in various stages of drunkenness. While he watched, more men entered the bar every few minutes, as it grew darker outside. It would be easy to plant spies into the crowd, their job to watch over the mermaids and gather additional information from the drunks as they did so.

"What is your name, and please tell me it's not Ariel?" Alex asked as he returned his attention to the redheaded mermaid.

"I know an Ariel, but I am not she. I am Kelby. Why do you ask?"

"Not important," Alex replied, noting that a singing crab joke would be wasted on this audience.

"So, Kelby, which houses are in league with Renfeld?" Abrianna asked, obviously shrugging off another of Alex's private jokes.

"Just one. The House of Drakon."

# Chapter 5

Rather than risk the trip back to the port after dark, considering what happened to Amelia's bodyguards, Kelby suggested that the group take rooms in the tavern for the night. In addition, one of her sisters delivered a message to *Cassie's Quest*, written in Alex's hand for Captain Yeagars, explaining their delay on returning to the ship.

For the moment at least, the mermaids were treating the four as honored guests. The implied promise of Alex's intervention in the oppression they were enduring was incentive enough to be exceptionally cooperative. Privately, Alex wasn't exactly sure if he could do anything on their behalf, but it was at least implied that they shared a common enemy.

"Let's go someplace more private," Kelby suggested as she rose from her chair, indicating the stairs on the far wall.

As everyone followed suit, Alex paused as he looked over at the bar where one of the mermaids was pouring drinks to be delivered by another. Stopping in place, he turned to Kelby.

"Only mermaids work in this bar?" he asked.

"Yes," the little redhead replied, confused at the question.

"You don't happen to serve coffee?" he asked, thinking it too much to ask for.

"What's coffee?' the mermaid replied as she shook her head at the question before continuing on her way.

Ushered upstairs into the mermaids' private quarters and away from the general population below, the group met with several of the women, each imparting what little they knew about the Drakon operation. By now, Alex had confirmed his earlier suspicions and believed Tantalus was the mystery conspirator in Amelia's kidnaping.

While Leander and Abrianna were more than comfortable with the situation, Alex could tell Cassie was not in the least happy with the circumstances.

"Why must we stay here tonight?" she asked during one of the breaks in interviews.

"It isn't safe to travel right now. I am sure Tantalus is well aware we are talking to the mermaids and will have his assassins out in force."

"Let them come, it's been too long since I've been in a good fight," she replied sharply. The comment brought an image to mind of the first time Alex had seen his bride-to-be. She was encased in plate armor, sword in hand, ready to take on four of Renfeld's minions by herself.

Since Alex and Cassie became involved, her uncle had placed her in classes intended on teaching her self-control for her wilder side. The inner nymph had a tendency to be rash and emotional, traits she initially turned to combat and weapons training. He had no doubt she meant what she said, but there was something else.

"What is really bothering you?" Alex asked. The question brought a blush to her cheeks and she looked away before turning to reply.

"I don't like the way they look at you!" she whispered, while indicating the mermaids.

"Welcome to my world," Alex replied with a laugh.

"This is different. What mermaid wouldn't want a wizard as her lover? Her child would be amazing!"

"And every man wants to be with a nymph. Please, let's just curb the jealousy and remember we are here to find your mom," he replied more sympathetically.

"Even so...." she replied before leaning in and kissing him. It was an act that every mermaid in the room watched with a keen eye.

"Does the line start here?" Kelby asked, as she took the seat on the other side of Alex.

"What did you learn?" Alex asked before Cassie could comment. Earlier, he had asked her to see if anyone remembered if or when Amelia had left the island, hoping she might be held nearby. While he had reports of her making the trip to Tazmain, he wanted to be sure.

"She was taken to the mainland. One of the sailors from a Drakon ship recalled the trip about a month ago."

"So she was held here in Freeport first?" Alex asked, doing the math in his head over the delay between then and her arrival in Freeport.

"Apparently so, though the sailor did not know where, only that she was brought to the ship under the cover of darkness and taken to Tazmain where they disembarked."

"How many were with her? Where did they go?" Cassie asked, anxious at the news.

"There were three men with her and he did not hear where their destination was, only that they required horses and supplies once they went ashore," Kelby replied in a sympathetic tone.

"She is your mother?" the mermaid finally asked.

"Yes, she is," Cassie replied emotionally.

"I lost my mother to the dark creature of the House of Drakon. I will help you find yours," the redhead said. With that, she rose and headed back downstairs. Alex could sense an intensity in Kelby that bordered on obsession and he suspected she was quite headstrong. As she left, Leander and Abrianna returned from their discussions with the other mermaids.

"Any luck?" Abrianna asked as she sat.

"They took her to the mainland. Kelby's sources say they landed in Tazmain and got horses there."

"We can contact the Rangers in Tazmain and try to find their trail," Leander proposed, noting how distressed Cassie was.

The four talked for a while longer before Cassie and Abrianna retired for the evening. Cassie was not at all satisfied with the sleeping accommodations, but with only two free rooms, she had her cousin's needs to consider. While Abrianna and Leander's relationship was blessed by the king, they were not at the same point as Cassie and Alex. That meant that the two would not be sleeping together now or in the near future.

Trusting in Alex's good judgement and Leander's chivalrous nature, she slowly made her way to the room provided. As Kelby, who had returned from below, led the women away, Leander leaned into Alex.

"Have you noticed how much the mermaid resembles Lady Cassandra? Shorter, but they could be sisters. Were I not entranced by Abrianna, I could see the attraction."

"Leander my friend, observations like that have led to many a man's early death!" Alex replied while indicating Cassie watching the two men talk as she turned the corner.

----*----

Leander and Alex spent part of the night reviewing all that they had learned from their day's work and the mermaids. Kelby had come by several times to check on the two men, but without Cassie present, her interest in Alex was much more subdued. Apparently, tormenting his fiancée was part of the fun.

"What's with this sea creature Kelby keeps talking about? Is it a threat to the ship?" Alex asked Leander.

"While I am not as well read as Abrianna, I suspect it's a Sea Dragon. If we are truly dealing with dark magic again, they are the minions of evil in the east. While not evil themselves, I am told they can be coerced by someone with special powers," Leander replied.

As the two men talked, Kelby returned with a stack of papers, dropping them on the table between the two.

"We keep things the customers lose, mostly their money, but you might find something useful in this stack," she said before turning and sauntering off.

Alex found he and Leander were both watching her without even realizing they were staring. Both quickly recovered and began sorting through the pile.

"Look at this," Leander said as he handed Alex a sheet.

Alex reviewed the paper Leander handed him. It appeared to be a ship's manifest, tied to a shipment from the House of Drakon. The items listed were of no real interest, mostly fabrics and nonperishables headed to a port he was unfamiliar with. It was the shippers mark that had their attention. In the lower right corner was a seal, authenticating the document. It held a winged dragon rising out of the waves.

"If it is Tantalus, I would expect he would hold her someplace remote. Somewhere he could be certain of. He couldn't afford rumors in town of his treachery," Leander proposed.

"You don't suppose Tantalus keeps any records on his holdings on the mainland? You know, estates, farms, mines," Alex asked.

"I would imagine so," Leander replied, catching the suggestion. What better place than somewhere he owned and controlled access to for hiding a hostage.

At that, Alex waved to Kelby, who was in the corner of the room, sitting and talking to other mermaids.

"Yes, Wizard Alex," she asked, mixing respect with a familiarity he was sure was meant to insult.

"Leander and I are going to do a little research. Should Lady Cassandra come looking for me, please tell her I will be back shortly."

"You going to House Drakon? Are you sure this is wise? No doubt Tantalus has men everywhere. Perhaps I should go with you?" she blurted out with some concern.

"That is not your concern, we will be fine. It's best you stay here," he replied.

With that, Alex made himself and Leander disappear in front of the mermaid.

"I will let Cassie know if she inquires," the mermaid replied with a smile after they reappeared.

"Call her that at your own risk. I would hate for her to kill you, now that I am becoming so fond of you," he replied with a smile. The two men started downstairs, and disappeared from view before reaching the bottom step.

----*----

Alex and Leander were standing outside the House of Drakon in a small alley between the warehouse and its neighbor. Still invisible, they had managed to slip out of the Siren's Song with little trouble. Sticking next to the walls, they skirted most of the foot traffic in the bar and slipped out the front door with ease.

Alex had Leander hold on to his shoulders behind him as he led the two clear of the tavern and well out into the darkness. On the way, he had detected two separate groups of men in hiding, surely watching the people coming and going from the tavern. Their progress had been slow, but they remained unnoticed.

Now they were assessing their options on how to enter the offices of the House of Drakon undetected. Along the way, they had acquired a rope and a few tools left unattended in a wagon. As they stood in the darkness, Alex was scanning the building with his senses, trying to determine if it was occupied.

"There are two people inside, one in the office area on the first floor where we entered today, and one upstairs. I sense the one below is asleep… not sure about the other," Alex whispered to Leander.

Scanning the area, Alex found a spot where a one-story wall connected two of the nearby buildings. Climbing up onto the wall, he then tossed the rope over the corner of the building, where a beam protruded up, giving him a purchase to hold the rope in place.

First Leander, and then Alex climbed up the rope, until both found themselves on the rooftop of the warehouse. Crossing over to the peak as quietly as possible, they reached a vent in the roof where hot air escaped the open space below. Prying up the rectangular lid, Alex first scanned the area, and then lowered the rope for the two to descend into the darkness.

Once inside, they found themselves on the second level of the warehouse, next to the open gap in the center of the floor. Peering into the gap, Alex could see the stacks below.

"Follow me," Alex whispered as he let his senses lead the two through the darkness. Moving across the wooden floor in near total quiet, they reached the far wall where Alex found a door. Beyond the door, he detected the second occupant, seemingly stationary, but apparently conscious as he could sense small movements as if the person was working.

Alex slowly cracked the door open, trying not to make a sound. Inside the room was a single candle, lit on a desk, next to a redheaded woman facing away from him. She was apparently working late, making her way through a stack of papers, methodically reading each one before setting it aside.

He was considering what kind of magic he could use on her, to render her unconscious without killing her, when she spoke.

"About time you two got here."

As she turned, Alex and Leander could see Kelby was working through a stack of documents on Tantalus's private desk.

"What are you doing here?" Alex asked pointedly.

"Why in the world would you expect me to wait for you?" the mermaid replied, her tone betraying her disbelief.

"How did you get here?" Alex asked in a hushed tone, remembering the other below them.

"Oh, you don't have to whisper. The guard is sleeping away downstairs," Kelby replied with a smile.

"How?" Leander asked?

"Mermaid magic. I lured him to sleep with a song and a smile," she replied, her dazzling face lighting up the room.

"Spiked his drink?" Alex replied, less inclined to be sucked in with a magical explanation.

"Yes," she replied, still smiling, "I came to the door, explaining that his mates had sent me with drink. He never questioned it and was soon fast asleep."

"How did you know we were coming here? And how did you get past Tantalus's men?" Leander asked.

"I suspect mermaids have exceptional hearing. She heard us talking," Alex said as a question directed at Kelby.

"We see exceeding well too," she answered, "and his men were not looking for me, they were looking for you. Now help me with these things. Reading, we are slow at. What are we looking for anyway?"

"We are looking for any references around the House of Drakon holdings on the mainland," Alex supplied.

"And anything on dragons," Leander added.

"Is that what killed my mother? A Sea Dragon?"

"We think so. Here, look at this," Alex replied while shuffling through several papers until he found one with the

House Seal they had seen at the tavern. Both men watched as the mermaid examined the seal, slowly nodding her head in understanding.

"I will gut Tantalus," she said slowly.

"Not just yet, we don't want to tip our hand until Lady Amelia is found. Then, I will help you," Alex replied.

Kelby looked at Alex, her eyes partially filled with tears. He could see the hurt there, but only for a moment, before she buried the vulnerability and was hardened once more.

"I will take your word on that," she replied, and then all three started going through the documents.

It was Leander who found the first lead.

"Sire, look at this," he said while handing Alex a piece of paper.

"Why do you call him sire?' Kelby asked as Alex scanned the paper.

Alex looked up and nodded to Leander, giving him permission to expose their cover. He then went back to his reading.

"Alex is Lord Protector of Windfall and Mage Apprentice to the Wizard King of Great Vale. Lady Cassandra is the King's niece and cousin to Lady Abrianna, the king's daughter."

"So you are all royalty?" Kelby asked, shocked at the revelation.

"Not me, I am the Ranger Guild Master of Great Vale," he replied, somewhat embarrassed.

"And I am not royalty, I just work for the King," Alex added without looking up from his reading.

"Close enough," Kelby replied sarcastically.

"Ok, so back on topic, why is a wagon train of beef going to someplace called The Dragon's Teeth of any concern?" Alex asked.

He noted an exchange of looks between Leander and Kelby, before the mermaid spoke.

"The Dragon's Teeth are a mountain range to the east, which was once the home of wild dragons. There are many farms and ranches there, all raising their own livestock. The only reason anyone would be going there with beef is to feed one."

"And the source of the meat is a holding belonging to Tantalus, heading to another at the base of those mountains. A perfect place to detain someone, as the locals stay far away from that area, lest they become dragon food themselves, or so they fear," Leander added.

Setting that aside, the three continued to search the office, until Kelby came across a map of the region, with notes on particular areas. They could see the reference at the Dragon's Teeth, where they had discussed the wagonloads of meat, but there was another mark on the map, located on a body of water, that got their attention.

"I know this lake, Lake Vishap, it is attached to the sea by an underground river," Kelby said as she pointed to the map.

"It looks as if Tantalus has a villa on the shores there," Alex pointed out.

"Wait," Leander said as he shuffled through more papers until he found what he was looking for. Handing the paper to Alex, he read the paper, comparing the names on the document to those on the map.

"Why would anyone ship large quantities of fish from the coast to a lake?" Alex asked, noting the document referencing large shipments from costal fisherman to the location noted on the map.

"To feed a Sea Dragon?" Kelby stated more than asked.

"If one wants their dragons to remain hidden, they need to feed them rather than allowing them to hunt," Leander said solemnly.

# Chapter 6

The three cleaned up after themselves and removed any telltale signs they had ever searched the place. Alex took a risk and kept the map they had found, leaving everything else behind. After replacing the roof vent and retrieving the rope from the warehouse, the three went downstairs to find the guard still sleeping soundly in his chair.

It took Alex a moment to rig the door so that the bar dropped in place once closed, giving the guard the impression that he had dreamed the mermaid visit. With that, the two men followed Kelby as she led them through the back streets, emerging near the bay. She then followed the trail heading back to The Siren's Song, with Alex making himself and Leander invisible for the final part of the trip.

Upon entering the tavern, Alex waited until she had closed the door before dropping the spell. The room was almost deserted, it being very late. Unfortunately, one occupant was wide-awake, and sitting front and center of the door. It was Cassie.

"And where have you been?" she asked in a tone no man wants to hear, as her eyes passed over the three.

"We think we have found where your mother is being held," Leander replied, appearing very uncomfortable under Cassie's steely-eyed glare.

Alex could see her soften a bit at the news, but he knew he was not out of the woods just yet.

"Kelby helped us get past the guards in the House of Drakon warehouse. There, we located two spots on the mainland where she could be hidden away," Alex supplied.

Cassie sat staring at the three for a few seconds, before rising and walking up to Alex. Giving him a quick kiss on the cheek, she then approached the redheaded mermaid.

"Thank you," she said quietly before turning and heading up the stairs, presumably to return to bed.

----*----

The following morning, Alex woke to the smell of baking downstairs. The room he and Leander were provided was small, with barely enough room for the two men, but the beds were comfortable and he had slept soundly after their late night activities.

After waking his roommate, he quickly dressed and went downstairs to find both Abrianna and Cassie in conversation with several of the mermaids. Alex experienced a momentary flash of panic as he spied Kelby next to Cassie, as they all chatted pleasantly.

Although he had nothing to be guilty about, his previous experiences with women told him that hardly mattered.

"About time you got up," Alex heard Kelby say.

Cassie turned with the comment, but said nothing as he crossed the room and kissed her cheek.

"Good morning," he added as he took the open seat next to her.

"Is there any more of that?" Kelby asked sarcastically.

Rather than take the bait, Cassie smiled and looked at Alex.

"So you took the mermaid with you last night and not me?"

Panic-stricken, he looked at Abrianna and then Kelby for assistance, before all three burst out in laughter, supported by the other women nearby.

"Kelby explained everything," Abrianna said, as she laughed with the others.

"Women can be very cruel," Leander announced, as he entered the room late. Evidently, he had caught just enough of the conversation to understand Alex had been the butt of their humor.

"Then she explained what we found?" Alex asked, trying to put the previous conversation as far behind them as possible.

"Yes, she did. So we are to believe that Aunt Amelia is either being held at the base of The Dragon's Teeth, or on Lake Vishap?" Abrianna asked.

"That's our best guess, yes," Alex replied.

"Dragons make excellent jailers. Once they latch on to something it is very hard to get them to relinquish it," Kelby added.

"And we believe both locations contain dragons," Alex supplied.

"Kelby says the lake is connected to the sea by an underground river," Leander added.

"Vishap means water dragon, in the ancient tongues. It is a sea dweller," Abrianna said thoughtfully.

"Yes and we think we know what this sea dweller has been doing," Alex added while glancing at Kelby.

"I gave it some thought after we returned last night. I fear we need to split up and pursue both leads. Once Tantalus knows we are on to him, he might move her again, or worse," Alex finished.

"Why don't we just capture Tantalus and make him return my mom?" Cassie asked, upset by the conversation.

"I very much doubt he would cooperate. I fear he is not the only player in this game and she would likely perish at the hands of another. We must find and rescue her to be sure of her safety," Leander explained.

"I agree. So, when do we leave?' Kelby asked.

"We?" Alex asked as the others turned to look at the mermaid.

"Whomever goes to Lake Vishap needs me to come along. There are underwater recesses there ideal for securing a hostage."

"I can reach such places," Cassie replied defiantly to the mermaid.

"Yes, but you will be traveling with your Lord, will you not? And from the look in his eyes, I sense he is bound for the Dragon's Teeth," she replied, just as defiant.

"She is right; my gut says that's the place they are keeping her. That, however, is not why she wants to come along, is it Kelby?"

"I have lost a lot of family to that Sea Dragon. It would be my pleasure to kill it."

"Mermaids are not known as warriors," Leander replied.

"Try me!" was the reply from the redhead with a flash of anger. Alex wasn't sure if it was the red hair, but her reply had a lot of Cassie in it.

"How does one kill a dragon?" Alex asked, interrupting the glaring match between the two.

"We will need to acquire magical weapons for that effort," Leander replied.

"We can address that in Tazmain, once we land there. How soon can you be ready to leave?" Alex asked the mermaid.

He detected a slight flash of anger in Cassie's eyes, as the mermaid replied.

"I can leave now, I don't need much," she replied while indicating a small satchel against the wall.

As everyone got up, preparing to depart, Leander pulled Alex to one side to speak in private.

"Is this a good idea my friend? Do not be deceived, Lady Cassandra and the mermaid do not like one another, and I suspect it is because of you," he said quietly.

"And that is why the mermaid goes with you," Alex replied with a smile.

----*----

The five travelers left the tavern and headed straight down to the wharfs of Freeport. Before leaving, Kelby had requested one of the other mermaids go to Captain Yeagars, asking that the jolly boat be sent to retrieve them straight away.

As they traveled the path to town, both Leander and Alex were on guard for any attempts on their lives, but none manifested. He suspected that Tantalus preferred the protection and anonymity of darkness to direct confrontation.

Reaching the port, they found the little boat waiting for them and the First Officer pleased to see the party. "Sire, I am very glad to see you. After the message from the mermaid last night, the Captain and I had concerns," he said while eyeing the new member of the party.

"Kelby, this is our First Officer, Mr.…" Alex paused, realizing he had never been properly introduced to the man.

"Sikes, Sire. A pleasure, ma'am," he replied, saving Alex the embarrassment of asking.

"Sorry," he whispered quietly to the man, as everyone loaded into the boat. Alex took special care that Cassie sat between him and Kelby, assuring her there was no hidden intent in bringing her along.

The boat was launched quickly and they were soon beside *Cassie's Quest*. On their approach, Alex could see Kinsey's head through the rails, her tail flying madly. As they passed the bow, Kelbly looked up to see the name on the ship.

"He named it for you. How sweet, he must like you," she said sarcastically to Cassie.

"You have no idea," Cassie replied with venom of her own.

Alex was overjoyed to see the boarding ladder, helping Cassie up and then Abrianna, saving Kelby for last.

"Listen, if you want to be part of this, then you better learn to behave!" he said as he blocked her from climbing the ladder.

She stared up into his eyes, providing him with her best innocent, angelic, face. However, he could see the mischief in her eyes.

"As you wish," she answered, waiting for him to release her. With the reply, he stepped away from the ladder and watched her ascend.

"You, my friend, are a very brave man," Leander said as he stepped up next to Alex, and then followed the mermaid up.

"Sire," Mr. Sikes said, as Alex started to climb, "mermaids are dangerous creatures that will lure a man to his death."

"It's not the mermaid I fear," Alex replied, as he continued up the ladder and onto the deck. There he found Captain Yeagars and Kinsey waiting, with the others gathered around. The wolf charged Alex, demanding attention before everyone else.

"Welcome aboard, Sire. What are your orders?" the Captain asked, while watching the mermaid. Alex was beginning to think he underestimated the superstition sailors held around them.

"We sail for Tazmain… how long a trip is that?" he asked, realizing he had no clue where it actually was beyond Tantalus's map in his pocket.

"We can make it by midday tomorrow, Sire. Ah, are we all going?" he asked while looking at the new addition.

"I am sorry, forgive me. Captain Yeagars, this is Kelby. She will be traveling with us. Can you see that she gets appropriate accommodations, please?"

"In the hold with the horses," Cassie commented, before turning and heading below with Kinsey on her heels.

As she left, the Captain turned and gave Alex a questioning look.

"A cabin will be fine," he replied.

With that, the Captain assigned a sailor acting as an orderly to assist the mermaid, while the rest of the crew recovered and stowed the jolly boat. Before he left, the Captain pulled Alex aside.

"Sire, it is wise to tempt the fates so, by bringing a mermaid on board? Surely, there must be other options available to you. Perhaps we should put her ashore while we can?"

"Captain, I understand your concerns, however, it is too late for that. Besides, she is far more interested in killing Sea Dragons than anyone here."

Alex noted the mention of Sea Dragons did nothing to relieve the good captain of his worried expression. At that point, he turned and headed below to check on Cassie, concerned at the reception he was about to receive.

----*----

Cassie was in the cabin she shared with Alex, brooding as she rubbed on Kinsey. She didn't know what it was about the mermaid, but her comments about Alex struck a nerve deep inside her, making Cassie an easy target for her harassment.

So long as he was not present, she had no issues with the redhead, she even found her pleasant company... well sort of. However, the moment Alex stepped into the room, all semblance of civility vanished. In part, she knew it was the mermaid's natural attraction to Alex.

As a magical creature, Cassie knew Kelby reacted to males as her nature dictated, projecting her sexuality to entrance them. She herself had practiced much the same thing for years, learning how to control and later manipulate the effect to her advantage.

It was the fact that Kelby didn't even try to turn hers off that so irritated Cassie. It was like having your little sister trying to steal your boyfriend. Though she trusted Alex, her inner nymph was ablaze in jealousy and rage.

She heard a soft tap on the cabin door before she saw Alex stick his head through a small opening.

"May I come in," he asked quietly.

"Of course," she replied while rising from her bunk and crossing over to meet him as he entered. Kinsey took the cue, and curled up on a blanket provided for her in the corner. Wrapping her arms around his neck, Cassie planted a kiss on his lips intended to remind him how much she loved him.

"Wow," he replied after she relaxed her grasp.

"Why did you bring the mermaid?" she asked calmly without releasing him.

"I will do whatever is necessary to find your mother safely. If that means I saddle a dragon and ride it to the moon, then so be it."

Cassie actually giggled at the description before asking, "So you think she can help us?"

"Yes, I do. Besides, she has a huge motivation to help us. I am sure the thing that killed her mother was the Sea Dragon at Tantalus's lake house. I don't think your mom is there, because it is too close to Tazmain, but to be sure we must investigate. For that, she is ideal."

"Well, I don't like the way she looks at you, but I agree," Cassie replied.

Reaching over to bolt the cabin door, Alex turned back and led her to the bunk.

"Well, I love the way you look at me," he said.

----*----

It was just after sunset when Alex and the rest returned topside from below deck, after eating dinner. Cassie and Kelby had managed to keep the barbs to a minimum while everyone else enjoyed the food and drink. Alex noted that being out on the sea had the same calming effect on the mermaid as it had on Cassie.

"What a beautiful evening," Cassie commented as she went to the rail and watched the last rays of sunlight disappear.

"For once we agree," Kelby added, standing close by and inhaling the sea air.

They had no more than started to talk when the entire ship suddenly shook, as if they had run aground.

"Have we hit a reef?" Leander asked aloud.

Abruptly, there was another jolt. However, this time it came from the other side of the ship. Grabbing the rail, Alex closed his eyes and attempted to sense what was below them. All he could feel was open water, the bottom too deep to detect easily. Then there was a flash as something large shot under the keel and paused just off the port side of the ship.

"It's the dragon," Alex said calmly while remaining at the rail with his eyes closed so he could try and track the creature.

"There!" he heard someone shout, and then, as he opened his eyes, he was treated to a flaming display as the creature lit up the night with its spout of fire. While he focused on the beast, he heard a commotion behind him as the captain called his crew to defend the ship.

Alex watched the dragon rise out of the water like a snake, its head and upper body as high as the yardarm of the mizzenmast. The head was larger than Shadows, and its eyes were planted firmly on Alex, as he stood at the railing.

He watched as the creature drew in a breath, and all the while Alex was gathering what loose energy he could find. As the flame burst forth from the dragon's mouth, Alex formed a shield between the ship and dragon. Slammed by the impact of the blast and struggling to deflect the flames away from the ship, he turned the fire back at the dragon's head. Engulfed in its own flames, it howled in rage and retreated, only to return to try and ram the vessel by lunging forward.

"Brace yourselves!" Alex shouted, as he wavered under the force of the creature and then fixed himself to the ship, wrapping shielding around himself and the decking. Slamming itself into the shielding repeatedly, the dragon rocked the ship, but left it otherwise undamaged. Alex watched as the shields prevented the creature from reaching the ship and those aboard. He could see its flaming red eyes glaring at him over the short distance

Taking advantage of a pause in its attack, Alex gathered a burst of energy. Pulling from his internal reserves and slamming it into the exposed serpent-like body of the dragon, he sent the energy blast forth. The force of the impact took the dragon by surprise, sending it flying into the darkness and scorching a gouge in its side.

Everyone on-board stood motionless, scanning the darkness and listening for any indication of the dragon's location.

"He has gone," Alex announced, after his magical scanning of the area produced no sign of the creature. Walking slowly back over to the railing, Alex concentrated, forming a shield that covered the entire hull of the ship. Once he was satisfied, he opened his eyes to see the Captain and crew forming a semicircle around him, with his companions mixed in among them.

"Sire, we would like to thank you," Captain Yeagars stated humbly.

"My pleasure. I have placed a shield around the ship's hull. Should the dragon return, we are protected from damage if it tries to ram us. Please post a watch throughout the night, though."

Alex stood in place, holding the rail while the crowd dissipated. Cassie came to his side, studying his face, but saying nothing. Finally, after everyone had left, he looked at her and smiled.

"Please get me something to drink before I pass out."

## Chapter 7

Alex sat in the small common area below decks, set aside for the royal family. With him were Leander, Abrianna, Kelby and Cassie, and all had their eyes on him as he drank from the large flagon Cassie had provided. Kinsey was lying near Alex, doing her best to stay out of the way.

"I have never seen that much magic used in one action," Kelby said, as she watched him drink, clearly in awe.

"Let us hope it will not be necessary to see such again," Leander replied as he handed Alex a round of bread.

"I thought the Elves taught you how to channel energy, Alex?" Abrianna asked. "I haven't seen you use that much of your own since the orcs in A'asari."

"Yes, but the dragon wasn't providing me energy as the red mages did. This was raw fire and I could only absorb small amounts while fighting. In case you didn't notice, that thing was big and strong. Did anyone see you help me below?" he asked Leander.

"No one noticed," Cassie replied to the question.

"Why do you care?" Kelby asked.

"The men have faith that Alex will protect them. He cannot appear weak in front of them," Leander answered.

"That's their ignorance! That much magic would kill most wizards, yet he stood there as if it was a game," she replied, dreamy-eyed and smiling.

"Easy, mermaid," Cassie responded as the redheaded nymph slipped into the seat next to Alex.

"Regardless of their ignorance, we need them to feel safe and protected," Abrianna added to the conversation.

"Well, I know I do," Kelby said while mooning at Alex.

"There is one bright side to this," Alex said between swallows.

"And that is?" Abrianna asked in reply.

"They no longer fear Kelby," he said with a smile.

----*----

The night had passed without incident, and Alex rose early, feeling famished. Grabbing whatever he could find in the galley, he and Cassie went on deck to watch the morning sunrise as he ate. They had left Kinsey below, still sleeping in their cabin.

"Isn't it beautiful?" Cassie asked as the sun cleared the horizon, lighting up a clear blue sky.

"Yes, it is," Alex answered between bites. When he had finally had enough to eat, the two sat on deck as the crew performed their duties around them. Soon enough, the others appeared from below, having either already eaten or brought their meals up with them as had Alex and Cassie.

"We will be in Tazmain in a few hours," Kelby announced, while pointing to the direction of the port city.

"Have you been there before?" Abrianna asked curiously.

"Not ashore, but I have been in the bay many times. When I was younger, before I started working at the Siren's Song, we would come and tease the sailors. Eventually, the patrol would chase us off. We weren't going to hurt anyone, but I suppose they didn't know that."

Alex was actually impressed that the little redhead was considering the feelings of others; the moment passed quickly.

"It was really funny though, when the sailors saw we were bare from the waist up, and jumped in the water to try and catch us," Kelby finished with a giggle.

"I'm sure it was hilarious," Cassie commented, thankfully only loud enough for Alex to hear.

"So Leander, what do you know of Tazmain?" Alex asked trying to change the subject before things escalated between the two redheads.

"It is about as large as Windfall, and is one of three major cities on the coast. As we have discussed, most of the shipping actually goes through Freeport, however the major houses also ship directly from Tazmain. Once we land, we should go straight to the Ranger's Guild. They are our best chance at gaining information on the House of Drakon."

While they talked, Alex could see the coastline as it came into view. Watching as they grew closer, he could see the green forested hills behind the more barren brown coast. Next came the masts of ships, he presumed at anchor outside those in the harbor itself. It was then that Alex heard the conversation around him.

"Alex, what do you think?" Cassie asked.

"I'm sorry, what?"

"Do you think we should go ashore right away or wait until we are warped to the docks so Shadows and Rose can be offloaded?" she asked, the others watching intently.

"Ah... what is warped?" Alex asked, completely unfamiliar with the term.

"It's how larger ships are brought in. We launch a boat with a line, and then we use the capstan to pull us into the dock," Leander answered. Alex had actually seen ships perform the task in Windfall harbor; he had just never known what the action was called.

"I think we should check in with the Guild while the ship gets settled. The quicker we get out of Tazmain, the better, I suspect."

"We can land with the boat that takes the line to the dock," Kelby proposed.

"Let's do that," Alex decided.

----*----

The five, plus Kinsey, were following the main road into Tazmain, having left the First Mate and his men securing the line for warping *Cassie's Quest* into position. There had been a short delay as they negotiated with the Harbormaster for a spot on a prime pier. A few well-placed coins from Alex's pouch had settled the issue.

Kinsey was drawing more than her normal number of stares, as wolves were not all that common on this side of the sea. Glued to Alex's side, she seemed delighted to be off the ship and back on firm ground again. He and Leander used Kinsey's influence to help clear a path in the busy street, with the three women close behind.

Leander made quick work of their trip, taking a few side streets and circumventing a large portion of the daily traffic to and from the port. With his guidance, the group soon found themselves as the doors of the Tazmain Ranger's Guild.

"Please inform your Master that the travelers from Great Vale have arrived," he said to one of the Rangers manning the door. In his exchange with the Master here, Leander had informed him they would be traveling anonymously, and without the need for the ceremonies a traveling Guild Master and royalty would demand.

Quickly, the man returned with another, both men doing a bad attempt at masking the hurried pace of their return.

"Our Master bids you welcome. Please follow us," one announced.

Waving everyone inside, they led them through the halls of a familiar structure. Though not identical, the building was very similar to the one in Great Vale.

"Welcome!" they heard as they entered a small office in the rear of the building. Inside, its single occupant rose from behind a desk and crossed to greet the party. Once everyone was inside, the Rangers who had led them there exited.

"Please, sit. Would you like something to drink?" the man in Ranger's colors asked. While older than both Leander and Alex, he appeared fit and weathered. It was Alex's guess that he spent far more time outside than in. He took a liking to the man straight away.

"I am Guild Master Thomas Robeck, and it is my great pleasure to meet you," the man announced, the smile genuine, in Alex's opinion.

Leander introduced himself as Guild Master of Great Vale, and then introduced the rest of the party, Kinsey included. With that, everyone found a seat, and Robeck opened the conversation.

"Your last message about the House of Drakon only confirmed a suspicion we have harbored here for some time. In the last year or so, they have risen from an small trading house to one of the most influential in the region, not just in Tazmain. There have been several mysterious accidents and disappearances among their competitors that have advanced their position in the guilds."

"They have been coercing the mermaids to assist in that," Kelby informed the Guild Master.

"That is most unfortunate," Thomas said somberly.

"We were attacked by a Sea Dragon on the way here," Leander added.

"And you survived?" the Guild Master asked in surprise.

"With a little luck," Alex replied before anyone else.

"That is a lot of luck. You are the first I've heard to survive such an encounter," he replied with a skeptical expression on his face.

"Our ship's master is very experienced. What can you tell us about dragons, and specifically how to kill them?" Alex asked, closing the discussion on the attack.

"That is a very difficult thing to do. Dragons are creatures of dark magic. That is to say, they tend to align with those that practice the dark ways. I understand that the recent attack on Great Vale was, at least in part, promoted by the dark elves?"

"That and they contributed in the corruption of the Rangers. Although they were defeated there, we fear their influence is not gone," Abrianna replied.

"Yes, we have felt the pressure here as well. However, since you uncovered the plot in the east, we have been able to root out the influences here."

"Can we get back to finding my mom, please?" Cassie asked, her impatience clear to all in the room.

"My apologies, Lady Cassandra," the Guild Master said, before continuing.

"I concur with your opinion that Lady Amelia is being held in the presence of a dragon. The House of Drakon is rumored to be in possession of at least one. While not the most gracious of hosts, they are renowned for protecting what is theirs. It will not allow any harm to come to her, but should she try to escape, the creature will pursue her mercilessly until it reclaims its prize."

"So it will be necessary to kill the thing before we can get Amelia back?" Alex asked, hoping to avoid a fight with something he wasn't even sure he could kill.

"Not necessarily; if that were so then Tantalus would never be able to reclaim her either," Leander inserted.

"Yes, the dragon must be willing to relinquish its prize. Unfortunately, we need to discover what the particular creature values. Most hoard gold and jewels, as a magpie, stealing shiny objects. I have heard of others more enamored with offerings of food, even casks of ale or wine. That is how Tantalus might recover Lady Amelia when the time came to return her."

"Maybe he just uses the dragon to guard his gold?" Kelby asked,

"A dragon's lair is a poor choice to store anything you intend to recover at a later date. It is only their desperation that drives them to place her there. Were she anywhere else in the city, we would have reclaimed her already," Thomas said to Leander and Alex. "Enough then. Let me take you to the archives to see what we can find about slaying dragons."

"My Ladys, and mermaid, might I show you to our VIP quarters where a hot bath is available for each of you?"

Alex noted both Cassie and Kelby perked up at the mention of a bath, over Abrianna's mild interest.

"That would be lovely," Abrianna replied for the three.

----*----

Captain Yeagars was conflicted at the current state of affairs. Usually he wasn't pleased to be tied to a dock, figuratively landlocked until whatever he was transporting was transferred to or from his ship. Today, however, he was delighted to be in water too shallow for a Sea Dragon to maneuver. In his many years at sea, that was the first time he had actually seen one of the legendary beasts. He hoped never to see another.

While they had no cargo to transfer, he had the crew ensure that all four mounts, still safely below decks, were ready to go ashore at the whim of the Lord Protector. Before yesterday, he had not given much thought about the man or the rumors of his magical capabilities. To Yeagars, he had been just been another Royal to ferry about.

He had since revised that opinion greatly. He did not know what invisible manipulations the man had performed in defending the ship and crew from the dragon. He just knew they worked. Wizard or Mage, he neither understood, nor cared for the difference. He was just happy to have the man aboard.

Therefore, it was with a broad smile that he greeted the five, plus wolf, as they crossed the gangway and returned to the ship.

"Your orders, Sire?" he asked as the Lord Protector came on deck.

"We have supplies being delivered within the hour. Once they arrive, we need to get the horses out of the hold and readied."

"Yes, Sire, and where would you like us to moor? Or would you prefer we anchor in the bay?" the captain asked cautiously.

"At your whim. I will gladly pay to leave you right here if that is your wish."

"That would be most satisfactory," Yeagars replied with a smile.

----*----

After leaving the captain, Alex and Cassie went below to their cabin to prepare to leave. He was happy to be back on the ship and working to rescue Cassie's mom. While the women had gone with the Guild Master, he and Leander were led to the Guild archives to search for any references on the local dragon population.

After several hours, the two were able to determine which types of dragons they were dealing with. In the Dragon's Teeth Mountains, they expected to find a Red Dragon. A fire breather, they were notorious gold hoarders, and preferred to fight with their claws to prevent damaging any treasure their opponent might carry, but would use a fiery exhale if necessary. A confirmed meat eater that preferred mountain caves, it fit everything they knew.

As for the Sea Dragon at Lake Vishap, it was most closely described as a Wyvern. Although neither Alex nor Leander remembered seeing more than one pair of wings, high on its serpentine back, and no front legs, its fire breathing abilities were without question.

"Were you able to locate weapons to use on the dragons?" Cassie asked, as she packed the saddlebags.

"I have other ideas about dealing with the Red Dragon in the mountains, but the Wyvern's scales can be pierced by a fire glass tipped spear. I think they mean obsidian, but Leander seemed to understand the reference," Alex replied.

"I have never heard of obsidian, but fire glass is very rare. It comes from the same fires, deep in the earth, that heat the eggs dragons are born from."

"Well, supposedly, there is such a spear held in a temple on the coast, south of Tazmain. While not exactly on the road to Lake Vishap, it is a necessary detour. The best part is it's a temple to the sea god, so hopefully Kelby can convince any retainers to lend it to Leander."

"We are going to the mountains then?" Cassie asked, as she finished closing her saddlebags.

"I still feel that's the most likely place to hold your mom. We only hear about Tantalus sending the Wyvern to do his dirty work at sea, not the Red Dragon, and that would leave the lake unprotected."

"But we need to be sure," Cassie stated more than asked.

"Yes we do," Alex replied as he indicated to Cassie to lead him out of the cabin to begin their quest.

# Chapter 8

All five walked their four mounts through the streets of Tazmain, as they crossed from the waterfront to reach the far side of the city. Kinsey helped lead the way, again looking pleased to be active and free of the confinement of the ship.

There had been a conversation-- well, argument really-- at the docks concerning Kelby and her mode of transportation.

"Alex, do we need another mount for Kelby?" Cassie asked, showing a rare moment of concern over the mermaid.

"Mermaids do not ride horses," the little redhead announced.

"Then how do you propose to keep up?" Alex asked, assuming they would pick up a horse at a location provided by Guild Master Robeck near the town gates.

After a moment's consideration, she slid up next to Leander, making the man visibly uncomfortable.

"I could ride behind him," she said with a dreamy smile, her flirt turned up to full.

"She will ride behind me," Abrianna stated flatly, showing visible signs of self-control over the flash of jealousy.

Alex smiled at the exchange. While he sympathized with Leander, he was just happy not to be the recipient of her unsolicited attention, for a change. By the time they reached the far side of the city and passed through the city gates, the groups split into two, and headed off into the countryside, one south and one west.

----*----

Cassie and Alex had been riding for the better part of the afternoon, moving at a steady pace, but not rushing. They did not want to attract undue attention to themselves, so did their best to appear unhurried. The forested countryside outside of the port city quickly gave way to rolling green hills with clusters of trees intermingled throughout the area.

Alex had Cassie to his left, with Kinsey trotting along at his right side, as they moved along the well-traveled dirt road. It always amazed him that no matter how long or hard he rode

Shadows, the mare never seemed fatigued. Rose appeared to be made of the same stock.

It was as they were trotting along that Alex heard a low growl from Kinsey. Scanning the area, he discovered a small herd of wild horses grazing in the open field to his right. Upon closer inspection, he noted something strange about the group. It was when one of the larger members, likely a stallion, lifted its head that he clearly made out the horn protruding from its forehead.

"Unicorns?" he asked aloud, attracting Cassie's attention.

"So they are," she replied, apparently uninterested.

"No, Cassie, those are real unicorns!" Alex replied as they drew closer. Stopping Shadows and hushing Kinsey's growl once more, he dismounted and started out, walking into the field toward the herd.

"Ah, Alex…" he heard Cassie say from behind. Waving her to silence, he continued to close the gap between himself and the small herd. By now, several of the adult unicorns had stopped grazing as well, and all were watching his slow approach.

Suddenly, when he was no more than ten feet away, the one he took for the male snorted loudly, pounded one hoof, and then sprang forward. With its head lowered, it drove hard toward Alex as if to skewer him on its point.

A surprised Alex dove to one side, narrowly avoiding the horn, only to find a second unicorn charging in his direction. Leaping again, he hit the ground, and then rolled to clear the hooves of the first, stamping the ground where he had just dropped. Alex continued to scramble, never making it completely to his feet, before a horn or a hoof caused him to leap, roll, or dive.

It was then that Kinsey leaped into the open space, growling and startling the two aggressors, causing them to retreat. She continued to threaten the pair as they paused their retreat, watching to see if they were being pursued.

With that, Alex took the opportunity to regain his feet, and began to quickly back away from the first unicorn as it watched his every move. With Kinsey at his side, the two hastily returned to an astonished Cassie, while brushing off the dirt and grass sticking to his clothing.

"What were you thinking?" she asked in an irritated tone.

"They are unicorns! They are supposed to be friendly," Alex replied in frustration.

"Says who?" she replied in an exasperated tone. "Alex, a unicorn is a wild horse. A nasty, temperamental beast at best, and it has a weapon on its forehead! Where would you ever get the idea that they were friendly?"

Alex quickly mounted Shadows as Cassie sat shaking her head while watching him. Soon the three were quickly out of the area and away from the herd, who had returned to grazing.

"Friendly Unicorns!" was all Cassie would say, as she shook her head in disbelief.

----*----

Elion stood by the scrying pool next to the elf monitoring Alex. As he watched, both Alex and Lady Cassandra were astride the two winged horses he had provided the pair, headed to the Dragon's Teeth. Elion had required around the clock observations of the group beginning with their departure from Windfall.

They had tracked his activities across the sea, into Freeport and on to Tazmain. Although still far from a full-fledged wizard, Elion was impressed with the way Alex handled the Wyvern as they crossed from Freeport to Tazmain. He was also concerned at its appearance.

As Alex's powers continued to grow, and with that, his ability to control them, Elion was becoming worried. Harmony was about balance and Alex was brought here just for that purpose. Putting the kidnaping of Lady Amelia aside, as Royals were always being ransomed for one cause or another, the escalations involving Tantalus and his dragons were alarming.

Dragons had been a devastating weapon used by the Dark Elves in the last conflict. Banishment rather than extinction, as the humans believed, had been their punishment. For them to be brought forth in this fashion indicated that Alex was perceived to be a threat to the balance. His powers were unmatched by any human aligned with the dark side and therefore something to be countered.

His thoughts were interrupted as Elion observed the two riders stop at the edge of a field. He saw Alex dismount and approach a small herd of grazing unicorns. He watched in amazement at the encounter, with the black wolf finally intervening on Alex's behalf.

Elion turned and left the room after he saw the two riders resume their trip. As he did, he considered that maybe the Dark Elves were overestimating things.

----*----

Abrianna was riding along next to Leander, with Kelby behind her on her horse. While the mermaid had not uttered a single complaint in the last few hours they had been riding, Abrianna couldn't imaging sitting behind her saddle was all that comfortable.

That's not to say she had been quiet the entire time, as she had asked a million questions about Windfall, Great Vale and the lands east of the sea.

"So you have never made the journey to the east?" Leander asked curiously.

"That is a great distance, ever for a mermaid. To make the effort to travel so far, one usually has a reason and until now, I had none. Besides, I hate to admit it but mermaids can be a bit cliquey."

"You would not be welcome?"

"Maybe, maybe not. That's why you don't make the trip on a whim."

"We should be thinking about a place to stop for the night," Abrianna said, interrupting the exchange. She didn't mean to intentionally break up the conversation between the two, but she wasn't sorry. There was just something about that flirty mermaid that set her on guard.

"There isn't an inn between Tazmain and the temple. It's meant to be reached by travelers giving thanks to the gods of the sea. Such gratitudes are delivered by sailors, survivors of great storms, or their families upon their loved ones safe return," Leander explained.

"So we will be camping then?" Kelby asked, appearing excited at the prospect.

"It would seem so," Abrianna replied, confused at the question.

"Wonderful! I have never camped before, this will be fun!" Kelby answered, more excited than before.

"Yay," Abrianna said quietly to herself.

----*----

The unicorn encounter had left Alex in a less than cheery mood. He thought he had finally encountered a magical creature he could enjoy, only to have his delusions crushed as they nearly got him killed. He pushed the thoughts aside as he considered the road ahead. The route they had chosen to travel was a major roadway, reaching deep into the eastern countryside; they soon reached a travelers inn.

Stabling both Shadows and Rose for the night, the three entered the inn, finding it to be about half-full of patrons. Kinsey received the usual stares and whispered comments, but no one stepped forward to prevent her from following Alex and Cassie to a table in a corner. As they entered, Alex noted two Rangers sitting at a table on the other side of the room.

He was tempted to go speak to them, but remembered he no longer wore the colors of the Ranger's Guild. Their presence did give him an odd sense of security in the strange surroundings. Once seated, the two waited quietly until a serving woman approached, keeping one eye on Kinsey, tucked behind Alex next to the wall.

"What can I get for you?" the woman asked politely, while drying her hands on her apron.

"We would like a room for the night," Cassie replied before Alex.

"With or without a bath?" the woman asked.

"With, please," she replied with a smile.

"Room with a bath is eight coppers for you two," she replied quickly, and then added more slowly, "and three more for the wolf."

"That will be fine," Alex replied before Cassie could challenge the increase. Pulling a silver from his pouch, he placed it on the table before speaking.

"I believe we would both like strips, with today's bread. Also a bowl and a bone for Kinsey, and a pitcher of water, please," he said while indicating Kinsey laying against the wall.

"Yes, sire," the woman replied, while snatching the coin up and hurrying away.

"That's robbery!" Cassie hissed, after the woman was out of earshot.

"And we are trying to be inconspicuous. Fighting with the help over prices will just draw undue attention to us," Alex replied.

"I'm sorry," she replied, "I think I am a little on edge."

"It's ok, and yes I would expect you are. We are still a day's ride to the lands listed on the map," Alex said while producing the map he had lifted from Tantalus's office. Unfolding it, he placed it between himself and Cassie, and away from prying eyes.

"We will arrive here by late afternoon tomorrow," Alex said pointing to a spot just past a split in the road. The map showed they would hang to the right, heading towards the mountains labeled Dragon's Teeth, while the left fork led around the southern end of the mountain range.

"You think my mom is there?" Cassie asked hopefully.

"Maybe," Alex replied slowly, "but be prepared that she may be further into the mountains."

Before Cassie could reply, a sound indicating the server was returning caused Alex to casually refold the map and tuck it away. The woman set the water pitcher and cups on the table. She had also included the bone and bowl for Kinsey in the trip. She then left without a word.

"We must be prepared to venture into the mountains if necessary is all I am saying," Alex added after she left.

"I understand," Cassie replied, a bit disheartened.

Dropping the subject for now, Alex did a quick check of the water in the pitcher, both cleansing and chilling it in the same exercise. By the time the woman had returned with their food, he had poured for both Cassie, Kinsey and himself.

After she had set the plates down, she began to turn before Alex interrupted her.

"Excuse me, but we are not from here. Could you tell us anything about the House of Drakon holding up the road? We heard they raise cattle there."

"You don't want anything to do with that place!" the woman replied sternly, the fear clear in her eyes.

"We were told in Tazmain that the trader raised beef there. We were thinking of approaching the master of the house, but wanted to view the herds before doing so," Cassie replied, expanding on the fiction Alex was creating.

"We buy a small amount from them, but most is never sold. Even so the herd never grows," she replied quietly.

Feigning curiosity, Alex asked, "Where does the beef go?"

Leaning in to the couple, the woman looked around before replying.

"There are rumors that Tantalus keeps a dragon in the mountains. He keeps it happy by shipping cows, sheep, and pigs for it to feast on."

"Why would anyone do that?" Cassie asked, making even Alex believe the question was genuine.

"Do you not recognize the name? Drakon, in the ancient tongue, means dragon. Long ago, Tantalus's family ruled much of these lands, using their flying dragons to overcome any who would challenge their rule. They were a great power during the last war, and their dragons ruled the sky. One day, a powerful white wizard came from the east, and vanquished the dragons, overthrowing the House of Drakon. The loss of the dragons removed the tyrants' power, permitting the people to rise up and take their freedom back."

The mention of a white wizard from the east caused both Cassie and Alex to look at each other.

"So, the dragons are back?" Alex asked.

"No one knows for sure, but if there were more than one, we think Tantalus would already be king. People whisper that he is in league with a Prince in the east, although those stories have dried up. News from the sailors talks of a great battle with a powerful white wizard, and Prince Renfeld in exile," she finished.

"If he has one, why didn't Tantalus send his dragon to help Renfeld?" Alex asked, curious now himself. Had there been a dragon on the battlefield, he wasn't sure he sure the outcome would have been the same.

"House Drakon lost their dragons to a white wizard once before, he would not be willing to risk a repeat of that," she replied.

"How do you know all this?" Cassie asked, looking somewhat suspicious of the serving lady's knowledge.

"You have never worked in a tavern, or you wouldn't ask such a question," she said with a smile, before turning to leave.

"Wait," Alex said; he retrieved another silver and tossed it to her.

"I think it best that we forget this conversation ever took place," he said with a smile. Catching the coin in midair, the woman quickly pocketed the silver, and nodded in agreement before leaving.

"Do you believe her?" Cassie asked, once the two were again alone.

"No reason not to; she certainly supports everything we learned in Freeport," Alex answered.

The two had been eating the whole time they talked to the server, neither realizing how hungry they had been. Alex pushed his plate aside, allowing him to take Cassie's hands in his as they sat. He could see out the windows of the inn that the sun had set and it was now quite dark outside.

"Can we go to our room now?" was all Cassie would say as she got up, not waiting for the answer. Waving the server over,

Alex requested she show them to their room. With Kinsey close behind, they headed upstairs to settle in.

----*----

Leander had located a small stand of trees to make camp for the night. With the knowledge that their journey was mostly over open land, he had made sure to provision them for several nights out in the open. Once they had stopped, he tried to busy himself in such a way as to avoid extended interaction with Kelby.

At several points in their trip so far, he had seen a look on Abrianna's face that he took to be disapproving. Each time, he had been engaged in animated conversation with the mermaid. While he had no personal interest in her, he found her fascinating. He had never before had an opportunity to see a mermaid, much less talk to one. He had never been the type to frequent the bars and taverns.

He suspected that Abrianna misunderstood his interest and, as such, decided the less interaction he had with the mermaid, the better for his love interest. Therefore, while he gathered wood for the fire and performed other such tasks, he left Abrianna to directing Kelby in her participation.

Returning from a second wood gathering trip, he found a fire burning and Abrianna providing instruction on cooking over a campfire.

"Thank you for the wood," Abrianna said with a smile.

"My pleasure," Leander replied as he sat next to her, and opposite Kelby. He noted that the bedrolls had been placed with his and Abrianna's a respectable distance apart, but both opposite Kelby's.

At that point, Abrianna passed Leander a skewer, with meats strips partially cooked. He noted Kelby's skewer had a fish of some sort.

"Fish?" he asked absently, not recalling packing any.

"We packed a few for her," Abrianna answered first.

"Mermaids are not particularly fond of red meat. As you might assume, we prefer seafood," she answered with a dazzling smile. "We also usually eat it raw; however, I have acquired a taste for cooked fish since working at the Siren's Song. It upset the patrons to see us eat uncooked fish."

"Alex tells me that, where he comes from, eating raw fish is considered a delicacy. I think he called it sushi?" Leander commented.

"I can tell he is a man of culture and good taste," Kelby replied in a tone that implied a longing for the man.

"I would suggest you put any thoughts of desire aside. He is betrothed to Lady Cassandra, and she is not one to tolerate fools," Abrianna stated, in a tone Leander had never heard from her before.

"As you say," Kelby replied, with no sense of concern in her voice.

"Perhaps we should discuss other matters," Leander interrupted, before things escalated, "like how we are to retrieve the dragon slaying weapon from the temple?"

"According to the materials in the Ranger archives, the spear is hidden in the temple. It can only be retrieved by someone blessed by the sea gods to do so," Leander supplied.

"Why does a temple to the sea gods have such a relic?" Abrianna asked.

"The manuscripts suggested that a Sea Dragon once terrorized the coastline there, sinking ships, and burning the villages along the coast. A brave sea captain fashioned the spear from an ironwood spar and a shard of fire glass that he had acquired during his travels. When his ship was attacked, he jumped from the rigging, driving the spear through the dragon's skull," he finished.

"So why the temple?" Abrianna asked, her curiosity displacing her irritation at Kelby.

"The sea captain claimed he found the fire glass when a storm grounded his ship off a small volcanic island. While working to free his vessel, he found the shard on its shore. After killing the dragon, he proclaimed that the divine intervention of the gods gave him the weapon and he helped erect the temple in their honor. In its construction, he placed the spear in a secret place to be revealed in a time of need. It is said that only someone worthy may find its location."

"Well, I guess tomorrow we find out if we are worthy," Kelby said between bites.

# Chapter 9

Alex and Cassie rose early, she waking in a much better mood after a bath and a good night's sleep. He took Kinsey outside to relieve herself while Cassie found them a table in the dining room for breakfast.

Again, the room was about half-full of patrons, most appearing to be travelers like themselves. Sitting with his back to the wall so he could survey the room, Alex noticed a table of four men. Alex didn't remember them from the night before, but then they had retired early.

What bothered him was they had the look of soldiers, or at least former soldiers. Every so often, he would notice one glancing their way; however, between Cassie and Kinsey, he hardly blamed them. The problem was their expressions were not of lust or fear, more like a predator tracking its prey.

Eating quickly, Alex paid at the bar and the three departed the inn at a casual rate. Alex paused in the street, looking to see if the men followed, but none appeared. They reached the stables without any visible signs of pursuit, and Alex had both mounts saddled in minutes.

Stopping only long enough to transfer his sword from his side to a position across his back, he quickly mounted Shadows. Cassie, already astride Rose, watched him without comment. As they departed the stables, with Alex and Kinsey in the lead, he began to wonder if he had misread the situation.

"Are you going to tell me what's up?" Cassie asked as they left the stable and quickly turned up the roadway, continuing toward the mountains.

"The four men in the tavern?" he asked, sure that Cassie had seen them as well.

"Yes, I saw them. They watched you pay, and then went back to eating. I assume they are fighting men of some kind, from their build and manner, but didn't see anything suspicious in their actions."

"Maybe not, but I don't like the look of them, so let's keep a lookout," he finished, before continuing to scan the woods and fields around them as the rode.

----*----

Abrianna woke to find Leander coaxing the fire back to life. She could see Kelby, still fast asleep, on the far side of the fire pit from her. Moving quietly, as to not wake her, she slipped from her bed and began to assist Leander.

Unlike the mad scramble she had endured with Alex and Cassie when evading Prince Renfeld's troops through the dark woods, they had planned this trip. She pulled out a pot for heating water on the fire, as well as tea for a nice hot cup to fight the morning chill.

It was while she was heating the water over the fire Leander had rekindled that Kelby began to stir. As she slowly sat up, she flashed a dazzling smile that even Abrianna had to admit was enough to attract her. No wonder sailors would jump ship to try to catch a mermaid.

"Good morning," Kelby announced.

Abrianna watched as Kelby slipped out from beneath her blanket, completely naked, and began to dress. While not shocked at the behavior of the mermaid, Abrianna was unprepared for the display. Glancing at Leander, she caught the look of complete surprise on his face, just before he quickly turned away.

Abrianna was beginning to understand why Cassie was so relieved to learn that the mermaid was not traveling with her and Alex. Doing her best to ignore Kelby, she began pulling their breakfast out of the saddlebags.

----*----

Alex and Cassie had been riding for quite some time, putting as much distance between themselves and those left behind at the inn as possible. Initially they had started at a fast walk, but had since slowed to a more sustainable pace.

Having ridden in silence for most of the morning, Alex finally broke the stretch with a question.

"Cassie, I don't get it. As I understand it, dragons are huge. How can the occasional cow or pig be enough to keep it fed?"

Cassie laughed at the question, taking Alex by surprise.

"I'm sorry," she replied, catching the hurt expression on his face. "It's just that I asked my uncle that exact same question when I was younger. Abrianna and I were in lessons with our tutor, and we were learning about magical creatures."

Alex nodded, responding to her apology, and waited for her to continue.

"I couldn't imagine that something so large wouldn't eat everything in sight."

"And what did he say?" Alex asked.

"He explained that dragons are magical creatures. They don't eat, like you or I, to sustain ourselves, they eat for flavor. For a dragon, food is a treat, not a meal."

"Then how do they survive?" he asked, now more confused than ever.

"You know how you draw in free energy, and then use it to perform whatever magical purpose you have?"

"Yes," Alex replied.

"Well dragons never release the energy; they absorb it as we do food. That's how dragons can lay idle for hundreds of years, never leaving their caves. They just continue to draw in the free energy around them."

"So, if a dragon is out eating cattle, it's a treat, not dinner?" Alex asked, looking at Cassie to confirm the statement.

"Yes, that's why people say, 'Let sleeping dragons lie!' An idle dragon is not looking to entertain itself by snacking on the local population."

Suddenly Tantalus's arrangement with the dragon made a lot of sense. He would toss it the occasional treat, as one might throw a bone to a dog, and it remained content to sit and guard whatever was placed in its cave.

Before Alex could say any more, the three rounded a bend in the roadway; just beyond was the fork in the road they were looking for. That fork determined if you went around the southern end of the mountains, or as in their case, continued on into the foothills of the Dragon's Teeth. Kinsey's growl betrayed the presence of three men on foot, blocking their path.

Alex immediately recognized the three as the men from the inn. However, they had been with a fourth there. Quickly using his senses, he scanned the area on both sides of their path, locating the fourth hidden nearby, behind the bushes and trees that lined the roadway. He could feel the tension in the man as he held the bow, drawn and waiting for release.

Unfortunately, that man was on Cassie's side of the roadway, with his fiancée stopped in between

"What is your business here?" one of the three before him asked in a less than inviting tone.

"I guess you must have ridden hard, to beat us here?" Alex asked, while edging Shadows forward, slightly ahead of Cassie.

The question seemed to take the man by surprise, but he recovered quickly and repeated his question.

"Why are you here?" he demanded.

"We are here to see the master of the House of Drakon; we were informed he has cattle for sale." As he spoke, Alex casually let his righthand rest at his belt, the horse's reins in his left. He also began forming a shield between Cassie and the archer, should things go badly in the next few seconds.

"You were misled. There is nothing for sale here. Be on your way," the man replied, while all three placed their hands on the hilts of their swords in a threatening gesture.

"And who are you to represent the intent of House Drakon?' Cassie asked in a tone dripping with disdain, one only a royal could produce with such venom.

"That is not your concern. Now be on your way or we will have to take action," the man replied, his meaning quite clear to Alex. Just as he was considering retreating and trying a different route to the mountains, an arrow flashed from the hidden fourth man, intended for Cassie and slamming into the shield with great force, splintering into flying shards.

Without a second thought, Alex dropped the shield, and while the man was nocking a second shaft, he let fly with his right hand. It contained one of the throwing knives he had been fingering at his belt. Next, leaping from Shadows, he drew his sword, and with Kinsey to his left, confronted the three obstructing the road.

Two charged him, while the third found both Kinsey and Cassie blocking his way. By now, Alex had drawn his fighting dagger in his left hand, using it to block the swing of one man, while engaging the other with his long blade.

Spinning to his right, he was able to slip the guard of his attacker with the dagger, driving his sword through the man's chainmail and exposing the tip of his sword out the man's back. The move momentarily startled the second swordsman, as he realized their chainmail was no protection. He snatched the fallen man's sword and pressed the attack on Alex, with both swords flying.

Concerned for Cassie and Kinsey, Alex could ill afford more than a glimpse of their engagement, before being forced to retreat due to the flashing blades before him. In that brief glance, he could see Cassie and Kinsey spread wide, giving the third man the fight of his life.

Returning his entire attention to the man before him, Alex had to acknowledge that he was very good. Although he was able to press Alex, the man wasn't able to get past his guard. Unfortunately, Alex was having the same problem. The man was able to wield two swords in a devilishly clever fashion, presenting Alex with a wall of steel.

Accepting the impasse, Alex was concentrating on a blast of energy that would send the man flying. Suddenly, an elven blade exploded from the man's chest, causing him to freeze, and then fall forward, exposing Cassie and Kinsey, her blade covered in blood. Kinsey's muzzle was bloodied as well, giving Alex the impression that the effort to dispatch their opponent had been a mutual effort.

"Are you OK?" Alex asked as he stepped forward to look her over.

"I'm fine," she replied, while allowing Alex to see with his own eyes that she wasn't bleeding anywhere. Next, he checked Kinsey, who seemed delighted at the attention.

"These guys were good, not your average hired guns," Alex commented as he began to search each of the fallen, looking for anything helpful.

"Yes, thankfully Kinsey was able to jump mine, while I had him distracted," Cassie replied, ignoring the gun reference.

Tossing Cassie the coin purses from the three on the road, Alex went to search for the bowman. Returning from the tree line with a pouch, parchment, and bow, Alex tossed the pouch to Cassie. He had learned on his very first encounter here that you could learn a lot from the coins these men carried.

"Cassie, look at this," Alex said as he presented the bow. Similar in shape to the one Alex carried, a present from the Woodland Elves, this one was a deep red to his black. Handing it to her, he watched, as she looked the bow over.

"That is a Dark Elf bow," she replied while examining the weapon. She quickly returned the bow to Alex, as if she didn't want to hold it any longer than necessary. He examined the bow in more detail, while Cassie started on the pouches.

Since he was waiting for Cassie to go through the coin pouches, he set the bow down and began unfolding the parchment.

"Alex, these guys are not just armed ruffians. Each has four or five golds and twice that number of silvers!"

"And I think I know why," Alex said as he lifted his eyes from the parchment.

Handing the paper to Cassie, he watched as she read the words inscribed there. After a pause, she began to read aloud;

*"... I am uncertain if Renfeld is dead or alive, but see no harm in continuing to hold Amelia where she is. Ensure no one makes their way into the mountains until I notify you otherwise. Most importantly, a small group arrived here today, claiming to be Amelia's envoys. I have little doubt they are actually searching for her. Should two men and two women appear, on pretense of trade, dispose of them in a way that no one can trace them back to us."*

"He must have sent that the same day we landed in Freeport," Alex commented as she finished.

"And a second to whomever controls the Sea Dragon," Cassie replied thoughtfully. And then added, "Does it mean what I think it does?"

"Yes, I think your mom is in the mountains ahead. I also think there may be others, besides these four, guarding the approaches to the mountains," Alex said. Stopping to check the position of the sun in the sky, and then pulling out the map they had been following, he took a moment before speaking.

"I suggest we hide these bodies, and then find a place to wait for darkness. From here on, I think we need to travel at night," he finished as he tucked the paperwork into a pocket and then began dragging bodies into the woods near the fallen archer.

----*----

Leander rode ahead of the two women, following the trail along the coastline, leading to the temple of the sea gods. Kelby's display, earlier that morning, had left him most uncomfortable around the mermaid. It was one thing to have a mermaid teasing and taunting you, it was quite another to have your love interest watching it all as well.

Once Kelby had dressed, and Leander was free to move about without risking the appearance of improper behavior, he then busied himself with their preparations for departure, while the women ate. Abrianna appeared unfazed by the mermaid's behavior, chatting casually, but Leander hardly spoke until the broke camp.

"Once we reach the temple, we will need to decipher the clues inscribed within," he explained as they rode along.

"Is there no temple priest or guardian?" Kelby asked, curious at the situation.

"Temples such as these are not usually inhabited," Abrianna explained, "they are predominately simple structures, some even without walls. They can be nothing more than pillars and a roof. All are intended to provide the devotees a place to focus their devotions."

"I was able to find sketches in the Ranger Archives that depicted a more elaborate structure, with external walls and several antechambers off a main altar room. Travelers are permitted to stay overnight, but prolonged residence is forbidden."

"We will only stay as long as necessary," Kelby replied with a smile.

"Were there any hints in the archives regarding how the spear might be found?" Abrianna asked.

"Only an obscure comment that the spear will present itself when it is most needed," Leander replied, skeptically.

# Chapter 10

Alex and Cassie had moved up the roadway a good distance before retreating into the woods. The two had removed as much evidence as possible of the earlier battle, covering the bodies with brush and releasing the horses to the wild, stripped of their tack. Alex had used cut brush to remove any signs of the disturbance caused in the dirt where they fought the four men, covering the blood pools with more loose soil.

Once they had settled in, waiting for darkness, Alex noticed Cassie was moving a bit gingerly. He asked her what was wrong, but she brushed the question aside, dismissing it as nothing. Refusing to let it slide, he lifted her tunic and protective undershirt to see a swelling on her side, just beginning to bruise.

"That is gonna hurt. What happened?" Alex asked her, as he continued to check her out, concerned about a possible broken rib.

"He slipped under my guard and got me good. That's when Kinsey jumped him. I think he was surprised he didn't wound me. The protective elfware kept him from cutting me, but he hit me hard," she finished, wincing as Alex probed her ribs.

Using his senses, as Abrianna had taught him, he could tell the ribs were not broken, but there was a lot of trauma to the area. While he dared not attempt a total healing, as he was far from accomplished in this type of magic, he was able to sooth some of the irritation caused by the blow.

"Is that any better?" he asked as he dropped the two shirts he had bunched in his left hand.

"A little, thanks," Cassie replied as she carefully shrugged and wiggled, checking for pain.

With the horses unsaddled, and the two sitting as comfortably as possible, they sat waiting for darkness to come before they resumed their trek to the mountains.

----*----

Leander spied the temple as they crested a small rise in the trail. They had been riding for most of the day, and it was now sometime past noon. Similar to most temples he had seen in his life, it had a gently pitched roof with pillars running the lengths of both the sides he could see from the road.

It appeared as if the entrance to the temple was on the side facing inland, away from the sea. That was something he thought odd for a temple honoring the sea gods.

"Our goal is in sight," he announced to his companions.

"Finally," Kelby replied

"I do not think mermaids were intended to ride horses," she finished, as she squirmed behind Abrianna, obviously uncomfortable with the long ride.

It was still close to an hour before they reached the temple itself. As they got closer, Leander could make out more of the details of the structure. The columns did run around the entire structure, providing a covered walkway completely around the inner walls. He could make out the carved reliefs in the stone walls, all depicting scenes of the sea.

Under the roofline, he could see small windows cut high into the walls that he assumed allowed light and fresh air into the structure. The steps wrapped around the building as well, allowing access to the covered area from any approach.

"Well, here we are," he stated as he dismounted in front of the temple entrance. Leading his horse over to his right, there was a circular stone-lined basin; he assumed was intended for watering the horses. Turning, he saw Kelby and Abrianna follow his example, Kelby heading into the temple, while Abrianna followed him to the water with her horse.

"This is beautiful!" he heard Kelby remark. Turning, he could see her studying a part of the stone relief depicting mermaids, swimming in the sea. By now, his horse had stopped drinking and started grazing on the nearby grass. Satisfied his mount wasn't going anywhere, he looped the reins where they wouldn't drop to the ground. He then headed up to the temple himself, waiting for Abrianna to follow.

Climbing the stone steps, he turned to watch Abrianna follow him, and then scanned the surrounding area. They hadn't seen a single traveler on their way here, so it was no surprise that the area was empty of human life beyond the three.

A movement to his right caught his attention, and he watched Kelby and Abrianna enter the temple. Following the two women inside, he stopped just inside the doorway, allowing his eyes to adjust to the change in lighting. The inside was one long great hall with a large statue in the center of the room. Behind the statue, a large opening in the back wall opened to a vista of the sea.

The statue was of a bearded man, exposed from the waist up, and bursting from waves. In one hand was a three-forked trident, while the other was extended forth, toward the entrance, as if casting a spell on those that dared enter. In the waves were smaller sea creatures, a mixture of fish, porpoise, crab, and other sea life. Leander even found a mermaid and a Sea Dragon in the waves.

He found it quite clever, how the open window, in the back wall, both framed the statue and provided a backdrop of the sea for the god who ruled there. Approaching the statue, he discovered it was also a fountain, with the circular pedestal formed to catch the water that cascaded over the carved stone waves, pooling at the base.

The temple must have been built on a spring, as the water was clean and fresh. Leander suspected the watering trough outside was supplied from the statue overflow, via an underground pipe. Looking to his right and left, he noted more carved reliefs, as well as open doorways, leading to anterooms.

Both the women were exploring the temple, wandering from room to room and pausing from time to time at various locations.

"Any clues?" Leander asked, as he scanned the walls near him.

"I am going to need some time to read the scripture on the walls. Most of this is devotions to the sea gods, but some speak of the great battles of the sea," Abrianna answered.

"Yes, I can see references to many heroic struggles. However, nothing about a weapon," Kelby added.

"Ok, I am going to unpack our things. I think we are spending the night here," Leander replied.

"Hopefully, just tonight," Abrianna said while shaking her head with a look of frustration.

----*----

Cassie was hurting more than she wanted to let Alex see. She had taken quite a blow from the man on the road, and had Kinsey not been there to assist her, she might not have survived the encounter. She could not imagine how Alex had confronted two at once, as these guys had been really good armsmen. Absently, she stroked Kinsey, who lay beside her, as if in thanks.

The treatment she had received afterward had helped some with the pain, but was far from a complete recovery. As such, she was thankful that they were sitting idle while waiting for the sun to set. Alex had chilled their water skins and the two were enjoying an early dinner.

"It's best we eat now, as I don't think we will be stopping again until very late," Alex had said. Even with the exertion of the earlier fight, neither was overly hungry. Soon enough, the sun started to set, and the woods were quickly dimming.

"We can probably start heading toward the mountains. I haven't heard anything since we stopped here," Alex said as he started to saddle the horses, beginning with Rose.

Cassie wasn't sure if it was gallantry or the fact that he suspected she was still hurting, but either way, she didn't challenge the move. Once he had everything packed away and the horses ready, he handed her Rose's reins.

"Follow me on foot," he said, while indicating the direction he was planning to go.

Nodding, she watched as he grabbed Shadow's reins and then started in the direction indicated. Moving through the trees at a steady walk, Cassie actually started to feel a little better with the movement, her bruised muscles uncramping with the activity.

By the time they reached the road, again much further down than where they entered, it was completely dark out.

With only a sliver of a moon in the sky, they could just make out the road ahead. She felt Kinsey bump her leg as the wolf stood next to her.

"Alex, I can't see a thing," Cassie whispered as the two stopped before passing the last line of trees and regaining the roadway beyond. Standing beside him, with both horses side by side, she could tell he was concentrating.

"You won't have to," he replied quietly. She watched as he paused again before leading them all out onto the road. She could see him whispering something to Shadows, as the unfiltered moonlight was a little stronger here in the open.

"Mount up," he whispered again, as he mounted. The pain in her side returned as she mounted Rose, the extra exertion of more than a simple walk in the woods irritating it. She watched as he called to Kinsey, catching her mid leap and draping her across his lap. She doubted Shadows appreciated the extra passenger.

"Ready," she said to Alex, once she was firmly settled in the saddle.

"Hold on," he said in a clear voice, as Shadows seemed to launch forward, her wings spread wide. In no more than a few steps, she could see Alex rising off the ground. Before she could register the fact, Rose repeated the action, lifting them both skyward and up into the night air.

She hoped the mares could see in the dark, because she could just make out Alex and Shadows close ahead and nothing on the ground below. Acting on faith, she just held on.

----*----

Darkness had required Leander to light the oil lamps and braziers to illuminate the temple interior, the latter more for the chill in the air that appeared after sunset. As Leander hadn't the slightest idea what to look for in their search for clues, he left the women to their research while he handled everything else.

Cooking over one of the braziers, he provided both Abrianna and Kelby a meal, preparing his last, once they had eaten. Each of the women had continued to work while they ate, and were working from a different approach to solving the riddle. Abrianna was reading all the available text, while Kelby interpreted the scenes depicting sea life and creatures of the deep.

Leander was studying the statue in the center of the temple itself as he ate. Quite exquisite, he imagined it had cost a fortune to construct, beyond the money spent on the temple itself. The artist had spared no expense on the elaborate decoration. With a crown of gold atop flowing white hair, the sea god had been given lifelike color to enhance the impact of his presence.

The trident he held appeared to be made of bronze, with black, sweeping, triangular tips, making Leander cringe at the thought of being skewered by such a weapon. Even at its base, he could see the different materials used in the creation of the waves and the creatures in the waves.

"I'm exhausted," he heard Kelby proclaim as she dropped to the temple floor, sitting next to him in a particularly uncomfortable close proximity. Without asking, she grasped his hand, the one holding the drinking cup, in both of hers, and guided it to her lips. Sipping, while staring into his eyes, she released it with the sound of Abrianna's voice.

"Ahem, am I interrupting something?" she asked, a distinct lack of concern in her tone.

"No, nothing!" Leander replied, while scrambling to stand.

"So, I assume you are done for the night?" Abrianna asked Kelby. Thankful for the change in subject, Leander moved away from the mermaid and pretended to stoke the brazier.

"Yes, it's hard to see in this light, and I can find no reference regarding the spear beyond the story of its creation."

Rising from her place on the floor, she led the others across the room to a carving in the far wall. Leander didn't need anyone to explain the meaning, as it was quite obvious. The scene before him showed a man leaping from up high in the ship's rigging, a spear clutched over his head in both hands and descending on a great dragonhead ravaging the ship below.

As he examined the relief, there was something familiar about the spear. Moving closer, he ran his fingers over the figure holding the spear, outlining the shaft, and more importantly the tip.

"I know where it is!" he proclaimed.

Turning, he began removing his boots, while the women watched him in confusion. Then he carefully waded into the pool at the base of the statue. Climbing up the torso until he was standing on the god's shoulders, he was holding onto the trident for stability.

"Leander, what are you doing?" Abrianna asked, not seeing the point of all this.

"Look at the spear in the carving," he replied, pointing at the relief on the wall. He saw both women turn to examine the relief in more detail.

"OK...." Kelby replied, obviously unsure of his meaning.

Once both women had turned back to him, he pointed up to the trident. "Look at the tips of the trident."

He could see the recognition on their faces as they realized what he had. The black tips were shaped identically to the one in the relief. Stretching to reach the closest, he carefully examined the point where the black blade touched the bronze. After a moment, he tried to turn the blade, being extremely careful not to cut himself on the razor-sharp fire glass.

Resisting at first, it slowly gave way, turning until he pulled it up and free from the statue.

"Not much of a spear," Kelby commented as Leander displayed a weapon with about a foot-long blade and no more than eighteen inches of ironwood shaft. The point where the two were joined was a brass ring, threaded to mate with the statue.

Carefully passing it down to the women, Kelby having climbed half way up the statue, Leander tried the center prong of the trident head. Just like with the first, it resisted and then spun free, this time producing a proper spear with a five-foot shaft of ironwood.

The third prong yielded a weapon identical to the first, giving the three each a fire glass tipped dragon killer. Leander climbed down and the three sat examining their find.

"So much for the legend," Abrianna commented.

"Well the spear is accurate; maybe the others were made later?" Leander offered, and then handed her the item before rising and heading to the relief once more. Wetting his hands in the fountain, he rubbed the relief before nodding.

"And there is the answer!" Leander replied with a smile. Waving both the women over, he pointed to the belt of the man dropping onto the dragonhead. Discernable, but not obvious, were the two smaller weapons tucked in the man's belt.

"That certainly gives support to the part where they say the captain built this temple, only someone who was there would know a detail like that," Abrianna commented.

"Then let's also hope it confirms these will kill a dragon!" Kelby stated while holding up one of the shorter weapons.

"I suggest we get some sleep then, as we are on the road at first light," Leander said, turning to start collecting their gear in preparation of an early departure.

"Where are we all sleeping?" Kelby asked, beginning to move in Leander's direction. Abrianna intercepted her before explaining.

"You and I are over here," she said guiding the mermaid into an antechamber towards the rear. It was set up for two, with bedding spread atop benches intended for sitting or sleeping.

"And him?" she asked, in pointing Leander's direction.

"I am over there by the entrance to the temple, where I can better protect you two," he replied while continuing to gather the belongings he could pack away in advance.

The fact that the rooms were as far apart as possible in the temple was apparent to the mermaid. Leander suspected that's what made her smile.

----*----

Alex couldn't see a damn thing... with his eyes anyway. Using his senses, he could make out the mountains ahead, and the trees and larger life forms below them. Besides the expected wildlife and cattle, he had detected several small bands of men, similar in number to the four they had encountered on the road.

Camped at this late hour, he suspected they were part of Tantalus's security force, placed to intercept anyone headed into the mountains. As they continued to fly through the cool night air, he hoped Cassie wasn't in too much pain. He had done what he could for her earlier, but he could tell she would be uncomfortable, until time, or Abrianna could heal her more. As for himself, his legs were starting to go numb with Kinsey across his lap.

Focusing ahead once more, he figured it would be an hour or more before they could safely land in the foothills of the Dragon's Teeth and begin their search for Lady Amelia.

# Chapter 11

It was well after midnight when Shadows and Rose set down in a secluded spot at the base of the Dragon's Teeth. Alex had her make several wide circles before landing, giving him time to scan for nearby life. Finding nothing of concern, he nudged her down. Kinsey leapt off Shadows as soon as they touched down, much to Alex's relief.

"Where are we?" Cassie asked quietly as she dismounted and stretched her legs, somewhat slowly in Alex's estimation. Alex noted that in flying or riding, the effects on the rider seemed to be the same.

"This appears to be the path used by Tantalus to run wagons into the mountains. I spotted his ranch on the way in and had Shadows follow the road from there," he replied, taking a few liberties in the description.

"Won't there be guards?" she asked, not even questioning his ability to see in the poor moonlight.

"I sensed quite a few on the way in, but none after we passed the ranch."

"Could that mean she is there and not in the mountains?" Cassie asked, confused as to why they didn't investigate.

"I can't explain it exactly, but as we passed over the buildings there, I didn't get the feeling of anything good there. When I try to sense things, I get a feeling from people or animals. You, Leander, and Abrianna give me a feeling of happiness and joy. Tantalus made me want to strike out in anger. All I felt at the ranch was hostility and violence. I think they use it to house the guards and those tending to the animals intended for the dragon."

"Shouldn't we get word to the others?" Cassie asked, indicating their belief that her mom lay hidden in the mountains, just beyond their current location

"Until we see your mother with our own eyes, we dare not risk the possibility we are wrong and misdirect them. Besides, Kelby has reasons of her own for joining this quest. I doubt we could dissuade her from killing the Sea Dragon that took her mother's life."

"OK, so what now?" Cassie asked, her nervousness obvious. Even the suggestion that her mother was close by had her anxious.

Pulling his bow and quiver from its place, he strung the bow and slung the quiver opposite his sword. Pulling a pair of water skins off the load on Shadows, he handed one to Cassie. He also pulled a coiled rope from one of his saddlebags.

"A must in any cave exploration," he commented absently as he held it up for Cassie to see.

"I think we walk from here. The road ahead enters into the mountain and I don't think either of the horses would appreciate the experience."

Not bothering to tether either horse, Alex, Cassie, and Kinsey left them to graze on the little patch of grass and brush available near the clearing. With that, the three headed up into the mountains, following a narrow road. As they walked, he could see the roadway was cut into the mountain dirt, and he could see the tracks where the wagons had traveled in and out, many times before their arrival.

Within a few miles, they could see the opening into the mountain, the road proceeding straight into the cave with no other option. Alex paused to check his and Cassie's gear before pulling an arrow from his quiver while she drew her sword. With a nod to her, he led the way toward the opening ahead.

----*----

Leander, Abrianna, and Kelby left the temple of the sea god before first light, each carrying one of the three fire glass tipped weapons they'd recovered there. Breakfast was eaten in the saddle, and was nothing more than water and bread, with a few dried meat strips of beef and fish.

Unlike the day before, Kelby was not light and flirty, parading naked. Leander suspected the prospect of confronting and killing the Sea Dragon, and thus avenging her mother's death, removed any of the flirty mermaid behavior from her mind.

The three rode mostly in silence, the sound of hooves on the hard-packed dirt road the only constant sound. The road itself was a gently increasing grade, rising from the coast and heading into the hilly interior. Turning back, Leander could see the temple in the distance, standing out against the backdrop of the sea in the early morning light.

They continued this way for the remainder of the morning, stopping once to water the horses in a stream and once again to eat a quick lunch, giving their mounts a much-needed rest. With each stop, he noted Kelby would take one of the shorter weapons and practice with it as one might a sword or dagger.

During the entire trip, Leander constantly scanned the area looking for any signs that Tantalus's men might be watching their approach. He wasn't sure whether to be concerned or relieved that no one appeared to challenge their passage as they traveled deeper into the hills.

Cresting a rise, late in the afternoon, Lake Vishap appeared in the valley ahead. The holding of the House of Drakon was still not visible, as the map had shown it was further up the lakeshore. However, the appearance of the lake seemed to electrify Kelby, her red hair flipping from one side to the other as she scanned the lake, looking for signs of the dragon.

"We must be alert for signs of the dragon," she announced, gripping her weapon in one hand. Leander and Abrianna acknowledged her statement with a nod, and then the three continued down the road, scanning the water for any signs of movement beneath the surface.

----*----

The sun was just up when Alex and Cassie entered the mouth of the cave, with Kinsey close behind. The additional sunlight was a welcome supplement, giving them a good look at what lay just inside the opening. Laying in a stack on one side of the opening were a pile of pitch soaked torches and a bucket with more of the liquid for replenishing them.

Grabbing two, he handed one to Cassie and then ignited them both with just a passing thought. He had to admit his focus and control were improving, but he still had much to learn. His hope was they would address the issue of Cassie's mom quickly, and then he could begin proper training with Ben soon.

Using the light from the torches, they continued to follow the wagon tracks deeper into the mountain.

----*----

The road Leander had been following from the temple to the lake had slowly edged its way over until it ran along the shoreline of the lake. Once, as it jutted along a point out into the lake, they had caught a glimpse of what they thought was Tantalus's property. A white, two-story structure, they could make out the walled compound surrounding the buildings in the distance.

"Stop," Kelby said, as she stared out into the lake.

Acquiescing to the request, all three dismounted and Leander and Abrianna watched as Kelby slowly walked to the edge of the lake, as if in a trance. Standing there for several minutes, she suddenly turned on the two.

"I'm going in," she said. Slipping out of her things rapidly, Leander had little time to consider looking away before he found her standing naked before him. Both of her hands were outstretched, one motioning for the spear he carried, while handing him the short version she had been carrying with the other.

"Are you sure about this?" Abrianna asked the mermaid, appearing to be concerned about her welfare.

"If I get in trouble, I will lead it here. Be ready with those and we can kill it together," she replied while exchanging weapons with Leander.

The two watched as the little redhead waded out into the water, diving in when she reached waist deep water. As her head reappeared, so did a tail, flipping water in the air as she dove again. This time neither Leander nor Abrianna saw her reappear.

Leading the horses away from the water's edge and to a place where they might graze, Leander and Abrianna prepared as best they could for a possible dragon attack.

----*----

The light from the torches provided more than enough illumination for Alex and Cassie to find their way through the cave. In addition, he would pause every so often, and let his senses wander into the various side tunnels they encountered. He wanted to be sure they didn't accidently pass up a hidden or obscured pocket holding Amelia, and with the network of caves here it was challenging.

Most of the tunnels were detours that led to dead ends or routed back to the main passage they were following. Sniffing the air at each stop, Kinsey seemed disinterested in each, affirming a lack of occupants. The main tunnel they followed was wider than any cave Alex had ever seen, and it had a strange resemblance to the Dwarf tunnels he had seen in Two Thorns. In that way, it appeared artificial rather than a naturally occurring channel into the mountains.

"Are there dwarves in these mountains?" Alex asked Cassie quietly.

"I have no idea, but I can say if there is a dragon here, then the dwarves are long gone. Dragons and dwarves crave the same things, and neither is known for sharing."

Alex nodded in understanding, if dwarves were mining gold or gems, the dragon would be interested in stealing their find. If the dragon had a hoard, the dwarves would do their best to claim whatever they could as their own.

"Let's keep moving," he said as he waved Cassie on, walking deeper into the cave network. They continued this way for well over an hour before Alex touched something with his senses that caused him to stop in his tracks. Kinsey let out a low growl as well, requiring Alex to silence her with a soothing pat.

"There is something up ahead," he whispered, and reached for Cassie's torch. Taking the two, he did something he had never tried before. Concentrating on the flames, he drew the energy from them until both were extinguished.

He took Cassie's hand, and with Kinsey following, he led her in the darkness, taking a side tunnel and moving as quietly as possible. Following the winding tunnel, they started to see a dim glow ahead. Peering around a corner, Alex could see the tunnel opened into a large cavern.

Both stepped up cautiously, peered out the tunnel opening and discovered they were a good twenty to twenty-five feet above the floor below. Why anyone would cut a tunnel into the wall of a cavern this high up, he had no idea, but had it not been illuminated, they might have walked out and dropped to injury or even death.

The illumination in the cavern was coming from various points high in the ceiling, glowing and providing a blueish hue. Scanning the cavern itself, Alex could see a rocky pedestal in the center of the open space, a good twenty feet tall, and with furniture and crates stacked all over.

The cavern floor was hard rock and swept clear of loose dirt. There were piles of loose stone and earth pushed to the outer walls, as if someone had cleared the center of the cavern floor around the pedestal on purpose. It was then Alex noted the piles of gold, silver and other precious object scattered here and there all over the open floor space.

The amount of treasure was impressive. There was not nearly enough to cover the vast cavern floor, but there was more than enough to ensure anyone who recovered it could live a life of untold luxury. As he was scanning the corners of the cavern, looking for another way in, Cassie grabbed his arm.

"Alex, look!"

Following her gesture, he saw a woman on the pedestal, moving over to one of the chairs by a table. While her hair wasn't red, the resemblance to Cassie was unmistakable. Cassie was about to shout to her, when a movement on the far side of the pedestal caused Alex to clasp his hand over her mouth.

As the two watched, a huge red dragon rose up from behind Amelia and gently dropped a cloth bag, dangling from its mouth, onto the table. Amelia opened the bag, pulling items out one by one and placing them on the tabletop. Kinsey began another, louder growl, requiring Alex to quickly quiet her again.

They watched as Amelia produced a bottle from the bag, and unsealing it, poured herself a cup.

"It's feeding her," Cassie said in wonder.

The dragon watched Amelia for a few minutes, as if checking to be sure she was eating ok. Finally, it wandered off, eventually curling up around the pedestal and closing its eyes. With that, Alex understood why the floor appeared brushed clean, as the dragon's tail slowly swept back and forth while it slept.

The dragon had to be at least forty feet, nose to tail, with large interlocking scales protecting its upper body. The head was bigger than the Sea Dragon they had encountered earlier, with two distinct horns at the top of its head. Alex could see talons on both the front and rear legs, long as his sword and slightly curved.

He had little doubt that it could breathe fire and the wings folded tight against its back were fully functional. The spikes on its tail were also of note; he could imagine they were used with deadly effect when whipped back and forth.

"How are we going to get past that thing?" Cassie asked as she pointed to the dragon.

"I have no idea."

----*----

Kelby was delighted to be back in her element, swimming fast and free. Riding a horse hadn't been as bad as she feared, and it was a necessary evil to acquire the weapon she now held in one hand. She had every intention of driving it straight through the dragon's heart.

Sweeping right and following the shoreline after her dive, she headed to where they had seen the House of Drakon compound near the lake. Sure enough, near the dock that extended out into the lake, the lake bottom was torn up, as if by huge claws pawing at it.

Using that as her starting point, she swam out into deeper water, looking for anything that might serve as the dragon's lair. This lake was well known to the mermaid community for not only its access to the sea, but for the numerous underwater caves.

Unlike mermaids, who could breathe underwater as well as in the air, she knew the dragon would require a dry den, one where it could rest easy. That was why she had been serious about looking for the nymph's mother. The air pocket in the Sea Dragon's lair would be ideal for holding an air breather without concern of escape. A captive would likely drown before escaping to the surface, as the distance was too great to swim unassisted.

The thought of the nymph and her human companions caused Kelby to pause her search. Before this, she only thought of humans as objects to be used, and then only the males had value. Female humans had no value to mermaids whatsoever. Her taunting of the Princess over her man was typical for the disdain they held for women.

Her time with these people, however, had given her cause to reconsider. Yes, she was helping them, but they were helping her as well. They had provided her with the first real lead she had in finding her mother's killer, and in arming her for battle with the same.

Originally, she had planned on killing the dragon, and returning to the sea through the underground river, leaving the humans behind. Now, she was considering, for the first time, returning to Abrianna and Leander to help find the nymph's mother.

It was as she debated her decision that the dragon's head appeared from the cave mouth behind her.

# Chapter 12

Alex and Cassie stood at the mouth of the tunnel, examining the cavern before them. Amelia still had not noticed the two as she sat eating a meal on the twenty-foot high stone pedestal in the center of the space. The red dragon continued to slumber at its base, presumably unaware of their presence.

Drawing Cassie and Kinsey back away from the mouth of the tunnel, he whispered to her when he thought it was safe.

"I can try and reach her by becoming invisible. Maybe there are stairs on the back side, where we can't see them," he suggested.

"No, Alex. You cannot use magic. Dragons are magical creatures, and very sensitive to such things. Even though you would not be visible, the dragon could see the energy around you," she replied in a panic.

Thinking again, he asked, "Would it feel the use of the bow?" referring to the magical properties of the elf weapon.

"I doubt it. Why? What are you thinking?" she asked.

"I think I can fire an arrow, with the rope attached, across the open space without waking the dragon."

"How will that help? My mother cannot shimmy down a rope!" Cassie commented, snapping at Alex in irritation.

"No, I was going to cross over," he replied patiently, understanding her frustration at being so close to rescuing her mother, only to find a dragon blocking their way.

"Once I am there to protect her, I can shield us both," he finished.

"How will you get back?" Cassie asked.

"I just need to get her off the pedestal, and then we can take any of the tunnels out and meet you back at the horses. Once there we can all fly back to Tazmain," he finished. What he didn't say was he neither saw a path down from the stone Amelia sat atop, nor a tunnel large enough to allow the dragon to exit. That indicated there was far more he didn't know about the cavern than he did.

Unfortunately, he didn't see another option and they certainly couldn't afford to delay much further. And so, gathering his bow, rope. and arrow, he prepared to execute their plan.

----*----

Kelby felt the change in water flow around her, just in time to miss the snapping jaws of the dragon as it surged out of its lair. Darting to one side, she prepared to spear the creature, but it performed a spinning move of its own, leaving her with no target. As the two maneuvered to gain the advantage over the other, they moved back down the lake.

Twice, she was able to strike at the dragon, creating nothing more than flesh wounds, but startling the dragon who had not experienced a fire glass weapon. As she was swimming about, looking for an opening, the dragon slammed her with its tail, sending her flying out of the water and high into the air.

As she spun in the air, preparing to land in the lake, she just made out Leander and Abrianna, standing on the shore with their fire glass weapons in hand. Hitting the water, she immediately shifted right, rather than straight down and into the waiting jaws of the dragon.

The forward surge from the dragon caused it to break the surface, allowing the humans on the shore to get their first view of the creature she was fighting. She could see the bright flash from underwater, where the dragon had spouted fire in rage.

Darting forward, she managed a quick jab with the spear, inciting a second flame burst that she took to indicate a painful response. She almost lost her weapon though, as the dragon spun away from her, nearly ripping the shaft from her hands. The force did cause her to fly away into the air again, landing in the shallows.

Rising up, she found herself standing on two feet, in waist deep water and backing toward the shore, spear still in hand. Before her, the dragon was howling from her latest strike, thrashing about, blindly searching for its antagonist.

Standing naked between Abrianna and Leander on the beach, all with their fire glass weapons in hand, she heard the man speak to her.

"I see you found the dragon," he commented dryly.

"Any sign of Amelia?" Abrianna added more seriously.

"No. But, I couldn't get into the lair. She may still be there," Kelby answered, as they saw the dragon cease its thrashing and focus on the three.

"I think we have trouble coming," Leander commented absently as the creature started forward. When its head reared up, the three dove to one side or the other, to try to avoid the fiery blast that scorched the area they had just occupied. Kelby felt the heat on her skin as she rolled away, returning to her feet with her spear held before her.

Glancing to her left, she saw Leander regaining his feet as well. His gaze caused her to return her attention to the dragon, who was preparing to release another blast of flame. As it drew a breath, she caught a flash from her left as Leander launched his weapon as one might throw a knife. The fire glass drove deep into the dragon's neck, right below its head and piercing one of the ducts used to make fire.

Kelby knew that dragons had glands, one on each side of their necks, that produced the liquid they combined to spit fire. Leander's blade had pierced one of the two, causing the liquid to shoot out before reaching the point where it could combine with the other.

Moving quickly, she raced forward, driving her spear into the side of the creature, her reward a new howl of pain. Unfortunately, the dragon also reacted instinctively, its wing swinging at the source of its agony. Unlike four-legged dragons, Sea Dragons were of the Wyvern type, their forelegs and wings combined.

The swat sent Kelby flying, her spear knocked to the ground, and her body slamming so hard she passed out. Her last vision as she hit was Leander snatching up the fallen spear, and he and Abrianna guarding over her prone form.

----*----

Alex securely anchored one end of the rope to the shaft of the arrow. He needed it to support his weight just long enough to cross the distance between the tunnel and the pedestal. Rather than try to embed the shaft in the stone, he decided to try for one of the large wooden crates stacked atop the plateau. He suspected they contained supplies for Amelia, or more of Tantalus's treasures, all well-guarded by the dragon below.

Leading Cassie and Kinsey back to the opening, he scanned the area again, ensuring nothing had changed, before drawing the bow and selecting a very large crate at the bottom of a stack of similarly sized objects.

He let the shaft fly, making sure the coil of rope fed out cleanly. He heard a soft thud, as his arrow bit hard into the wood of the crate. The sound was soft, but caused Amelia to spin, scanning for the source of the unfamiliar sound. Cassie quickly caught her attention, creating excitement for both women. Soon, though, Amelia paused and then began waving them away, indicating the sleeping dragon.

It was clear to Alex that she feared the danger to her daughter over the promise of her own rescue. Using the bow to sink a shaft at his end, he wrapped the rope several times around the anchor, before handing the free end to Cassie.

"Hold this until I am across. We might need it to descend from the rock later," he whispered.

Slinging his bow opposite his sword and parallel to the quiver, he checked his weapons to verify all were secure and none would drop when he was over the sleeping dragon. Then he began crossing the open void, hanging beneath the rope and using both hands and legs to work his way across.

On the far side, he could see Amelia had ceased trying to dissuade them and was now alternating between watching Alex and the dragon below. At one point, about half way across, he froze as the dragon shifted, and then settled quietly back into a new position.

Reaching the far side, Alex was greeted by Amelia. Her first words to him not exactly what he expected.

"You shouldn't be here! Cassie is in great danger!" she hissed at him in a whispered tone.

"Lady Amelia, I am Alex Rogers. Cassie and I have been searching all over for you," he replied while leading her away from the edge and the sleeping dragon below.

"Why would you bring Cassie into a dragon's den? Are you insane?" the woman replied, frustration in her tone.

Glancing across the open space, Alex could see Cassie watching the two intently. Unsure of how Cassie wanted to inform her mother of their relationship, Alex decided to take a different approach.

"Look, your brother, Ben Griffin of Charleston, sent us to come find you and bring you home. You need to trust me," he replied.

"How do you know that name?" she paused and asked suspiciously. Alex knew that Amelia was the only other person that knew his real name and where he came from.

"Because he told me. We come from the same place," Alex finished, hoping the information closed the issue for the moment.

It was then that Alex caught a movement from the corner of his eye and turned to see Cassie crossing the rope. Kinsey still stood in the opening, clearly not happy with this turn of events, but thankfully quiet, for the moment.

"Shit!" Alex commented in a low tone while rushing to meet his fiancée as she reached the crate.

"Mom!" Cassie cried quietly as she let Alex help her from the ledge, and then passing him by to embrace her mother.

"You shouldn't be here! It's far too dangerous," her mom hissed while hugging her daughter.

Moving everyone over to the far side, away from the dragon, Alex started looking for a way down while the two women talked in whispers.

"Uncle sent us to find you. Prince Renfeld attacked Great Vale, trying to take the valley. If it wasn't for Alex, he would have succeeded."

Alex glanced over to see the look of skepticism on Amelia's face. He could hardly blame her, as he was completely unknown to her. He watched as the two women stood looking at one another, before Amelia spoke.

"There is something different about you," she commented, causing Cassie to blush.

"Mom, I'm getting married," Cassie replied with a broad smile.

"WHAT?" Amelia burst out, her composure gone.

That was more than the sleeping dragon could miss. It reared up, spying the three standing on the stone. As it raised its head, it pulled the rope free of its anchors and had it dangling across its back.

In one quick motion, the dragon snapped at Alex, separating him from the two women as he dived out of the way. The creature followed up by then swatting at Alex with one paw, the claws crashing down on the stone mere inches from their goal.

Alex rolled away and gained his feet, stable enough to fire off two bolts in quick succession, temporarily blinding the beast as they burst across its face. The dragon howled, shaking its head, trying to clear its vision, then swung a second paw at its target.

Cassie clambered away from her mother, and over to the crates, looking for a weapon to use against the dragon. This left her mother alone, as she watched Alex duck another swipe of the dragon's clawed paw. The action left him face down on the stone but he then scrambled to a position where he could fight back.

The distraction allowed the dragon to snatch Amelia up with its other paw, causing Cassie to dive from the sweeping claws as she returned with an ornate spear. The weapon appeared more decorative than functional, but was all she could find.

By now Alex had regained his feet and was facing the dragon. He dared not take action that might cause harm to Amelia, but needed to do something to make it release her.

Suddenly, the creature belched a ball of fire that caused both Cassie and Alex to dive away from the center of the stone. While neither was hurt, the table and chairs nearby were now aflame. Alex ended up half hanging over the sheer edge of the stone tabletop and had to quickly scramble back.

The separation of its antagonists had caused the dragon to shift to one side, closing the distance to Cassie so it could better confront Alex. This movement caused the creature close to the stone pillar.

Cassie watched the dragon move ever closer to her while focusing its attention on her fiancée. In one swift motion, she was able to drive the weapon into the arm holding her mother, snapping it in half in the process and leaving one end embedded in the beast. The dragon bellowed in pain but maintained its grip on Amelia.

By now Alex had closed the gap between where he had been and Cassie's position. The beast soon recovered and turned to face the two. It then reared its head back to blast Alex and Cassie with flame.

Thinking quickly, Alex formed a shield, blocking and deflecting the blast and its heat, sending it harmlessly around himself and Cassie but not back at the dragon. Looking up, Alex could see the dragon appeared confused that the two survived the prolonged spout of fire, and so, shot off a second, and a third as it moved around the cavern.

Alex had placed another shield at the mouth of the tunnel they had entered, now holding Kinsey, preventing her from attacking the dragon and likely saving her from death. He also tried several times to contain the dragon, without injuring Amelia, as it held her tightly in its grasp.

Each time the creature tried to use one of the many passages in and out of the cavern, it found its way obstructed by Alex's invisible constructs. In one case it attempted to smash the barrier with a swing of its massive tail, but had no success.

Apparently, the dragon realized the impasse, and it suddenly launched an enormous fountain of fire at one part of the cavern ceiling. As Cassie and Alex watched, the stone turned to melted slag and the sun came bursting through. Before Alex could react, a second blast enlarged the opening, and the dragon spread its wings, launching itself through the hole. The two watched in frustration as the dragon then continued up with Amelia still in its grasp.

Alex turned to see Cassie, devastated, with tears running down her cheeks, staring skyward after her mother.

----*----

Kelby awoke to find herself fully dressed and lying in the shade of some trees. There was a fire nearby and Abrianna was cooking something that smelled wonderful. She turned her head to see Leander down by the lake, attempting to spear fish with something other than the fire glass tipped shaft that lay on the ground near him.

"What happened?" she asked Abrianna in a raspy voice. Abrianna provided her a drink from a pot she had on the fire. Kelby could see one of the shorter fire glass weapons by her side on the ground.

"Drink this, it will help you heal," she responded while watching the mermaid sip from the cup.

"You were sent flying, the landing providing a considerable jolt, but otherwise you are uninjured. Leander and I were able to keep the dragon from killing you."

"And the dragon?" she asked after a second drink.

"It escaped. We haven't seen it in several hours now," Abrianna answered absently.

"It escaped, retreating while I'm down and the two of you are hindered by the need to protect me? That hardly sounds likely," Kelby replied skeptically at the simple explanation.

Abrianna was occupied at that point, checking Kelby's various bumps and bruises before she replied. Kelby could feel the easing of the pain due to whatever it was in the cup provided earlier.

"Once we realized you were unconscious, Leander charged the beast while I dragged you out of harm's way," she replied in a matter-of-fact tone.

"Leander charged an enraged dragon on his own, and it retreated?" Kelby replied, glancing once more at the man now waist deep in the water. Although she had a growing respect for the warrior, it hardly sounded plausible.

"Yes, well, I did manage a quick illusion spell before he did so," Abrianna offered with a smile.

Closing her eyes, her arms quickly flew wide. Suddenly, Kelby saw over a dozen Abriannas flaring out from either side of the original. As one, they opened their eyes, smiling down on the prone form of the mermaid. With another sweep of her arms, they all disappeared, leaving the original alone with her.

"So the dragon saw an army of Leanders, all charging with fire glass spears," Kelby nodded in understanding.

"Funny how the parlor tricks you learn as a child occasionally have a practical use," Abrianna added with a laugh.

"And then?" Kelby asked, trying to fill in the blanks.

"As I said, it retreated into the lake and we haven't seen it since. You have been unconscious for several hours now and since I am not as up on Mermaid physiology as I could be, our concerns for your welfare were growing," Abrianna replied.

"Hours?" Kelby replied unbelieving as she tried to rise. The effort sent pain shooting throughout her body.

"Easy, you need to rest. Yes, you have been out for several hours now and we were becoming concerned."

"So, she is alive?" Leander commented, as he presented a large fish to Abrianna at the end of a spear.

"Thanks to you," Kelby said aloud, acknowledging it as much to herself as to her two companions.

"Once you are feeling up to it, we had hoped you might be able to check the dragon's lair for any sign of Lady Amelia," Abrianna asked hesitantly.

"I can go now." Kelby tried to rise again.

"No, rest for a bit longer. I suspect that if she were there, she is long gone. The dragon's departure would not be without its charge. There would remain, however, evidence of her occupancy. That alone will tell us what we need to know."

With that, the three sat by the fire and discussed the battle, eating and resting from the encounter. By late afternoon, Kelby was feeling up to a short trip into the depths of the lake. She did laugh to herself as she undressed, for the humans standing nearby had apparently gotten over her nudity, particularly the male.

Fire glass spear in hand, she descended to the place where she had first encountered the dragon. She cautiously approached the mouth of the den, looking for any signs of the creature. Seeing nothing of concern, she slowly entered, following the passage until she broke the surface.

In the dimly lit area, she could see the signs of dragon residence, with bones scattered about. Climbing out, her legs returning in the process, she searched the area for any indication a human had been imprisoned here.

She scoured the cave, covering every crack and crevasse. In one spot she located the short spear she had seen Leander throw earlier disrupting the creatures ability to spout fire. Clearly the beast had returned here to lick its wounds before vacating the area for good. Her search complete, she quickly exited the den, positive Amelia had never set foot inside.

----*----

Alex and Cassie searched the pedestal that had held her mom, looking for clues as to where the dragon might have taken her. Kinsey sat glaring at the two from across the cavern. Fortunately, the dragon, whether by accident or on purpose, had avoided the area containing the crates with its flames.

Sorting through some of the crates, they found exotic fabrics, carpets of the finest weaves, and other works of art. There was statuary of gold and bronze, with jewel-encrusted enhancements. There were paintings and gilded carvings that had to be worth a fortune.

"I gather we can assume this is Tantalus's wealth?" Alex asked.

"At least a portion of it," Cassie replied, her frustration clear in her voice. Then she added, "Alex come look at this."

Moving beside her, he looked at what she had uncovered. One of the smaller crates was filled with scrolls of paper and parchment, all organized in a latticework of dividers. Pulling one out, Alex scanned its contents.

"Bingo! This is a list of all the House of Drakon's holdings in the south."

"And this talks about lands across the sea, in the north of Windfall. Renfeld granted Tantalus unrestricted use of the western part of the Northern Mountains," she replied, sounding confused at the description.

"Cassie, were there ever dragons in the Northern Mountains, any place where they might have lived?"

"Long ago maybe," she replied thoughtfully. "You think the Red Dragon might have gone there?"

"I know one way to find out. I think it's time we revisited our friend in Freeport," Alex answered.

"Alex, how are we getting off of here?" Cassie asked while looking around the plateau.

"That's a good question," Alex replied as he spied the rope laying on the floor twenty feet below.

# Chapter 13

It was late afternoon when Leander led Abrianna and Kelby into the compound owned by the House of Drakon. Having scouted it while Kelby was searching the dragon's lair, he discovered it occupied by only a handful of retainers and none suitable to challenge his intrusion.

Once inside the walls they had gathered everyone in residence and ushered them into a small courtyard for questioning. Leander had to admit that the place was quite beautiful. Were he in a position of wealth, he would have enjoyed such a retreat himself.

"Have any of you seen Lady Amelia?" he asked the assembled group. Scanning the faces, he saw only looks of confusion at the name.

"Has Tantalus asked you to detain anyone here?" Abrianna asked in a more general reference.

"No, my Lady. We have not seen the master in over a season. Nor have we received any visitors, but yourselves, in just as long," an older woman Leander took to be the head of the house staff replied. He noted several nods of agreement from the others.

Leander looked at his two companions, their looks confirming his thoughts. There was no way Amelia had been here, particularly as unguarded as it was. Further questioning confirmed that Tantalus had pulled his armsmen away from here for other duties. None here knew where they had been sent, but Leander suspected it was to guard Amelia.

"We apologize for the intrusion," Leander announced as he waved Abrianna and Kelby back outside of the compound and to their mounts.

"What now?" Abrianna asked, with Kelby looking particularly interested in the reply.

"We return to Tazmain and await word from Alex and Cassie, I expect," he answered.

"I would suggest we return the weapons to the temple first. We are likely to return to the sea and I would not want to anger its gods," Kelby finished with a frown.

"Is that wise?" Leander replied as the three started their ride back.

"Well we can't stay here tonight, so let's get going. We can still make it to the temple if we move quickly and decide what to do when we get there," Abrianna replied

Leander was about to push harder that the weapons might be needed on the voyage home, but decided against cursing the trip before it even began. With that, he pointed his horse toward the temple, leading the group away from Lake Vishap and on to who knew what.

----*----

Kinsey was extremely happy to see Alex and Cassie back on her side of the cavern. It had taken them a while to find something they could use to lower themselves down off the rock. Alex was positive Tantalus had never intended his fine fabrics to be used in such a fashion, but he hardly cared.

Once they were on the cavern floor, Alex retrieved the rope the dragon had snagged and driven a shaft into the ceiling of the tunnel above, where the impatient Kinsey stood watching and waiting. Alex assisted Cassie, steading the rope as she went up.

He then climbed up behind her, with the additional load of select items tucked in a sack he had looted from Tantalus's private stash. The papers they had found there made references to things Alex suspected might interest Ben.

All three then retreated to the main tunnel, where Alex relit the torches and they then made a hasty retreat back out the passage. Before reaching the opening to the cave entrance, Cassie stopped the group.

"I hear someone ahead!" she whispered. Retreating to the first side tunnel they could find, all three quickly ducked in and Alex extinguished the torches. After a moment, Alex could hear voices.

"I told you someone was up here. Those horses had saddles," he heard a man say.

"How did they get past the patrols? Tantalus will have our asses if they reached the chamber. Even if the dragon eats them, they shouldn't have gotten past us," another replied. Alex reached out with his senses and counted four in all, the other two apparently not much for conversation as he had only heard two.

He could see the light from their torches as they passed by the entrance of their hiding spot.

"We need to get out of here fast!" Alex whispered to Cassie once the men passed. Taking only one of the torches, he quickly relit it and led Cassie and Kinsey back out into the main tunnel, picking up the pace as he did so.

The trip out of the caves seemed to take far longer than it had in. He was sure it was just an illusion, but he was anxious to be out and gone from here. As they approached the entrance, he could see a man with horses at the entrance. Evidently the four who passed them earlier had left someone with their horses outside the cave. Driving the torch head into the dirt quickly, so as not to give them away, Alex drew his bow and patiently waited for the man to expose himself.

Still hidden deep in the cave, they were cloaked in darkness, as compared to the fading daylight outside. Kinsey let forth a soft growl, something Alex did not stop. As the man stepped away from the horses, he drew his sword while peering into the cave. Raising his free had to shield his eyes from the dimming sun, he searched in the darkness for the source of the sound. He quickly sprouted an arrow from Alex's bow, driving him back before he dropped.

"Come on," Alex said aloud as he waved Cassie and Kinsey forward.

Rushing to the fallen man, he checked that the prone form was dead, before grabbing two of the horses, and cutting the rest free. Handing Cassie the reins for one, he drove the rest off, sending them running down the road in a cloud of dust. Mounting his ride, he waited for Cassie to do the same, and then the two, plus Kinsey, headed down the road at a run.

Riding the mounts hard and herding the others before them, they soon reached the point where they had left Shadows and Rose earlier that day. As Alex had expected from the comments of the men in the cave, there were two more men there, tending the mounts. Both men had been sitting in the shade, so the appearance of Alex, Cassie, and the running horses, had taken them by surprise.

Ramming his horse into the closest man, who was drawing his sword while attempting to rise, Alex leapt from the saddle. His leap landed him squarely on the second, driving his dagger into the man's chest on impact. As he rolled free, he was in time to see Kinsey dispatch the first man, grabbing him by the throat and crushing his windpipe.

Watching the mounts run off in all directions, Cassie commented, "Without horses, it's going to take them a while to get the word out," indicating the men they had left back in the cave. She had dismounted her borrowed horse and was tending to Rose as she spoke.

Brushing himself off after rolling in the dirt, Alex gathered his things from his borrowed mount, and began preparing Shadows for the trip to Tazmain.

"Unless you can think of a reason not to, I suggest we fly all the way back," he said working at cinching down all the loose items in his arms. He saw Cassie glance at Kinsey before replying.

"I'm not the one who might object," she replied with a smile while indicating the waiting wolf.

----*----

The return trip to the temple had been uneventful for Leander, Abrianna, and Kelby, even with the coming darkness. Abrianna had been able to provide a dim glow, giving them enough light to travel safely. The horses had little difficulty getting them to their destination.

Kelby seemed in good spirits as they rode along. Although the mermaid was disappointed at not having vanquished the Sea Dragon, Leander suspected that she was more than appreciative at surviving the encounter.

He, himself, was still sore and bruised from the engagement after she had passed out. Both he and Abrianna had managed to inflict a considerable amount of damage on the beast, forcing the creature to retreat into the lake. Fortunately,

Kelby had recovered the fire glass tipped weapon he had driven into the beast's neck before it vanished beneath the lake's surface. Leander's greatest concern was he suspected that it was not the last they would see of the dragon.

It was several hours past sunset when they finally reached the temple, and as before, they found no one in residence there. It was apparent to all that they would not continue any further this night.

"If you like, I can get us settled, while you return two of the fire glass weapons to the statue," Kelby offered as she dismounted from behind Abrianna. It had been decided on the way here that they would keep the spear, but return the others. All three pledged to return the spear once the quest was completed.

Both Leander and Abrianna looked at one another, questioning the offer; Abrianna finally answered.

"That would be lovely. Can you help me with the horses first?"

Leander watched Kelby take the reins of his horse. She then followed Abrianna to the watering trough they had used the first time they had arrived.

Turning and entering the temple, Leander lit the torches and again removed his boots before attempting to climb the statue. Working carefully, he was able to replace both shorter weapons before the women entered, carrying various items for the night's meal.

"We settled the horses for the night, with plenty of grass to graze," Kelby announced as they entered, causing Leander to stifle a laugh. She was acting as if she were an old hand at all this. In a way, he appreciated the effort she was making; he suspected it was her way of thanking them for saving her life.

Climbing down, he put his boots back on and, with Kelby's assistance, prepared dinner for the three while Abrianna got them settled for the night.

----*----

Cassie and Alex landed a short distance outside of Tazmain, selecting a small meadow surrounded by trees to shield them from unwanted attention. The sun had set long ago, something that worked in their favor should anyone be looking from Tazmain. On their descent, they could make out the lights of the city, showing them the way back.

Upon touching down, Kinsey leapt from Shadow's back, digging her hind claws into Alex's leg as she did so. Though it didn't break the skin, as he wore protective clothing, he got the idea that she had enough of flying.

"Ready?" he asked Cassie, nodding his head in the direction he intended on going.

"Lead on," she replied. Alex could see the tired in her eyes as he turned east. They had been going on adrenalin now for a good 24 hours and both were starting to drag. He wandered through the trees until they came to the edge of the road.

Heading out onto the same road they had traveled on their trek west, the two soon found themselves at the edge of Tazmain. Passing through the gates once more, they had to dismount to make their way through the late night crowd. Though not thick, the darkness made things more difficult

Ever since they landed in the meadow, Alex had been debating on the best time to confront Tantalus. Their current level of exhaustion made the risky activity a bad choice at present, however, with each day's delay the likelihood that the man would discover the events in the cave was greater.

Then there was the possibility that even Tantalus didn't know where the dragon had taken Amelia. Unlikely as that might be, it was something to consider. And finally, he would sure appreciate Leander's assistance in any confrontation with Tantalus's men. If they were anything close to the quality of those in the woods, he did not want Cassie to risk herself again, he needed a soldier.

It was with all that going through his head that Alex led Shadows out onto the dock, *Cassie's Quest* still right where they had seen it last.

"Lord Protector, you return without your companions?" Captain Yeagars declared, meeting them on the dock, at the base of the boarding ramp.

"So, the others have not yet returned?' Alex asked, as several sailors hurried down the ramp to assist the two with the horses.

"No, Sire. You are the first."

Following the others on board, Alex escorted Cassie and Kinsey to the ship's ladder that led to the lower decks.

"Please have the men see to the horses, and notify us immediately if the others arrive," he asked as he waved to the Captain and the crewman handling Shadows and Rose.

"Also, be prepared to set sail for Freeport as soon as the others arrive. We have need to visit the House of Drakon as soon as possible."

"Would that be to meet with the house master?" Yeagars asked.

"Yes, he has information we require," Alex replied, confused at the Captain's question.

"Sire, his ship made port the morning you left. I am told he was aboard and is now at his warehouse here in town. That is his ship there," Yeagars supplied while pointing to a large cargo ship nearby.

"Thank you, Captain, that is very good news," Alex replied, with a smile.

"Yes, Sire. Would you care for food or drink?" Yeagars asked before he disappeared below. Looking to Cassie for an answer, she nodded negatively.

"No thanks," Alex replied before he disappeared below. Following Cassie and Kinsey, the three entered their shared cabin, one reserved for the king, and within minutes were all sound asleep.

----*----

Leander woke with the others still fast asleep, and before the sun had risen. He was anxious to prepare for their departure. He had been surprised to find all three beds had been prepared in the same anteroom, and even more so when he learned that Abrianna had been the one responsible for doing so.

It was his experience that those appreciative of rescue tended to forget fairly quickly. Only time would tell as to the sincerity of the mermaid's feelings. As the two women slept, he gathered their things and prepared the horses. He secured the spear for travel and used the spring in the statue to refill their water skins.

"You've been busy," Kelby announced, as she exited the antechamber ahead of Abrianna.

"If we push hard we can reach Tazmain just after nightfall," he replied, in the way of an explanation.

Kelby nodded at that, with no sarcastic remark in reply, and just started following Leander's lead of packing their gear. He found the change in the woman very unsettling. By the time Abrianna woke, everything was ready to go, save her bedding. Once she was up, she was packed within minutes and the three were back on the road just before sunrise.

Leander noted that Abrianna dropped several golds into the temple collection as they were leaving. In his opinion, it was money well spent considering the extended loan of the weapons. Spurring his mount forward, he planned on more than walking the animals today.

----*----

Alex woke the next morning, surprised at the late hour. Both Kinsey and Cassie were still lying quietly; although Kinsey had her eyes open, staring at Alex. As no one had come to wake him, he assumed that their missing companions had still not returned. While attempting to slip out of bed, Cassie spoke, though her eyes remained closed.

"Where are you going?" she said as she reached out and drew him closer, her arm wrapped across his chest. Cassie then snuggled up beside him, resting her head on his chest.

"Are we going to be able to save my mom?" she asked after a moment. Alex could see her eyes were still closed and a tear was slowly running across her face, finally landing on him.

"Yes, of course we will," he replied as he hugged her, wrapping both arms around her body. The two lay in that position for a while, neither speaking, just enjoying each other's company.

"I do think it's time we got something to eat," Alex said, breaking the silence. At the mention of food, Kinsey got up and stretched before wandering over to the cabin door with a look of anticipation.

He could feel Cassie slowly release her grasp and he began to slide out from under her. Laying on her side, she gradually rose until she was resting on one elbow, the blankets falling to her waist, revealing a lack of clothing. Alex paused, taking in her beauty and fighting the urge to return to bed. As his eyes followed the curve of her body, he noted the nasty bruise on her side, snapping him out of the trance.

"I am hoping Leander and Abrianna return today, so we might pay Tantalus a visit. While we wait for them, I want to look through the documents we recovered from the dragon's lair," he said while pointing to the sack of things he had taken when they escaped the tunnels. Alex figured anything Tantalus felt was valuable enough to place under the protection of a dragon was something he needed to check out.

Following his lead, Cassie gingerly slipped out of bed and began dressing. Soon after, all three made their way to the ship's lounge, well suited for the royal passengers, and ate breakfast quietly while Alex sorted through the documents in his sack. Cassie took Kinsey ashore to permit her time to relieve herself in a more wolf-like location as he stayed behind to read.

# Chapter 14

Leander was never so happy to see a city gate as he was to see the one at Tazmain. The three had pushed the two horses harder than they probably should have, particularly given the two riders on Abrianna's horse. However, the anxiety over the unknown status of Alex and Cassie had driven them to ride without a break.

They had arrived at sunset, as the street lamps were being lit, and the daytime street traffic was starting to diminish, though the nightlife was yet to begin. They were still required to get off and walk the horses through the streets, but that was a welcome change to spending the day in the saddle. Upon entering the city, Leander had expected Kelby to make her excuses and depart for the Siren's Song the relatively short swim to Freeport was nothing for a mermaid, or so he was told. However, she did no such thing.

Instead, she continued walking at Abrianna's side, scanning the streets as if looking for familiar faces. By the time they reached the waterfront, where they found *Cassie's Quest* alight, it was completely dark out. They had barely stepped foot on the dock leading out to the ship's ramp when the sailor at its base sprinted on board, presumably to announce their arrival.

Leander was extremely relieved to see Alex and Cassie rush down the ramp, with the wolf right behind the two.

"Am I glad to see you!" Alex declared as he embraced Leander, while Cassie and Abrianna repeated the gesture. Alex was surprised to see Abrianna hand Cassie off to Kelby for a welcome as well.

"Brie, we saw mom. We almost had her!" Cassie announced for all to hear.

"Almost?" Leander asked Alex.

"Let's get you settled and then we can compare notes," Alex replied, waving to the waiting sailors to take the horses.

Pausing for a moment, Lander removed the spear from its place tied to his saddle. Handing the weapon to Alex he pointed to the jet-black tip.

"Fire glass," he commented.

Alex inspected the weapon as they boarded the ship and headed below. Leander could see a look of confusion on Alex's face as he studied the weapon. Once below, Alex set the spear near his bow in the lounge they used as a gathering place.

Once everyone was seated in the lounge, with food and drink for all, including Kelby, Alex explained what had happened in the Dragon's Teeth. After he had finished, he could see the frustration on Abrianna's face, knowing Cassie had been so close to rescuing her mom.

"And you have no idea where the dragon went?" Abrianna asked.

"We have some clues," Alex replied while pointing to the pile of papers stacked on a desk in the corner of the lounge.

"Are these the papers you took?" Abrianna asked, crossing the room to examine a few.

"Yes, I expect they are whatever passes for a land grants or deeds here," Alex replied, getting the expected looks of confusion from everyone.

"This one speaks of obligations owed the holder. There are no names assigning said holder, but the obligator section is signed by the King of the Vassal Lords," Abrianna observed.

"Who is that?" Alex asked; his ignorance of things beyond Great Vale was well known.

"They reside in the lands beyond the Northern Mountains. Each Vassal Lord controls a section and is sovereign there, subjugate only to the Vassal King," Leander explained.

"That's interesting," Alex commented, rising and searching through the papers until he found what he was looking for. Handing it to Abrianna, he waited patiently as she scanned the scroll.

"This says Renfeld grants a portion of the Northern Mountains, that area in the western end of the range near the sea, to House Drakon as payment for allegiance in the war with Great Vale," Abrianna said looking up from the document.

"Cassie tells me there were once dragons living in those mountains. Might their lairs still exist?" Alex asked.

"Yes, and the allegiance of the northern lords would provide whatever support they needed to survive there. It is quite cold and hostile north of those mountains and those that live there are a fiercely independent bunch," Cassie added to the conversation.

"Sounds like your kind of people!" Alex said with a smile.

"I propose we cease the speculation and go pay Tantalus a visit. I am sure I can coax the location of your mother out of him," Kelby said while holding an knife up for all to see.

"The good news is he's here. I am told he arrived the morning we departed for the mountains," Alex replied.

"Then what are we waiting for?" Kelby said as she started to rise from her chair.

"Best we wait until morning, when everyone is rested and we are at full strength," Alex replied, recalling the last run in with Tantalus's men.

----*----

As things wound down, Alex asked if Abrianna would have a look at Cassie. Not bothering to lift her shirt and expose the area indicated, Abrianna gently placed her hands on the nymph's side as directed by Alex. The wince from Cassie was more than enough warning for her to proceed gently.

"Oh cousin, what did you do?" Abrianna commented as she closed her eye to better concentrate on her work. She stayed like that for a long while everyone watched. Finally, she sighed and straightened up while opening her eyes.

"Well, that should help some, but you are going to be quite sore for a few days. I hope the other guy looks worse," she replied with a concerned look on her face.

"Thanks to Kinsey," Cassie said, pointing to the wolf laying on the floor nearby as she flexed, testing her cousin's work.

At the mention of her name, she opened her eyes, without raising her head. Her tail beat out a steady thumping displaying her delight.

Leander, Abrianna, and Kelby then retired early, leaving Alex and Cassie alone to go up on deck and enjoy looking out over the harbor at night. The torch light reflections danced on the calm waters, with the warehouses closed, but the taverns and inns full.

"Why is Kelby still here?" Cassie asked, as they sat together. Alex didn't detect any jealousy in the question, just curiosity.

"Leander told me about the fight with the dragon at the lake. Kelby nearly died. After the dragon was driven off, she returned to the water to search for signs of your mother, though she could hardly walk," he replied.

Cassie seemed to think on the description of Kelby's heroics, and the search for her mom, before speaking again.

"Do you think Tantalus knows where the dragon might go? Do you have any ideas?" she asked, changing the subject.

"I don't know about dragons, but I do know greedy men. There is no way all of Tantalus's wealth was that lair, in the Dragon's Teeth. He would never risk losing everything by keeping it all in one place. Placing half his wealth in the Northern Mountains ensures he has a place to retreat to, no matter what the local politics. Should things go bad for him here, I could see him escaping there, where people are obliged to help him."

Cassie nodded in agreement before taking Alex's arm and wrapping it around her. The two sat in silence, watching the activities around the harbor until they decided to call it a night and head below.

----*----

The following morning found all five of the on the dock, just after breakfast. Alex had conferred with Captain Yeagars and, with his assistance, selected five more of the crew particularly noted for their fighting skills. With everyone armed, including Kelby, who had selected a long dagger from the ship's weapons store, they all headed into town.

The trip to the warehouse district was uneventful, although they did draw a stare or two from the early morning crowd. By the time they reached the House of Drakon, most of the shops and warehouses were open and starting their workday. Alex had the armed sailors hang back at the mouth of the street, suggesting they keep watch and come running should he signal for them.

As they approached the loading dock, there were two wagons at the House Drakon warehouse loading dock, with several men busily loading crates from inside the building. Stepping forward, with the others spread out behind him, Alex hailed the man he recognized as Tantalus's assistant in Freeport.

"We wish to see your master," Alex declared, in a tone not intended to alarm the man. Should Tantalus still be unaware of the activities in the mountains, he wanted to catch him by surprise. If he was already informed of the losses there, no eyewitnesses could identify them as the perpetrators.

"The master is away," the man replied without even looking up from his papers.

With a boost of magic, Alex pressed a force shield off the roadway, propelling him up onto the loading dock as if he had made the leap in one stride. His booming landing caused the man to start, tearing his eyes off the paperwork and onto the man now standing a head taller than he.

"Can you tell me where he is?" Alex asked in a far less pleasant tone.

"I do not know, Sire, he had a large ship hastily prepared the day before yesterday, and sailed with the evening tide, last night after dark."

"And you have no idea where he is headed?" Alex asked again, noticing everyone had stopped work to watch the exchange, but none had stepped forward to intercede on the man's behalf.

"He gave no destination to the ship's captain while I was with him, but he took one of our largest ships, so I would speculate he was headed east, across the sea," the man replied, now visibly nervous.

The man appeared sincere, and Alex doubted a search of the warehouse would turn up anything of value. Tantalus had obviously been told of the events in the Dragon's Teeth and was running.

"Thank you," he replied to the man as he took the steps down to the street to rejoin the others.

"What now? He's got half a day's start on us," Cassie asked after they walked out of earshot from the men on the dock. They all had heard the exchange.

"Other than Windfall, where would a ship that large make landfall?" Alex asked as they headed back to the docks and *Cassie's Quest*.

"There is a seasonal port in the north. Half of the year it is frozen over and unusable, but currently it is free of ice," Abrianna replied, clearly tying all their clues together. Between the oath of obedience from the Northern Lords, the grant in the Northern Mountains and the need for a deepwater port, it was the likely destination.

"Kelby, I am sorry, but I fear we will not make port in Freeport. Can I book you passage on another vessel to take you home?" Alex asked as they reached the docks.

"Why?" she asked, clearly not interested in the offer.

Now it was Alex's turn to be confused. Stopping, he turned to face the little redheaded mermaid.

"Kelby, you risked your life in search of Cassie's mom, something we appreciate very much. We cannot ask you to continue to do so."

"Wizard, you are no fool and know damn well I joined this to try and avenge my mother's death. In that effort, I would have died, had it not been for my companions. They risked their lives in defense of mine, and after I treated them so poorly. Now, the dragon still lives and I am in the debt of others. I will continue on this quest until we succeed or perish."

With that, she turned and started for the ship, with the others close behind.

"Technically, I'm a mage, not a wizard. I am apprenticed to the Wizard of Great Vale," Alex confessed as he caught up and then followed behind her.

"That's OK, I'm only a junior mermaid. We are required to work in the bar until we can demonstrate the ability to control men to get what we want from them."

"Interesting, and how is that going for you?" Alex asked as they reached the boarding ramp.

"I think you just got me a step closer," she replied with a smile, as she slipped past him to be the first onboard.

----*----

*Cassie's Quest* set sail within the hour of their boarding. Alex was pleased that Captain Yeagars had anticipated their departure and added fresh provisions while they were away. They were still stowing cargo as they exited the harbor.

"Set a course for home," Alex instructed.

"Will we be stopping at Freeport?" Yeagars asked, glancing at the mermaid.

"Kelby will be going to Windfall with us," Alex replied,

"Will there be more dragons, sire?" Yeagars asked quietly so the men didn't overhear.

"Let us hope not," Alex replied, knowing the Sea Dragon was still out there somewhere, doing Tantalus's bidding.

----*----

Alex knew the voyage home would take longer than their trip to Freeport, as they were now traveling against the wind. Tacking back and forth across the chosen course would get them home a few days longer than the original trip west.

It had occurred to him that it might be possible to catch Tantalus at sea; their schooner was surely faster than the merchantmen Tantalus was in. Though it likely held three masts, to their two, it sat deeper in the water and was made for hauling cargo, not speed.

Unfortunately, it was a big ocean and, without a good idea of their precise course, they would probably never find them before they made landfall in the north. He had also considered making a run directly for the northern port, but without men to fight for him, they would be in a poor position to take on Tantalus and his crew.

On the plus side, Cassie and Kelby appeared to be getting along, although certainly not the best of friends. A ship this small ensured that they were in close proximity most of the time. Abrianna helped with any potential conflicts, though Alex had noted a tinge of possessiveness in her own interactions when Leander was involved.

Alex took the opportunity to go through the entire cache of documents they acquired in the dragon's lair. As he did so, he set aside several exceptionally damning documents, intended for Ben's review. There were several outlining the deals between Renfeld and Tantalus. One in particular described the sections of the Great Vale Tantalus was to gain dominion over as well as another suggesting a possible union between Renfeld and Abrianna, should she survive the war.

Another document went on to propose a marriage to Amelia would gain Tantalus a royal standing while giving Renfeld the ally he needed. Alex shuffled those specific scrolls aside, not wishing Abrianna or Cassie to happen upon them unnecessarily. He suspected Leander would be even more irritated at the suggestions contained on the parchment, including references to creating an heir.

In his off hours, Alex frequented the ship's workshop, where he fashioned new arrows, utilizing objects taken from the dragon's lair with the documents. Alex wasn't sure they were what he thought they were; they were completely different from what he had seen, so he chose not to tell anyone what he was up to.

----*----

Cassie was at the bow of *Cassie's Quest*, enjoying the sights, sounds, and smells of the sea. Alex had been busy below, working on the pile of scrolls they had taken, and she was more than happy to let him handle things there.

Kelby was nearby, appearing dreamy eyed as she gazed out over the open sea. While Cassie comprehended the mermaid probably better than anyone aboard, she doubted they would ever be more than acquaintances. The mermaid had been helpful, and Cassie certainly understood her desire to avenge her mother's death.

So long as she kept her references about, and distance from Alex, they could coexist just fine. With all this on her mind, she watched as the expression on the mermaid's face went from relaxed to worried. She seemed to pause, as if straining to see something below the surface of the water.

"Dragon!" she suddenly shouted. No sooner had the words burst from her lips than the water off the starboard bow erupted with a winged serpent. There was a mad scramble as sailors hurried to their stations.

"Alex!" Cassie shouted, watching the creature approach the ship, its head bobbing as it moved closer. Cassie looked on as the serpent raised its head high, and it opened its mouth. She saw the ball of flame gathering there and then watched it spring forth, driving right for her. The small flying form of the redheaded mermaid hit her side, creating a shooting pain and sending both skidding down the deck.

Glancing back, just where she had been standing, flames bathed the decking from the dragon's head above. No sooner had the dragon began to spout fire, than Alex appeared from the stairwell, bow and spear in hand. She had no idea what he thought the bow was going to accomplish, however there was no time to ask.

Alex tossed the spear to a nearby sailor, then drew an arrow from his quiver as he focused his attention on the dragon. Cassie could see him scan the deck ahead, apparently planning his next move.

Rushing past her and Kelby lying on the deck, she watched as he deflected the second fire blast, diverting the flames down into the water. At this point, the ship had come abreast of the beast, giving everyone a good view of the scaly hide and leathery wings, as the dragon spread them in anger.

The beast turned to keep pace with the ship, this time directing its blast high, catching Alex off guard, and setting the upper rigging alight.

"Douse the fires!" Cassie heard Captain Yeagars bellow from his station at the helm. Turning, she watched Alex nocked an arrow in his Elf bow. Knowing full well the power of the weapon, she still didn't understand the action as she expected the missile to simply bounce off the dragon's hide.

Closing in on the ship's railing, the sailor with the spear was able to jab at the dragon's head, startling the beast and causing it to back away from the ship. Cassie could see the beast reassess its attack and it raised its head high once more.

As she watched, the dragon began to release another fountain of fire, just as Alex released the arrow. It flew at a blinding speed, flying directly at the dragon's throat. To both Cassie and the dragon's surprise, the arrow drove through its scaly hide and buried deep into the creature's neck, halting its actions as it clawed at the injury.

Taking advantage of the pause in the attack, Alex let fly with a second arrow, and then a third, each driving deeply into the dragon's hide. Cassie watched as the dragon thrashed about, flailing as it tried to remove the arrows embedded deep in its skin. A forth arrow drove into the dragon's exposed eye, causing it to howl in pain and rage before descending into the sea, disappearing from sight.

"How was that possible?" Cassie called to Alex as she and Kelby joined him at the rail, looking for any signs of a return of the creature.

Alex smiled and pulled another arrow from his quiver, not risking the one nocked and ready for use. Taking the arrow that Alex passed to her from his quiver, she noticed the tip was not of metal. Instead, it was a polished reddish glass, fixed in place with brass wire. The smile he had on his face gave her the suggestion Alex had just attached it to the shaft. She passed the shaft to Kelby for examination, who then returned it to her.

"What is that?" she asked passing it back.

"Fire glass, I assume, but nothing like Leander's spear," Alex replied with a smile.

"From where?" Kelby asked in return.

"The dragon's lair. Tantalus had a small box full of it. I grabbed the box with the scrolls before we left. I thought it might prove useful."

She watched as Alex displayed a quiver full of the modified arrows, all with razor-sharp, red-glass tips. Turning to the mermaid, Cassie paused before embracing her. While holding her tight, she knew Alex could see her squeeze the mermaid before she finally released her. Taking a step back, all heard her say, "Thank you for saving my life."

# Chapter 15

*Cassie's Quest* made port in Windfall a few days later. After the dragon attack, they had seen nothing more of the creature, attributing its absence to Alex's injury to its eye. Alex was gratified that his fire glass tipped arrows had been as successful as he hoped. He was also thankful he had many more; he suspected he would need them again.

The fire damage to the ship had been minimal; most of the broken and burnt rigging had been replaced while underway. Overall, it had delayed them less than a day, so everyone was happy to be home on time. Kelby was the exception, as she appeared ambivalent to the homecoming.

Captain Yeagars was able to expedite their docking, pulling royal privilege in commandeering space along one of the commercial piers. Alex could see several of his soldiers clearing workers from the pier, allowing others room to help the men warping the schooner into place.

"Alex, uncle is here," Cassie said as she pointed to the banners flying above the castle keep. While still very new to the whole social protocol part of his job, he knew that when royals visited, their banners were prominently displayed for all to see.

"Look there," Leander announced, pointing to a small group of men approaching from one of the streets than ended at the waterfront. Alex could make out Ben and several of his military commanders.

"The Ranger Guild Master of Tazmain had dispatched a message when we returned there, informing His Majesty we were coming home. He felt obliged to notify the king that Princess Abrianna was safe and well. I suspect King Ben wished to meet us here rather than waiting for us to reach Great Vale," Leander added.

By the time *Cassie's Quest* was secured to the dock, Ben's party had arrived and all were patiently waiting for the ramp to be put in place.

"Father!" Abrianna proclaimed, as she was the first to descend, embracing the man at its base.

"I am glad you are home safe," Ben replied returning the hug warmly. After they separated, Alex could see Ben scanning the group as they disembarked, stopping at Kelby for a moment, and then looking to Alex.

"We have a guest?" he inquired as he returned his gaze to the mermaid.

"Sire, may I present Kelby of the Freeport mermaids. She was instrumental in the search of Lake Vishap for Lady Amelia and has been a great asset in our continuing pursuit," Alex announced with some fanfare.

"I thank you for your assistance," Ben replied as he took the mermaid's hands in his and gave them a warm and welcoming squeeze.

Before leaving the pier, Alex turned and gave instructions to the captain on returning Shadows, Rose and their other mounts to the stables, a welcome change for them, he was sure. He could also see Ben eyeing the sack and spear he carried, but felt that explanation could wait.

He caught the tail end of Cassie's embrace with her uncle before the nymph took the mermaid, and arm in arm, led her away up the dock ahead of the others. As Alex and Ben watched, she seemed to be excitedly explaining all the sights around the bay.

"I am guessing that there is a story there," Ben commented quietly to Alex.

"If you have anything to contribute, I am all ears. Those two have gone from the fiercest of enemies to the best of friends," Alex commented as he shook his head in disbelief at what he was seeing.

"Is there a reason the two appear so similar they could be sisters?" Ben asked as they headed away from the activity at the ship as it was being unloaded.

"You are the second person to ask me that question. We met Kelby in a tavern in Freeport. She helped us get a lead on Amelia's location and was almost killed by a dragon in the effort to locate her."

Alex decided to withhold the description of Cassie's near death experience on the trip home until later. After that event,

Cassie and Kelby had been nearly inseparable, spending the remainder of the voyage giggling and gossiping like a couple of schoolgirls. At points during the trip, he would see the two looking in his direction while they whispered, making him decidedly uncomfortable. When he asked Cassie about it later, she would just reply it was girl talk.

----*----

The women went to get cleaned up from the long sea voyage, with Cassie insuring Kelby had VIP quarters on the Royal family's level of the keep. While they did so, Alex, Ben, and Leander went to the same small study, where they had planned their cross-sea adventure earlier.

"So, you saw Amelia?" Ben asked when Alex described his portion of their experience.

"Yes, in the dragon's lair. Tantalus has been using dragons in the west to establish himself as the prominent trading house there. In the sack are all of his contracts and correspondence with Renfeld and others in the east, helping establish his foothold here," Alex explained while indicating the bag he had placed on the table.

Ben nodded, now understanding the importance of the sack Alex had been carrying himself, rather than delegating the task.

"And the spear?" he asked while pointing to the weapon now standing in the corner next to the elf bow and quiver.

"The only weapons we have that pierce dragon hide," he replied with a shrug.

"And you have no idea where the dragon took her?" Ben asked, returning to the main objective.

"We were hoping you might have an idea," Alex replied, indicating Leander.

Pulling out a few of the documents he had set aside, Alex handed them to Ben for his review. As he and Leander waited for him to read the contents, Alex had one of the guards standing outside send for food and drink. By the time the refreshments arrived, Ben had finished a quick review.

"Northern Lords, huh?" he replied, tossing the last scroll onto the table.

"Do you know any of them?" Alex asked.

"Met a few a ways back, though they may all be dead by now. They are a stubborn, independent bunch. For Renfeld to get this commitment, he had to promise them something big."

"Or had something big to threaten them with?" Leander asked.

"You mean the dragon? Yes, that is also a possibility. Either used in support of their efforts or as a threat against them, it would have a great influence in gaining their allegiance."

It was then that there was a soft tapping at the door, causing the three men to look.

"Yes?" Alex replied.

With that, the door opened, and Cassie, Abrianna, and Kelby entered. All three had changed into fresh, clean clothes, each a simple, yet elegant, design. Alex was sure Kelby must have borrowed some of Abrianna's things; Cassie's clothes would have been far too big on her.

The mermaid appeared slightly uncomfortable in both the fine clothing, and at the sight of Ben. However, she followed the others into the chamber, and quickly took a seat to one side, while Abrianna went to her father and Leander, kissing each on the cheek before finding a seat of her own. Cassie went to Alex and remained standing at his side, after their own personal greeting had completed.

"What have you determined?" Cassie asked, pointing to the pile of paperwork on the nearby table.

Everyone was looking at Ben, hope clearly expressed on their faces.

"I agree with the consensus that the dragon came east, likely to the Northern Mountains. We once had dragons there, long ago, before the great purge drove them close to extinction."

"Uncle, I don't remember learning anything about a purge," Cassie said.

"It is not discussed. In the last confrontation with the Dark Elves, the dragons sided, or were forced to fight with, the dark forces. Many perished in the destruction of A'asari and even more were hunted and killed in the years that followed. It was assumed that they were gone, but obviously, some remained, hidden away."

"And it's House Drakon and Tantalus, in particular, that seem to have the ability to control the dragons?" Alex asked.

"Yes," Ben replied as he turned and scanned the books on the shelves of the small library. After a few minutes, he located what he was looking for and pulled a large volume from one of the upper shelves.

"This is the Book of Families. All the royal families have a copy. It contains a history of all known houses, both royal and notable," Ben explained, placing the book on the table.

"I remember that book," Abrianna said as she lit up in excitement.

"Cassie and I used to flip through it when we were kids. We could hardly wait for the latest updates."

"Updates?" Alex asked, confused at the reference.

"All copies of this book are magically linked. The master volumes are held by the elves. Every time they make a change, it automatically updates all the copies as it occurs," Ben explained.

"You can search by House or by location," Cassie commented, looking over Alex's shoulder.

Alex opened the book and began flipping through the pages until he found a reference to Great Vale. His heart skipped as he read. On the page before him was a reference to House Griffin, noting King Ben as the first of his line and listing Abrianna as his sole direct heir, with Cassie next in line. Apparently the name was not a complete secret.

Alex realized that while Ben never used his last name, the Griffin was tied to his house in symbol. The royal seal, on the page for House Griffin, was not the blue emblem Alex had seen denoting Great Vale, but was rather a yellow Griffin on a gray background. The creature was part lion, and part eagle, its wings spread wide behind the body. He wondered if the colors referenced his Confederate roots, yellow and gray being confederate cavalry colors.

Continuing on, he found the pages referencing Windfall. Here, he scanned the notes referring to Renfeld, his father and the demise of their house rule in Windfall. He noted it didn't reference Renfeld's death, just the loss of the crown. As he continued on, he suddenly stopped and looked at Ben.

"I have a house?" Alex asked, pointing to the page entitled House Rogers. The crest emblazoned on the page displayed a black Pegasus, its stance reminiscent of the Ferrari emblem of a rearing horse, but its wings spread wide. Behind the horse were two crossed white lightning bolts, an obvious reference to his magical powers. Both were on a light blue background with white trim, something Alex assumed linked him to Great Vale.

"The elves apparently feel you are noteworthy enough to grant you such," Ben answered with a touch of sarcasm.

Ignoring the reply, Alex continued until he found the House of Drakon. As he scanned the pages, he nodded when he reached the part he was looking for.

*"....House Drakon is noted to possess an innate ability to communicate and control dragons of any type. They are immune to dragon fire and can telepathically link, seeing through the dragon's eyes as well as communicating instructions."*

"So, that's how Tantalus knew we had breached the lair," Cassie declared.

"Yes, he likely saw everything that happened there through the dragon's eyes," Alex replied.

"I wish we could do that now and see where the beast is hiding," Leander added.

There were several nods from the group, as they all considered the statement.

"We need to start looking for contacts in the north," Alex commented as he pulled a map of the area north of the mountains toward him.

"I could scout the mermaid bar here and see if any of the sailors know of a Tantalus ship in the area. The sailors love to try and impress the barmaids, so they are always spouting off," Kelby suggested with a knowing smirk.

"You are sure we have a mermaid bar in Windfall?" Alex asked.

"All large seaports have a mermaid bar," Ben stated, appearing distracted as he considered the map as well.

Alex almost burst out laughing as Ben realized both Cassie and Abrianna were staring at him as if he had grown a second head.

"From time to time I have had need to charter a vessel, and mermaid bars are the best source of reliable information," Ben replied with a smile.

"Not ignoring the fact that mermaids have a particular fondness for men of power or Royalty?" Kelby asked slyly.

"I had noticed," Ben replied, not shying away from the implications.

"Do we know which bar here is run by the mermaids?" Alex asked, rescuing Cassie and Abrianna from any further unwanted disclosures on Ben's private life.

"I believe it's called The Sailor's Folly," Ben replied lightly.

"I don't even want to hear how you know that," Abrianna declared.

"Ok, tomorrow I will stop in and see what I can find out," Kelby commented, smiling at the ladies' discomfort. It was clear she was warming to Ben's presence.

"I should probably go with her," Alex added protectively.

"I think not!" Cassie snapped back, "If anyone goes, it should be me."

"Cassie is right," Kelby replied, "Alex would be an unwelcome distraction to those in residence there, while a nymph and mermaid traveling together would be more welcome."

While Alex had no desire to have his fiancée hanging out in a sailor's bar, he doubted there was much in the way of danger beyond drunk, groping, sailors. On that, though, he feared for those men.

With the subject closed, the group retired to the downstairs dining hall for an evening meal. That time was spent in tales of their trip and speculation on the future.

----*----

The following morning Cassie found Alex and Ben in the large meeting hall, taking care of things considered too important by his surrogates to be decided until his return. She left them both with a kiss and a hug before she and Kelby set off to The Sailor's Folly. Although everyone agreed it would be impossible for Alex to accompany the two even to the door, Leander was another thing entirely.

Predominantly unknown in Windfall, he was an excellent alternative as a discreet bodyguard. With two of his Rangers, all in local garb, the three alternated following the women at a respectable distance. The Rangers had accompanied Ben on his trip from Great Vale in hopes of assisting their Guild Master in his return.

As the destination was known, there were no concerns of losing the women in the crowds. The three men simply stationed themselves along the route and watched.

"You know Alex was not happy with you this morning?" Kelby said as they walked along the street. Every so often, she would stop and examine the merchant's wares, doing her best to look unhurried.

"You have no idea. All I heard before bed last night were his complaints," she replied while rolling her eyes.

"If that's all you got from him last night, you have my sympathies," Kelby replied with a smirk.

"I quieted him down soon enough," Cassie responded with her own look of knowing.

"I don't see our escort," Kelby commented as she casually scanned the street behind them.

"There's one of Leander's men standing by the fruit vendor," Cassie replied as they turned the corner and headed to the waterfront north of the castle.

Wandering into a less prosperous section of the city, Cassie caught two more changes of their guards before they turned onto the street known for its bars and taverns. The majority of the foot traffic here was male and far from affluent. The two redheads drew plenty of attention from all they passed, though none impeded their travel.

That morning, Abrianna had provided both women clothing more appropriate to their destination. While clean and well fitting, it was neither fine nor new in appearance. The two might be assumed to be shopkeepers or possibly in the trades, but certainly not affluent.

Two things easily identified the Sailor's Folly as they approached. The first was the sign hanging over the entrance, depicting a well-endowed mermaid, the tavern name emblazoned beneath. The second was Leander, sitting at a table just outside the door, flagon in hand and in deep conversation with another patron.

Kelby stopped and turned to Cassie.

"Let's bait the trap, shall we?" With that, she reached over to Cassie and opened a few buttons, adjusting her clothing until her attributes were well displayed. Her inner nymph flared with excitement at the prospect of titillating the men inside, while her proper self was mortified at the response. Repeating the process on herself, Kelby then gave them both a once over and a nod of approval.

"That should be good enough," she said with a smile.

"To wake the dead!" Cassie replied with a blush, but did nothing to adjust Kelby's work.

Cassie and Kelby passed Leander by without a glance, receiving the same treatment from him. The man he was speaking with, however, paused midsentence as he gawked at the women entering the tavern. Pausing to allow their eyes to adjust to the darkened interior, they had barely stopped when someone shouted from across the room.

"Kelby?" came the call from the far side, behind the bar.

"Oh, crap!" Kelby said quietly, as both watched a young woman jump the bar and rush across to snatch Kelby up in a bear hug. It was then that Cassie could see the newcomer was the spitting image of Kelby, flaming red hair and all.

"Cassie, this is my twin sister, Leena," Kelby said, as she broke free of the hug, gasping for air.

# Chapter 16

Alex and Ben had spent the entire morning dealing with everything but the one issue they were most interested in addressing. It had been a steady stream of merchants, factors, and shipping moguls petitioning for one favor or another. Alex was just happy to have Ben there to address most of it; he had a hard time detecting the fact from fiction in most of the petitions.

Some were looking to gain unfair advantage over their competition, while others had valid complaints regarding taxes, tariffs, and levies placed on their livelihood. Alex had made a good start at fixing the injustices of the past, but there was still a lot to correct from Renfeld's short time in power.

Ben was quite pleased with the shipyards under construction, and had suggestions of his own on other civic projects. Both men subtlety probed all that came before them on the subject of Tantalus and dealings in the north. More than one of those claimed no direct knowledge but were more than happy to share rumors.

With each petitioner presenting privately, uninfluenced by the previous audience, the two were able to stitch together which rumors were more prevalent. The facts around any of the rumors was still to be substantiated. The complaint of piracy Alex was able to personally verify, based on his own experiences, and was eager to ensure the complainant that he was on it.

"Well its lunch time and still no Cassie," Ben commented as the two left the audience chamber, on the way to the royal dining room.

"If it weren't for Leander, I would be scouring the streets now myself," Alex replied.

"Let's take their delay as a good sign then," Ben said as he motioned for Alex to sit. With that, the two men ate mostly in silence, anxiously waiting for women to return with information guiding their next steps.

----*----

Cassie sat at a wooden table in the upstairs area of The Sailor's Folly, waiting quietly as she watched Kelby console her twin sister. The news of their mother's passing at the hands of Tantalus had yet to reach Leena, or any of the mermaids here. As she watched the two, she marveled at the resemblance, unable to detect the slightest physical difference between the two mermaids, beyond the tear streaks Leena now sported.

Once Leena was able to speak, she peppered Kelby with questions surrounding their mother's death and all that had occurred in serving justice to the killer. Kelby patiently delivered an extended tale of the actions taken to date, including the search for Cassie's mother and their eventual battle with the dragon at Lake Vishap.

The wounds inflicted on the creature during the trip home brought a smile to Leena's face, but that soon faded as she learned of its escape. Kelby ended the tale with their arrival at The Sailor's Folly, in search of a new lead.

"Leena, have you heard anything that might help us find out where Tantalus is hiding?" Cassie asked after a pause.

Cassie could see the mermaid considering the question. Glancing at her sister before replying, she nodded yes.

"Before coming here, I was in Nyland," Leena declared. Cassie must have given her a look of confusion, because she added in irritation.

"Its north of Gundor Stronghold, on the coast," Leena provided.

"Yes I know. That's why I never expected to see you here. We sent word of mother there," Kelby supplied. The comment brought a sniffle from Leena, but she quickly gathered herself and continued.

"It was miserable up there. Freezing seas, snow on the ground most of the year, not a fit place for nymph nor mermaid," Leena declared, indicating Cassie in her statement.

"You picked it!" Kelby replied sharply, momentarily forgetting her sister's distress.

"I couldn't very well stay in Freeport with you, always second place to my prettier sister!' Leena snapped.

"Ah... you two are identical," Cassie commented, confused at the reference.

"Now! But once we transform in the water, someone's tail is all the rage!" Leena said, then rose and headed to a nearby counter, looking for something to drink. As she spoke, she swirled one leg behind her as one might flip a tail.

"My tail fluke is, well, shapelier than Leena's, and she's always been jealous of it," Kelby said quietly.

"I've never been jealous of you," Leena replied, returning with a pitcher and three mugs. Evidently, Kelby had not been quiet enough.

"Then why are we discussing it now?" Kelby snapped as she watched Leena pour for all three.

"Ah... ladies, the topic at hand, please?" Cassie interjected before Leena could counter Kelby's statement. She had to wonder if nymphs had issues like these.

"Yes, well, as I was saying, I was in Nyland for a short time before heading south to warmer waters. While I was there, I saw several Tantalus ships make port with nothing to deliver to town or pick up. What little they landed was shipped straight to Gundor Stronghold."

"Any idea what they were delivering?" Cassie asked after listening to the mermaid.

"No, but whatever it was, they had guards from both House Drakon and Gundor escorting it," Leena replied.

"How long ago was this?" Cassie asked.

"Last month. I came down here about three weeks ago," Leena replied.

"We should get back to the castle and tell Uncle about this," Cassie replied after some consideration.

"You are not leaving without me!' Leena announced.

"Leena, we are going north, and likely inland, and away from the sea," Kelby replied, obviously trying to influence her sister with the last comment.

"Then you need me, I know the way!" Leena replied as she rose and led them downstairs and into the tavern below. Cassie watched her exchange a few words with one of the other women Cassie took to be the owner. The woman examined both Cassie and Kelby before nodding, and then Leena turned and joined the two.

"I'm good to go when you are," she stated while waiting for them to lead the way.

"Let's get the rest of our party then," Cassie replied while Kelby simply glared at her sister. Scanning the room, Cassie found Leander and his two Rangers covering all the exits and ready for action, while appearing casual. With a nod from Cassie, all three rose, and with her leading the way, the entire party exited and headed south, down the street.

"We have another one?" she heard one of the Rangers comment to Leander, as they followed closely behind.

----*----

Alex had gone down to check on Rose and Shadows, with Kinsey by his side. His unease over Cassie's prolonged absence had him restless. Besides distracting him, he suspected they would soon need the mounts as the next part of their quest formed around them. As he checked on Rose, it occurred to him that the gift from the elves had been well timed; something he very much doubted was a coincidence.

To date, he found nothing related to elves as accidental. It was with these thoughts running through his head that he exited the stables in time to see Cassie and Kelby enter through the main gate. Kinsey rushed to Cassie, but Alex did a double take, seeing two Kelbys following his fiancée. He was also taken with his fiancée's appearance.

"I love your new look!" Alex said while indicating the considerable amount of cleavage on display. He assumed it was part of their tavern disguise as Kelby was even more exposed.

Cassie appeared to realize she had forgotten the alterations; she blushed bright red and quickly rearranged her attire.

"Kelby, you've come up in the world," Alex heard the Kelby clone say in awe as she surveyed the castle courtyard.

"Alex, this is my sister, Leena," Kelby proclaimed. She made no attempt to adjust her clothing to cover anything on display.

"Sister? A pleasure to meet you, Leena," Alex replied wrapping an arm around Cassie's waist as she came to him.

"Leena was in the north when Tantalus landed several shipments there. She can help us," Cassie commented as a way of explanation for their growing numbers.

"Let's get you inside to see the king before you all start a riot," Alex said, indicating all the gawking guards on the walls and in the courtyard.

"King?" Leena said nervously as they made their way inside.

----*----

"That's quite a story," Ben commented as he sat listening to Leena describe her travels from Freeport to Nyland. She had then added her time in the north before coming south to Windfall.

"I was in Nyland once, many years ago. That was before I married your mother," Ben added with a smile, telling Abrianna as if preparing her for any further disclosures. The seven were sitting in the small private dining room, reserved for royalty. None of the three women had eaten lunch, so Alex had them served while Ben took the opportunity to question Leena on the things she had seen in Nyland.

"The Drowning Man, isn't that the name of the bar there?" Ben asked to everyone's surprise.

"Yup, that's the place," Leena replied with a bob of her red head.

"They still go out to all those hot springs inland?" Ben asked absently.

"Oh, yes. That was what saved me while I was up there. Some people will tell you that a mermaid doesn't feel the cold water, but they are liars. I would visit the hot springs almost every day while I worked in the north," Leena said, looking to her sister for agreement.

"Geothermal?" Alex asked Ben, wondering about the relevance and getting confused looks from the others.

"Yes, there is volcanic activity in the area, very close to the surface. It makes the valley very fertile and they have a productive growing season. In addition, there are rumors that the Gundor Stronghold sits on top of a volcanic vent, buried deep within the mountain," Ben replied. Alex noted several of the others nodded in understanding at Ben's reference.

"I don't get it, what's the connection?" Alex asked, not seeing the relevance of volcanic activity and the quest for Amelia. He took a moment to toss Kinsey a morsel from the table. She had found a spot to one side of the room and curled up.

"Dragons are born from eggs hatched in volcanic fissures. Because of that, they are very fond of anything volcanic," Abrianna supplied.

"Gundor Stronghold was once a dwarf city, carved right out of the stone on top of a small mountain in the central valley. The walls and buildings are solid structures, left after the surrounding stone was removed. It is said that the dwarves exhausted the precious metals and gems in the mountain, leaving a maze of tunnels and caves beneath the castle. They dug so deep they struck lava," Ben explained.

"With nothing left to mine, the dwarves moved on. It was then that the dragons moved in, laying claim to the inside of the mountain and driving anyone away that dared try and claim the abandoned city above," Abrianna added, smiling at her father's acknowledgement of her contribution.

"Finally, after the last great battle, the dragons were thought extinct and humans took possession of the castle. With no dragons left to contest ownership, the Vassal King took control of the surrounding valley and port of Nyland," Ben finished as if ending the lecture.

"So are we now assuming that the dragon is hiding in the Gundor Stronghold?" Alex asked, confused at the turn of events.

"Not in the Stronghold itself, but likely deep in the mountain it sits upon. The occupants above may not even know it is hiding there."

"Then what's with the land grants to Tantalus in the Northern Mountains?" Alex asked, not quite willing to relent on their earlier suspicions of the dragon hiding there.

"The dwarves that built Gundor still exist in the mountains north and south of the valley. From time to time, they rattle their sabers, making threats on retaking Gundor for themselves. While Renfeld bestowed said lands upon Tantalus, his ability to claim them rests on his dragons driving the dwarves away. I am beginning to see a very uneasy set of alliances here," Ben said as he stared up at the ceiling.

"I don't understand, Uncle," Cassie said, speaking up for the first time since accepting the seat by Alex. She had been eating quietly while the others talked.

"Renfeld sought help from both the Lords of the North, and Tantalus in the west. The Vassal King would take nothing less than assurances that their lands would be defended against any dwarf claims. Tantalus and his dragons would be a great aid there. A single dragon can go a long way in intimidating dwarves.

"Tantalus wanted access to the volcanic chambers beneath Gundor, most likely to try to expand his dragon collection," Ben said, then paused.

"But neither participated in the attack on us?" Abrianna commented.

"They likely were to assist in his planned attack south on Great Vale but Alex accelerated the timeline. Burning the supplies in A'asari required Renfeld to move up the attack earlier than expected, and necessitated leaving them out. Neither Tantalus nor the Northern Army could arrive in time," Leander suggested.

"I wonder what was in those crates shipped from the west and destined to Gundor. If they were dragon's eggs, it would scare the hell out of both the dwarves, and the Northern Lords. Renfeld would have been unstoppable if he fielded several dragons at once," Ben finished as the others considered his theories.

"So Tantalus would have to drive the dwarves out of the Northern Mountains to take possession of his claim there. I am sure Renfeld spun tales of gold and gems in those mountains to spur his desire." Alex began again.

"That move would likely cause the dwarves to attack Gundor, who would then retaliate against Tantalus. The fighting would decimate them all," Leander said.

"And the Renfeld would be free to move into the north and claim those lands as well as the south they all had helped him conquer," Abrianna completed the thought.

"Wow, what a conniving bastard Renfeld was!" Alex stated.

----*----

Naga was not so unhappy with the latest turn of events. Yes, the White Wizard that had confronted her in the Dragon's Teeth had forced her to leave her beloved den and make a hasty exit, that was for sure. Had it not been for her charge, she would have pressed the man much harder before relinquishing her home.

As she considered this she watched the human female as she made herself comfortable in the pit next to her. Unlike her previous location with the stone pedestal, this cave had a deep pit set to one side to prevent the woman from escaping. Items had been provided on their arrival from the humans above to make the prison more comfortable for her.

Naga had cleansed the area with a bath of flame to remove any traces of previous detainees, a gesture the woman seemed to understand and appreciate. Naga took her responsibility very seriously, for she understood that Tantalus held hostage her most precious treasure. Should she fail in her duties, the results would be devastating. While she would act with integrity, she was all too aware that the man had none.

As she settled down next to the pit, her one piece of satisfaction was in knowing that this relocation placed her very close to those treasures taken from her so long ago. She could feel its presence and it comforted her.

# Chapter 17

After a late lunch, everyone had gone their separate ways, with Ben and Alex headed back into town to deal with issues of state. Cassie, Abrianna and the mermaids had gone upstairs to change, while Leander dealt with his own duties involving the Rangers of Windfall.

That evening, everyone gathered in the small study after dinner, and the group considered their next move. Alex noted that since the arrival of Leena, Kelby had been far less flirty with him and Leander. Even though Kelby and Cassie seemed to have settled their initial differences, the mermaid attention still made him very uncomfortable. He hoped that it was a thing of the past.

As he was considering this, he was suddenly drawn back into the conversation in the room.

"What do you think Alex?" Cassie asked, an expectant look on her face.

"Ah..." he replied, trying to recall what they had been discussing.

"We were discussing which of us you wanted to kiss more," Kelby supplied with a seductive smile; she leaned forward causing her charms to become more exposed. While wearing different attire than earlier in the day, it was no less provocative.

"So much for that hope," he sighed to himself.

"We were discussing the legends on how to control a dragon," Abrianna returned sharply, rescuing him.

"And?" Alex asked, trying to draw Cassie's question out again.

"We were thinking that the crates Leena saw might contain the dragon's eggs," Cassie explained.

"While Tantalus can interact and even communicate with dragons, it's quite another thing to get them to do your bidding," Ben commented, the Book of Families spread across the table. Alex suspected he had been referencing the page on Tantalus's family traits.

"Dragons by nature are reported to be quite honorable and neutral to the ways of elf and man. It's only by consent or coercion that they can be influenced to act on our behalf," Ben added.

"And how do the eggs help?" Alex asked, clearly far behind on the topic of conversation.

"Blackmail, my boy," Ben answered with a knowing look. As both Ben and Alex came from the same world, there were certain subjects that had special meaning to just the two of them.

"So he takes the eggs as hostages, and the dragon cooperates or he threatens to destroy them?" Alex asked, the ruthlessness of it a clear indicator of whom they were dealing with.

"In a word, yes. So long as the dragon cooperates, the eggs are safe," Ben replied.

"How long do dragon eggs last? I mean, won't they go bad...and why not just lay more?" Alex blurted out.

"A dragon will only lay a few eggs in its lifetime, and they can last for a thousand years before hatching. Only in a lava bed will it hatch, so the dragon must take it there when she is ready. The eggs that Tantalus hold now could have been collected by his great, great, grandfather and hidden away from the mother to control her," Abrianna answered.

"And, given the opportunity, the dragon would choose to reside near their hiding place. I have little doubt she can sense their presence," Ben supplied.

"It is said that of all the items a dragon hordes, her eggs are her greatest treasure," Leena added to everyone's surprise, as it was almost poetic.

"OK wait. So are we thinking that the Red Dragon from the Dragon's Teeth is now in the caverns beneath Gundor Stronghold with Amelia? In addition, the eggs Tantalus uses to control the dragon are being kept in the same place. Am I the only one that thinks that this is a bad thing?" Alex proposed to the group.

"On the plus side, this is a strong indication that Tantalus will use Amelia to try and influence me," Ben replied.

"However, should the dragon recover her eggs, she will likely kill everyone in the Stronghold, Amelia included," Ben added emphatically.

"We should move quickly then," Cassie stated, a worried expression across her face.

"We do need to move quickly, yes. However, it is not as dire as it appears. Tantalus is no fool. He will have the eggs well protected and hidden away from anyone looking to take them for themselves. It is also not likely a full-grown dragon can roam the castle unnoticed as it looks for them," Leander posed.

"And as for human threats, it is a strange thing, but just possessing an egg does not guarantee the ability to control the dragon. One must also be able to communicate with the creature," Ben said while turning his full attention to Alex.

"Why are you looking at me?" Alex asked; suddenly he was the center of attention in the room.

"It is possible *you* can communicate with the dragon," Ben answered after a moment.

"Why in the world would you think that? The only times I have ever been close to one, it's been trying to kill me," Alex replied, visions of fire and snapping jaws in his head.

"Precisely. Your brief encounters were centered on violence and you had no opportunity to reach out to either of the creatures. Dragons are actually quite intelligent, and delight in mental games, like riddles and puzzles. More importantly, they are creatures of honor. If a dragon agrees to something, it's good to its word," Ben stated.

"And in the cave, it was sleeping when we got there," Cassie added thoughtfully.

"So why me?" Alex asked Ben directly.

"Remember our conversation about the colors you see with magic. Specifically how differing colors represent core talents or abilities?" Ben asked, referring to their discussion on the return trip from Renfeld's camp the night before the battle.

"Yes," Alex replied, remembering the night they spent booby-trapping Renfeld's war machines.

"And what did I tell you about white?" Ben asked as an instructor might quiz a student.

"They are a mix of everything and considered unstable," Alex replied. The comment brought out a snort from Kelby, who obviously found the reference humorous.

"Not unstable," Ben corrected, smiling at the mermaid's insinuation, "unpredictable".

"The combination of all the magical colors gives white a little bit of everyone's abilities and disposition. Remember, the color represents a combination."

"So how does one speak dragon?" Alex asked, curious for the first time.

"It's not verbal, it's telepathic," Abrianna answered.

"We can discuss the hows later. For now, I think we need to get to Nyland and scout the castle, if at all possible. Kelby would you and Leena consider returning to the Drowning Man and see what you can dig up?" Ben asked the twins.

"Sure," Leena replied before Kelby could answer. The sister appeared excited to be included in their plans.

"Yes, Leena and I can go and see what we can find out. Leena says the castle guards come down from the mountain. I am sure I can get them to talk," Kelby added, making a move with the last part that left little doubt she would be successful in convincing lonely men to talk.

"It would be best if you went separately from the rest. Possibly swimming in on your own?" Ben said, clearly uncomfortable with asking the two to travel alone and in mermaid form.

"No problem. We can leave in the morning," Kelby replied with a shrug, while Leena gave a shiver. Alex assumed it was at the return to cold water.

"Excellent!" Ben replied.

"And us?" Cassie asked her uncle anxiously.

"We will prepare *Cassie's Quest* to follow right behind them. However I expect they will arrive well in advance of the schooner," Ben replied, indicating the mermaids as he answered.

Alex had no idea how fast a mermaid could swim, but given the comments from Ben, he suspected it was much quicker than the ship. The thought of *Cassie's Quest* brought another subject to mind.

"Pirates," Alex blurted.

"I beg your pardon?" Ben replied, confused at the outburst.

"We ran into two brigantines on our way west. Captain Yeagars told me that pirates were returning to the area with the demise of Renfeld," Alex explained.

"Well, the mermaids will have little to fear, however, general shipping is at risk," Ben replied thoughtfully. He then turned his attention back to Alex.

"How did you address the threat? Two brigantines against that schooner are hardly great odds," he asked, a curious look on his face.

"The Captain was preparing to repel boarders when I sent an arrow from my elf bow, threatening to fire their sails."

"Well, that would do it. So they knew you were of magic?" Ben replied with a laugh.

"No, but firing an arrow beyond the range of their ballista probably was good enough," Alex replied, with a nod from Cassie.

"I didn't see the shot, but they were showing us their rudders by the time I came on deck," she added with a laugh.

With that, they called an end to the evening, and everyone headed off to their own rooms. Alex kissed Cassie and told her he would be along shortly. Ben noted the exchange and waited to see what Alex wanted to discuss in private.

"Ben, why no cannons?" Alex asked, once the others had left the room.

"Ah, yes. I wondered about that when I first arrived, as well. Here, let me show you," Ben replied as he went to the wood box next to the fireplace and withdrew a small sliver of wood.

"Can you light this from there?" Ben asked as he held the stick out, but indicated Alex should remain where he was.

"Sure," Alex answered, confused at the change of subject.

"With your eyes closed," Ben added.

"Easy," Alex quipped at the added challenge.

Well practiced by now in diverting enough free energy to set just the tip ablaze, he did so with little effort.

"Great," Ben replied as he tossed the burning stick into the fireplace.

"Now imaging holding a revolver and have all six cartridges go off at once," Ben said, giving Alex a knowing smile. Suddenly it was quite obvious to Alex why there were no guns, cannons, or other explosive weapons. A nimble magic wielder could turn them all against you.

The image of an exploding powder magazine, ripping a ship in half was more than enough to justify the lack of powder. Alex nodded to Ben in understanding. He then watched as the older man went to the bookshelves, searching for several minutes before finding what he was looking for. Turning back to Alex with a smile, he extended a small volume.

"If you can resist my niece's charms for just one night, I suggest you read this before retiring tonight."

Alex took the book and examined the title along the spine: "*How to Communicate with Dragons*" was emblazoned in gold letters on the brown leather.

----*----

The following morning found Alex and Cassie out on the end of a dock with the mermaid twins. It was still very early, just after sunrise, and there was hardly a soul about. The sisters were both in thin robes provided by Cassie, and apparently unaffected by the morning chill. Cassie had suggested the robes to both reduce the number of items they would need to carry back and to derail the suggestion that they simply walk naked to the dock. While she personally had no issues with that, she was all too familiar with the effect such an act would have on the males involved, her fiancée included.

"Are you sure you are ok with this?" Alex asked the women once more as they reached the end of the pier.

She couldn't decide if he looked more worried or tired. After returning to their room, he had spent a good portion of the night reading a book. He explained that her uncle had provided him the copy after the rest had left the study that night. While her inner nymph was crying out for him, she had conceded to his point in choosing the book over her. If the book gave him insight into rescuing her mother, it held top priority.

"We will be fine," Kelby replied as she stepped forward and kissed his cheek in an almost sisterly fashion. Almost.

Taking one-step back, the act was followed with a quick shrug as she dropped her robe. Cassie watched as it slipped off her shoulders, with Kelby catching it deftly in one hand just before it fell to the dock. The mermaid performed the act without ever taking her eyes off Alex, and she finished by extending her arm to him, robe in hand, as she stood there naked.

As Alex took the extended garment, Cassie was drawn back to the moment by Leena. The twin was offering her the robe she wore. With that, both women turned, and as one, dove into the bay. Surfacing just a few feet from the pier, Kelby waved to the two on the dock before both mermaids turned and dove once more, their tail flukes exposed as they extended skyward before slipping into the sea.

"Leena was right," Cassie said as she took Alex's arm in hers and led him back to the castle.

"How's that?" Alex asked, looking unsure of the comment.

"Kelby's tail is nicer," Cassie answered with a smirk, knowing she has just tainted Alex's memory of a naked Kelby on the dock.

----*----

The rest of the day was spent in preparations for taking *Cassie's Quest* north to Nyland. As luck would have it, Captain Yeagars was well acquainted with the harbor and the town. He had visited many times, it being a regular stop for the cargo ship he had mastered years before. As such, they left it up to him to prepare the ship, and provision its stores. Yeagars relief at hearing that the passenger list was limited to the original four was visible, his distrust of mermaids evident.

Ben was not to partake in this endeavor either, as both Alex and Ben could not be absent from their leadership responsibilities for more than a few days. While the goal was to retrieve Amelia as quickly as possible, the probability that it might take longer than desired precluded his participation. It was better not to artificially rush things, just for a hasty return.

Ben and Alex did take the opportunity to do a little magic tutoring. As Ben's apprentice, Alex's magical education was dependent on their time together. Although Ben acknowledged that Alex was a natural in many ways, things like dragon telepathy were not intuitive.

It was for that reason that the two sequestered themselves in the small study for the better part of the day. Alex noted that after his time with the elf tutors, Felaern and Alduin in E'anbel, Ben was an easy study. With barely a break for lunch, the two emerged just after sunset to find Cassie and Abrianna waiting patiently for them in the private royal dining room. Kinsey was curled up in her designated corner, a meal of her own already in place.

"About time you two appeared," Cassie declared rising to greet Alex as they entered. The move gave Ben plenty of time to seat himself at the head of the table. Alex wasn't sure if Cassie had done it on purpose to prevent him from making a social faux pas, but as tired as he was, it did the trick.

Seating Cassie and then himself, he noted for the first time that Leander was not there.

"Where is Leander?" he asked as he watched the food being delivered to the table without anyone asking. He personally feared he might someday become too accustomed to this treatment.

"He went to the local Rangers Guild today to see what they had on Nyland. He also wanted to search for any references to the Gundor Stronghold, especially any maps of the layout," Abrianna replied after thanking the server who placed her meal before her.

Alex did the same when his plate was place before him. It looked like some kind of fish, with a white sauce and greens. Although not a huge fan of fish, he had caved to local eating customs. With it came the discovery that he really liked several of the more popular dishes.

"I wonder how far the twins got today," Cassie asked absently between bites.

"I expect they will continue on through the night and make Nyland by late tomorrow morning," Ben replied.

"Won't they get tired?" Abrianna asked.

"I understand they can go many days before requiring a stop. I would never have said this in their presence, but I gather it's similar to how sharks swim while sleeping," Ben replied with a grin.

"I'm glad you didn't mention it," Alex said with a sigh. Somehow, he doubted the two would have found the comparison a compliment.

# Chapter 18

Alex headed down to the docks early the next morning, leaving Cassie and Kinsey to meet her cousin for breakfast. He wanted to check with Captain Yeagars and see how soon they could depart. He was sure that if he pressed the good captain, he would rise to the occasion, but he felt rushing off ill prepared was a recipe for disaster.

Yesterday's lessons had been monotonous, but necessary if he was to have any hope at all of talking to the dragon. Since they had no dragon to practice with, Alex was left with visualizations and written accounts from books in the late Renfeld's library. As no one had actually seen a dragon in these lands in a very long time, there was no one available with that kind of experience.

Both men found it quite interesting that Renfeld had so many references in his library on dragons. It was just one more nail in the coffin of their suspicion that Renfeld had planned to turning on Tantalus after conquering Great Vale.

"Permission to come aboard," Alex shouted at the base of the boarding ramp leading to the deck of *Cassie's Quest*. Before receiving a reply, he had to move aside as deck hands carrying cargo made their way up the ramp.

"Granted," Alex heard in reply as Captain Yeagars appeared at the railing. While he knew the request was unnecessary, Alex's intent was to reinforce the Captain's authority onboard the vessel, as well as show respect for the man.

Heading up the ramp, the captain met him as he stepped onto the deck, he hand extended in greeting.

"How's it going?" Alex asked the older man after receiving the handshake.

"We will be ready to sail at the next tide. I assume you will want to load your horses before then?" the Captain replied. Alex was aware that they used the receding tide to assist in leaving the harbor. It was one of the many things he had learned in assuming responsibility for the trading port of Windfall.

"And that is?" Alex asked, unsure of when the next time change actually occurred.

"This afternoon. You have plenty of time yet," Yeagars replied with a smile. Alex had never proclaimed himself a seaman and Yeagars patiently addressed his boss's lack of knowledge.

"I'll make arrangements to have them brought down about noon?" Alex asked.

"That would be splendid," Yeagars responded.

With that, Alex made his way back down the ramp and into the castle, where he made good on his commitment to Yeagars. Once the stable hands had their instructions, he headed into the keep in search of his traveling companions. He found everyone, Leander included, still eating in the small dining room.

"There you are," Cassie announced as Alex entered the room and took the vacant seat next to her. No sooner had he seated himself than a plate appeared before him, complements of one of the nearby serving staff.

"Yeagars says we can leave this afternoon. I have arranged to have Rose, Shadows and your horses in the hold by noon," Alex said, indicating Abrianna and Leander with the last.

"I have reviewed the Ranger archives here in Windfall, looking for anything they might have on Nyland and Gundor Stronghold. There wasn't a lot, but I did find maps of the tunnels below the castle as well as diagrams of the castle itself. Apparently, the Rangers had considered occupying the abandoned bastion at one time, but it was found to be too far from Nyland or any other village to be useful. The maps are incomplete I fear, but better than none at all," he finished with a smile.

"And the rest of you, are you ready to go?" Ben asked as he looked to Abrianna and Cassie.

"Yes Uncle, We packed warm clothing, and fire glass weapons," Cassie replied; she referred to Alex's glass-tipped arrows and the spear from the temple.

"Let us hope Alex can find a less dangerous way to gain Amelia's freedom," Ben replied with a concerned tone in his voice.

----*----

Kelby and Leena arrived in the harbor of Nyland by midday. The two had swum continuously since leaving Windfall, but were still in good condition, neither requiring a break before heading to the Drowning Man. It was a common practice for harbor towns frequented by mermaids to have a safe house at the waterfront. There, one could stop and find clothing or rest in security.

Although no mermaid had issue with appearing unclothed in public, it was frequently troublesome with either the female occupants or the more aggressive males. On more than one occasion a presumptuous sailor had been found face down in the harbor after accosting a mermaid transitioning from the sea to land.

Since Leena had been here before, she led her sister straight to the safe house before anyone noticed them. In short order, both were dressed in what passed for conservative mermaid attire, although Kelby was sure Abrianna would have considered their appearance scandalous.

The thought brought a smile to her face as well, as the memory of Alex holding her robe on the pier returned. Even though her relationship with Cassie had improved to the point of friendship, she couldn't resist tormenting the wizard. Even with all his power, he was still just a man and susceptible to all the manipulations a mermaid could offer. She respected his commitment to the nymph though, and kept her flirting to a minimum.

Putting that out of her mind, she followed her sister out of the safe house and onto the streets of Nyland. The mermaid bar was purposefully located away from the safe house and closer to the more active part of the harbor. It wasn't long before the two found themselves entering the tavern, the pub sign depicting a mermaid rescuing a drowning man. Kelby laughed as she envisioned the rescued man being dunked by his rescuer soon after.

Entering the darkened room, Kelby watched as her sister rushed to greet several of the women working the room before heading to the bar. Apparently, they did a brisk lunch trade here as almost all the tables were occupied with men eating and drinking. The only women in presence were working the tables, flirting and otherwise fleecing the patrons of their wages.

"Right, we are good. Felicity says we can have free rein so long as we turn over the house share of any money we make and don't drive off customers," Leena said, indicating a tall blonde behind the bar.

"Got it. Okay, game time," Kelby replied as she loosened the ties on her blouse while she scanned the room looking for anyone resembling a Gundor guard.

----*----

Ben was at the pier as Alex, Cassie, Abrianna and Leander boarded the schooner bound for Nyland. He smiled as he watched Kinsey slip between Cassie and Alex, nudging Cassie's hand with her nose, looking for attention. He was concerned about sending Cassie and Abrianna on this trip north, but had little doubt that he was powerless to prevent them from going.

The trip west had only steeled Cassie's resolve to find her mother and return her to Great Vale. While sending Abrianna only compounded the worry, he knew she would keep Cassie from being reckless.

Normally he might expect Alex to watch out for her, but in this case, the boy was more likely to charge in himself. Ben appreciated a good many things about Alex, but when it came to Cassie, he was a hopeless wreck in telling her no. Therefore, as he stood at the dock watching them depart the harbor, he crossed his fingers and prayed that they would all return safe.

----*----

Alex found Cassie at her usual spot near the bow, as the Captain went to full sail and headed north after clearing the harbor. He noted Kinsey had found a spot nearby where she could curl up, out of the way of the sailors doing their jobs, while still maintaining a good view of her charges. Alex was quite pleased at the way she had taken to Cassie, saving both their lives on more than one occasion.

Not saying a word, he simply slipped up behind her and wrapped his arms around her waist. He could feel her lean backwards, pressing into him as her free hand rested on his arms around her waist, while the other maintained its grasp on the rail. As they stood there silently, Alex began to wonder what was going through her head.

With the quest to save her mother back on track, he imagined her tremendously worried over Amelia's welfare. That was why, when she finally spoke, it took him a moment to reply.

"Do you think they made it safely?" she asked.

"Do you mean Kelby and Leena?" Alex asked, surprised at the question.

"Yes. With a Sea Dragon about and pirates sailing the coast, they could have been killed," she replied without turning.

"They are very worldly; I am sure they made it to Nyland just fine. In fact, I expect they are this very moment fleecing customers and chasing leads on gaining your mother's freedom," he replied with a smile.

With that comment, Cassie turned slightly so she could lay her head against his shoulder. Her head came to rest in the nook between his shoulder and his neck, giving him a chance to squeeze her tighter.

"You know she doesn't mean it," Cassie said quietly.

"Mean what?" Alex asked, completely confused by the conversation.

"Kelby and her flirting. We have become quite close and you would be surprised to learn she actually respects you a lot," Cassie explained.

"She has a funny way of showing it," Alex commented dryly.

"It is very difficult for her to control a lifetime of prejudice. Since she was born, she has been taught that men are to be deceived and taken advantage of. It's only been recently that she has had cause to question that," she finished.

"Well, she has been helpful. Also I have no doubt she wishes to avenge her mother's death, and make Tantalus pay," he added.

"Sire, a word if I may?" Captain Yeagars asked, approaching the couple from behind. As they turned, Cassie gave Alex a quick kiss before leaving him and the Captain alone. Kinsey got up slowly and followed the nymph below decks.

Alex could see Yeagars had a chart rolled and carried under one arm as he motioned for him to follow. The Captain led Alex over to one of the lower cabin rooftops, conveniently protruding up from the deck about table height. As he watched, Yeagars spread the chart out on the rooftop, moving to one side to give Alex a better view.

Alex slid over to review the map depicting the coastline they now followed north. He could see the ports of Windfall and Nyland as well as other landmarks noted along the way between the two.

"We have a bit of a problem," Yeagars started as he motioned to the map.

"I understand we want to make Nyland with all haste," he began.

"Yes, the sooner the better," Alex replied. He could see the Captain nod before continuing, acknowledging Alex's statement.

"Well, to do so, we will need to hug the coastline all the way north, which brings us to our problem. I had intended to do just that, hugging the coast and taking the shortest route. That requires us to pass between this point of land and the islands off the coast," Yeagars explained as he pointed to the map.

Alex could see where the mainland jutted out, almost skewering a cluster of islands just offshore. The chart noted that the islands were a hazard to shipping, with shallows and underwater obstructions throughout. He could see Nyland was not far beyond the point.

The islands extended well out to sea, and Alex suspected they were once part of the mainland, attached at the point. Some geological event had broken them away, dispersing the land mass into disparate islands. There were notes of small settlements on a few of the larger, homes to fishermen he assumed.

"OK, sounds reasonable…" Alex replied, unsure of the problem.

"I had hoped to pass that point in the night, where darkness would cover our passage. Unfortunately, the winds are not so favorable and we will cross between the point and the islands at early mid-day tomorrow," Yeagars explained.

"Why is that a problem?" Alex asked, confused that the Captain would want to run the risk of navigating a narrow passage in the dark.

"This area is favored by pirates. They hang back in the narrows between the islands or just inside the point here. They had been driven out by Renfeld's father but have since returned to the area," Yeagars answered while indicating the spit of land jutting forward.

Alex was beginning to understand. Moving through the narrow channel under the cover of darkness would allow the schooner to slip past any would-be bandits. Now, they could be jumped from either side of the channel well before they had a chance to avoid the conflict.

"Can we go around?" Alex asked indicating the mass of islands.

"Yes, but it will add more than a day to the trip," Yeagars replied solemnly.

"I guess I had better go get my bow then," Alex said.

----*----

Later that day Alex updated his traveling companions over their evening meal. No one seemed particularly surprised at the information and Leander added to the subject.

"Yes, I was informed at the Rangers Guild that the pirates had returned to those islands. I wasn't paying close attention; I assumed we were going around them. The Guild is doing what it can to assist travelers in that area but they can do little more than track and report on the pirates' activities off the coast."

"Well I'd rather not burn their ships to the waterline so we will have to come up with a better idea before tomorrow morning," Alex replied.

"Why do you care?" Abrianna asked, her curiosity evident.

"I talked with Yeagars and some of his officers earlier, looking for ideas and they gave me rather detailed accounts of pirate raids they had experienced. Unlike the villains of my world where they use can… er, explosive weapons to subdue their victims, here they chase them down with minimal loss of life. Mostly they board you and take valuables and goods."

"And that's not bad?" Abrianna, now shocked, let slip.

"Deadly force in defense of life and limb is well justified. Its use in protecting goods and valuables is subjective at best," Alex replied with a shrug.

"You would have them board us and take whatever they pleased?" Cassie now asked.

"I would do my best to avoid such an encounter to begin with. But if pressed to heave to and allow boarding versus risking the lives in this room and on deck, then yes," Alex responded firmly.

"What things of value are aboard that are worth your life?" Alex continued.

"The coins in my purse, the provisions in the hold?" he added.

"OK, point made. However, what if they want the *Quest*?" Leander proposed, referring to the ship.

"Then we fight," Alex replied with conviction.

# Chapter 19

The next morning found everyone on deck early after a quick breakfast. Captain Yeagars had men high in the rigging, acting as watch for telltale signs of approaching vessels. From his spot near the bow, Alex could make out the islands off the port side while the coastline was still visible on the starboard.

The air was clear and he could detect the slightest chill as the northern temperatures started to make themselves known. Ben had indicated that by the time they reached Nyland, Alex should be prepared for ice and snow as the winter was just beginning to set in up there. He recalled Leena's dislike of the cold and felt a pang of guilt.

With the thought of Leena, Alex wondered how the twins were doing in their quest to unearth leads regarding Amelia and Tantalus' whereabouts. With the last, Alex had little concern that Kelby would rest until she had the Dragon Master in her grasp.

With that vision in his head, he returned to scanning the horizon, looking for telltale signs of ships stalking unwary travelers.

----*----

Kelby was sitting in the downstairs great room of the Drowning Man, waiting for the morning crowd to trickle in. Like any other seaport, there was always that group of men that started the day in a bar. She had never given much thought as to why that was the case nor cared to ask. She was simply anxious to start the day's hunt for anyone connected to the Gundor Stronghold.

Yesterday, she had heard references to Tantalus from several men either sailing or warehousing for him. All confirmed they had not seen him since arriving in Nyland, and most suspected he had left to join Renfeld somewhere inland.

From her previous experience with Cassie and Alex, she did not think Renfeld was still alive. That meant Tantalus was more likely hiding in Gundor. Working the room until closing, she had been unable to locate any of the Gundor personnel whom might be able to shed light on the question.

Every time she thought of Tantalus, she seethed with anger. She constantly envisioned pulling his struggling body deep into a watery grave, or slitting his throat and watching him gurgle as his life's blood ran from the wound. While she hoped to assist in rescuing Cassie's mom, her focus never wavered on avenging her own mother.

Noises from the front door brought her attention back to the present. As she watched, four men came in, all laughing and already staggering for so early in the morning. What caused her heart to skip a beat were the clothes they were wearing. Rather than the typical attire the local fishermen and dockworkers sported, these were some kind of uniform.

"Can I help you boys?" Kelby asked as she slid up to their table in a seductive fashion. The four had seated themselves at a table near the center of the room and away from the front door.

"Hell yes!" the closest one of them replied as he slid his arm around her waist, but not before hovering on her behind for a moment.

"A pitcher of wine!" another announced, and then asked, "Do we want food?"

"You can't drink food, fool!" a third replied with a laugh.

"Looks like you got an early start?" Kelby asked, not in any hurry to run off just yet.

"Barton liberated a few bottles for the trip, so we got to start our leave early!" the fourth offered, while pointing to the first.

"Never seen you before," the one called Barton asked as he looked up at her from his chair; arm still firmly around her waist. With the question, she deftly spun in place, allowing her to sit crossways in the man's lap while she wrapped both arms around his neck

"I'm new here, just came in yesterday. Where are you all from?" Kelby replied coyly while entrancing the man with her charm.

"We are on leave from Gundor," the fourth replied, apparently hoping to attract Kelby into his lap as well.

"Are you the only mermaid here today?" replied the second, suddenly doing the math, and determining Kelby wasn't going to be able to entertain them all at once.

"Leena?" Kelby called without looking away from the man she was sitting on.

"Yes?" came the reply as the twin appeared from a room behind the bar.

"There's two of em!" number four declared as they watched Leena approached the table with a smile and carrying a pitcher with four mugs.

Leena and Kelby had worked it out earlier that if either located a Gundor lead, they would call for the other. It was common mermaid tactics to pair up to keep the mark distracted and confused, as the women got what they wanted from him.

"On the house boys!" Leena announced as she set the mugs down and filled them from the pitcher. Kelby knew the contents were the strongest drink in the tavern, something intended to loosen tongues and purses. As she watched, still seated in Barton's lap, all four emptied their mugs and then waited as Leena poured another round.

"This is wonderful!" the man across from Kelby declared as he took a breath between draws from his mug. She watched as Leena worked the table, rubbing up against each man as she refilled the mugs.

"So, what do you big, strong men do in Gundor?" Kelby asked with a dazzling smile.

----*----

The sun was high overhead as *Cassie's Quest* headed into the narrow channel created between the offshore islands and the point of land jutting out from the coast. Alex couldn't see any telltale signs of inhabitants on either side of the channel, nor did he see any masts.

Sailing ships had one fault in concealing their presence, and that was the tall masts required for their sails. With the coast on either side devoid of trees, just lingering next to shore wasn't possible without early detection.

However, as the islands and mainland here had high cliffs along the rugged coastline, it was easy to just hang back outside of direct view. With men still high in the rigging and every available body manning the rails, the thought that any slip on the pirate's part would go undetected was unlikely.

The men on deck were there to serve another purpose as well. Should they be set upon, showing so many able bodied fighters at hand was hoped as a deterrent to attack. Alex suspected that it was a small hope indeed, but it seemed to make Cassie and Abrianna feel a little more secure.

His earlier comments on avoiding a fight were said in earnest, but he privately held no desire to allow anyone to board the ship without some resistance. He had a few magical tricks up his sleeve, things he had conferred with Ben on when cannons had been discussed.

While he was considering this, one of the sailors high in the rigging gave the alarm.

"Masts, starboard side."

Sure enough, as they cleared the point, Alex could see the masts of two ships, but with the sails still furled. He would have expected men in the rigging, preparing to drop sails and ready to make a hasty pursuit. Instead, he could clearly see men staffing the decks, but giving the schooner no more than a passing look.

"Captain?" Alex asked as he joined Yeagars near the helm. The man was using his binoculars and was scanning both vessels as they sat at anchor.

"Those two are the brigantines we saw on the trip west," Yeagars replied without lowering the glasses.

"Why are they just sitting there?" Alex asked in reply.

Rather than reply, Yeagars handed Alex his binoculars. Taking to offered field glasses, he focused on the nearest vessel and began a scan from bow to stern.

"Wow, that's a lot of damage. Did you see the burned decking and rails?" Alex asked as he moved to the second ship.

"Yes. I am guessing they ran afoul of a dragon," Yeagars replied.

"There is a lot of high quality metalwork on those ships," Alex commented as he handed the binoculars back. He could see the confused look on the captain's face, but chose not to elaborate.

"Captain, heave to and lets drop anchor a safe distance away," Alex asked as he considered the situation.

"Sire?" Yeagars asked as if he questioned his hearing.

"I think we might have an opportunity here," Alex replied and he turned and scanned the deck for the first officer. Spotting the man, he shouted to get his attention.

"Mr. Sikes, can you please have Shadows brought on deck?"

----*----

Kelby and Leena had moved the Gundor soldiers to a table in the back of the room, far away from anyone else. They had been fighting with the desire of the men to overindulge, keeping the four just drunk enough to continue talking, but not so they passed out.

By now, the tavern had filled to near capacity, and the entire mermaid staff had descended on the unsuspecting patrons. It never ceased to amaze her how much money a man was willing to spend for time talking to a pretty face and the possibility of more intimate activities.

Her four victims had nearly run out of coins by mid-morning, not that they even realized it. She would have let them drink free, but the mermaid in charge wanted fair compensation for their participation. Leena and Kelby had made sure they were well distracted as the two entranced them with seductive attention and suggestive banter.

What the men failed to realize was the banter was wrapped around questions on Tantalus, the Stronghold, and what secrets lay deep in the bowels of the mountain. It took far less effort than she expected to get them to divulge that Tantalus was in fact hiding out in the Stronghold, a guest of the king. The four constantly complained about the extra duties and cramped quarters having the additional men with Tantalus placed on their meager resources.

Just as surprising though was the total lack of knowledge they had on anything dragon related. They knew of mysterious crates stored in a room near Tantalus's quarters. They were also up on the rumors of Sea Dragons and attacks on shipping, but had no idea that one might be hidden away in the abandoned dwarf tunnels deep in the mountain.

She began to wonder if maybe King Ben and Alex had been wrong in their estimation that the Red Dragon had taken refuge in the mountain caves. But then they commented on the regular meal deliveries made to the dungeons, where no prisoners were being held. Also, regular hunting parties were sent out to kill game that never made it back to the castle.

Satisfied that they had bled the four dry of money and information, Kelby gave her sister a nod. The twin smiled as she pulled a pitcher off the bar and poured each of the men another round, taking care not to fill the cups more than half way.

Within minutes, all four were face down on the table and sleeping peacefully. With a smile, the twins returned to the bar, taking time enough to drop the four coin pouches with the bartender and drain the drugged wine from the pitcher lest it be delivered unintentionally to another table.

Arm in arm, the two headed upstairs to compare notes and wait for the arrival of the rest of their companions.

----*----

Alex could see that Cassie was not in agreement with his decision to visit the pirates. As he saddled Shadows, she was hovering nearby, mumbling obscenities. Since dropping anchor a respectable distance away from the two damaged ships, neither had made a move to challenge the other.

Captain Yeagars had his lookouts stationed high in the rigging, tracking the pirates every move. Alex noted the man's discomfort at the situation; however, he kept his concerns to himself.

With the schooner's sails furled, the boom amidships was pushed aside, providing Alex the room he needed to mount Shadows and for the mare to spread her wings. The look of awe from the nearby sailors reminded Alex that what was becoming routine to him was still something special.

"Are you sure this is really a good idea?" Cassie asked again, obviously not satisfied with the last explanation.

"We need information, and I hardly expect they will suddenly attack when their ships are barley afloat as it is," he said while pointing to the two vessels at anchor.

Mounting the mare, he adjusted himself in the saddle while guiding her over to the ship's railing. He could see Cassie was not accepting his explanation, so he felt a sense of urgency to get moving to put the issue to rest.

With a single step, Shadows launched skyward, and giving the mare her head, they circled the schooner twice before rising to a height sufficient to clear the mastheads. Alex nudged his ride toward the pirate vessels and scanned the decks below, looking for indications of the kind of reception he might receive. He had moved his sword to rest across his back with an easy draw should things go poorly.

As he circled the two vessels, he could see some confusion below as the men scrambled about. From the confusion, Alex was able to determine the leaders of the vessels and selected the one he thought to be the flagship of the miniature fleet.

Pointing Shadows to the deck of the ship he had chosen, they circled once to lose altitude before she landed firmly between two of the square-rigged masts. She had to take particular care to miss the deck grate centered in the opening on the deck.

Once settled, Alex watched as the pirates made a large circle around him and the mare.

"I would have asked for permission to come aboard, but as you saw, that was not so easy to do," Alex declared to the crowd. A movement to his right drew his attention as a larger man moved through the crowd to stand inside the circle with him.

"And what brings you here?" the pirate captain asked.

"You appear to be in need of assistance; that is some serious damage," Alex replied as he pointed to the section of ships railing missing with burned decking all around.

"A cooking mishap, nothing more," the Captain answered nonchalantly.

"Not dragon fire?" Alex asked directly, getting weary with the banter.

"I recognize that ship you are on. We met a few weeks back. You threatened to fire our ships, is this what you meant?" he asked in a more hostile tone. Alex could see the words put an edge in the attitude of the crew.

"I did prevent you from making a very big mistake," Alex replied while he looked to a nearby sailor. Gently, without causing the man injury, he wrapped him in shields and used them to levitate the sailor about ten feet above the deck. Then he slowly floated the man over to the captain before softly placing him on the deck once more.

"I don't need dragons to do my bidding. If I had wanted your ships to burn, they would be at the bottom of the ocean right now," he replied calmly. From the murmuring of the crew, Alex hoped his demonstration had the desired effect, however, he partially cloaked himself in shields just in case.

"What is it you want, Wizard?" the captain asked, more civil in his tone this time.

"Tell me about your dragon encounter and who does your iron work." Alex asked as he slipped off Shadows and pointed to some ornate bands binding a cabin door. He then turned and approached the captain with a smile.

"Today may be your lucky day!" he finished as he led the captain away from the crowd.

# Chapter 20

It was late the following day that Kelby caught word of *Cassie's Quest* making port in Nyland. Rather than meeting the ship at the docks, the twins decided to await their arrival at the Drowning Man so as to not raise any suspicions with the locals. As for the four Gundor guards, they had slept off their binge, all none the wiser that they had been pumped for information.

Kelby and Leena laughed as they heard the four boast of the entertainments provided them by the mermaid staff as they left. One of the effects of the elixir used to knock them out was vivid dreams, undisguisable from a drunken reality.

It was just before nightfall that Kelby watched the four companions enter the tavern and take seats at a table well away from the other patrons. While waiting for their arrival, she and Leena had killed time working the bar and fleecing the customers.

It was funny, but she didn't feel the same rush as she did with her time at the Siren's Song, or just recently with the Gundor guards. She almost felt sorry for these men as she automatically worked the same swindles she had performed over the last few years. Shaking it off as she crossed the room, while subtlety waving off the brunette that was headed to the table, she slid up behind Alex and placed her arm around his shoulders.

"Now, what can I get you?" she asked, turning on her sex appeal as she made a show of rubbing against Alex. She hadn't actually meant to do that, but for some reason, every time she got near the wizard, she just couldn't turn it off.

Kelby noted the slight flush in Cassie's face and immediately regretted the action. Thankfully, Leena appeared at Leander's side, mimicking the move, and distracting everyone at the table.

"We are interested in rooms for the night," Abrianna replied while looking daggers at Leena. Even though everyone here knew this was all a charade, Kelby wondered how much of the women's response was an act.

"Well, let's go upstairs and see what's available then," Kelby suggested as she backed away from Alex and turned to lead the group to the back stairwell. Unlike other taverns she had seen, the Drowning Man had three floors. The first floor was the bar, the second provided lodging for travelers or patrons too drunk to leave safely in the winter months and the third was mermaid territory.

No sooner had they cleared the third floor landing than Kelby spun on Cassie and wrapped her up in her arms.

"By the gods, I am so happy to see you!" she declared, surprised at her own outburst. She was additionally shocked at the strength of Cassie's return hug.

Leena motioned everyone over to a large table, and gathered mugs and a pitcher of ale for the group.

"Did you have any problems getting here?" Cassie asked, as everyone took the offered seats. Kelby noted that the nearby mermaids vacated the area and was thankful for the privacy. She did see several confused expressions at her outburst over the nymph's arrival.

"No, the trip was uneventful, but I still hate the cold water!" Leena replied. Kelby was sure she did not want to be left out of the discussion.

"I expected you earlier today. Did anything happen?" Kelby asked. She noted a look pass between Cassie and Alex before the latter replied.

"We ran into pirates as we passed through the channel off the coast," Alex answered.

"Yes, we passed those ships at anchor on our way. They seemed to be damaged, I can't imagine they could give you much in the way of trouble," Kelby replied while focusing on Alex. With what she had seen him do to a dragon, she hardly expected a few pirates would even matter.

"Oh, they were no trouble; he wanted to make friends!" Cassie replied, the irritation in her tone clear to everyone.

"Let's not rehash this again. Were you able to find out anything?" Alex said while diverting the conversation away from the pirate encounter and back to Kelby.

"Yes, we landed four Gundor guards yesterday," Leena interrupted before Kelby had a chance to speak.

"And?" Cassie quickly asked, her earlier distraction completely forgotten with the news.

"Well, Tantalus is definitely holed up in the Stronghold. The four were adamant on that part. What was not so clear was the dragon and Amelia. They gave us indications that something was going on deep in the mountain, but no one had seen either," Kelby replied while eyeing her sister. Her sister's need to blurt out answers first was becoming an irritation.

"What indicators?" Abrianna asked, her earlier anger apparently forgotten as Leena had seated herself between her and Leander without a reaction.

"Big game hunters that never return with a kill, human food delivered to empty dungeons, and everything below ground declared off limits," Kelby replied.

She smiled as Alex nodded in agreement.

"We need to find a way into the mountain without attracting attention from the residence above," Leander stated sourly.

"I may have found a way," Alex replied with a smile of his own.

"How?" Cassie asked.

"With a little help from our new mix of friends," he replied cryptically.

"Who?" Leander and Abrianna asked in unison.

"Dwarves and pirates!" Alex replied with a grin.

----*----

It was well past sunset when the six returned to *Cassie's Quest* at her spot on the docks. While the original four had gone on to the Drowning Man in search of the mermaid twins, Captain Yeager had been tasked with finding them a place to tie up on the waterfront where they could unload the horses safely.

Alex had proven that flying Rose and Shadows off the deck was more than possible, but it did little to get the other mounts off ship. It would also generate far more attention than any of them wanted. As it was, just having the mermaids aboard was a risk to creating unwanted attention, but one that was unavoidable.

"Ok Alex, share!" Cassie said once they had settled in the lounge below decks. He had insisted that they retreat to a location more secure before outlining his plan.

"When we spotted the two pirate ships anchored off the coast, it struck me that the ironwork on both was of such high quality. It was consistent between the two so it was unlikely that it was part of the original build."

"So?" Abrianna asked, not catching the point.

"Who do we know that considers ornate metalwork as run-of-the-mill?" he asked the group.

"Ok, so the pirates got hold of some dwarf metal work... so?" Kelby replied.

"Not some, a lot! The pair of ships had been reworked bow to stern in quality metalwork. And not just decorative, the ballista on deck had obviously been redone by a master weapon smith," he added.

"I am beginning to understand," Leander said with a smile.

"Well I am not!" Cassie replied, frustrated.

"The pirates are trading with the dwarves. The mountains push out to the sea at that point, which is why it towers above the coast there," Leander supplied.

"Yes, and also why it's such a good ambush point. You cannot see what's on the other side until you pass the point. My new friend, the pirate captain, says there are tunnels that exit close to where they were anchored. They meet the dwarves there and trade stolen goods for repair work," Alex explained.

"So they were waiting for the dwarves to come help fix their ships?" Cassie asked, starting to understand Alex's insistence on meeting with the pirates.

"That and trade for weapons capable of killing dragons," he replied with a nod.

"Oh, dwarves hate dragons," Leena added with an ominous tone.

"Alex, that bay is leagues from Gundor Stronghold," Abrianna stated.

"Yes it is. Regas insists, though, that the dwarves have tunnels going from the bay into the Stronghold itself and beyond. He has personally traveled deep into the mountains, emerging high above the valley, at a peak looking down onto Gundor Stronghold, so he knows it to be true."

"And why would they want to help us?" Cassie asked as her mistrust of pirates appeared evident to all.

"Two reasons. The first is they have a debt to settle with that Sea Dragon. The captain had the misfortune of selecting Tantalus's ship as a target on its way to Nyland. He lost a third of his men between the two ships."

"And the second?" Leander asked.

"I bought both his ships," Alex said with a smile.

----*----

Captain Yeagars was not completely surprised with the order to sail at first opportunity. He had been working for the Lord Protector long enough now to understand you couldn't predict his decisions. He was, however, unsure of the choice of destinations.

It was one thing to parley with pirates from a distance, it was quite another to ask him to drop anchor within shouting distance. He had complete confidence in his crew's ability to protect the ship, but with three to four times their numbers, he was at the mercy of Lord Alex to address the shortfall, should they come to blows.

It was still dark when they warped away from the dock they were tied to and made their way back out to sea. The massive hulk of the House of Drakon's cargo vessel was still discernable where it lay anchored in the harbor. Yeagars was positive that the owner was the target of this search, so he was confused at their departure.

It struck him as odd that the ship still sported so many men aboard, and all so well-armed. Usually once a ship was set at anchor, only a minimal support crew maintained the vessel until needed.

He paid no more attention to the ship as the cleared the harbor mouth. Once safely in deep water, he turned the command of the helm over to Mr. Sikes and headed below for a nap. He left orders to be awakened just before they arrived at the point.

----*----

Alex had discussed more than dragons and dwarves with the pirate captain before leaving for Nyland. The comment about the purchase of the pirate fleet was a simplistic way of describing a complicated negotiation. Alex suspected Captain Regas would better describe his new position as head of the Windfall Navy.

Prince Renfeld had gutted his sea forces when creating a land army to threaten Great Vale. Alex was aware he now owned many empty ships sitting at anchor in the bay that had once patrolled the seas off the coast of Windfall. Without willing sailors to operate them, they were just a backdrop for merchant vessels passing in and out of the port.

Alex had left the former pirate captain with orders to make his ships seaworthy, a task already underway, and instructions to contact the king of the mountain dwarves for a meeting upon his return. Though unsure of his influence, he hoped his relationship with King Brokkr of Two Thorns might carry some weight in his favor.

So it was, that by sunrise, Captain Yeagars had *Cassie's Quest* within a stone's throw of both vessels. Alex was on deck as they approached the two ships, positioned exactly as they had left them the day before. He noted there seem to be a lot more men working on both ships than when they had left.

"Try not to freak them out," Alex commented to Kelby who was standing nearby, noting the slightly bizarre fascination/fear that the sailors had with the mermaids. His own crew, now somewhat accustom to the mermaids' presence, still watched them with a wary eye as they moved about the schooner.

The little redhead nodded in reply, even if he suspected she had no idea what he had just said.

"Captain, once we are settled, can you put a boat in the water for us to cross over in, please?" Alex asked while indicating the party of five standing with him. Kinsey gave him a look of anticipation, one he was going to have to disappoint.

"Kinsey, you stay here," he said apologetically.

"Sire, are you sure about these men....." Yeagars began.

"It will be fine, Captain, I promise," Alex replied, but he was interrupted, as there was a sudden jar. He could feel the ship slammed from below, as if they had hit a reef.

"DRAGON!" he heard someone yell as the beast they had encountered at sea appeared from the water between the three ships.

"Cassie, my bow!" Alex screamed. He took the dragon's first fire blast and funneled it skyward, while collecting free energy into a fire bolt that the dragon took full in the chest. He could smell the burnt flesh as he drove the bolt hard into the beast. The thrashing of the beast in the water rocked all three vessels, sending men into the sea all around them.

He continued to concentrate energy into the wound as he waited for his bow, where a fire glass tipped arrow could provide a lethal strike. A flash to his right caught Alex's attention as he saw three splashes hit the water below. Nearby were two piles of clothing on the deck that he recognized from the twins and his bow with no arrows, well out of reach.

"Where is Cassie?" Alex asked no one in particular, as he sent a second blast directly into the face of the beast, interrupting another fire bath. The energy bolt slapped the dragon's snout, forcing it up and away from the ship.

"There!" Leander said while pointing to a head bobbing in the water nearby. He could see Cassie as she tread water off to his right.

It was then that the dragon howled in pain as Kelby exploded from the water, fire glass spear in hand, propelled high by the dragon's tail. As the dragon's head snaked out to snatch her from midair, Alex slammed a shield into its head, diverting the lunge.

The mermaid landed safely near Cassie as the nymph began an attack of her own. Alex had just begun to gather an overpowering charge of free energy when someone called out.

"Look there!" Leander pointed.

As the two men watched, a whirlpool started to form around the point where the dragon's body emerged from the water. It quickly became a vortex so strong that it threatened to pull all three vessels from their anchors.

The dragon however, acting as the center point of the vortex, had no means of countering the action. Within seconds, it was spinning violently out of control, flailing in all directions as Cassie directed the forming waterspout away from the ships and into deeper water.

With more water to work with, she created a massive spinning waterspout, one that appeared to tear at the dragon, working to shred the beast. Whether by Cassie's manipulations, or by acts of the dragon trying to free itself, the beast suddenly went flying. As they watched, it tumbled uncontrolled, sailing farther out to sea and landing by one of the nearby islands. Alex swore the thud he heard indicated a shallow-water landing, one not conducive to avoiding injury.

Scanning the horizon, with both his eyes and senses, he detected no trace of the creature attempting to return. Turning back to the space between the three ships, he watched as the two mermaids returned sailor after sailor to the safety of ship or shore. Cassie had moved to a spot between the ships and open sea, holding the spear and acting as a guard should the beast return unexpectedly.

Soon enough, all were safely returned to ships or sat on dry land. Alex quickly had dry towels brought up as he first helped a soaking wet Cassie aboard. He greeted her with a hug and a kiss, unsure of what to say at the moment, but angry at the risk she had taken. Taking the offered spear, he handed it off to a nearby crewman.

"We will talk about this later," Alex commented as she left his embrace, wrapped in a towel, and went below to change. The twins emerged from the water naked, as expected. Abrianna quickly wrapped the two in towels, while Yeagars, Leander, and Alex ushered the overly interested sailors on to their duties. Now was not the time for mermaid distractions.

With the flurry of activity, Alex had barely time for more than a few words with Cassie, and she appeared in no mood to listen to his lecturing on her safety. Within the hour, all was back to normal and the six had been ferried to the ship commanded by Captain Regas.

The man was there to greet them as they climbed aboard the brigantine from the jolly boat. As he was the last to board, the others saw Alex greeted with less respect than he deserved, but far more than a pirate would normally provide.

"You said nothing about nymphs and mermaids when last we spoke," Regas declared as he embraced Alex as one might a fellow sea captain.

"Are you complaining? They just saved your ass!" Alex replied after the man released him.

"I believe proper introductions are in order," Abrianna announced before the captain could continue.

"So they are," Alex responded while stepping over to his five companions.

"Captain Regas, may I introduce the Crown Princess of Great Vale, Lady Abrianna. Next to her is her Royal Cousin and my fiancée, Lady Casandra," both women dipped slightly at the introduction, but received hardly a nod from Regas.

"Fiancée, huh? Too bad," Regas replied softly as he eyed Cassie. Before she could reply, the fire in her eyes evident, Alex continued.

"This fine gentleman is Leander, Guild Master of the Ranger's Guild of Great Vale."

Alex noted the wince from Regas at the mention of the Rangers. While not technically law enforcement, Rangers of the Ranger's Guild were not to be messed with by those in a thieving profession. Regas was quick to move past Leander and on to the twins.

"And what of these angels of mercy?" Regas asked, showing some gratitude to their efforts in saving his sailors in the water. He stood smiling as he eyed the mermaids up and down.

"Kelby and Leena are here to avenge their mother by killing that dragon," Alex replied, indicating the beast they had just driven off. As he spoke, he watched the twins slide up to either side of Regas with their flirt turned on high.

"Easy girls," Regas said as he gently guided both back to where they were standing while retrieving his coin pouch from Leena's hand at the same time.

"Where did all these men come from?" Alex asked as he motioned to the work going on around them.

"Once word got out about our change in profession, we had recruits from all over the islands show up. We can probably man one or two more of those ships in Windfall you mentioned once we are seaworthy," Regas replied.

"And the dwarves?" Alex asked slowly.

"King Teivel will meet with you tomorrow, inside the tunnels there," Regas replied as he pointed to openings in the hillside just up the point.

Alex considered that the name Teivel didn't sound very dwarfish to him, but then everything here had been a learning experience. It did have a familiar ring to it, but he couldn't place it.

"Ok until tomorrow then, let's see what we can accomplish today," he replied as he pointed to the incomplete work all around.

# Chapter 21

The rest of the day was spent in ship's repairs and other preparations. Alex surprised more than a few people as he applied some of his engineering knowledge to the effort. The mermaid twins did their part as well, assisting in any underwater activities as well as getting into some mischief. With three ship's crews on hand, it was more of a temptation than either could resist.

With every trip they made into the water, flashes of skin or enticing looks had more than one sailor accidently overboard. Several times that afternoon, Alex had to reprimand the two, reminding them that the goal was to help not hinder.

As a way of making amends, the two provided a lavish seafood spread for dinner, with some things Alex had never seen before. Using modified gaffs as spears, they had skewered several large fish and collected a bounty of crab and lobster. The ships cooks appeared overwhelmed with the offering.

It was decided to take the affair to the nearby beach in order to accommodate all the crews at one time. Alex kept a watchful eye as the evening progressed, concerned about the crews and biases from previous encounters. His fears we unfounded, as it turned out, mainly due to the mermaid twins, and their innate talent for handling men.

While he, Cassie, Abrianna, and Leander sat with the Captains and other officers, planning the next few day's efforts, the twins did what they did best and handled the sailors. Kinsey sat nearby, thankful for returning to dry land and hopeful for the occasional tidbit tossed to her by one of the revelers. Every so often she would get up and wander, taking offerings as they came available, only to return to sit by Cassie.

Alex watched in fascination as the two mermaids worked the crowd, nudging conversations and participants from one group to another, insuring a good mix in crew and attitudes. Every time a temper might flair, or a voice was raised, they were right there to defuse the situation and bedazzle the antagonists into submission.

"You two are amazing!" Alex commented to Kelby at a lull in the evening. By this time, it was very late and the lion's share of the participants had returned to their ships for the night or simply dropped in the sand to sleep, passed out cold. The night air was comfortable, and made for a pleasurable evening out.

"It's nothing really, we do this all night, every night," Leena replied before her sister, who shrugged in apparent agreement.

"We usually have help though," Kelby added as she stroked Kinsey who lay nearby. Both sisters had taken a liking to the wolf, spoiling her at every meal. Alex had watched her follow the twins all over last night, appearing as an enforcer to whatever the women had on their hands. Alex knew though, she was just looking for handouts as they wandered from group to group, who were all eating, and drinking.

----*----

Alex led the small group down the beach and toward a tunnel, the same Captain Regas had identified as the one intended for the meeting with the dwarves. With him were Cassie, Abrianna and Leander with Kinsey following close behind. The wolf had been particularly playful, running up and down the beach as she enjoyed the return to dry land and open spaces.

The twins were still aboard *Cassie's Quest*, peacefully sleeping the morning away. Besides showing no interest in meeting the dwarves, both mermaids had put in quite a night, furthering Alex's goal of converting the pirate crews into a more presentable force for good. Between the evening's frivolity and the influence of the twins, he felt his mission accomplished and they earned the rest.

As the four walked, Alex could see the remnants of the previous night's festivities, the various smoldering fire pits spread around the beach. The embers were all that remained of the raging fires from the night before. Sprinkled amongst the fire pits were still sleeping sailors, from all appearances, dead to the world.

He suspected they had overindulged, as the drinks provided from all three vessels were heavily laden with some form of alcohol. Not much of a drinker himself, he had sampled a few of the flagons offered him, only to pass them on to those more eager to imbibe.

"Is it this one?"

Cassie's question brought Alex back to the task at hand. There were several openings in the cliff, some natural and some with the telltale tool marks left by hand tools. The one she had indicated was one of those with the tool marks.

"That's what Regas said," he replied as he cut right, heading away from the water and straight toward the tunnel opening. They had taken no more than a few steps before Kinsey stopped and started a low growl. She had darted ahead of the party and was positioned at the mouth of the tunnel, between the opening and the group.

They stopped as two dwarves, short, broad, and heavily laden with weapons and armor, appeared from the shadows.

"You're farshpetikt; about time you goyim got here," one of the two commented to the humans.

"We were not given an exact time for the meet," Abrianna tried to explain.

"No time to kibbitz. This way then," the other dwarf directed, apparently not interested in an explanation for the perceived tardiness.

With one dwarf leading and the other bringing up the rear, everyone entered the tunnel. Kinsey had stopped growling and closed in, walking between Alex and Cassie. Neither dwarf appeared particularly intimidated by the animal, something that didn't surprise Alex considering his last experience with dwarves.

Within a few hundred feet of the tunnel entrance, the passageway widened into a large circular room. While the ceiling heights were not much more than the tunnel providing access, the walls were pushed out a good twenty feet in both directions.

Were it not for the fact that it was solid stone, Alex would be very concerned about the integrity of the ceiling. Dirt would have come crashing down long ago with such an open span containing no supports.

Light was provided by several torches, all in wall sconces lining both sides of the chamber. To his left, Alex could see additional torches, held by dwarves, lining both sides of a stone chair, rising from the stone floor itself. While very plain, with no ornamentation whatsoever, he suspected the dwarf occupying it was King Teivel.

"Oy vey! Get your toches over here already. You think we have all day?" Alex heard the dwarf on the throne bellow as he waved them over.

Crossing the open floor space, the four, plus Kinsey moved quickly until they stood before the dwarf king.

"King Teivel?" Alex asked hesitantly.

"You went to all the tsuris to set this meeting up and think I won't show? Of course it's me!" the King replied, appearing somewhat irritated at the question.

"I was led to believe you were a Yiddishe kop?" the king added.

Alex had no idea what tsuris or a Yiddishe kop was but he suspected, from the short conversation so far, it wasn't the last unfamiliar words he would encounter. He then went through the introductions of those with him, emphasizing Abrianna and Leander's status as principals in Great Vale.

"And your little tchotchke?" the dwarf asked, indicating Cassie standing next to him.

"My fiancée, Lady Cassandra," Alex replied with an edge. He didn't understand the reference, but had little patience for the disrespect it might imply.

"Your Majesty, we were led to believe you might know a way into the tunnels beneath Gundor Stronghold?" Abrianna asked, stepping forward to defuse things.

"And you are here to schmooze me into helping you? Do I look like a shmendrik?" The king asked sarcastically.

"Ah, no Sire, but we feel you might find value in our proposition," Alex replied, shooting from the hip; he was completely at a loss as to what the dwarf had just said. The king seemed to be considering Alex's statement for a moment and then waved to someone behind the four. Chairs were brought forward and the group was invited to sit.

"Ok, let's hear your spiel, but cut out the shmaltz," King Teivel said finally.

First, looking at his companions to see if anyone had a desire to jump in, he then detailed the quest to recover Cassie's mom from Tantalus. At the mention of Renfeld and Tantalus, Alex heard murmurs of discontent from the dwarves surrounding them, with what he thought was a "feh!" from several in the crowd. King Teivel sat stone faced the whole time.

References to the two dragons also got a rise out of the crowd and the king, the Red Dragon being more interesting to them than the Sea Dragon. At the suggestion that there may be a dragon's lair in the base of the stronghold, he got more whispers, with a few questions from Teivel regarding potential treasure.

Alex outlined the plan to enter the stronghold from the tunnels in the mountains and retrieve Amelia and the dragon's eggs, thus removing further threat.

"And you are a maven on dragons?' the king asked Alex after he had finished.

"Expert," Abrianna whispered, as his confusion must have been visible. Apparently, she could understand at least a portion of the dwarf's references.

"Hardly, however, I do have a few tricks up my sleeve. With that he held out his hand, palm up, and created a glowing white ball. The sphere, pulling in free energy from the torches, blasted a white light that illuminated the entire room.

"Nu? Am I to be impressed?" the king responded to the demonstration.

"That is just a small sample of his power, Sire. He has faced both dragons numerous times now and has successfully driven them off each time," Cassie replied, omitting her own contributions to the efforts.

"Couldn't kill the things, heh?" the King replied, looking unimpressed at the statement but decidedly more interested in the conversation.

"So will you take us?" Alex asked after a pause in the conversation.

"We have no love for Renfeld or Tantalus. They have encroached on our mountains as the Vassal Lords have done in the valley to the north. However, I don't see how this is our fight," the king replied.

"You can help vanquish Tantalus," Abrianna replied.

"And I get bupkis for my efforts?" The king asked.

"As described, we have no idea what's in the lair or the stronghold, but beyond the eggs, it's all yours. It is a sure thing that Tantalus has brought some of his wealth with him to Gundor. In addition, should you be interested, we will lead you to the lair in the Dragon's Teeth where we can personally vouch for the dragon's hoard we saw there," Alex replied. The king sat quietly for several minutes as he considered the offer. Alex could see the dwarves nearby watching their king with interest.

"Ok, I'll be a mentsch, but I'm holding you to the payment. And you are going to need more of a shtick than a glowing ball if you plan on defeating a dragon," the King said as he stepped down from the thrown. With a smile, he slapped the now standing Alex on the back warmly.

"Enough of this kibbitzing. Come, let's nosh while we make plans to schlep our way into Gundor Stronghold and steal from a dragon. It will plotz when it finds out! What mishegoss, what chutzpah!" The King announced while leading the group deeper into the tunnels to a place where stone tables lined the side of the widened space. Alex had no idea what the dwarf had just said, but at least he was agreeing to the plan.

"So I have to ask, your name, Teivel. It's familiar but I can't place it. What does it mean?" Alex asked as they approached the tables covered with food. He had seen dwarves eat before and wondered if this was going to be enough.

"Devil," Teivel replied with a broad grin.

----*----

Finishing what the dwarves considered a light meal, the four bid them goodbye and returned to the schooner with a promise to return before nightfall. As the trip was to be made through the tunnels riddling the Northern Mountains, it hardly mattered if it was day or night when they traveled.

As they walked along, Alex considered the conversation with the King and then asked Abrianna a question.

"What language was that?"

"It's a rare dialect not normally taught. I learned it as a young girl because the words sound so funny. My father wasn't so pleased with some of the things I learned," Abrianna answered with a laugh.

"I remember the day uncle caught you wandering the halls repeating that one word, what was it? He had a fit!" Cassie commented with a laugh of her own.

"Schmuck! It just sounded so funny. I had no idea what it meant," Abrianna replied, laughing.

"Uncle had a fit and made you promise not to use it ever again," Cassie cried, tears of laughter streaming down her face.

"It was only later, when I learned what it referred to, that I really understood his attitude about a young girl skipping down the halls saying it," Abrianna replied, her laughter adding to Cassie's.

Leander looked over to Alex, who returned a shrug at the two laughing women. By this time they had reached the small boat they had beached earlier, their transportation to and from the schooner. Both men assisted the women into the boat before they both gave a solid shove, slipping the boat off the sand and back into the water.

Alex grabbed one set of oars with Leander operating the second set. By the time they had the boat turned around, they were coordinated in their efforts and heading smoothly back to the ship. There was a sailor waiting as they brought the boat parallel to *Cassie's Quest*, with another at the top of the ladder.

Alex got Kinsey into the makeshift harness they had been using to hoist the wolf in and out of the boat, as she was just too large to carry easily. She wasn't particularly pleased at the process, but waited patiently nonetheless as she seemed to understand its purpose.

Soon everyone was back on deck and Alex found Captain Yeagars there waiting with several members of the crew.

"Sire, I presume you will be departing soon?" he asked as he greeted the party.

"Yes. Can you and anyone you require meet us below? I will also need Captain Regas. Oh, and have someone wake the twins, they will want in on this."

As he watched, Yeagars waved several of his men away while holding his first and second officers. He sent the officers to retrieve the mermaids while everyone else followed Abrianna below decks and into the lounge they had been using as a meeting room.

Once everyone had gathered, Alex did a quick headcount, insuring all the necessary members were present, and then gave an audible sigh.

"Ok gang, here's the plan," he began.

# Chapter 22

It was late in the afternoon when Alex, Cassie, Abrianna, and Leander returned to the beach with Kinsey in tow. Each member had their necessary items in easily carried satchels or backpacks. In addition, their weapons were all accessible; they held little hope of this being a bloodless rescue.

King Teivel had indicated the trip would require several days of hard travel, walking long hours, particularly for the goyish travelers, whatever that was. Alex suspected that the trip with the dwarves was going to be filled with incomprehensible conversation.

With a favorable breeze blowing, Alex could see Captain Yeagars preparing *Cassie's Quest* to make sail. He viewed Leena and Kelby at the railing, watching them. The twins were not entirely happy with their part of the plan, but agreed their contribution would be far greater as Alex had outlined, rather than following the four into the tunnels beneath the Norther Mountains. He suspected they were not all that excited at the prospect of an underground trip taking them so far from the sea.

At the tunnel mouth were two dwarves as before, waiting impatiently for the humans to arrive. He could tell their irritation by the way one paced back and forth across the opening. As they closed the distance to the entrance, Alex could hear the one pacing speaking to the other.

"Farshpetikt again. I hope they don't make a habit of this."

"Vos ton ir zorgn, so long as the wizard does his part," the other replied to his impatient comrade.

Alex had no idea what the dwarf was referencing, much less understood half the words, as he had not committed to any particular action. He wasn't particularly concerned however, so long as the dwarves did their part and got them to the Stronghold.

Without a word, one dwarf took the lead with Alex following. Behind him, Cassie, Abrianna, and Leander followed with the other dwarf trailing the group. Kinsey planted herself at Alex's side, sniffing at both dwarves as if to ensure their identity.

Entering the same cavern as before, Alex was surprised to see so many dwarves in the traveling party. He had expected a few to act as guides, however there was a good dozen of the King's men and all were armed to the teeth.

"Are we expecting trouble?" Leander whispered to Alex, who replied with a shrug.

"Ah, here at last!" King Teivel declared as they entered the chamber. His statement had none of the sarcasm that the others had displayed. With nothing more to say, Teivel turned and started down the tunnel on the far side of the cavern.

"Not one for small talk," Alex commented as they followed behind the leaders. The four found themselves in the middle of the column of dwarves as they headed deeper into the mountains. Interspaced throughout the group were torches, lit for the benefit of the humans, Alex was sure.

What surprised him was the lack of grumbling amongst the dwarves as they progressed along the winding tunnels deep in the Northern Mountains. Unlike their previous experiences with dwarves, this group included, these dwarves were not complaining about every insignificant inconvenience they encountered.

Alex and Leander had heard King Brokkr's men complain about the torches, carrying the torches, and why they even needed torches in their encounter in Two Thorns. If he did not know any better, Alex would suspect that they were headed into a fight.

They had been traveling for several hours before Teivel called for a rest stop. Alex had been keeping tabs on both Cassie and Abrianna, insuring that the two were not overly taxed by the pace. He was happy to see that both were reasonably wearied, but still more than capable of continuing the trek.

After a brief rest, they returned to follow the tunnel, taking the occasional branch as chosen by the lead dwarf. By Alex's reckoning, it was well past midnight when the King called a halt. The tunnel they were following had widened slightly beyond the width of a single dwarf, allowing the group to spread out a little.

It seemed to Alex that the dwarves built their tunnels to accommodate a width of little more than one dwarf. Fortunately for him, the height of the passage was tall enough for the shorter dwarves to swing a pickaxe overhead.

By now, the dwarves had spread out along the length of the tunnel opening, providing for a length of tunnel specifically for the humans to stretch out to sleep. They had left two torches with Alex and Leander, and then extinguished the others as they settled in.

"Alex, is it just me or are these dwarves hiding something?" Cassie whispered as the four closed in to talk privately. Kinsey had decided to curl up in the middle of the tunnel next to her human companions.

"They are certainly being uncharacteristically cooperative," Abrianna added.

"Cooperative?" Alex replied with a tone of sarcasm.

"Have you ever known dwarves to be so considerate as to carry our supplies for us?" Leander asked while pointing to the additional water and bedding for the women, dropped in place upon their arrival. It had been a surprise to all.

"OK, so you have a point, but what could they be hiding?" Alex asked.

"I don't know and that's what worries me," Cassie replied.

By this time, there was a solid snoring from both sides of the tunnel as the dwarves had apparently nodded off. With nothing more to discuss, the four took Kinsey's example and settled down to sleep.

----*----

Captain Yeagars set sail early the morning following the Lord Protector's departure. All activities he performed the night before marked his last obligation here. While he was told the nearby vessels were now allies, he needed to see more proof before he believed it. The sunlight had barely touched the tops of the masts when he had the crew make sail north, intending to return to Nyland as instructed.

With the main party accompanying the Lord Protector ashore, his only passengers were the mermaid twins, who remained aboard for the return trip north. Although they had proven themselves valuable over the last few days in particular, the superstitions of the crew remained strong. Yeagars was just happy the cruise to Nyland was a short trip.

The Lord Protector had left Yeagars and the others with a specific set of instructions, to be followed once they had reached Nyland. The captain was used to the unusual behaviors of the man, him being of a wizardly sort, but these were the craziest yet. Thankfully it had all been written out for him to follow, should anyone question the accuracy of the requests.

As the helmsman guided the ship out into deeper water, farther from shore, he scanned the horizon for signs of danger. He was less concerned about pirates these days and far more worried about the beasts that lay beneath the waves. Since taking command of *Cassie's Quest*, he had experienced more encounters with Sea Dragons than in a lifetime of sailing.

To compound his concerns, their previous survival had been achieved due to a resource that was no longer aboard. With the magic of the Lord Protector no longer available to them, his only hope was the few fire glass tipped spears the wizard had fashioned for them before leaving. Hardly an equal trade, but he had to be satisfied with the gesture.

"Steady as she goes," Yeagars said absently to the sailor at the helm, as he corrected from the northwesterly track to one due north.

"Aye sir," the man replied.

Yeagars couldn't help but note the nervousness in the man's reply.

----*----

It was at the end of the third day of their trek that Alex learned what the dwarves had been hiding. Well, hiding probably wasn't the best description, more like withholding. The group had continued to travel for anywhere from fourteen to sixteen hours a day, with short breaks interjected. By his estimate, they had to have traveled a good one hundred twenty miles underground.

As everyone was settling in for the night, King Teivel made an uncharacteristic appearance.

"So Wizard, how are you faring? Not tired from schlepping all over the place?" the dwarf asked as he entered the glow of the torches the humans used.

Alex indicated the dwarf should sit, and watched as the king dropped in place next to him.

"Look, I don't want to be a nudnik, but we have a bissel tsuris ahead. I don't want to be treger fun shlekht nayes, but it seems the tunnel that takes us directly to Gundor Stronghold has been hijacked by a gonif," the King replied casually.

Alex stared at the dwarf for a moment, not sure how to reply. Finally, he turned to Abrianna, with a pleading look on his face.

"He needs help, something is blocking the tunnel ahead, I think," she replied

"It's a real shtunk of a Lindworm, actually might be more than one. It's going to take more than a zetz to remove them," the King added.

Alex was beginning to smell a rat. It wasn't likely that a Lindworm had just moved into the tunnels while they had been traveling. There must also be something there as he was sure the dwarves could have cut a new route to the stronghold, bypassing the Lindworm, long ago.

"Why can't we go around?" Cassie asked, apparently on the same thought as Alex.

"Look bubbele, you can go around, but that will add days to the trip. You are in a hurry, and this is the fastest way, fershtay?"

"Ok, so you need me to convince the Lindworms to leave. What else are you not telling me?" Alex asked directly, tired of dancing around the issue.

"Well there might be a bissel of gold nearby," the king replied softly.

"Alex, a Lindworm is a type of dragon," Cassie added, pointing to the significance of a dragon family blocking the only tunnel into Gundor.

"How are dragons getting in and out without using these tunnels?" Leander asked, looking as if he suddenly realized they might be blocking the path to the sea.

"There is an underground river that passes through the tunnel there. We were working the find there a few weeks ago when they suddenly appeared and drove us out. I don't want to sound like an alter kocker, but the mine is all fershlugginer since they arrived."

"So you have been planning this all along! You needed Alex to chase off the Lindworms for you!" Cassie snapped at the dwarf.

"Listen sheyna punim, your promises of dragon gold were bupkis, but helping us reclaim the mine is a metsia!"

Alex sighed as he listened to the exchange. He should have considered that Tantalus would be aware of the dwarf tunnels and post guards to protect his back. He did a quick mental inventory of dragon lethal weapons on hand; he was thankful they had brought the spear along, but knew they were woefully short.

"Ok, let's move on. Tell me everything you know about Lindworms," Alex asked the assembled group. For the next few hours, the party discussed their next move, before finally settling in on a plan of attack. With that, everyone separated to try to get some rest.

"Alex, do you think we can do this?" Cassie whispered as she lay next to him in the dark.

"Oh, sure," he replied, trying to sound more positive than he was.

----*----

Kelby and Leena were working the main room of the Drowning Man, gathering as much information as they could from the patrons there. They had been there since Captain Yeagars had put them ashore shortly after anchoring in the harbor in Nyland. Kelby had found it humorous that they provided a boat to ferry the twins ashore rather than making them swim the short distance.

Leena had expressed her gratitude at not having to enter the cold water, while Kelby had simply kissed the Captain's cheek as a daughter might do to a loving father. The flustered man nodded shyly in reply as he escorted the two to the rope ladder draped over a railing.

There had been several sailors sent ashore at the same time, each with a specific mission of their own. She had no idea as to what they were up to; they didn't offer and she didn't ask. Once they hit the docks, each went their own way.

Since their return to Nyland, neither twin had seen any of the Gundor guards, as they had before. There were rumors aplenty however, all suggesting that the Vassal King and his guest were at odds over some arrangement they had struck. Merchant's employees, who delivered supplies to the stronghold, reported a very tense atmosphere between the guards of Gundor and the armsmen of House Drakon.

It would soon be time for the twins to head out, per the plan outlined before Alex's departure with the dwarves, but they still needed a way in. The thought of the wizard gave her a sense of desire she had felt for no man before. Were it not for her growing respect for Cassie, she would consider taking a shot at stealing the man from her.

Putting that thought aside, she began wandering the floor, looking for likely targets who could add to their knowledge of Gundor and provide access to the stronghold.

----*----

Tantalus was coming to the end of his patience. He had been forced to flee the west, barely escaping before the minions of King Ben of Great Vale had cornered him in Tazmain. He had been fortunate enough to connect with the Red Dragon as she was fending off the rescue attempt.

Now, holed up in the freezing north east, teasingly close to the lands promised him by the inept Prince Renfeld, he had another idiot to deal with. The Vassal King had taken him in as an ally in support of his own ambitions. Tantalus was discovering Renfeld had promised a great many things to a great many people in the north.

He was now trading his dragon's protection from dwarves and southerners for a safe haven from the magical upstart that was intent on rescuing Lady Amelia. The problem was the Vassal King seemed to have a neverending list of demands tied to that sanctuary.

In an effort to bring the insanity to an end, Tantalus had sent word to the King of the Dark Elves, requesting assistance in ending his pursuers and permitting him to release his dragons. If they supported his claim, he could regain the fame and power his family lost in the last war.

Until he received a reply, he was tied to the Vassal King and his stupidity.

----*----

Alex and Leander led the small group into the area where the tunnel widened. As King Teivel had described, the area was broad and flat with pillars intermingled in an uneven spacing where the dwarves chose to leave supports for the ceiling. The ceiling was not much higher than the tunnel they had entered from, making it impossible for Alex to perform an overhead swing of his sword should the need arise.

He could just make out the river that sprouted from the wall to his right and crossed the room, to disappear on his left. The openings on either side of the chamber where the water passed through were as tall as a man, and twice as wide. Alex hoped that didn't indicate the size of the Lindworms that used the river as their personal road to the sea. He could see markings in the dirt on this side of the river where the serpents had disturbed the soil as they moved.

Alex had been gently summoning the free energy around them to power the glowing sphere hanging above their heads that illuminated their path. Its glow was bright enough to cut through the darkness and give the humans a good view of the area around them in all directions. On his left, Cassie had Alex's elf bow with a fire glass tipped arrow at the ready, while Leander had the fire glass spear. Alex had his sword out as well, the black leather grip warm in his hand.

King Teivel and his two dwarves, on Alex's right, all carried double-bitted battle axes, and without the need of Alex's light, had wandered wide to the outer edge of the chamber. It had been decided earlier that flooding this chamber with bodies would do little to aid their cause. As such, the remainder of their party held back in the tunnel, waiting. Kinsey was not at all pleased at being left behind, but Abrianna was able to coax her to stay.

The dwarf king had explained earlier that the weapons they carried had not been completely ineffective on the Lindworms in previous encounters, inflicting some damage. However, they had been unable to deliver a lethal blow, while the Lindworms had eaten several of his subjects. In addition, the poison they produced was toxic on contact. Fortunately, they didn't spit poison, you had to come in contact with the mouth of the creature, something Alex hoped to avoid.

In that regard, Alex was unsure if his elf sword would do much better than the dwarf axe. The only successfully tested weapon they had among them were the fire glass tipped arrows and spear. He was also prepared to create shields and fire lances, the latter successful against the Sea Dragon, but with limited amounts of free energy, he would need to draw on his inner reserves.

Motioning for the others to halt, Alex moved out into the center of the cavern, using his senses as much as his eyes, trying to discern the slightest movement. His effort was unnecessary, as two sets of red glowing eyes appeared across the river, reflecting the light from above. Emerging from the darkness were two huge Lindworms, with heads as tall as Alex.

As they came forward into the light, he could see a large numbers of coils behind the heads, indicating a substantial body. It was only the low cavern ceiling that prevented the serpents from raising high overhead. Both dragons halted at the edge of the stream that split the room.

"Well, we found them," Alex said absently as he took a step back, glancing at the others. From the look on Cassie's face, he confirmed his suspicion that he wasn't the only one surprised at their size.

He jumped at the sudden outburst from his right.

"ATTACK!" screamed King Teivel, as he charged the pair of serpents with axe overhead, his two men close behind.

"Oh dear god," Alex said absently as he watched the dwarves charge forward.

# Chapter 23

Captain Yeagars had received word from the two mermaids that they had located a willing merchant to take them to Gundor. He asked no questions on how they had convinced the man; he just delivered the supplies they would be taking with them. Besides the two flying horses, there was a third packhorse that would be required.

It had taken him some time and effort to acquire all the materials on the Lord Protector's list, and in the necessary quantities. For certain items, they had to travel inland to visit farms now well past harvest with the coming winter. They had been only too happy to sell whatever they had available, the necessary items unneeded until next spring.

Yeagars had been forced to go to the local Alchemist for the final item on his list. That worked out well as he was able to contract with the man to complete the Lord Protector's instructions. While appearing to question Yeagars' sanity, as the Alchemist had never received such a request, he nonetheless followed the written instructions precisely and packaged the items as required.

The Captain had no idea what the Lord Protector intended to do with the things the Alchemist delivered, but he was relieved to hear the mermaids were ready to leave. Once all was put ashore, there was nothing for Yeagars and his crew to do but wait.

----*----

Kelby and Leena were each astride one of the flying horses, following the merchant's last wagon as it headed up the road to Gundor Stronghold. There were three wagons total, all containing supplies intended for the castle kitchens. Kelby had attached their packhorse to the last wagon, letting it act as guide while the inexperienced riders followed.

Her riding experience with Leander and Abrianna had given her a small idea of what to expect, but both she and her sister just allowed the horses to go where they pleased.

Fortunately, that seemed just fine with the mounts, as they never wandered from the trail.

The wagon train had left at first light with the expectation of reaching Gundor before nightfall. It was tradition that they would spend the night inside the castle, and return to Nyland the following morning. That worked just fine for the twins' needs.

----*----

Alex hardly had time to create a shield wall before the two creatures sprang forth at the charging dwarves. He couldn't tell who was more surprised, the dwarf king who slammed into the shield on this side, or the two serpents who crashed into the other side, their bodies strung out into the water.

The river was now washing up on both banks as the Lindworms created a partial dam in the river. The party of six were all in ankle deep water, except Teivel, who was drenched and regaining his feet.

"WHAT THE DREK WAS THAT FOR? Are you meshugener?" the dwarf screamed at Alex.

Before he could answer, both dragons slammed into the shield again from the far side, causing the ground to shake all around them. Without replying, Alex turned his entire attention to the two serpents. He watched as the two fixated on his movements, striking out every so often, as if to test the barrier between the two groups.

With his people regrouped on either side of him, Alex pushed the shield toward the pair of dragons; following their movements as they retreated until all six were knee deep in the river. He could see the Lindworms almost pacing back and forth, pressing against the shield as they looked for the edges of the barrier.

He watched as the pair suddenly retreated, and then split as one rose up, disappearing into the ceiling, while the other dropped into a hole in the floor.

"Where did they go?" Cassie asked quietly.

"There are levels above and below this one, dug out as we chased the gold veins," King Teivel said thoughtfully.

"Now you tell us?" Leander cried, mimicking Alex's own thoughts.

"How does the river flow?" Cassie asked as she realized the space below their feet was hollow.

"The river bed is stone. We took great care to ensure we wouldn't flood the mine," Teivel replied, sounding somewhat offended at the question.

Before anyone else could speak, one of the dragons burst through an opening in the floor behind the six. Popping up like a jack in the box, it snapped at one of the dwarves behind King Teivel. The dwarf leaped to one side as Cassie released an arrow that drove solidly into the side of the beast's head, both surprising and injuring it.

The creature howled in pain and rage as it started to retreat. King Teivel managed to leap forward and slam the edge of his double bitted axe into the side behind its head. The wound it left, while not deep, sprouted blood before the dragon disappeared back into the hole.

With everyone was distracted, the second dragon dropped from above, with the intent of attacking Cassie. Alex spun in place, driving his sword out while grasping and pulling Cassie by the arm. The Lindworm turned its head sideways to allow it to open its jaws wide, and surged forward, snapping at its intended target.

By pulling on Cassie's arm, Alex had maneuvered her body out of harm's way, leaving only one leg exposed to the Lindworm's bite. He heard her scream out in pain as the jaws clamped down on the limb. Next, it was the creatures turn to howl, as Alex's elven steel bit deeply into the soft, exposed under chin of the dragon's jaws.

He withdrew and stabbed over and over until the creature released Cassie, but not before thrashing her about in its attempts to avoid the demon blade. Alex was covered in dragon's blood as he had closed in on the creature that was holding his love.

Once released from the dragon's jaws and down on the ground, Cassie attempted to edge away. Alex could see the bleeding skin of her leg from where the tattered garments and elven underpants had been pushed aside. She tried to crawl, only to find Leander there to drag her clear of the battle between Alex and the dragon, holding the spear out in defense. Never relenting, Alex continued to stab at the Lindworm as it tried to dodge and parry his thrusts.

The dragon feinted a retreat, only to spring forward at Alex, its jaws agape, but limited by the ceiling above. Side stepping the strike, Alex drove his blade into the passing eye. With the strike, the creature slammed its head up, wrenching the sword from his hands and tossing him several feet away.

It was then the second dragon sprang from another hole in the floor, slithering to the spot where Leander crouched over the prone Cassie. Picking himself up, he checked on the location of the dragon he had been battling before returning his attention to the new threat. He could see two of the dwarves pounding their axes into the side of the serpent; it ignored their efforts on its way to Leander and Cassie.

Leander rose, spear held out in preparation to defend the prone Cassie.

"ENOUGH!" Alex screamed as he fired off a concentrated bolt of energy, drawing the power from deep inside himself.

The bright white beam struck the approaching serpent straight between the eyes, leaving a burned tunnel the length of its head, near splitting it in half. His overhead light extinguished with the effort, the burning dragon was the only illumination left for the humans. The last thing Alex saw before he passed out was the second dragon charging him as he hit the floor, his sword still protruding from its eye.

----*----

The road to Gundor Stronghold was nothing more than a single cart track worn into the usually frozen earth. Over half the year the area was covered in snow and ice, and it was as firm as stone and easy to follow. The area on both sides of the trail was flat, providing little impediment should wagons need to pass going the other direction.

That however, was an unnecessary concern, as they hadn't seen a soul the entire trip. Kelby and her sister had been riding for most of the day and were now within sight of the keep. It rested at the top of a small mountain in the center of the broad flat valley.

To the south, she could see the Northern Mountains, where deep in its bowels, Alex and the others were making their way here. To the north was another range of mountains, all capped in snow and ice, which marked the boundary for the desolate north.

Having spent her life in the warmer southern waters, she was beginning to understand her sister's dislike of the cold, though she would never admit to it. Both she and Leena had acquired the proper attire to both protect them from the cold and provide the illusion that they were servants of the merchant.

Upon their arrival at the castle, the packhorse contained everything they required for the next stage of their plan. Until then, Kelby spent the idle time studying the castle.

----*----

Alex woke to torch light and the smell of burning flesh. He immediately gagged, as the water that was being forced between his lips required an unexpected swallow.

"He's awake," he heard Leander announce; Alex realized it had been his friend force-feeding him the liquid.

"Alex, get over here, I need you!" he heard Abrianna's voice call out as he sat up.

Looking about to get his bearings, he could see both dragons lay dead nearby on either side of him. He could also tell everyone from the tunnel had filled the chamber around them. His head was splitting from the previous magical effort and he had no idea how long he had been out or how the second dragon had been slain.

He could see that Cassie had been moved, and she and Abrianna were now partially in the river, Cassie was laying on her back with Abrianna kneeling next to her and holding her head in her lap. Scrambling to regain his feet, he required Leander's assistance before he was steady enough to walk the short distance to the water's edge.

Kneeling in the cool water, he could feel it seeping into his clothing as he examined the pair before him. Cassie was looking pale and a bit worse for wear, the thrashing the dragon provided obvious in her disheveled condition. Looking down toward her feet, he could see blood running in the water where it washed from her calf.

"She's been poisoned," Abrianna offered as an explanation, her own efforts showing in the strain on her face. Alex closed his eyes and gently used his magical senses to explore his fiancée's condition. In his mind's eye, he could see the fiery redness of the poison coursing through her cool turquoise form.

Countering the destruction racking her body was a soothing green emanating from her cousin as she worked to counter the poison. In addition, he could see more turquoise drawing from the water surrounding the nymph, as her own magic worked to battle the illness delivered from the serpent's venom.

"What do I do?" Alex asked hoarsely, as he struggled to sit upright. A bleary-eyed Abrianna took a moment to look at him before replying.

"Close your eyes and concentrate on the red you see surging through her body. Try to wrap the discrete pieces in your own energy, until it disappears. Be careful to attack only the red, as anything else is Cassie. It could kill her," she finished.

With the explanation, Alex again closed his eyes and concentrated on what Abrianna was doing. He could see small green tendrils wrapping themselves around streams of red. They would be engulfed and squeezed by the green as it worked to destroy the red. He could feel the energy flair as the red was consumed and destroyed. He could see it was a tedious and exhausting process, one that Abrianna had been obviously working hard at to keep Cassie alive.

"Cassie is helping us by drawing strength from the water, but you must hurry because she is fading," Abrianna whispered as if to answer the unasked question of the turquoise he had seen earlier.

Concentrating on the red wisps floating in a turquoise sea, he isolated one and started summoning his own energy to the area. Even as he tried to be gentle, he heard the admonition from Abrianna.

"Be careful, you are near her heart!" Abrianna snapped at him.

Probing more cautiously, he could indeed detect the struggling heart beating an irregular rhythm as she worked to fight the poison in her system. Backing away from that location, he located another concentration of red near one hip. He again worked to encircle and contain the wisp of red, feeling the heat of the battle between the white and red.

He was beginning to understand the delicate balance that was needed. He could actually snuff out the red in an instant, but the heat released from the attempt would burn the area, killing the tissue nearby.

The object was to work more at a rate where Cassie's body could dissipate the heat, as it coursed through her body. He could see the cool water helping her release the trapped body heat they were generating with their efforts. Alex absently wondered if this was how the body actually fought off illness, having experience his share of fevers.

He and Abrianna continued to work on the unconscious nymph for what seemed like hours. Every time Alex thought that they were making progress, another piece of red would flair up, increasing the amount coursing through her body.

"Something's wrong, she's not healing properly. Leander, check Cassie's leg," Abrianna asked in a voice that sounded hollow. Alex could tell the healer was reaching her breaking point as the energy drain continued.

As both magicians continued their work, Alex could hear the splashing sounds of someone moving into the water nearby. With his hands on Cassie, he could feel her body move as she was being inspected.

"I found it. There is a tooth fragment in her calf muscle," Leander replied.

"Well, pull it out," snapped Abrianna, her irritation quite evident. There was a moment's silence before Leander responded.

"Got it, but its bleeding badly now," his concern portrayed in his voice.

"Let it bleed for a bit and then bind it tightly. The flow will help clean out the poison," she replied in a much calmer tone. Alex could see for himself why Abrianna was less tense.

The two had worked nonstop the entire time, and for the first time since he began there was a notable reduction in the amount of red he detected. The pair continued to work until Cassie began to stir. There was a slight moan as she tried to roll away from Abrianna's grasp.

"Easy, don't try to move," Abrianna whispered to her cousin.

"We can stop now. She's out of danger," she added, speaking to Alex this time.

"Thank God!" Alex replied as he opened his eyes. Looking down at Cassie, he could see the color had returned to her face, but her eyes were still closed. He reached out and gently stroked her cheek, still covered in dirt from her earlier struggle.

With a sigh of relief, he leaned back and started to get up from his kneeling position. He stopped as he saw Abrianna start to sway. In an attempt to catch her, he surged forward with both arms extended to catch her. His last memory was the water hitting him in the face as he passed out and dropped in place.

----*----

Kelby and Leena continued to follow the wagons as they traveled the stone causeway leading up the mountain, headed directly to Gundor Stronghold. She could see the series of switchbacks they needed to travel that had been cut into the mountainside so long ago. As it was late in the day, the sun was low in the sky and the starting to cool down.

Kelby hoped they wouldn't be on this road for too much longer as the cold was starting to seep into her clothing. She pulled her cloak tight around her, and she could see her sister doing the same. Both women were quite ready for this trip to be over; neither particularly enjoyed the ride or the cold.

Kelby was mentally reviewing their next steps as they turned the final corner leading up to the massive gates to the castle. She watched as the lead riders halted the wagon train and began an exchange with the gate guards that would eventually allow them to enter.

She could see the merchant speaking to the two guards at the gate, while a third, high on the wall above, shouted something to the men below. She caught reference to the two women on horseback, understanding the reference to herself and her sister.

They had removed their hoods, allowing their long red hair to be visible to the men at the gate. Although she couldn't hear the merchant's reply, she expected it to be the one they had rehearsed before leaving Nyland.

Unlike a nymph, the mermaid's magic wasn't limited to water. While their form changed from one medium to another, their magic was constant. This was a fact they chose to conceal, aiding in the perception that a mermaid couldn't influence you unless they were in water.

Kelby and Leena had used their magic liberally in influencing the merchant and his men in aiding them in their efforts to infiltrate Gundor Stronghold. Now they would do the same, once inside. She watched as the guards opened the gates, waving the lead wagon past while keeping a keen eye on each passing load. As the two women neared the gate, they adjusted their clothing to increase their appeal.

"Bolter says you are here looking for work," the guard commented while looking the sisters up and down. Kelby and Leena made sure he had plenty to see, while the men completely ignored the packhorse passing through the gate behind them. Both sisters had their charm turned on full, entrancing all three guards at once.

"He was kind enough to offer us work and suggested you might have need for us here," Kelby replied with her flirt directed at the first man.

"I am sure we can find something for you to do," the guard replied, the leer in his tone obvious as he waved the sisters inside the gates.

# Chapter 24

"It's about time you woke up," Alex heard the familiar sound of Cassie's voice. He opened his eyes to a redheaded blur. As his vision cleared, he closed his eyes again as he winced at the splitting headache and pounding in his ears. All around them were lit torches illuminating the cavern.

"What hit me?" he asked as he tried to sit up, only to feel someone pushing him back down.

"Just lay still," he heard Abrianna say, as he turned to see her kneeling next to him. With her help, he slid up until his head and shoulders were slightly elevated, resting on something soft. Turning back, he could now see Cassie propped up as well, leaning against a pile of supplies. Neither woman looked terribly great, but he was just happy to see Cassie conscious.

"How do you feel?" he asked, while still having trouble focusing on her.

"I hope I feel better than you look!" she replied with a smile. He could hear the weakness in her voice, but the smile was genuine. He could just make out the leg the dragon had savaged, the bandages covering her from ankle to knee. He was finally able to sit upright slowly, discovering another stack of items behind him to lean upon.

"She will be fine, thanks to you. I was losing the fight with the poison," Abrianna replied as she was busy with something.

Before he could reply, he discovered Abrianna forcing a cup full of a warm liquid at him. He saw where they had started a small cooking fire with a pot in the middle. Where they had obtained the firewood, he couldn't imagine. He sipped from the cup, and found the flavor similar to chicken soup.

"What is this?" he asked Abrianna, who had seated herself next to the cooking pot, still looking very tired.

"It's a healing potion. I have already had some and so has Cassie. Drink it, it will give you strength," she replied while indicating the cup next to her cousin. With the reference, Cassie lifted her cup to show Alex hers was completely empty. With every sip, Alex could feel a warming sensation spread throughout his body. When the cup was about half empty, he had the energy to lean forward and survey the area around them.

Near the river lay the dragon he had been battling before passing out. It now lay motionless, head separated from its body, the enormous mouth agape. Turning the other way, he could see where the second dragon lay, still burning where he had sliced it with his blast of energy.

It must have been the pounding in his head that had prevented Alex from hearing the dwarves digging away at the far wall behind the dragon. He could see dirt flying as a small group attacked the dirt and stone.

"What are they doing?" Alex asked turning back to Abrianna.

"It seems your energy bolt passed right through the Lindworm and blew a rather sizable hole in that wall. It exposed a considerable gold strike that sent the dwarves into a frenzy. It likely saved your life as the dwarves set upon the remaining Lindworm in mass, charging in from the tunnel and pummeling the beast to death," Abrianna replied with a smile of her own.

"By the time I entered, you were down and the dwarves and Leander had beheaded the dragon," she finished.

"AY YAY YAY, you are still alive, boychick!" King Teivel cried out as he crossed the open area between the diggers and where the three lay, his arms spread wide.

"I said a bracha over you as we finished off the vilda chaya there, you looked pretty fershlugginer I might add," he said as he pointed to the severed dragons head and then back to Alex.

Alex was as lost as ever with the dwarf's statement, but he could read the joy in his mannerism.

"What happened?" Alex asked the dwarf, while pointing to the beheaded dragon.

"When you fried that shlimazel there, the bolt kept going and made the wall plotz. The smell of gold had the rest of my men in here mach shnel and we finished off that shlemiel," the king explained pointing from one dragon to another.

"When I saw the gold you exposed, it left me ver clempt," the king replied. Alex almost swore he had a tear in his eye.

"OK, well that's great, but we need to get moving," he replied as he attempted to rise. He had gotten no farther than half way up before his head began to spin and he dropped back down.

"Gay shlafen, we will stand guard until you are rested enough to travel," the king declared as he waved Alex back down to his resting position. With that, the dwarf walked back to where his men were carving away at the chamber wall. He could hear them cheer every time a gold nugget was released from the stone and dirt.

"He's right, Alex; we need to rest before we continue. As it is, Cassie is not going to be able to walk for a day or two," she said, pointing to the bandaged leg.

It was then that Leander appeared, carrying Alex's sword and looking somewhat chagrined.

"Here is your sword," he announced as he set the exposed blade next to Alex.

"I had hoped you wouldn't mind me borrowing it as I scouted the tunnels on the other side. It worked quite well against the dragon, better than the spear, I think," he said in way of an explanation as he pointed to the dead dragon and the other side of the chamber.

"You used it on that thing?" Alex asked as he point to the beast.

"After you dispatched the dragon charging Lady Cassandra and myself, I saw you fall. I was able to close the distance before the beast reached you and drove the spear into its side. From there I withdrew the blade from its eye. With the help of the dwarves, we were able to dispatch the creature in no time," Leander finished.

Alex suspected that there was much more to that tale as Leander would have had to fend off the dragon for several minutes before the dwarves could arrive. From his appearance, torn clothing and covered in blood splatter, it must have been a hell of a fight.

"It's my pleasure," Alex replied with a smile as he offered his hand to his friend. Leander accepted the hand and then continued to speak, the show of affection embarrassing the man.

"The dwarves tell me that the tunnel runs straight and true from here to the base of Gundor Stronghold. Once we reach the mountain, there is a labyrinth of tunnels we will have to explore to find the dragon's lair."

"And they have no suggestions?" Cassie asked, her discomfort obvious as she constantly shifted, looking for a more comfortable position.

"Only that we do so cautiously," Leander replied, acknowledging the lack of helpfulness in the statement.

----*----

Kelby had managed to locate a small room near the kitchens to store the contents of the packhorse, its condition indicating a lack of use. With all the activity from the wagons to the kitchens, no one paid them any attention as she and her sister transferred the goods. It was also their good fortune that most of the kitchen staff was male, so all felt the sisters' influence.

By the time the wagons were unloaded, both women had secured positions as kitchen servants, providing almost unlimited access to the castle. Kelby's biggest concern was that Alex and the rest of the group would appear before the sisters had an opportunity to search the floors above the kitchen.

With the day's work complete, she set about organizing the quarters they had been provided, while fending off the various men nosing around the new arrivals. She did have to acknowledge that while her talents in manipulating men were valuable, at times she wished she could just turn it off.

With the last suitor for their affections turned away for the night, Kelby watched Leena bar the door before each settled into the spartan beds. The two quietly discussed the tasks to be completed in the morning, splitting the workload. With nothing more to say, she doused the candle and silently slipped into a deep sleep.

----*----

Cassie was the first to wake after the four had taken King Teivel's advice and gone to sleep. There were only two torches burning, and those had been set far enough away to provide a soft glow where the humans had set up camp. She could still hear the sounds of digging from across the chamber as the dwarves continued to pursue their gold strike.

She smiled as she saw Kinsey curled up between her and Alex, her eyes open and watching Cassie. She hadn't bothered to lift her head, but she watched Cassie's every move as she slowly sat up. The shooting pain she felt throughout her body at the effort reminded her of the thrashing she had received while in the dragon's grasp.

She was thankful that Alex had not had the opportunity to inspect her more closely, as she was positive she was bruised from head to toe. While she was very appreciative of his protective nature, she feared he would send her back with the dwarves rather than allow her to continue the quest.

Earlier, while Alex was unconscious, Abrianna had been emphatic that, had he not been able to assist her, Cassie would have perished due to the poison's effects. She had described the amazing strength of his magic and how she had to temper his efforts. Both cousins were becoming very aware of his growing capabilities.

She knew that once they rescued her mom, Alex and her uncle needed to spend some serious time together for his training. She had heard him comment more than once about the need to learn control, particularly when one had great power. What bothered her was the look of concern her uncle had when he talked about Alex.

"What's wrong?" Cassie heard from nearby. She turned slightly to see Abrianna watching her from her bedroll.

"You were frowning," she added once her cousin faced her.

"I'm just worried about Alex, he took quite a beating," she lied. There was no point in voicing her concerns now. Abrianna laughed softly at the comment before replying.

"Cassie honey, of the four of us, you are by far the worse for wear. I am just drained," Abrianna replied while indicating Leander and Alex in the reference.

Cassie scanned the motionless forms of the two men, both still sleeping soundly. Even in the dim light, she could see the battered forms in tattered clothing. She recalled they had barely enough strength to wash the dragon's blood away, finding a few contributions of their own in the process.

"And he is always trying to protect me," she added as an afterthought while motioning to Alex.

"Lady Cassandra, if he hadn't pulled you out of the way when he did, that dragon would have killed you," Leander declared, apparently now awake as well. While the three continued to talk in hushed tones, Cassie watched Alex sleep.

"As battered as we are, we need to be careful of the dangers ahead," Leander had just cautioned when Alex suddenly bolted awake.

"Danger, what danger?" he cried out as he sat up, bleary eyed and scrambling for his sword.

"There is no danger, Alex," Cassie replied as she leaned forward to try to calm her fiancée. It took a moment before he appeared to recognize his surroundings. While he did so, Abrianna and Leander began to move about their camp, relighting the fire and preparing breakfast.

She watched as Alex gingerly began the process of standing. He seemed to be testing each of his limbs to ensure stability before finally gaining his feet. It was then that the dwarf appeared and wrapped him in a bear hug that she was sure would do him in!

----*----

Alex was sore everywhere, but he knew he couldn't let it prevent him from continuing the quest. After awaking in a panic, he had been testing his arms and legs to see if anything objected. Next, he needed to see if he had the strength to stand, which proved questionable.

He could see Cassie watching him, concern written all over her face. He needed to put on a good show for her to allay any fears. He had just managed to balance on his own two feet when the dwarf king appeared out of nowhere and wrapped him in a bone-crushing embrace.

"Bubbele, you are up and around! What chutzpah!" King Teivel bellowed.

"Thanks," Alex managed after the dwarf released him.

"We have been digging all night. This is a gosys gefinen!" Teivel announced. Alex assumed that meant it was a good find.

"We are going to need to get moving soon. Can I beg a favor of you to gather supplies for us?" Alex asked Teivel

"You are no shnorror; you have earned anything you need!" Teivel exclaimed, pointing to the dead dragons and then the gaping hole where the dwarves had tunneled, following the gold vein. The sight of the dragons made Alex ache all the more, but he put that out of his mind as he did a quick inventory.

"I was told we are about a day's travel to the base of Gundor. I would think no more than two or three day's supplies," Leander provided. Alex smiled and nodded thanks to his friend.

"Keyn problem! I will have someone bring you what you need within the hour!" the dwarf answered

"You are welcome to come along," Alex offered, hoping for some extra backs to carry things.

"Gay ga zinta hate, we will stay here and dig, mazel tov," the King replied before giving Alex another bear hug and then heading back to the digging.

Alex turned to Abrianna, holding up both hands in a gesture of confusion.

"He said go in good health. It is a nice way of saying we are on our own from here on," she interpreted.

"I had to try," Alex shrugged as he began sorting through their gear, separating the must haves from the niceties. He still wasn't sure how Cassie was going to travel, and had to force her to sit several times.

"I'll be fine!' she replied after the third attempt.

"Abrianna, will you please watch her while Leander and I get things ready?" he asked in exasperation.

While sorting through the gear discarded by the dwarves turned miners, he was able to piece together a set of crutches. In addition, he fashioned a pair of backpacks, allowing he and Leander to carry the bulk of the supplies they required.

They sat down to a simple but filling meal, Abrianna insistent that everyone eat as much as possible to help restore their strength. Alex was surprised to see the healer put away more than he or Leander. She continued to snack as they finished their preparations to leave, including Leander and Alex in the tidbits.

After a quick lesson with Cassie and the crutches, the party bid farewell to the dwarves and headed into the tunnels. If anyone noted that Alex had gathered torches instead of using magic to illuminate their path, they choose not to speak of it.

# Chapter 25

Leena had started early, working with the kitchen staff in preparing the meals for the guards while Kelby headed upstairs to begin her search. Using the guise of one of the chambermaids, she worked her way into the royal quarters, learning the layout.

Each sister had a list of people and locations to find before the day was done. Leena was to locate the guard's quarters for both factions in the castle while Kelby was to locate the private quarters of the notables in residence. Both sought any references to the dragon's lair below the stronghold.

It didn't take long to discover which part of the castle was occupied by Tantalus and which was not. The guards had staked out positions in the halls on various levels, challenging anyone who entered. It was becoming quite obvious that the Vassal King had an unwelcome guest.

Rather than wander the halls in the brazen fashion of an oversexed mermaid, flirting her way past the guards, she had chosen to downplay her appearance. The last thing she wanted to do was raise suspicions with either Tantalus or the Royal Family. As it was, most Ladies of the castle had issues with overly attractive maids near their husbands.

Before long, Kelby had managed to locate everything on her list, so she delayed as she completed the chores assigned by the castle's head steward. She needed to maintain her charade for as long as necessary without raising suspicions. The problem was that the head steward had taken a fancy to her and she was supposed to finish her duties in his quarters.

He was a nasty, overweight man who she doubted had seen a bath this year. The idea of drowning him by enticing him into a bathtub occupied her thoughts as she wandered from room to room cleaning up after the departed occupants.

"Girl, are you new here?" Kelby heard from behind as she made the bed in one of the rooms on the Royal side of the castle. Turning, she discovered a woman, likely the Lady of the castle, emerging from a dressing room off the main bedroom.

Kelby noted that she wasn't completely dressed yet as her gown was loose about her shoulder.

"Yes my Lady," Kelby answered as she did her best to curtsy, an action she had never even seen done before.

"I thought as much. Most of the staff knows not to enter this room until asked. Well, come here and help me since you are here. Come, make yourself useful!" the woman snapped as she turned, indicating Kelby should help with her dress.

"Yes, ma'am," Kelby replied as she hurried across the room to help the woman dress. As she did, she smiled as she realized this was the solution to her problems with the head steward.

----*----

Leander, torch in one hand and spear in the other, led the four through the tunnel with Abrianna, and then Cassie right behind him. Alex and Kinsey were bringing up the rear where he could protect their flank and watch over Cassie at the same time. She was maneuvering fairly well on the crutches, thanks to the dwarves' handiwork in the tunnels.

Alex hadn't paid much attention before, but with his fiancée hobbling along, the quality of the tunnel floors had become of great interest. He was grateful that Leander had kept a reasonable pace that allowed Cassie to not overextend herself trying to keep up.

As it was, he was happy that they were not being pressed for time, as his own strength was in question. If everything was going according to plan, the twins should be just gaining access to Gundor and delivering Alex's special packages.

During one of the many rest breaks where everyone consumed food and water, he noticed that the pounding in his head had subsided. He was also more alert as he observed, for the first time, Abrianna inspecting Cassie's leg.

He could see the green energy streams emanating from Abrianna and wrapping themselves around the bandaged limb. Closing his eyes and using his senses, he could see the healing taking place.

"Enough, Brie," he heard Cassie say as she pulled away from her cousin's touch. Alex could detect the depletion of Abrianna's own strength from the effort. Alex stepped forward as she straighten up, wrapping both arms around her and hugging her.

"Thank you," he whispered in her ear as he held her tight. Not in water, Cassie couldn't see how he enveloped her in a cloak of white energy, restoring her strength before Abrianna realized what he was up to.

Abrianna took a step back after Alex released her, the flash of anger in her face soon replaced with a warm smile of thanks. Only the two of them knew what had taken place, and Abrianna was not about to divulge Alex's sacrifice. What was done was done, and she understood why.

Returning to his resting spot, he reseated himself and watched as Cassie flexed her leg, apparently happy with the improvements.

----*----

Kelby was still upstairs in the same bedroom when the head steward burst in on her. She was seated quietly on a small bench at the end of the bed, and appeared to be waiting for something.

"What are you still doing up here? You were supposed to meet me an hour ago," the man shouted as he crossed over to her.

"What is the meaning of this?" the Lady of the castle asked pointedly as she emerged from the dressing room.

"Forgive me, my lady. I was just looking for this lazy maid," he replied as he bowed before the woman.

"This girl has been helping me all morning and is far from lazy. We are in the process of exchanging my fall wardrobe for a more appropriate winter look!' she snapped at the man as he groveled before here.

"Yes, my lady. I was unaware," the man answered while looking daggers at Kelby as she did her best angelic face.

"I suggest you find another girl to harass as she will be busy helping me for quite a while," the Lady replied as she motioned the steward out of her chambers.

"Now, where were we?" the Lady said absently as she returned to her dressing room. Kelby had discovered an entirely different kind of flirting as she continued to endear herself to the Lady of the castle. She watched as the woman appeared with another ensemble in hand.

"Oh no, my Lady, that will never do for a winter look," she stated while batting her eyes.

----*----

Alex caught up with Leander and the women as they stopped for a rest. They had passed another spring in the tunnels and, while everyone else pressed on, Alex stopped to top off the water skins and let Kinsey drink her fill. As he approached, he noticed the three looking around from their seated positions.

"I think we are here," Leander commented as Alex came into view. Sure enough, the tunnel had taken on a different appearance, as it widened slightly, and was much taller. Alex passed the seated forms and ventured ahead, only to find where the tunnel split into two passages. Turning back, he returned to the three and found his own place against one wall.

"We should sleep here before going any farther," he informed the rest of the party. He could see Cassie struggling with her reply before she finally agreed.

"I know we are close to mom, but I agree. We need to rest in case we have another fight on our hands."

Alex passed out the refilled water skins and then began preparations for a meal. While he did that, the other three worked at getting themselves settled in for the night, although none actually knew if it was day or night outside.

He wondered if the twins had been able to complete their tasks, or even access the castle itself. He had to rely on their ingenuity and creativity and hope they were ready when the time came. His last thought before retiring was: *What I wouldn't give for a cell phone right now.*

----*----

Kelby and Leena were just settling in for the night. The two hadn't seen each other all day and spent this quiet time catching up. Leena seemed outwardly pleased at Kelby's new status, and that it had given her the ability to access those areas of the castle previously unavailable to them.

Privately, Kelby could see the jealousy that always seemed to come between the two. It was that same jealousy that had driven Leena to come to Nyland in the first place. Leena had been very successful in placing the packages she was responsible for, but seemed to be selling herself short.

With only one task remaining for the twins, they agreed on a plan of action for the early morning, and bid each other a good night.

----*----

Alex awoke from a less than restful sleep, opening his eyes to complete darkness. They had extinguished the torches before retiring, and he hesitated to relight them for fear of waking the others. Gently, he reached out with his senses, trying to feel each of his companion's state.

Cassie was closest and he was happy to find her resting peacefully. He suspected that the healing potion Abrianna had given her just before they all retired contained a sleep aid as well. Then again, he had always heard that sleep was the best medicine.

Moving to Abrianna, he suddenly felt her presence reaching out to him. Confirming that she was also awake, he projected what he hoped was warm, caring feelings before moving to Leander.

His friend was still asleep, but from the tension still in his body; Alex guessed he was not in a relaxing sleep. Projecting a calmness into the man's dreams, Alex could feel him begin to relax and he heard Abrianna start to move about in the darkness.

Alex assumed she was using her own senses as she maneuvered herself past the two sleeping forms and settled down near Alex in the darkness.

"I felt you," she declared in a hushed voice. "You are developing a very sophisticated touch," she added, a tinge of pride in her tone.

"And I sensed your hand in Cassie's slumber. Sleeping potion?" he replied with his own tinge of humor.

"Perhaps," she replied with some humor of her own.

"Can you sense the dragon?" she asked after a moment.

"No, not yet. I have reached out a couple of time, but so far I just see a maze of tunnels," Alex replied, a bit frustrated.

"Do you think the mermaids are ready?" she asked, changing the subject.

"I have to believe so. Kelby may be a hardheaded troublemaker, but I doubt she takes failure lightly. If we pull this off, she gets the revenge she is looking for," Alex replied thoughtfully.

"Someone want to light a torch?" Alex heard from a half-awake Cassie.

Without a thought, Alex fired up both while he moved to check on her. With a watchful Abrianna at his shoulder, he infused more healing energy into her leg, pretending to check her bandages. With an exchange of glances, he passed the limb over to Abrianna for final inspection.

"I think we can take these off," she commented absently as she started to remove the cloth wrap. Once she was finished, Abrianna had her test it while standing and walking in a circle.

"Good as new! Thanks Brie!" Cassie declared as she hugged her cousin.

"Great, now you can carry your own stuff!' Alex added as he hugged his fiancée.

With not more than a light meal, the four packed their things and started the search for the dragon's lair and Lady Amelia.

----*----

Alex could sense the dragon's lair just beyond the run in the tunnel. They had been searching the tunnels for several hours, eventually going up several levels in the mountain with Gundor Stronghold atop it. He had them extinguish the torches to prevent any telltale glow they might provide. He had to silence Kinsey as the wolf continued a low growl at the scent he was sure she had picked up from ahead of them.

With everyone in check, he guided the party forward in the darkness, assuming Abrianna was using her senses, as was he, to move them forward. As he approached where the tunnel gave way to the dragon's lair, he could see light ahead.

Stopping and checking to be sure Kinsey was in check, with Cassie holding on to her, he started forward again. Where the tunnel emerged into the lair, all four halted as they came face to face with the slumbering red dragon Alex and Cassie had encountered in the Dragon's Teeth.

Waving everyone back, out of view, he stopped out of sight of the dragon and prepared to use his senses once more. Just before he closed his eyes, he could see Abrianna had already begun her own reconnaissance of the chamber. As he started, he felt the others' eyes on him.

Alex let his mind wander back into the room, where he felt the overwhelming presence of the sleeping dragon.

"She's in the pit," he heard Abrianna whisper.

Trying to take in the entire chamber quickly, he found the pit Abrianna referenced, and inside, at the bottom he sensed Cassie's mom, Amelia. He could tell she was awake, and reading something in the dim light. Returning his attention back to the dragon, Alex let his senses roam over the creature.

As he was doing so, Alex felt Cassie's movement and he followed her as she crept to the entrance to the chamber. He was sure she was looking for the pit Abrianna mentioned. Alex knew the hole was not visible from her vantage as the dragon blocked their view, but dared not speak for fear of waking the dragon.

Moving his senses back to the dragon, he was much more confident now than the first time he had encountered the beast. Ben had spent a considerable amount of time and effort on preparing him for this moment. Alex was awash with emotion as he absorbed all he could from the dragon's presence. It was an impression of something very old and very angry.

He next tried to reach into the dragon's mind as Ben had tried to teach him. If he could influence the beast's thoughts, he might be able to manipulate its actions. What he found both surprised and shocked him.

"Alex, it's awake," he heard from Cassie as he sensed the dragon's detection of his attempts.

"Come here!" Alex heard in his mind. Acknowledging the jig was up, he opened his eyes, and with Leander and Abrianna following, he passed Cassie and entered the chamber, while motioning for her to stay put.

"What are you doing?" Cassie hissed as he passed her and walked over to face the dragon.

"He's talking to the dragon," Abrianna answered for him as she stopped Cassie from following. Alex stopped and turned, again motioning for them to stay where they were. He then turned back to face the Red Dragon that it lay before him, only now its eyes were open and fixed on him.

"Why are you here?" Alex heard the dragon ask, but not with his ears. He rationalized they were in some sort of telepathic conversation. Ben had indicated that those who could speak to dragons did so without another being able to hear them. From Abrianna's comment to Cassie, she suspected she had been able to catch the dragon's side of things.

"You have a hostage, a woman in the pit there. We would like to take her home," Alex projected into the dragon's mind.

"She is my charge. If I protect her, my eggs stay safe," the dragon replied without moving.

Things had moved so fast the last time that Alex had seen the dragon that he didn't have an opportunity to really assess the size of the beast. It was huge! The head was twice the size of the Lindworms they had battled in the tunnels, and the body bigger than a bus.

Alex couldn't help but scan the chamber around them, trying to see how the creature had been able to squeeze into this lair. Soon enough he spotted a large opening it the ceiling up and to his left where the dragon must have entered.

"And what if I return your eggs?" Alex asked finally.

With a swiftness he didn't think possible for such a large creature, he suddenly found himself nose to nose with the dragon. He heard both Abrianna and Cassie gasp as he waved a charging Leander back.

"You can return them, undamaged?" the dragon asked as it hissed a heated breath out both nostrils. Standing now, the dragon's back traveled half the height of the chamber and its long neck craned down so its head remained at Alex's level.

"If I do, you will release the Lady unharmed, take them and leave?"

"I have not seen them in over 200 years, but will know them on sight. Do not pretend you can deceive me," the dragon hissed in his head while exhausting more smoke from its mouth and nose.

"You haven't answered my question," Alex repeated, sounding far braver than he was feeling.

"You have a bargain, Wizard. Yes, I recognize you from the Dragon's Teeth. You bring me my eggs and the woman is yours."

"And what will you do with your eggs?" Alex asked, almost as an afterthought. He stood before the dragon for several seconds before it finally replied.

"Fear not, Wizard. If you return my eggs, I will take them and leave. It is obvious you have much to learn about dragons, but know we are good to our word. The time of dragons has not yet returned. I fear the elves have much more meddling to do before we can return to the realms," the dragon finished.

Alex wasn't entirely relieved by the reply; it sounded more like a warning.

## Chapter 26

Kelby and Leena rose early, before most of the other staff, and began the search for the dragon's eggs. They had been able to complete all the other tasks Alex had outlined for them but this. In part, they had been prohibited from accessing the parts of the castle that Tantalus called home. In reality, they had hoped to come across the eggs' location while performing their other activities.

Leena had been the one to discover the means of reaching the floors Tantalus occupied without detection. Kelby had attempted accessing the rooms there several times via the hallways, only to run afoul of the Tantalus guards posted there. Even with her flirt turned on high, the men feared death more than they desired her.

To complicate matters, there was a dedicated staff on the levels Tantalus used as his residence, and they were not allowed to leave at night. They were only rotated out on a weekly basis, and that was still days away. The Master of House Drakon was always present to inspect new servants to ensure none was of concern to his personal safety.

Leena's discovery of an elevator system used by the kitchen and household staff to deliver food and linens had been a boon. By using the manually operated system, they would be able to secret themselves upstairs before the regular staff arrived for their morning duties.

Part of their mission was to place a few of Alex's packages in strategic locations there as they had done in the other parts of the castle. Fortunately, these were not as large as some of the others and the two women carried them easily.

Leena led Kelby down through the kitchens to the small room that contained the service elevator. There was a small wooden door covering what amounted to a wooden box suspended by ropes. The two sisters closed themselves in the small room and prepared to lift each other into the upper floors. Both had dressed in common household attire, hoping to blend in with the floor staff should they be seen.

"You crank me up first, and then I can crank you up from there," Leena explained as she entered the box while pointing to the crank nearby.

The elevator was only large enough for them to go up one at a time anyway, so Kelby agreed Leena should go first while she operated the crank that lifted the box attached to a rope pulley system. There was an indicator by the crank that let the operator know when the box had reached each floor.

Kelby stopped at the floor Leena specified she had been sending things intended for Tantalus, and waited. Once Leena had verified all was clear, she sent the box back down and then operated the crank at her end to elevate her sister.

It was still dark when the two left the small room that housed the elevator. Peering out the doorway, Kelby checked to see if the hallway was clear, and then both sisters exited the room. The hallway lighting was still low with only interspaced candles, since the morning chambermaids had yet to light the wall sconces.

Kelby had hoped this part of the castle resembled the other areas she had explored. She quickly realized that Tantalus had been given the less opulent floors, most probably used by staff and lower-class visitors. The frustration she felt at having to search for their objectives was tempered with the delight she experienced over the slight the Vassal King had paid the Master of House Drakon.

Kelby had no idea what these packages were that Alex had them hiding, but if he hadn't insisted they were important, she would have skipped the whole thing for a chance at killing Tantalus. The thought of the packages brought her back to the task at hand. The twins had been moving quietly down the passage together when Leena stopped short, pulling her sister to one side.

Down the hall, they could make out two guards, standing to either side of a door on their right. The guards seemed to be half dozing as they used the wall to hold themselves upright. Kelby imagined that the duty must be considered the most mundane assignment deep in the protection of castle walls.

There was only one thing on this floor that warranted a twenty-four-hour guard, and that was the dragon eggs. Leena pointed to the small linen closet, a small half-height chest, opposite the two men and then the package she was holding. Alex had been very explicit in his instructions that none of the packages were to be placed with the eggs, however one should be as close as possible to any guards.

Backtracking, they found another linen closet, as they were spaced along the hallway for easy access by the room occupants. They each pulled out a small stack of folded linens, secreting their package in between. They then turned and brazenly headed down the hallway, to all appearances, chambermaids beginning their morning duties.

As they neared the chest closest to the guards, Leena stopped and opened the top, placing her stack inside, while slipping the package to the bottom where it would remain hidden. Kelby paused, giving the men a shy smile before she turned away, preventing them from getting a good look at her face.

Once Leena was done, the two continued quickly down the hall until they were out of sight of the guards. By now, the morning sun had just started to creep into the castle windows, warning the twins that their time was almost up.

At an intersection in two hallways, they found a large set of double doors; they took this to be Tantalus's room. Here they placed two packages, one in the linen closet as before and one behind the tapestry hanging next to the doors to the room.

Their work competed; they quickly returned to the elevator room, entering just as the morning staff began to emerge from their rooms to begin their day. Kelby quickly lowered Leena into the kitchens, where she emerged in time to greet the laundry lady delivering clean linens.

"Oh, I'm sorry, I didn't see you enter," the woman said, clearly surprised to find Leena already in the room.

"No worries. I just sent a load up. Would you like me to handle that," she said while pointing to the stack of bedding the woman had in her arms.

"That would be lovely!" the woman replied, knowing it would relieve her of cranking the load upstairs and waiting until someone collected the delivery,

Leena relieved the woman of her load and watched her leave, closing the door behind her. She quickly cranked the bedding upstairs, until the indicator displayed the floor where she knew an impatient Kelby was waiting.

She got a surprisingly quick reply and rapidly cranked her sister down before anyone else appeared to use the device. Kelby exited the box without a word and the two beat a hasty retreat back to their quarters to change.

"I don't know what those things are but they better be worth all this trouble!" Leena complained as she finished dressing before heading to the kitchens.

"Alex said they were a game changer, whatever that is. Ok, how do I look?" she said as she turned in front of her sister. With her new duties assisting the Lady of the castle, the woman had insisted that Kelby dress better than the chambermaids. As such, she had been given some discarded clothing from the Lady's closet… a more honest person would have agreed they were things that were now far too small for her.

"Like a royal whore," Leena said sarcastically as she left the room.

"Perfect!" Kelby replied with a smile as she headed in the opposite direction.

----*----

"Alex, what was all that?" Cassie asked as he led the group out of the dragon's lair and back into the tunnels.

"He made a deal with the dragon." Abrianna replied. With that, Alex stopped the others and turned to face them in the torchlight.

"Yes, rather than try and steal your mom, possibly getting her or us killed, I made a deal," he replied.

"What kind of deal?" she asked suspiciously.

"We give up her eggs, and she releases your mom," Alex said simply.

"But we don't have her eggs," Cassie replied sarcastically.

"Not yet," he answered with a smile. He then bent slightly to kiss her cheek before spinning in place and continuing to lead the group out of the tunnels.

The four, plus Kinsey, continued their tour of the tunnels, with Alex stopping every so often, closing his eyes, and searching the way ahead for the path up and out of the mountain. It wasn't too long before they could all make out a distinct change in the route they were taking.

"Alex, these are masonry walls," Leander pointed out.

"Yeah, I think we are in the lower dungeons," he replied cautiously. As if to substantiate his guess, they began to come across wooden doors, set into the walls and bolts drawn shut.

"You think the eggs are down here?" Abrianna asked, the hope clearly obvious in the question. Alex stopped and closed his eyes again before answering.

"I don't think so, I'm not sensing anyone ahead. I seriously doubt Tantalus left them unguarded."

With that, he continued to lead the group into the upper levels.

----*----

"My dear, wherever did you get that dress?" the Lady of the castle asked as Kelby entered her chambers.

The dress had been one of several she had been given the day before as appropriate for a lady in waiting. Kelby was positive they were old clothes from the Lady's younger days, now unwanted reminders of a slimmer youth. One thing she had learned during her training at The Siren's Song was: it's not what you wear, it's how you wear it.

"My Lady, this is one of the dresses you gave me yesterday. Shall I change?" she asked, putting on her best innocent face in the process.

"Um, no. I suppose not. I just don't remember it fitting me quite that way," the Lady replied absently.

"I am sure it was far more glamorous when you wore it. I really don't have the figure for such things," Kelby replied dismissively.

"Well, never mind then. Come help me get ready for breakfast. That loathsome Tantalus has insisted on meeting my husband this morning to complain again," the Lady responded as she wandered into her dressing room.

It took Kelby the better part of an hour to get the Lady ready, while surreptitiously reworking her look to add sex appeal. At first, the Lady was startled at the attempt, but within minutes she was surrendering to Kelby's magical applications.

"Oh my, you are a wonder. I look ten years younger," the woman commented as she reviewed Kelby's handiwork in the mirror.

"Do you think his Lordship will approve?" Kelby asked shyly, knowing the answer before asking.

"Who cares? I love it," the Lady answered before sweeping out of the dressing room. "Come along, we don't want to keep them waiting," she added as she led the way out of her chambers and downstairs.

----*----

Alex had led the group undetected up to the first floor of the castle's lower levels. They stopped in front of a large set of heavy wooden doors. Placing both hands on the panels, he closed his eyes and stood there, letting his senses roam the area on the other side.

"Quick, in here," he whispered as the led the group back down the hall and into a storage area, closing the large wooden door behind them.

With Cassie holding on to Kinsey to help keep her quiet, they listened to a pair of servants that passed by, making small talk as they headed to another part of the level. Motioning for Leander to stand watch at the door, Alex found a place to sit and calmly settled down.

Closing his eyes, he began the task of searching the castle floors above, going from place to place in search of several things. Number one on his list was locating the dragon's eggs, the trade goods necessary for Lady Amelia's freedom.

Second, he needed to locate Kelby and Leena, to ensure their safety before all hell broke loose in the castle above. The reason for the concern was the last object of his attention, or rather objects. All the packages he had the twins' secret throughout the castle, needed to be located before he could begin his plan of action.

"Make yourselves comfortable, this is going to take a while," he whispered to the group as he began to realize how big Gundor Stronghold actually was.

----*----

The Lady of the castle led Kelby down several flights of stairs before they finally came before an extremely large set of double doors. There were castle guards on each side of the portal, and they jumped to open the pair quickly before the Lady reached their threshold.

Not even slowing, the Lady passed into the room Kelby assumed was the great dining hall of the castle. At the far end of an enormous table sat a single occupant, who she took to be the Vassal King.

While Kelby took the Lady to be in her late 40's or possibly even early 50's, the king looked well past 60. He first looked at his wife, a smile appearing at her handiwork. The smile was only to be replaced with a leer when he noticed the mermaid.

"Who is this, my love?" he asked as he took his wife's hand in greeting, only to pass over it all too quickly as she sat next to him, before motioning Kelby to come closer.

"Oh, she is my new lady in waiting. Come here, girl, and stand behind me," the Lady replied.

Kelby could feel the King's eyes on her as she passed by to stand behind his wife's chair. She had to take a step back as the kitchen staff appeared with the morning's meal. Kelby caught Leena's wink as she passed between her and the Lady, serving her plate while another girl filled the cups of the seated pair.

With everything set, Leena went to a corner of the room, patiently waiting for the missing guest. Their wait wasn't long as the doors burst open and Tantalus charged in.

"Sorry Dragon Master, but we had no idea when you might arrive," the King said between bites as he motioned the man to a nearby seat.

"We have much to discuss. I fear we are in trouble," Tantalus replied as he watched Leena slip a plate in front of him.

"Just a knife to the throat," Kelby thought to herself as she saw her sister standing next to the object of all their hatred. Still, she relied on the promise from Alex that he would set things right and avenge their mother.

"I have lost contact with the Lindworms guarding the southern approach. I fear we may soon be under attack," Tantalus said while ignoring his food.

"We have heard this all before," the King replied as he waved off Tantalus's concerns.

"Was it not just last week we had to stop allowing our men to relax in Nyland due to your fears of spies?' the Lady asked in a very condescending tone.

"And your dragons have gone astray before only to appear once more," the King said while pointing at Tantalus with his fork.

"Remember, Vassal King, it is those dragons that keep your lords in check and you in power," Tantalus warned, finally lifting a fork of his own.

"And it is my armies that keep the southerners at bay after that upstart Renfeld made such a mess of things," the King countered.

"Your armies may be of little consequence, soon enough. I have received word from emissaries of the Dark Elves. They look for a counter to the disaster in the south," Tantalus announced in a haughty tone.

"You think they look to you and your dragons for allies against the Woodland tribe?" the Lady asked, her interest obvious at the possibility.

"My dragons are a power to be feared," Tantalus replied.

"And yet here you sit, driven from your home by a southern White Wizard," the King answered, unimpressed.

"That was no Wizard, merely a mage apprentice of the Wizard of Great Vale," Tantalus snapped.

"More's the pity, then, that you were exiled by only a mage apprentice," the King laughed.

At that, Kelby watched the three drop into silence; they continued their meal while Tantalus sulked.

"Alex, where are you?" she thought desperately.

# Chapter 27

Alex had located just about everything he needed, except the twins. They had managed to place all of the packages, as he had requested, without the slightest idea of what they were for. He was particularly concerned about the one near the dragon's eggs; however, he was able to confirm all was well there.

Several times during his search, they had heard servants passing by the storeroom that was their hiding space. Alex knew he was pressing his luck in delaying much longer, however, he owed it to the twins to ensure their safety before proceeding. They had risked much in performing their tasks.

He was just getting ready to give up the search when he passed over the large dining area. Inside he touched on the familiar warm sensations of the twins and a very dark, cold essence that could only be Tantalus.

"Get ready," he told those around him as he considered the best way to let Kelby know they were there. After a moment's consideration, he came up with an idea that he was sure Cassie would not like one bit.

"Well, here goes nothing," Alex said quietly as he went into action.

----*----

Kelby was standing just behind the Lady of the castle as the three seated in front of her returned to their discussion. As was her intent, the King continued to leer at her, completely ignoring the demands from Tantalus to increase castle security. Suddenly, she turned, as she felt someone touch her shoulder, but no one was there.

Returning her attention back to the table, she felt a sensation as if someone were caressing her. It began at her ankles, electrifying her skin, and slowly made its way up her body. She gave an involuntarily sigh of pleasure as it caressed her neck and back. Suddenly she felt a pinch on her bottom.

"Alex!" she almost cried aloud, jumping slightly. Only he could have pulled off the magic, teasing a mermaid so. Glancing over at her sister, Kelby gave the slightest nod, receiving a reply, before she removed the last of the packages from where she had hidden it in her dress folds.

His instructions had been specific. Throw the package into the fire from as far away as possible, and then take cover. She glanced at the fireplace just a few feet away and in one smooth motion, tossed the small box into the flames while dropping to the floor.

"What are you doing, girl?" she heard the King say before the deafening explosion rocked the room, throwing the seated occupants onto the floor.

Kelby scrambled past the Lady, with only a fleeting sense of guilt as she reached her sister who had been farthest from the blast but still knocked to the floor. Just as the two started to rise, several more explosions rocked the castle, the sounds coming from all directions.

Before either of the sisters could act, they watched as Tantalus scrambled past them and out the door, heading away from the unconscious Vassal King and his Lady, and up to his part of the castle. Scrambling to follow, the sisters came face to face with one of the guards. Apparently, Tantalus had said something because the man had his sword drawn and was intent on using it on the sisters.

----*----

Alex had been waiting for the explosion, satisfied he had given Kelby a sign she couldn't mistake for anyone but him. Once it had gone off, he started on the charges placed in the guard quarters and watch stations holding both Tantalus and the Vassal King's men.

They had decided early on that harboring Tantalus made the Vassal King just as culpable as the Master of House Drakon and Renfeld in the kidnaping. As such, Alex had asked the twins to spread the charges equally among the forces.

His conversation with Ben about cannons and gunpowder had given Alex the idea about planting explosives throughout the castle. Once hidden in place, he would be able to detonate them at his convenience, creating chaos, disrupting the castle guard and taking out Tantalus's men.

Once he was satisfied that the major elements of the castle guard were incapacitated, he led the group out of the storage room and up into the first floor of the castle.

"Come with me," Alex announced as he burst through the cellar doors and into a service area of the castle. The startled servants retreated in fear as the four charged through and out into the common area.

Alex and Leander appeared first, swords in hand, with Cassie using Alex's bow and Abrianna his dagger. Kinsey wasn't to be left out as she bolted past Alex to drag a hapless guard down from behind at the dining hall doors, where he had been threatening the twins.

"Tantalus went up there," Kelby pointed, as she indicated the stairs to Alex's right.

He turned in time to see three men in House Drakon colors charging down the flight of stairs. One sprouted an arrow while the other two engaged Alex and Leander with their blades. Alex's elven blade made short work of his opponent, which confounded the man facing Leander as he fell on him.

Soon all six were charging up the stairs with Alex and Leander leading the way and the mermaid twins, unarmed, bringing up the rear. They encountered several more small groups of guards as they continued up the staircase, with Kelby shouting instructions from the rear as to the location of the eggs. Between the magic of Alex and the bow and blades of the three, they made short work of the opposition.

By the time they reached the level Tantalus had made his temporary home, they had encountered a good many Tantalus guards, though not of the quality Alex and Cassie had experienced in the west. Alex assumed these must be local recruits, and hastily assembled at that.

Their luck ended, though, as they approached the hallway leading to the eggs; a half dozen armed men stood in their path. Alex had barely enough time to throw up a shield to deflect the flight of arrows that greeted them upon their arrival.

"Alex, behind us!" shouted Kelby as another group of armed men appeared at their rear. A second shield prevented them from closing the distance and attacking the rear of the six.

While Alex could shield himself in armor, permitting him to attack, he couldn't protect the rest of the party at the same time.

"Stay behind your invisible walls, pretend wizard," they heard Tantalus say as he stood behind the men in front of them. Alex heard Kinsey growl at the sound of the man's voice.

"It will give me time to secure my treasures and be gone, leaving you to face my dragons," he finished as he waved more men toward the chamber holding the eggs.

"I think not," Alex said calmly, as he sent the fleeting thought to the package Kelby and Leena had placed in the linen chest.

The explosion ripped through the assembled mass, sending men flying in all directions, some solidly into the invisible wall protecting the six. Alex paused before pressing forward, never dropping the boundary to their rear, where Tantalus's men were pounding in an attempt to assist their fallen comrades.

As they moved to the egg chamber, Alex allowed the bodies of the fallen to pass through the boundary. Those not killed had been rendered unconscious and were left unharmed. Alex could see Tantalus had been thrown back, landing farther up the hallway. He lay on the rug, rolling slowly from side to side as he attempted to shake off the effects of the explosion.

Once at the door to the chamber, Alex waved to the others, indicating he wanted them inside.

"Alex, the door is bolted," Leander commented.

Taking his eyes off Tantalus, Alex motioned Leander back and then concentrated a small charge of energy around the lock. As they watched, the lock shackle melted away, allowing the bolt to be lifted free. With that completed, he waved the group, minus Leander, inside and then formed a shield over the entrance, insuring only he could access the contents.

Turning, he was just in time to see Tantalus regain his feet and stagger away from the fight.

"You ready?" he asked Leander, before he dropped the shield between themselves and their adversaries at their rear, not waiting for a reply. With a second push, he slammed a new shield into the surprised men, sending them flying while he waved to Leander.

"This way, Tantalus is escaping," he shouted as he turned and sprinted off, Leander and Kinsey at his heels. Behind, he could hear the very unladylike comments coming from Kelby as she discovered they had been sealed in.

----*----

Kelby was furious! She had done everything the damn wizard had asked of her with only one request. She wanted to kill Tantalus. Now, here she sat, sealed in a small room with three others, and a bunch of small crates.

"I can't believe he did this to us! Sealing us in here like that," she screamed in frustration as she turned to the others.

"Better believe it, sister. It's not the first time for me," Cassie said absently as she inspected the nearest crate.

"We had a deal. Do you have any idea what Leena and I have been through? The things we have had to endure?" Kelby ranted.

"Yeah, I think I do," Cassie replied as she took the time to expose the leg mauled by the dragon. Kelby could see it had healed a little, but it still bore the signs of the event. She knew in time it would be almost undetectable.

"Help me with this," Cassie said as she changed the subject. Kelby stepped over to inspect the crate Cassie was attempting to open.

A sudden thud behind them caused all four to jump. They turned to see several of Tantalus's men pounding at the shield Alex had put over the entrance. Try as they might, they made no progress in breaching the barrier.

"Trust me, you won't get through. I've tried," Cassie said sympathetically, while Kelby simply made a rude gesture at the men before returning her attention to the crate.

Under closer examination, she realized these were actually finely constructed boxes and quite old. Each one had a particular dragon carved in its top and was latched closed with some kind of internal locking mechanism.

"You think that's the dragon the egg belongs too," Leena asked as she ran her hand over the carved relief.

"That's a Sea Dragon," Kelby spat as she recognized the image on the box before them.

"This is the Red Dragon, and that one too," Abrianna said as she inspected others nearby.

In all they counted two Red Dragons, two Sea Dragons, one Lindworm and one dragon they had yet to encounter.

"So the Lindworms in the tunnel were just fighting to defend their egg," Abrianna commented sadly.

Kelby considered that the Sea Dragon that had killed her mother had been under the same burden. While it softened her feeling about the creature, it inflamed her rage at Tantalus even more.

"Let's open one," Leena said, breaking the spell of Kelby's anger and bringing her back to the present.

"I tried, it's locked somehow," Cassie replied.

"Here, try this," Abrianna said as she handed Cassie the elven dagger Alex had lent her.

Kelby watched as Cassie attempted to wedge the blade between the edges of the top and bottom of the box. Slowly she was able to work the blade in until they heard an audible snap, causing the box lid to pop up about an inch.

Kelby reached forward and slowly lifted the top, exposing the contents to the four. The egg inside was about two feet long and… egg shaped. It had an iridescent sheen to it that swirled in colors ranging from light red to various pinks.

"This is the Red Dragon's egg," Abrianna said absently as they all gawked at its beauty.

"We can get my mom back," Kelby heard Cassie whisper, tears appearing in the nymph's eyes.

----*----

Alex and Leander sprinted down the hallway, with Kinsey now leading the way. He used his senses to feel for the presence of Tantalus, insuring the man couldn't slip past them and double back. They came upon Tantalus's chambers, the doors blown off their hinges and the guards laying on the floor.

Alex had triggered the last of the charges when he saw Tantalus run this way, hoping to catch the man as he retreated.

After a quick check of the damage, they didn't see their target among any of the bodies spread around the hall.

A crash in the chamber beyond drew all three into the room, where they found things in disarray, as if someone had been scrambling to pack valuables. Alex saw clothing and other items tossed across the floor, with drawers and cabinets left open.

A loud flapping brought their attention to an open set of doors leading to an exterior patio, where they could see Tantalus mounting a small green dragon, hardly bigger than Shadows. They rushed to prevent the escape, but were met with a wall of flame as the dragon reacted to the threat.

Alex deflected what he could and by the time the flame had receded, Tantalus was aloft and gaining altitude. Both men ran to the edge of the patio, where they could watch as the green dragon circled the castle a few times, assessing the situation below, before finally turning and heading to the coast, and the city of Nyland.

Exchanging looks of frustration, both men turned and headed back inside where they were met by the stragglers of Tantalus's beleaguered guard. The three men stood, swords raised high, challenging the two men and the wolf.

"Really?" Alex asked, the frustration clear in his voice. "Your boss is gone, abandoning you to save his own hide, and you are going to die for him?" He pointing at them with his elven blade, the blood of other guards still evident on it.

The three glanced back and forth between themselves, before the man in the center finally spoke up.

"By your leave, Sire?" the man asked pointing back over his shoulder and lowering his blade. The others quickly followed suit, apparently anxious to avoid another fight.

"Go," was Alex's reply. The men backed away at first, suspicious of a trick, and then turned to quickly disappear down the hallway.

Motioning for Leander to follow, he led the way back to the egg room where he had sealed the rest of their party inside. As the rounded the corner, he was just in time to see the three men he had released gather the remainder of the guard, and retreat down the stairs at the end of the hall.

"Tantalus?" Kelby asked as Alex dropped the shield sealing the room.

"He escaped on a small green dragon," Alex answered calmly.

"Escaped!" Kelby snapped.

"Don't worry, I know where he's going. He won't get far."

"Alex, these are the Red Dragon's eggs," Cassie said excitedly as she pointed to two of the carved boxes.

"Excellent, and the Sea Dragon?" he asked, drawing confused looks in reply.

"Over here," Abrianna answered absently.

"Great. OK, here's what we are going to do," Alex began as he explained the next steps of his plan.

# Chapter 28

Tantalus was enraged beyond belief as he rode the small green dragon to Nyland and safety. He had his ship at anchor there; it could return him to Freeport or perhaps even Tazmain, and his holdings there. The loss of the eggs was devastating, as it removed the control he had over the most powerful weapons he had.

The small green dragon he now rode was a juvenile; too little to carry him across the sea and too young to break from his control. However, if he failed to collect her eggs once she matured, she would also be lost to him as well.

He knew that the dragons would have no knowledge that he no longer held their eggs until such time as the new owner made it known to them. He had a small window of opportunity to take advantage of this fact. It should be just long enough to permit him to escape safely.

He had managed to pack what riches he could carry into the satchel strapped to his back as well as his dagger and sword. Fortunately, he had left a good part of his wealth and personal effects on board his ship, so he wasn't entirely destitute and devoid of belongings.

He prided himself on distributing his wealth widely, insuring no single event could rob him of his way of life. Granted, this was a major setback, but he was optimistic that his new, closer relationship with the Dark Elves might compensate the losses.

In a short time, he found himself approaching Nyland, smoke rising from the chimneys marking its location on the coast. Rather than creating a major disturbance by landing a dragon in the town square, he had his mount land him far enough outside the city to avoid attracting unwanted attention.

As he started the short walk to town, his rage continued to build and he started plotting his revenge on the upstart Mage who had caused his misery.

----*----

Rather than do the heavy lifting he required himself, Alex sealed off the egg chamber once more and led his companions downstairs. Once they reached the main floor, they found the Vassal King rallying his guard, or what remained of them anyway, in the large common area.

"How dare you attack my kingdom!" shouted the Vassal King as Alex led the way onto the stone floor from the stairway.

The man had lined his troops up as a barrier between himself and the group, their blades drawn and at the ready. As a precaution and a warning, Alex formed a bright energy ball, held extended between his hands. The crackling ball was a clear demonstration of his power and a threat to terminate anyone he might pass it to.

"As Lord Protector of Windfall, I have every right to pursue fugitives of Renfeld's cowardly attack on Great Vale. You were unaware of House Drakon's support of the attack?" Alex proclaimed, as he eyed the armsmen lined up between himself and their king. He had given the fool an out if he was just smart enough to latch onto it.

"I don't care..." began the King, before his wife intercepted her husband's lapse of judgement.

"We had no idea, my lord, that Tantalus was in league with the criminal, Renfeld. Had we but known, we would have notified you immediately and had the villain thrown in a cell," the Lady declared, speaking over her husband as she stepped in front of him.

Satisfied that the woman had her husband under control, Alex let the ball dissipate, by passing the energy through the armsmen's chainmail. The effect was similar to passing low voltage current through their bodies, as a reminder of what was possible. He smiled at the slight shudder that passed through the men.

"Tantalus has escaped. I need several of your men to help me recover the chests he kept locked away upstairs," Alex instructed, while pointing to the men sheathing their blades. He noticed the King about to offer a comment on the contents of the boxes before his wife again cut him short.

"Yes, take whatever men you require. We are aware of the chests, but have no idea what was kept inside," the Lady replied as she waved several of the guards forward.

"If you have no further need of us, we wish to retire to our chambers until we can have the mess Tantalus created cleaned up."

With a nod, Alex watched as the Lady ushered her husband out of the room and up the stairs, insuring he kept his mouth shut the entire way. He had to laugh as he noted she blamed Tantalus for the damages and not Alex or Great Vale.

"You men, follow us," Alex said while waving at a dozen of the Vassal troops. Leading them up to the egg room, he assigned two men per crate. In a line, he led them back downstairs to the main floor and then out into the courtyard beyond.

Once everyone was outside with their crates, he separated the Red Dragon eggs from the rest and then dismissed the men. The six, plus Kinsey, quickly found themselves alone in the cold morning air, as none of the men wanted to test the wizard's patience.

"Ok, its showtime," Alex said absently as he closed his eyes, picturing the Red Dragon in the lair beneath their feet in the mountain. To his surprise, he received a mental image of the chamber, as he had seen it before, but different.

It was much brighter than he remembered, and had a strange hue, like he was seeing spectrums of light he had never seen before. Suddenly the view changed and he was looking down into the pit that held Amelia. He could see her sitting on some cushions, next to a small lamp, and reading. The lamp was far brighter than he believed possible.

He was startled for a moment until Alex realized he was seeing through the dragon's eyes. Regaining his composure, he concentrated on the dragon.

"We have recovered your eggs. Can you bring Lady Amelia safely up to the castle courtyard?" Alex projected. He must have succeeded, as he sensed the quick start of emotion from the creature, before receiving a reply.

"If this is a trick, you will all die," the dragon replied with enough force that Abrianna gasped and turned to Alex in surprise.

"She is on her way," Alex replied to the group standing around the crates. He noted a mix of excitement and concern across the faces of those gathered there. As they waited, Alex realized that with all the time he and Cassie had spent together, he had hardly exchanged one word with her mother. What if she objected to the wedding? Her initial response had been less than positive.

His concerns would have to wait as the sound of wings brought all eyes skyward. The sunny courtyard was completely cast in shadows as the massive wings of the Red Dragon were spread wide, slowing its descent.

Alex refused to relinquish his spot between the two Red Dragon crates as the creature landed before him, while everyone else backed away. Even Kinsey took a step back before returning to Alex's side.

They had opened both Red Dragon boxes, giving the dragon a clear view of the contents. As the creature halted before him, Lady Amelia was placed gently on the ground, where Cassie, throwing all caution to the wind, rushed in to embrace her mother before leading her away.

Everyone watched as the dragon sniffed first one and then the other of the crates, a satisfied huff accompanying each inspection.

"You have fulfilled your promise, Wizard, the Lady is yours," the dragon projected into his head. Over his shoulder, Alex could hear Abrianna relaying the message to Cassie and her mom. Both broke out in tears.

"What of the others?" the dragon asked while motioning to the other crates with its snout.

"The Lindworm is dead, a casualty of Renfeld's war. The others I intend to return," Alex replied. The dragon stared at him for a long while before nodding at the statement.

"I believe you will. For that reason, I will give you some advice. Do not trust the one who rules here, he will turn on you the moment he has opportunity. Also, beware the elves. While they are your ally now, they serve their own purposes," the dragon relayed, with a tinge of concern in her thoughts.

"I thank you for the warning about the King here. On that note may I ask a small favor?" Alex replied. The dragon waited for him to continue.

"I need to go quickly to the coast, to address two issues. Could you watch over the ladies, Abrianna, Cassandra and her mother, Amelia, until my return?" He pointed to the Sea Dragon eggs and then to the three women, still locked arm in arm.

The dragon paused for a moment, and then understood when Alex pointed to the Sea Dragon's eggs. It was a clear indication that at least one of the two issues mentioned involved returning the eggs.

"I will watch over them until you return, but be quick, Wizard. It is said that dragons have great patience and integrity, but do not test either of mine," the dragon replied, tinged with a sense of humor. With that, the dragon settled down and reached out to draw her two crates toward her.

Turning to the others, Alex closed in and started to explain his intentions.

----*----

Tantalus had been able to cross Nyland unmolested and made the harbor carrying his load. It had been some time since he had been forced to walk such a distance, much less with a burden such as this, but he was well motivated.

He was quite annoyed that it had taken so long to get the attention of the ship's watch before they would dispatch a boat to retrieve him. While others might overlook the incident, considering the circumstances, he had no such intent. After berating the captain for the lack of diligence on his crew's part, he became further inflamed when he learned they would need to wait for the tide before departing.

He stood on the deck, venting his rage for a long time, watching those around him cringe at his wrath. Finally, exhausted from the morning's chaos, Tantalus headed down to his stateroom with orders to sail at the first opportunity.

----*----

"I don't like this plan one little bit, Alex Rogers!" Cassie proclaimed sternly as they prepared Shadows and Rose for flight.

Alex wasn't the least bit surprised at her attitude. He was however, quite determined that this was the way it had to be.

"Look, sweetheart, Shadows and Rose cannot carry more than two riders. While you could, possibly, ride the dragon, are you really going to ask your mother to do so as well? Or even worse, leave her here while you come with me?" He knew the last was a low blow, but it made his point.

"Why do they have to go with you?" she asked, changing the subject as she pointed to the twin mermaids. Both redheads were each holding one of the Sea Dragon's eggs in their arms as they waited to mount one of the flying horses.

"Leander and I cannot fly the horse and hold the eggs. Besides, when we reach Nyland, I may need them to help locate the Sea Dragon," he replied, holding Cassie at arm's length while staring into her eyes.

Out of the corner of his eye, Alex could see Lady Amelia intently watching the two as they talked. She had been particularly quiet after being released from the dragon's grasp. He wasn't sure if that was good or bad, but didn't have time to investigate. This part of his plan was on a very tight timeline, and he couldn't afford to miss the changing of the tide in Nyland.

"Kinsey, you stay here and watch over Cassie," Alex stated before turning back to Cassie.

Giving his smoldering fiancée a kiss, he turned to Kelby and lifted the woman up onto the back of Shadows. He watched as Leander mirrored the task, an over observant Abrianna nearby. With that, both men mounted their charges and slowly nudged the mounts forward until they were clear of the area occupied by the dragon.

Both mermaids slid forward into their rider, trapping the dragon's eggs between the bodies as they wrapped their arms around each man, insuring its safety. Alex didn't even bother to check Cassie's response to that action, he just spurred Shadows forward, and with a single flap, found himself shooting skyward.

Both mounts circled the courtyard once, giving the riders a chance to settle in. Alex gave the dragon below a parting thought of thanks before Shadows broke the pattern and headed to Nyland.

Alex expected that what would take most of a day on the ground would still require several hours in the air. He could feel Kelby's arms wrapped tightly around his waist and her face buried in his back, giving him the impression that the mermaid wasn't all that thrilled with flying.

Everyone had bundled up as the cold air was biting at exposed skin. Alex couldn't be positive, but he thought the horses were flying faster than he had ever experienced. It was as if they understood the need, without him driving them.

Sooner than expected, Alex could see Nyland ahead, and the harbor beyond. From this height, he was also able to verify the arrival of his reinforcements. Nudging Shadows down, he didn't bother with landing outside of town to avoid the undue attention it would cause. With what was about to happen, this would be the least of their worries.

Setting down close to the harbor, the four rode their two mounts out toward the docks passing startled workers. Clearing the warehouses, they could see that Tantalus had his ship preparing to make sail and exit the harbor. Alex and Leander dismounted, both assisting the mermaids as they followed suit.

Both women continued to carry the eggs, leaving the men free to lead the horses as they walked out onto one of the many piers extending into the harbor. Dropping the reins, Alex led his small party out to the end of the pier where they could see the activity out on the water.

----*----

Tantalus was throwing a fit on deck, shouting at the captain, his face red from the effort. He had been notified when the tides became favorable for them to set sail, and so came on deck to see them safely to sea. He had serious concerns over the possibility of pursuit from those he escaped from in Gundor.

His current rage had been spawned by the discovery of three ships blocking their exit from the harbor. While similar in style to the pirate vessels he had seen on the crossing over to Nyland, these ships were all flying the banner of Windfall.

"Where did they come from? Why didn't you see them before?" Tantalus screamed at the captain.

"Sire, they must have been waiting off shore for us to make sail. We had no idea they were there until we started to leave," the captain answered.

"Can't we just go between?" Tantalus shouted as he pointed to the gaps between the three ships.

"No, Sire, the way they are positioned, we would be grappled by any two of them before we made the open water. There is no escape," the captain replied, resigned to the berating he was about to receive.

However, rather than exploding, as the captain was surely expecting, Tantalus became very quiet as he calmed himself. He examined the three vessels blocking their way and suddenly smiled, noting the captain shivering at his expression.

"Oh, yes there is," he replied as he walked to the rail.

# Chapter 29

Alex could see all the commotion on the deck of Tantalus's ship as the man berated the captain standing nearby. He smiled as he watched the man flailing his arms and shouting at everyone. Beyond, he could see Captain Regas and the other ships Alex had placed under his command.

Before departing with the dwarves, he had drafted a letter to be delivered to Windfall, giving Regas the authority to take any of the inactive ships currently at anchor there for his use. It had been Alex's intent to deal with Tantalus in Gundor, but on the off chance the man escaped, he wanted the harbor blockaded to prevent him from sailing west once more.

He knew it was a gamble, as the pirate could have simply presented the document and then sailed off with the prize of the Windfall fleet. However, with the events around battling the dragon and his generous offer of command, Alex doubted the man would turn tail and run from the opportunity.

As he watched the scene before him, Alex did a quick check on the mermaid twins, while he waited to see if Tantalus would cooperate and finish the trap he had set.

----*----

Tantalus looked out to sea, past the ships blocking their exit and concentrated. He knew he was bluffing his way at this point, but had little choice. He smiled as he envisioned the devastation that was about to befall the hapless victims before him.

His wait wasn't long as he could see the disturbance in the water just beyond the blockade. He concentrated as he summoned the dragon to him. With an explosion of water, the creature breached the surface, towering over him and the others on deck.

He spread his arms wide, presenting himself to his minion as he had done many times before. Concentrating, he closed his eyes and focused his wish that the dragon clear a path to the sea, crushing and burning anything that blocked their way.

Tantalus opened his eyes, expecting to see the dragon facing him, only to see the side of its head. Following the dragon's gaze, he could see that damn wizard standing on the dock, with several of his followers next to him.

Tantalus did a double take as he realized what two of the females were holding.

----*----

Alex watched as the Sea Dragon breached next to the ship Tantalus was using to escape. He could hear in his mind as the man instructed the creature to destroy the vessels blocking his way. The arrogance in the tone was like fingernails on a chalkboard to Alex.

While Tantalus continued to shout his instructions to the dragon, Alex subtly projected images of the eggs held in the mermaid's arms. Doing his best to be calm and reassuring, Alex envisioned the dragon eating Tantalus and in return, receiving her eggs from those on the dock.

As he did so, he didn't feel the same sense of intelligence that he had from the Red Dragon. It was more an exchange of images, visualizations of what each was communicating.

In response to Alex's projections, the dragon responded with images of his death as well as those with him. In addition, he could see Nyland burning all around them.

The message was clear, deceive me and all will die. With that. Alex watched as the dragon turned and faced Tantalus once more.

----*----

Tantalus was at a loss for what to do. His bluff had been called as the dragon saw its eggs in the hands of others. His entire life, he had maintained control over the dragon's eggs, as had his father and his father before him. He had been taught how to control them, bend them to his will, but always in possession of the precious eggs.

His family had been the unquestioned masters over the beasts who could bring them prominence. Only Tantalus had been brilliant enough to bring them forth out of hiding and use them to propel him to greatness.

Now this upstart of a magician was ruining all his plans. He could see the stupid beast struggling to follow his basic commands, so he simplified them.

"Kill them and take your eggs!' he shouted, not bothering to think it at her. He watched as the dragon turned back to those standing on the dock. As he watched, the women stepped forward and set the eggs gently on the dock, insuring they were safe. Once completed, they stepped back behind the wizard as he stood alone, the eggs at his feet.

With nothing left to bargain with, Tantalus shouted at the beast, his anger turned to panic. His only hope was that the dragon would still follow his commands out of confusion and fear that it was all some trick.

----*----

Alex stood calmly with the eggs at his feet, projecting a simple message: Kill the man and take the eggs, yours to keep forever. He watched as the dragon switched back and forth between him and the frantic Tantalus, now almost hoarse from screaming.

Suddenly, the dragon lurched forward, snatching Tantalus up from the ship's deck as those around him scrambled to get clear of the snapping jaws. Almost playfully, the dragon tossed the struggling form into the air before bring crashing jaws down on the man, ending his struggles.

In one swallow, Tantalus was gone and the dragon turned its attentions firmly onto Alex. By now, the others had retreated several steps leaving Alex alone with the eggs at the end of the dock.

The dragon approached slowly, wary of any treachery, until it came within reach of Alex on the pier. He backed away with a flourish, indicating the eggs were now in the custody of their mother. All watched as she gently placed both in her mouth before retreating back into the harbor and disappearing beneath the waves.

Alex turned to face his companions, only to find both sisters teary eyed.

"You mother is avenged," was all he could say before he found himself engulfed by both women, arms wrapped around him tightly as they wept.

----*----

Alex was astride Shadows, with Rose flying without a rider, as they headed back to Gundor. He had left Leander and the twins to manage the chaos they had created in Nyland with the appearance of the Sea Dragon and the death of Tantalus.

With the loss of their master, the crew of the ship offered no resistance when Alex claimed the vessel and its contents for Windfall. He didn't hold the crew responsible for their master's crimes, but he warned them that any disobedience would be dealt with swiftly. He promised any who wished it a safe return west or employment in Windfall. From their faces, he didn't expect any problems either way.

He had also flagged Captain Regas from his position outside the harbor, suggesting they take shore leave before beginning their new role as coastal patrol. The Captain was eyeing Tantalus's ship as an unclaimed prize, one Alex reminded him was unavailable to him in his new position.

Once everything was in motion, Alex asked Leander to message Ben and let him know all were well and they would soon be returning with Lady Amelia, safe and sound. He really needed to send the man a progress report on all that had occurred and the new holdings they acquired in the west with Tantalus's passing.

It was with all this going through his mind that Alex arrived at Gundor Stronghold, the dragon still firmly seated in the courtyard below. He had Shadows pass over the area once to be sure everything was as it should be and nothing unexpected had occurred in his absence.

He could see the three women surrounding a small fire, warming themselves. Apparently, someone had provided a small brazier for them, rather than have them move inside. Alex was pleased at the decision.

He could also make out Kinsey parked in the open space between the three women and the dragon. He laughed aloud as he saw the wolf and the dragon nose to nose, as if facing off with each other, the wolf putting her on notice that she was on guard.

After the second pass, he nudged Shadows down until both horses set down lightly, the activity drawing the attention of those standing there.

"Leander?" Abrianna asked, as she noted the rider less Rose.

"In Nyland attending to matters for me there," Alex replied with a smile.

"And Tantalus?" Cassie asked as she stepped up to kiss Alex after he dismounted.

"He is now one with his dragon. We won't be seeing any more of either of them," Alex replied after releasing Cassie.

"You sir, are awfully familiar with my daughter," Lady Amelia declared as she approached from the far side of the horses, blocked from Alex's view.

"I beg your pardon, Lady Amelia, I do not believe we have been properly introduced," Alex replied, unsure of what had transpired in his absence. He had assumed that Cassie and her mother had time to discuss her relationship with Alex before his return.

As he stumbled to bow before the woman, all three burst out in laughter.

"Forgive me, we are being unkind," she said between breaths.

"Mother, may I introduce my fiancée, Lord Protector of Windfall and master of my heart, Alex Rogers. Alex, my mother," Cassie finished, completing the task while suppressing her laughter.

"My Lady," Alex began before being interrupted.

"Am I free to go now?" the dragon projected, strong enough that both Alex and Abrianna cringed at the outburst in their heads.

"Forgive me," Alex said to Amelia while stepping away from the women and walking over to where the dragon sat nearby.

"I assume all went well?" the dragon asked, less forcefully.

"The Master of the House Drakon is no more. The Sea Dragon has her eggs and while I have no idea whom else may be involved, you are free to leave."

"Then I will do as you say. Remember my warning, Wizard. Take great care, for the elves are not your friends," the dragon said with finality.

With that, Alex watched as she scooped up the two chests and took to the air. After no more than a few beats of her wings she was high overhead and heading west, to what Alex assumed was her lair in the Dragon's Teeth.

Turning back, he could see all three women staring at him.

"What did she say about the elves," Abrianna asked him.

"She warned me that the elves had motives of their own and not to trust that they had our best interests at heart."

"Maybe so, but for now our interests are aligned, and that's good enough," Abrianna replied.

Alex nodded at the comment, but privately wondered if that was still true. Unwilling to delay any further, he got Cassie and her mother mounted on Rose while placing Abrianna behind himself.

He had carried materials from Nyland that would allow him to secure the chests to the back of each mount's saddle. It created an awkward riding situation, but he couldn't leave the last two eggs behind with the Vassal King.

Lastly, Alex needed space for Kinsey. He was concerned about overloading Shadows, but doubted Cassie and Amelia would enjoy the trip with 200 pounds of wolf in their lap. Climbing into the saddle, with Abrianna sandwiched between him and the egg chest, he coaxed Kinsey into the spot across his lap.

Shadows made a disapproving snort, but made no other protests as Alex nudged his mount into the open space vacated by the dragon. He checked to see Cassie was following before he did one last check.

Once he was sure all were mounted, the flying horses took to the sky, winging their way west to Nyland.

----*----

It was several more days before all was well enough for *Cassie's Quest* to depart Nyland for Windfall. The people of Nyland were quite happy for the off-season boon to their economy as the ships' crews made use of the inns and taverns while Alex and the captains transferred cargo and crew between ships.

Alex and Ben exchanged several message birds during this time, Ben anxious for more information about the demise of Tantalus and the situation with the Vassal King. Alex doubted very much that they had heard the last of the Vassal Lords, but had no reason to doubt the desire for the peace currently proclaimed.

Captain Regas had found willing recruits from Tantalus's old crew to flesh out his ships' rosters. Those sailors uninterested in joining up would be provided transportation home once the ships were all safely anchored in Windfall harbor. Captain Yeagars assured Alex that there were more than enough men aboard each to make the trip safely.

Alex discovered a substantial amount of treasure still in Tantalus's ship's hold, thankfully all under lock and key. Apparently, Tantalus had not trusted the Vassal King to protect such riches, instead leaving it to the ship's crew to guard on pain of death. He would need to check with Ben on the final distribution of the wealth, but suspected some would find its way into the Windfall city coffers.

Once those questions had been addressed and everything was in order, he had Regas escort the cargo ship to Windfall before he began his patrolling of the shipping lanes. Yeagars gave Alex a look of astonishment on the orders, but kept his opinion to himself on Alex's sanity.

As busy as he was during the day, each night he found himself aboard *Cassie's Quest*, where they spent their nights. Alex was not entirely convinced they were safe in Nyland, even with the King's decree that they were to be treated as honored guests.

Enough people had seen the interaction with Alex and the Sea Dragon that he was confident none would risk attacking their ship by water. He was particularly happy to learn that Kelby and Leena had arranged for the local mermaids to patrol the harbor, insuring nothing approached the schooner without permission.

Cassie and her mom spent the entire span aboard ship, catching up on the time they had lost and discussing their plans for the future. Alex was gratified that he needn't worry about their safety during the day, but found his evenings to be a bit challenging. It seemed to him that every night was a quiz, testing his knowledge of weddings and life planning.

Amelia was extremely pleasant, seemingly quite satisfied with her daughter's choice. He did notice a disapproving look each night when they retired, but not a word was mentioned on the subject, and Alex was not about to broach it.

She also took the time to explain her outburst in the dragon's lair. The disclosure that Tantalus had threatened to marry Cassie off should they win the war caused Alex to flinch as he remembered the scroll proclaiming the same for her mother.

When the day came to set sail for home, Alex was the first to breathe a sigh of relief. After what seemed an eternity of searching, they had finally completed their quest and were homeward bound.

Alex was surprised to learn the Kelby and Leena would be accompanying the group home. He was even more surprised to learn that it was at the specific request of Ben. Alex had learned long ago that if Ben asked something like this not to ask questions.

## Chapter 30

*Cassie's Quest* arrived in Windfall harbor late in the afternoon. With their arrival in Windfall, the entire city turned out to see the Lord Protector and his bride-to-be. The delivery of Tantalus's ship and the accompanying wealth had everyone anxious to see the couple. After the failures of Renfeld, the stories of dragon slaying and pirates had glorified the couple to near god-like status.

Alex wasn't surprised to see the banners of Great Vale flying over the castle. He had little doubt that Ben was anxious to see both his daughter and adopted sister alive and in person as soon as possible. Leaving instructions with Captain Yeagars to get their belongings and the horses ashore as soon as possible, he joined the others in the long boat that met the schooner after it dropped anchor.

As they crossed the open water between their ship and the docks, Alex could see masses of people lining the water's edge. With the throngs of well-wishers on the docks, the group had to work their way to the gates of the castle before they were met by King Ben. Once in the courtyard, they crossed the open area to meet him on the steps of the keep.

"Father!" Abrianna cried out as she crossed over to meet him before the others. After a kiss and a hug, it was Ben's turn to speak.

"Amelia," he said warmly as he embraced his sister.

"I am so sorry for what happened, you are unhurt?" he asked as he held her at arm's length while inspecting her.

Cassie and Abrianna had been able to replace her clothing while in Nyland, but had been limited to what was on hand. Alex had been impressed that the Lady had not spoken a word of complaint over her ordeal nor in her treatment since. Like her daughter, he suspected there was a bit of a tomboy still in her.

"I'm fine, Ben. Please, let's get these kids inside and we can talk there," she answered as she led Ben by the hand past the door guards and into the stone keep.

No sooner had they entered the main floor of the keep than Ben had stopped and turned to the rest of the group.

"Can I have a word with Amelia and Alex privately?" he asked, inciting a look of surprise from both Cassie and Abrianna.

"Ah, sure, Father," Abrianna replied as she grabbed a confused Cassie and led her up the stairs to presumably get cleaned up. She had waved to the mermaid twins to follow as well. Leander took his cue and excused himself as well.

"Follow me," Ben said as he led the two up the stairs into the all too familiar private study. Once everyone was seated comfortably, he poured drinks and then seated himself. Kinsey had followed the group and found the place she usually occupied. If Amelia found the wolf's presence surprising, she made no comment.

"To Amelia's safe return!" he toasted. Alex and Amelia mirrored the action, with everyone drinking.

"I asked you both here for two reasons, the first being Amelia's opinion of this marriage," Ben asked as if Alex were not even present. Amelia stared at Ben for a moment, the question clearly unexpected. She then looked at Alex before turning to Ben.

"I have been watching these two for several days now. I never expected Cassie to find someone after all she has been through. He seems to be able to bring out things in her I have never seen before...but is he committed?" As she said the last, she turned to face Alex with a stern look on her face.

"Ben told me all about Cassie. I know what I am getting into," he replied, trying his best to reassure her.

"Do you? Cassie has told me many things about you. Who you were, where you came from. You and Ben come from a place very different from this realm and he struggled with that difference with Abrianna's mother," she replied. Alex presumed he was referring to something Alex knew nothing about. They had never talked about Ben's wife.

"Amelia, this is different. The boy was offered a chance to go home and he turned it down for Cassie," Ben replied softly.

Alex figured this was not the time to question Ben about his past, but his declaration softened Amelia.

"Is this true?" Amelia asked Alex as she turned back to face him.

"Yes," Alex replied flatly, seeing no need to expand on the subject. Now more than ever, he saw returning home without Cassie as no option at all.

"What is the second thing?" Amelia asked, apparently satisfied with her daughter's suitor.

"That is why we are speaking privately," Ben replied slowly.

----*----

By the time Alex had left Ben and Amelia, it was dark out. They had sent word earlier that everyone should eat without them, as they had urgent matters of state to attend to. In reality, Ben had uncovered a bit of disturbing information that if proved to be true, could change Cassie's life forever.

Sworn to secrecy, Alex departed the study and made his way to the royal chambers, his quarters as the Windfall head of state. Entering the room, he found Cassie already changed and ready for bed, with a plate of food on the table.

"I had the kitchen make you something in case you didn't eat," Cassie replied to the unasked question.

"Thanks. No, we didn't have time. Your Uncle has a pile of things for me to do and some of it couldn't wait," he lied as he picked up the plate and started eating while sitting on the edge of the bed.

"You know you can't lie to me to save your life," Cassie whispered as she leaned over to kiss his neck.

"That is true, but I am sworn to honor your Uncle's wishes. I can tell you he wanted to be sure your mother was ok with me," Alex replied between bites, knowing that subject would distract Cassie for the moment.

"Mom loves you!" Cassie replied.

"Yet she questioned my dedication to you," Alex responded, as he set the empty plate down, exchanging it for the nearby cup.

"She did?" Cassie asked in response.

"Well, of course she did. She really doesn't know you like I do," Cassie added almost immediately.

"Rest assured, after our conversation with your Uncle, she seems satisfied I am not merely taking advantage of you," Alex responded playfully, after taking a sip from the cup and then replacing it on the table.

In an effort to end the conversation, Alex gently pushed Cassie back onto the bed, kissing her passionately. Her eager response was more than enough to tell him the conversation was finished for the night.

----*----

Bright and early the next morning, Alex and Cassie chatted lightly as they descended the staircase leading to the private dining room. It had been a long time since the two had been able to enjoy each other's company, unburdened with a trip or task.

Upon entering the dining room, they were surprised to find Ben, Amelia, Abrianna, Leander and the mermaid twins all in attendance.

"Are we late?" Cassie asked as they found themselves seats among the group. Scanning the table, Alex could tell they must have been there for some time as most had finished eating.

"No dear, we just got an early start. I am told that you no longer have your own room so now have reason to linger in the morning," her mother said in a not completely disapproving tone.

"Mother!" Cassie replied with a tinge of a blush. Alex knew privately that he had been encouraged to delay their morning routine.

"It is just as well as it allowed us to address some questions before your arrival," Ben commented with a smile. Alex exchanged looks with the man, receiving the slightest nod in return. He then looked to Amelia and the twins, to see their smiles.

"Uncle, what issues?" Cassie asked.

"Come here, girl," Ben asked as he stood from the table. Cassie did as she was bid, getting up from the table and walking to Ben. Everyone watched as he led her over to a small round table, about waist high. On the table was a silver tray, and a long slender knife.

"Give me your finger," Ben asked as he extended his hand. Cassie gave a nervous glance about the room as everyone watched.

Taking her hand in his, Ben took the knife and pricked the tip of her finger, drawing several drops of blood in the process. The blood was dripped onto the silver tray, over to one side.

"Kelby?" Ben asked as he released Cassie, but motioned her over to one side of the table rather than redirecting her to her seat. Everyone watched as Kelby got up from her place and proceeded over to Ben.

Alex watched as Ben repeated the procedure with the mermaid, allowing the blood to drop on the opposite side of the tray. He repeated the process a third time with Leena until all three women were standing to one side.

"When these delightful ladies first arrived in Windfall, I could not get over the resemblance they shared with our Cassie. As I spent more time with them, I recognized behaviors that reinforced that opinion," Ben began.

"While you were gone, I did some research. To begin, I should explain that the ancestor Cassie got her nymph from was her father."

"Uncle, I don't understand," Cassie interrupted.

"You were never told that it was your father that was born of a nymph mother for fear of its influence on you. As he was a halfblooded nymph, you are far closer to true nymph than anyone we have encountered," Ben explained.

"Your father was male and therefore unable to connect with the nymph blood that ran through his veins," Amelia began to explain to her daughter.

"When you were born, we had no idea how much the nymph blood would affect you. Then that day in the river, we discovered the true extent of its influence over you," she finished.

Alex recalled the story Cassie had told him of her coming out, so to speak. As a young woman, likely a teenager, she had gone wading one hot summer day, only to find herself uncontrollably radiating sexuality. Her mother had to wade through the admiring boys to lead her back to the castle.

"What Amelia didn't know was that Cassie's father was aware of his linage from a very young age. Even without the connection to the nymph blood that you feel, Cassie, he was drawn to water. He struggled with his past, having difficulty resolving the mixed heritage."

"Before ever meeting your mother, he had gone to sea, sailing out of Windfall and traveling west with the shipping trade as a sailor," Ben continued, taking over from Amelia.

"He told me many times of his trips to the ports of the west, including Freeport and Tazmain. It is not a stretch to envision a lonely young man enticed by a beautiful young mermaid. Kelby can confirm that mermaids are drawn to men of power. A mermaid would be able to sense the magic in his blood."

At this point, Cassie began to see where this was leading.

"You don't think?" she said as she turned to the twins and then her mother.

"There is a way to determine if you are related. When I burn the blood on this plate, we will either see them all burn the same color, the smoke intertwining, or they will burn separately, with Cassie's smoke separating from Kelby and Leena."

With that explanation, Ben turned to the table and began to hover over the silver platter. Alex watched as the three nearby women closed in around him, their fates tied to the outcome of the results.

As he watched, Alex saw three aqua flames jump up from the plate, their smoke plumes intertwining into a single braided column. Everyone's eyes moved from the plate to the three redheads, all with tears running down their faces.

"Sisters?" Cassie said almost silently as she turned to the twins.

"Half-sisters actually, you share the same father. Since mermaids almost never meet their father, it would be normal for them to not know who he was," Ben corrected.

"Mother, what now?" Cassie asked as she gathered her new found siblings and all three cried together.

"Ben wanted me to know about his suspicions before he told you. As Cassie's father was my husband, I would gladly take you in as my own daughters," Amelia said as she stood, looking at the twins for a reply. Rather than speaking, all three rushed her, wrapping her in a blanket of arms and red hair.

# Chapter 31

The next several weeks were filled with activity as they planned for the royal wedding. Cassie had more help than she knew what to do with as the twins, Abrianna and Amelia took command of the preparations. With the popularity Alex was generating in Windfall with his economic programs and stability on the seas, they had been pressured to have the wedding in Windfall rather than Great Vale.

Fortunately for Alex, Leander had gathered the courage to ask King Ben for permission to marry Abrianna, which gave Great Vale a royal wedding of their own in the near future. Ben and Leander had to return home to deal with items neglected in their absence, while Alex was left to handle the barrage of questions from the women.

Ben had overseen the division of Tantalus's treasure before leaving, dividing equal shares for Windfall and Great Vale. He suggested, and Alex agreed, that the remaining eggs be placed in the vaults in Great Vale for safekeeping. With Alex's talents for dragon interactions, it reduced the possibilities of misinterpreted interactions should a dragon appear unexpectedly.

Alex was able to enlist several of the men destined to return to the west to return the fire glass spear they had borrowed from the temple on the mainland. They were to transport the spear to the Rangers in Tazmain, who would then return the relic to its rightful place in the temple. All were generously compensated and made to understand it was better to have a wizard indebted to you than angered at you. He had no fear that it wouldn't arrive safely.

In an effort to avoid the constant barrage of questions, Alex did his best to stay away from the castle and remain hidden amongst the businesses he was supporting. The shipyards had begun taking orders as well as performing repairs, to the delight of the tradesmen involved.

The port master was thankful for the return of his manifest, borrowed so long ago, and reported record trade passing through the warehouses. On that note, the Harbormaster reported Captain Regas had escorted two cargo vessels safely to port after chasing off the marauders attempting to pirate the cargo.

As a reward, Alex had treated the good captain and several of his officers and crew to drinks at the Drowning Man. While there, he was relieved to find neither of his newly adopted sisters-in-law still plying their trade in the tavern.

Earlier he had heard Amelia informing the twins that they were now royalty and above frequenting such places. Alex was not about to inform the good Lady that both her daughter and brother had other opinions on that subject. He had little doubt that should the twins choose to do so, the Drowning Man would have the pair patrolling the barroom, looking for victims to scam.

His real fear was the influence the pair would have on his soon-to-be wife. While Cassie was far from a prude, the twins did seem to have a liberating influence on her that made Alex blush. Several times in the last few days he had come home to find all three redheads in his and Cassie's room, wearing less than a swimsuit while performing some female grooming ritual.

Abrianna had done her best to balance their antics, but even she had thrown her hands up in exasperation on several occasions. Fortunately for all, Cassie did heed her mother's warnings and toned down the antics.

----*----

The day of the wedding was bright and sunny, the city of Windfall alive with celebration. King Ben had returned to Windfall just a few days earlier, bringing Leander and several other dignitaries with him.

Alex was beside himself trying to accommodate the traveling royalty that descended on Windfall. King Elion arrived via one of his flying horses, while Kings' Brokkr and Teivel arrived in more traditional fashions.

While Elion had already delivered Rose as his wedding gift, King Teivel offered an exquisite golden figurine depicting a tiny golden Alex, sword extended, facing a giant coiled serpent. The gift was incredibly detailed and caused Cassie to cringe at the memory it depicted.

Masters from all the Houses and Guilds paid their respects to the happy couple, providing tokens of appreciation and gratitude for Alex's improvements to the city. Even the common folk from the countryside came to see the festivities, as Ben had declared a day of celebration for all.

Privately, Ben had informed Alex that the spoils recovered from House Drakon would more than cover all the costs of the wedding while still providing a sizeable contribution to both Windfall and Great Vale.

Alex discovered he was required to be separated from his intended the day before the celebration, a tradition that seemed to transcend the differing worlds of their origin. He had actually taken up residence on *Cassie's Quest*, a few days prior, in an effort to give the women the freedom to share a single room.

Alex had asked Leander to be his best man as Ben would actually be presiding over the ceremony. Cassie had Abrianna as her maid of honor, but continued to outnumber the men with Kelby and Leena as bridesmaids. Poor Kinsey had been awash in all the new arrivals, her only respite when they retreated to the schooner at night with Alex.

When the day finally arrived, Alex found himself in the great hall of the castle, the galleries on both sides filled to capacity. The second tier had been reserved for visiting royalty, insuring them the best possible vantage point. As he scanned the gallery, he noted many a familiar face, with just as many unknown to him.

He was sure Lady Amelia, who would be escorted first in the procession ending with the bride, was the final word on the guest list. Even Ben dared not challenge her on the choices. Alex was just happy to be finally getting married.

As he watched Lady Amelia being led into the room, her position as mother of the bride insuring her the seat behind the bride, he gave a sigh of relief. He looked down to see Kinsey squeezing in between him and Leander, as if looking for protection from the crowds.

"Hang in there, my friend, it's almost over," Leander whispered, misunderstanding the exhale.

After Amelia was seated, passing Alex with an adoring smile as she did so, they began with the bridesmaids. Both Leena and Kelby were true visions in the extravagant dresses provided for the occasion. Alex had been told that special materials had been delivered from the elves to dress the entire wedding party.

He could see the material shimmer like nothing he had ever seen before as each of the women passed him by. The material looked alive as it changed colors from a bright pure white to a pearl with rippling streams of color, like the inside of an oyster shell. He could see the mermaid influence with the low-cut bodice presenting a generous amount of cleavage. Their red hair was done up, giving then a look of true elegance.

Next it was Leander's turn to gasp as Abrianna appeared. Her gown was like the others but with a much more modest cut to the design. In addition, her hair had been left down but clipped back, giving her a mane of brown to accent her green eyes and flawless complexion. The smile she gave both men as she past was absolutely radiant.

Finally, Cassie came into view. Framed in the stone archway that held the open doors, she was in a snow white flowing gown that seemed to cascade off her shoulders and flow out in all directions. Her veil barely covered her face in what appeared like a falling snow, each flake appearing and disappearing as it drifted past her glowing smile.

She seemed to be floating as she approached the altar, her eyes never leaving Alex as she stopped beside him. He reached out and took her hand in his, the warmth of her touch sending a thrill throughout his body. They both then turned to face her Uncle and the ceremony began.

Alex had no real idea what transpired after that, all he recalled was Ben speaking the words, "You may kiss the bride" and the ooh's and aah's of the crowd.

As they were presented to the witnesses, Alex believed they were beginning the greatest adventure of their lives.

----*----

Elion stood by the railing on the second level of the great hall, watching the festivities below with a smile. He had been one of the many witnesses of the royal marriage between Windfall's Lord Protector, Alexander Rogers, and now Lady Cassandra Rogers, niece to the King of Great Vale and now Lady of Windfall Castle.

The ceremony had been everything one would expect of a human nuptial, grand on their scale he was sure, but lacking when compared to an Elven affair. Alex had been dressed in a combination of Windfall colors with his symbol of House Rogers emblazoned across the ceremonial breastplate he wore.

Lady Cassandra was resplendent in her gown and accompanying train, all the materials provided as a gift from the elves. Adorned in white and trimmed in the colors of Great Vale, her beautiful red hair had been done up, adding to the elegance of her appearance. Elion had to admit she would challenge an elven bride with her beauty.

It was as he was enjoying the show before him that he felt the presence of another behind him. He didn't bother turning, as the overwhelming aura of neutrality that washed over him foretold the intruder's identity. He lost the joy he was feeling, only to have it replaced with ambivalence.

"Here to pay your respects Avenstore?" Elion asked flatly, as the Dark Elf King stepped up to the railing next to him.

"In part, Elion," Avenstore replied. Both elves stood patiently, each waiting for the other to broach the subject hanging over them.

"She is with child?" Avenstore finally asked, trying to make it sound a question.

"Yes, though unaware. The baby holds great promise as the mixture of wizard and nymph, if female," Elion replied, knowing it added to the unspoken problem.

"You know what must be done. The Balance has come unhinged," Avenstore responded, with an edge to his tone that Elion took as uncharacteristically emotional.

"The dragons live, pardoned by his actions. They now roam free, released from their slavery under the iron hand of Tantalus," Elion commented while motioning at Alex below.

"You say that as if it is a good thing. The dragons are indebted to the wizard who released them. At best, they are now neutral, and thus irrelevant to the Balance. Unless you act, there will be war, worse than last time, and many will perish," Avenstore answered somberly.

"There will be no war. I know what must be done," Elion stated without looking at his counterpart.

"Soon, Elion. It must be done soon," the Dark Elf warned.

"It will be done at an appropriate time. That is not today. Let them have their moment," Elion replied, this time facing Avenstore and sending a clear message to stop pushing.

"As you say, not today, but soon, Elion," the Dark Elf answered. With that, he gave a slight bow and then disappeared into the shadows.

With his departure, King Elion of the Woodland Elves turned back to the railing in time to see Alex take his bride in his arms and kiss her once more.

"Not today, probably not tomorrow, but soon," Elion said to himself sadly.

# Yiddish Reference

ALTER COCKER: An old and complaining person, an old fart
AY-YAY-YAY: A Joyous, or at times sarcastic, exclamation
BISL: a little tiny bit
BISSEL, BISSELA: A little.
BOYCHICK: An affectionate term for a young boy
BRACHA: A prayer.
BUBBELE: A term of endearment, darling.
BUPKES: Something worthless or absurd
CHUTZPAH: Nerve; gall,
DREK: shit, human garbage
FARSHPETIKT: late, being late
FEH: An expression of disgust, representative of the sound of spitting
FERSHTAY?: Do you understand.
FERSHLUGGINER: Beaten up, messed up, no good.
GAY GA ZINTA HATE: Go in good health.
GAY SHLAFEN: Go to sleep.
GONIF: A thief, a shady character.
GOY: A derogatory term meaning gentile
GOSYS GEFINEN: Goys find, a lucky find
KEYN PROBLEM: no problem
KIBBITZ: To offer comments which are often unwanted
MACH SHNEL: Hurry up
MAVEN: An expert
MEGILLAH: Long, complicated and boring.
MENTSH: a real gentleman
MESHUGANA: crazy
METSIA: a real bargain
MISHEGAS: crazy behavior
MAZEL TOV: expressing congratulations or good luck
NOSH: To snack
NU: so?; How are things?; how about it?;
NUDNIK: A pest, a persistent and annoying person.
OY VEY: "Oh, how terrible things are"

PLOTZ: To burst, to explode
SCHLEP: To carry or to move about
SCHLEPPING: Act of carrying or moving about
SCHMOOZE: friendly chat
SCHMUCK: A vulgarism, strong putdown for a jerk, a detestable person.
SHEYNA PUNIM: pretty face
SCHLEMIEL: A dummy; someone who is taken advantage of, a born loser.
SCHLIMAZEL: A chronically unlucky person,
SHMALTZ: a bit of dirt, smudge "You have some shmaltz on you"
SHMENDRICK: A weak and thin pipsqueak.
SHNORRER: A beggar, a moocher, a cheapskate, a chiseler.
SHTIK: refers to an individual's unique way of presenting themselves,
SHTUNK: A stinker, a nasty person or a scandalous mess
SPEIL: a long or fast speech or story intended to persuade
TCHOTCHKA: An inexpensive trinket, a toy, a sexy but brainless girl.
TEIVEL: Devil
TREGER FUN SHLEKHT NAYES: someone who brings bad news
TSURIS: serious troubles
TUCHES: rear end, bottom
VER CLEMPT: All choked up
VILDA CHAYA: a wild animal
VOS TON IR ZORGN: What do you care?
YIDDISH KOP: smart person
ZETZ: a punch

Made in the USA
Middletown, DE
20 January 2024